Also by Mary Manning

Mount Venus
Lovely People

The Last Chronicles
of
Ballyfungus

The Last Chronicles
of
Ballyfungus

by Mary Manning

An Atlantic Monthly Press Book

Little, Brown and Company

BOSTON/TORONTO

FIRST EDITION
T05/78

Four of the Chronicles appeared in *The Atlantic*, in different form.

Library of Congress Cataloging in Publication Data

Manning, Mary.
  The last chronicles of Ballyfungus.

  "An Atlantic-Monthly Press book."
  I. Title
PZ3.M3212Las   1978   [PR6025.A498]   823'.9'14   77–20176
ISBN 0–316–54523–6

ATLANTIC–LITTLE, BROWN BOOKS
ARE PUBLISHED BY
LITTLE, BROWN AND COMPANY
IN ASSOCIATION WITH
THE ATLANTIC MONTHLY PRESS

Designed by Christine Benders

Published simultaneously in Canada
by Little, Brown & Company (Canada) Limited
PRINTED IN THE UNITED STATES OF AMERICA

To Polly Starr

Chronicle One

In which we meet the Community and live with them through the vicissitudes of the Poetry Festival.

Chronicle Two

In which we suffer with the nymph Felicity through her unfortunate affair with a centaur — her subsequent humiliation — and the reaction of the Community to the same.

Chronicle Three

In which an American student encounters a daughter of Demeter, is seduced by her and leaves her sorrowfully, for his own country, but does not leave her completely alone.

Chronicle Four

In which Father Kevin encounters a siren who almost leads him on to a fate worse than death.

Chronicle Five

In which the Woods of Balooly are now seriously threatened by evil men. Tottenham arrives and plunges into battle. Events become more confused and mysterious when he falls in love with a dryad.

Chronicle Six

In which the Older People take the law into their own hands and pay dearly for it, but the battle is not yet over.

Chronicle Seven

In which the battle for the enchanted Woods is fought — involves the whole Community — and the result is a Pyrrhic victory for Tottenham.

Chronicle One

A FEW YEARS AGO, Ballyfungus was hardly on the map, it was so unimportant. It was a small market town situated on the River Fung which meandered through rich grazing country and pleasant woods into the sea at Fungusport.

The port was famous amongst other things for its tiny eighteenth-century theatre which had been built by "the bad Lady Cowperthwaite" for her private theatricals and as legend had it for her "terrible doings." Nobody has been able to explain why Lady Cowperthwaite was "bad." She was, it seemed, intelligent and artistic, qualities which were apt to arouse suspicion and animosity amongst the horsy gentry and surrounding peasants. The theatre, which plays a rather tragic role in these chronicles, was gratefully and reverently used by the Chamber Music Society, dramatic companies and sometimes for an interesting lecture. The beautiful little building was the darling of the Georgian Society and of all the local residents.

Ballyfungus boasted no such redeeming feature. There was one hotel, used mainly in the season by coarse fishermen who angled for coarse creatures like carp or pike which they threw back again into the river. There were two churches, one at either end of the town, Catholic and Protestant, Catholic very full and Protestant very empty; six pubs owned by one man, Patrick Rooney; one supermarket run by Frank Goggins (the Goggins family owned quite a slice of Fungusport); one drapery establishment which featured long underwear in the window; a Medical Hall owned by another Goggins. A Victorian-Gothic Castle with Norman keep (ruined), once the seat of the De Braceys (also ruined), dominated the town. There were an expensive Catholic boarding school,

"Convent of the Sacred Angels," and a Victorian-Gothic Post Office, presided over by a postmistress who was also Gothic — the gargoyle variety: when her upper dentures went awry, she looked like Dracula. The twelfth Lord de Bracey was a Victorian-Gothic madman (syphilis, they say) which explains everything.

Mainly because it was a backwater and within commuting distance of the madding crowd Ballyfungus attracted a great many retired persons. Within recent years some distinguished tax dodgers arrived, amongst them the well-known detective-story writer Colin Evans (creator of Tierney) and his friend Eddie Fox the distinguished interior decorator and last but not least the distinguished British artist Elizabeth (Liz) Atkins. In order to escape taxation one had to establish distinction. A slight touch of fantasy was added to life in Ballyfungus — if it could be called life — a dreamy torpor would be a more accurate description — by the restoration of a twelfth-century Cistercian Abbey, instigated and led by Canon Morragh P. P. who was not only the parish priest but also a devoted and some said a crazy antiquarian. The good Father spent most of his waking moments in the ruins directing operations so his two lively curates did more than their share of the parish work. The one hotel in Ballyfungus — the De Bracey Arms — besides being used during the season by anglers who were usually loud persons with strong Yorkshire accents also lodged commercial travellers and an occasional suicide. The food was outstandingly bad and the plumbing was, as one person described it, "reel savage." This dreadful hostelry was owned by John Fallon. He also owned the Grand in Fungusport which tried to live up to its name and he had bought De Bracey Castle but he did not reside in the noble ruin; he had other plans for it.

The pride and joy of Ballyfungus and indeed of the county were Balooly Woods which stretched between Ballyfungus and the neighbouring parish of Kinealy. The Irish name had been "Riocht na n-ein" (the Kingdom of the Birds). Once they had been part of the De Bracey demesne but that meant

4

nothing anymore, neither did the De Braceys. The widowed Countess, Alicia Lady de Bracey, lived in a gimcrack bungalow outside the town and ran a weaving industry in the basement of the Town Hall. As far as anybody knew the Woods belonged to the people and how they loved Balooly, and so did the birds and the other wild creatures who ran free there. You walked under the green canopy of trees reverently as if you were walking in a cathedral in the beautiful silence. There was no vandalism because it belonged to the people; the wild flowers were theirs and the regal ferns, and the birds sang there as they sang nowhere else. The Woods they said were older than Christianity, older than the druids. It was a pagan domain. The Old Doctor who was a devoted bird watcher said it was a left-over from ancient Greece, an Olympian protectorate, and he swore that nymphs, satyrs, centaurs, dryads, and fauns emerged at twilight and there they assembled for The Rites of Spring and later for The Fires of Autumn. Like the rest of the town he considered the Woods belonged to him and to the birds. A frightful vengeance it was rumoured would fall on anyone who cut down a primeval oak or pulled up the wild flowers or the ferns by the roots. The birds too were safe from the sportsmen with guns. Nobody dared harm a living thing in those enchanted Woods.

Ferncourt, a small Victorian mansion situated on the edge of the Woods, had been inherited from their father, Colonel Bing, by Mabel Lady Vigors and her sister, Mrs. Albinia Travers. They were widows. Mabel's husband had been governor of a British protectorate in East Africa which is now the Black Republic of Zonga. Albinia's husband had been a fashionable Dublin doctor who made a pile (no pun intended) out of his painless treatment of hemorrhoids. Mrs. T. was childless but Mabel's two sons were married and living in New Zealand. The two ladies lived very comfortably, waited on by an orphan, aged fifty-odd, and odd was the word, for Betty was known far and wide as "Batty Betty." However, in spite of her mental confusion, she was a superb cook and everyone longed to be invited to Ferncourt for dinner. Old Jamesy Nolan, a dirty old fellow with a straggly grey beard, lived in the broken-down lodge and helped with the cleaning. Nobody cared to probe too deeply into Jamesy's lifestyle. Suffice to say there was no inside sanitation and he slept on newspapers.

On this evening in November some years ago four people were seated at a bridge table in the Ferncourt drawing room. They were General Artie Ironside (Rtd) and Doctor Josh Browne (Rtd) and the two widows. Both the General and the Doctor were widowers which made everything so convenient and it also made a pleasant foursome for bridge twice a week. They were known indeed by the local society as the fearsome foursome. They were all around eighty years of age; the Doctor in fact was eighty-two but they were on the whole in excellent health. Their faculties were more or less unimpaired and they shared a great many prejudices in common, which included all forms of progress, developments, foreigners, social upstarts, new inventions, abstract art, poetry that did not rhyme, sexual nonconformity, and nonconformist type of Christian worship. Mabel, known as Mabs to her friends, was the older sister. She was nearly six feet tall and her complexion was withered and tanned by the African sun. Her sister, Albinia, Albie to you, was not quite so tall, wore different coloured wigs to suit her moods and was artistic. She painted water colours, indoor scenes of chairs, tables and corner cupboards. The General was plump, pink-faced with white moustache. The Doctor was small, resembled an elderly pixie; his clothes were usually on the side of eccentricity. This evening Mabs was wearing a black evening dress purchased hurriedly in Harrods in 1935 on the way to Africa. Albie was wearing a brown pyjama suit and gold wig.

"Your bid, Albie," snapped Artie. "On your toes, girl."

"Sorry, darling. Two diamonds. Incidentally did you boys get a notice about the Poetry Festival?"

"What poetry festival?" growled the Doctor; he was holding bad cards.

Albie removed a crumpled leaflet from her evening bag and adjusted her glasses. She read loudly and decisively because, to be frank, they were all a little hard of hearing. " 'You are invited to a meeting in the lounge of the De Bracey Arms at eight P.M. to discuss plans for the forthcoming Poetry Festival.' It's signed Liz Atkins."

"Poetry Festival." Artie laughed derisively. "In view of the fact that this nation is bankrupt I would think a festival of any kind is out of place."

"No, darling. Yes, I *did* say two diamonds — in times of crisis the human heart turns to poetry, as the bard said."

"What bard?" asked her sister suspiciously; "I pass."

"Haven't the faintest idea."

There was a knock at the door and in came Betty, a wild looking woman with hair straggling to her shoulders, wearing a dirty white uniform. She was leading a very old bloodhound who, when released, limped over to the fireplace and collapsed in a heap on the rug, not before he had left a trail of phlegm on the General's knee. Loving cries came from the ladies: "Adorable Dolphie; Mummy loves 'oo. Sweetest dog! Dolphie my petskee!" The gentlemen said nothing; they loathed the dog.

"Dolphie's fed, mum," murmured Betty confidentially; "He's fartin' terrible."

"Now I come to think of it I did get one," said the Doctor. "One of those notices I mean. I understand it's to commemorate the tercentenary of Tomas O'Sullivan's birth."

"And who was Tomas O'Sullivan?" asked her ladyship haughtily.

"He was a great Irish poet born here, my dear; he was blind and wandered all over Ireland reciting his poetry."

"They wander all over America now," said Albie brightly; she kept up with the times to a certain extent. "Rubber, isn't it?"

"Who told you all that, Josh?" asked Mabs. It was a habit with her to be suspicious. Everyone had to substantiate their stories.

"Father Kevin. The little curate with red hair. The one who runs the drama group."

"Both curates are adorable," Albie chimed in brightly. "But Father Dermot is much too handsome. A priest shouldn't be handsome at all. It's bad for the girls and bad for him."

"Not if he takes a lot of exercise." Josh lighted up his smelly old pipe. "And Father Dermot does exercise running that football team."

"So does the Archdeacon. Poor thing, he might as well be a celibate," sighed Albie. "I don't believe he's ever had a moment's sex with Muriel." She leaned forward and looked into the General's eyes or rather his glinting hornrims. "Artie, you'll come with us to the meeting. Say yes, like a good boy."

"I suppose so, though I haven't been asked.

"Nonsense, Artie. You never pick your mail up off the hall floor."

"I do, on the first of the month for the bills." (He hasn't noticed Dolphie's spit on his trousers, thought Albie. I hope he doesn't till he gets home.)

"John Fallon's going to be at the meeting. John Rooney told me." Living right in the town the Doctor was always more informed about social doings. The ladies exclaimed at hearing this piece of information.

"John Fallon." Mabs wrinkled her long nose as if she smelled a bad smell somewhere. "Are you sure? Who told you?"

"Rooney the great publican and sinner himself. You know he's an admirer and hanger-on of Fallon's. He says Fallon has some scheme on foot for a development in Ballyfungus. So he's supporting a festival to start with. He says it will put Ballyfungus on the map."

"A development. I don't like that." Mabs stood up. "Time for drinks. Boys, look after yourselves. Development means

8

devastation on a large scale. Look at Dublin." She poured herself a generous Scotch. Both ladies loved their alcoholic refreshment. Glass in hand, she walked with slow and stately Government House tread towards the fireplace and caressed the dog with her foot: he rolled over and released some digestive gas. The gentlemen exchanged significant glances. They had often discussed putting the animal out of its misery, or rather out of theirs.

"We must go to the meeting, Albie. You boys can pick us up. I hate driving in the dark. I'd like to look at this awful Fallon. I haven't seen him for years. How can he think Ballyfungus needs waking up when we have Father Kevin's drama club, the dear Archdeacon's and Father Dermot's football team, not to mention the Canon's ruins . . ."

"Yes, but there was a further threat," said the Doctor slowly. "There was mention of industrial doings in Balooly."

Both ladies screamed and the General banged his fist on the table.

"The Woods," exclaimed Artie purpling with rage. "He dare not touch the Woods."

"Doesn't he know about the curse?" Albie stamped her foot and glared at the Doctor, who remained calm.

"A man like Fallon ignores curses or any superstition. He fears nothing, believes in nothing except the acquisition of wealth. Wealth and power." Having delivered himself of this polemic the Doctor boldly thrust his forefinger into his mouth and adjusted his dentures.

"This vandalized Goth must not be allowed to touch the Woods." Mabs drew herself up; she was every inch the Governor's lady.

"Have a few words with Fallon tomorrow night, Mabs. I'll pick you up at seven-thirty. Come, Josh. Time to go. It's raining and blowing hard." The General rose to his feet, rather slowly. "That damn rheumatism! Seven-thirty? Right!"

"Right!" Albie obeying the clipped command saluted him and said, "Right, General." Dolphie also rose to his feet and uttered a noise between a bark and a belch.

Safely outside the hall door the General turned to the Doctor and said, "I wish to God Albie wouldn't wear those wigs, she's got perfectly good hair, hasn't she? You've seen her in bed? Eh?"

"She has plenty of hair; it's white of course. She has at least half a dozen wigs strung up in her room like Indian scalps. That dog. He's Cerberus. I'd like to push *him* in the Styx."

"A poisoned sop would be the answer." Artie laughed; it was an evil laugh. "Come on, Josh, you can lay hands on a poison any time. Gad what a night."

Inside the house the two ladies were discussing the other half of the foursome and they were not kind. "I do wish Josh would invest in modern dentures. The ones he has are Crimean War vintage, don't you think?"

"And Artie's feet. They spread out now at right angles and he has no control over them. I wonder what tomorrow night's meeting will bring forth?" Albie moved around emptying ash trays and putting out the lamps.

"This is Ireland, Albie. It will bring forth nothing but mutual recrimination and resulting confusion. Come, Dolphie dearest. You must take your little constitutional in the stable yard, my sweet."

The entrance hall of the De Bracey Arms smelled of a hundred years of cabbage and fried fish. The walls were lined with glass cases displaying stuffed fish with weight and date of catch. In one corner stood a large stuffed bear holding a box with "Give To The Little Sisters" on it! It was always empty, mainly because nobody knew who the Little Sisters were. The grandfather's clock in the other corner had stopped at five-thirty one sunny afternoon in May 1877. At least that's what Old Mick the porter told people; the old fellow was coming up to a hundred and in his spare time read the stars. Most of the staff except the barman were what Mabs Vigors described as "witless poor things." Quite a few people were already seated in the lounge adjoining the squalid bar when Mabs and Albie arrived with their two escorts. Lady de

Bracey motioned them with cheery smiles to sit beside her. Her Ladyship was handwoven from head to foot and clanked with handbeaten jewelry every time she moved. Her face was a pale withered pink from exposure to the elements (she cycled everywhere) in spite of her age, "seventy-seven, dear — to the minute." She was known to most people as "Auntie Al" which was what her beloved grandnephew Tottenham called her and we may as well do the same. Liz Atkins, tall, dark, haggardly handsome, was seated between Colin and Eddie. Colin was tall, thin and highly nervous; Eddie was short, fat and very very calm. The Boys, as they were called, had made over three ruined thatched cottages into a splendid thatched mansion, beautifully situated on the river, at times almost in the river. Liz had bought the Old Mill and built a huge studio onto it. It was only a quarter of a mile down the road from The Boys. Peering through her lorgnette, which was only used for intimidation, Mabs spotted John Fallon at the table near the fireplace, seated beside Goggins the T.D. (the Irish version of M.P.) who was in a wheelchair, "some wasting disease," they said; "a disease endemic to most T.D.s, quipped the Doctor. Goggins' wife was in close attendance, she hoped to take his place in the Dail when he had passed on.

The villain Fallon was wearing expensive tweeds with leather patches on elbows and knees designed to create an image of aristocratic shabbiness. He was fleshily handsome and did emanate steely power not altogether comforting to anyone with an income under five thousand per annum, *before* taxes. He rose to his feet when everyone was settled.

"Drinks are on the house. Order what you please," (he never drank himself; it didn't pay) "and I would like to nominate Father Hannigan for the chair. The Canon met with a slight accident in the ruins and is unable to be present. Archdeacon Musgrave is working with the Boys Club tonight." There was a muffled groan. Father Hannigan was obsessed it seemed by the subject of sex and wrote endless letters to the papers about the horrors of contraception and abortion and the collapse of the family. Apart from his obsession he was a pleasant fellow, played the violin and was a devoted member of the Fungusport Chamber Music Society. Father Kevin Sheedy, the red-headed Catholic curate (his obsession was Theatre), rose and said eagerly, "Mr. Fallon, ladies and gentlemen, the Canon has unearthed some interesting information about Tomas O'Sullivan, the wandering poet who wrote the classical narrative poem called *The Celebration of Spring* and it is this poem which the Ballyfungus Festival is to be built around."

He sat down again amidst applause; he was very popular in the town. Meanwhile everyone was ordering drinks in loud and determined whispers and by the time the orders had arrived and been consumed, not once, but twice, and double ones at that, it was hard to understand what the plans were and why anyone was there at all, at all.

Father Hannigan at last rose, thumped the table and called the meeting to order. "I understand our good friend Mr. Edward Fox is to act as organizing secretary for the Festival [applause followed]. With all apologies to the Canon, Tomas O'Sullivan wrote filthy drivel and I do not think we should celebrate filthy drivel!" There were boos and some liberal hisses.

"No problem, Father." John Fallon showed his teeth. "Everyone now writes filthy drivel. We have to move with the times." The audience laughed. Father Hannigan frowned. Eddie held up his hand. "If I may be allowed to speak. Do I not understand we are using the English translation of *The Celebration* by that highly respected English poet Marcus Brooks?"

In a flash Father Kevin was on his feet; "It is. We are, and a very fine piece it is too. My — our — Hodge Podge Players have already done a dramatic reading. We should use it again."

Father Hannigan excommunicated him with his eyes. The curate sat down as hastily as he had sprung up.

Eddie was up again; "I suggest we hold the Festival in

April, that would give us nearly six months to prepare for it, there are festivals all over the country, one for every month in the year it seems, but I've made some enquiries and April does seem to be free and after all O'Sullivan wrote about spring and April would seem to me just about right." There was some clapping at this but Father Hannigan shook his head. He was against spring; too many regrettable things happened during that dangerous season.

The irrepressible Father Kevin was once more on his feet. "I know April is free." He beamed around on everyone. "Croom and Kilrush were thinking of celebrating the Colleen Bawn murder with a festival but they haven't yet decided which town she was drowned in, so we needn't bother about that. I do think, Mr. Chairman, we need some theatre as well as the poetry." He sat down this time wildly applauded by members of the Hodge Podge Players, who were seated at the back of the room.

"Very good idea, Father Kevin." Eddie addressed the chair, "Incidentally I have a friend in the London National Theatre who puts on a delightful one-man show 'The Women of Shakespeare.' "

"Is she a man?" asked Father Hannigan suspiciously scenting sodomy. The Boys were presumed to be homosexual.

"No, he's a woman. I mean she's a woman. Pardon my error."

Everyone burst into laughter except Hannigan who again shook his head. Filth everywhere it seemed.

Now it was Mairin O'Kelly the postmistress' turn to object. She was a tall thin yellow-faced woman who came of a long line of patriots; her old "Pappy" aged ninety had been out in '16 in the G.P.O. "London? Then she's English and no English need apply, not while I'm here," she snarled. Eddie, Colin and Liz did not know where to look, being invading sassenachs, but the rest of the audience remained uncomfortably silent.

Father Kevin, for which everyone blessed him, rose to his feet. "The Festival is strictly non-political; however, if I may make a suggestion, Dairin McGivern does a good one-woman show, 'Yeats' Women' or 'The Women of Yeats,' I'm not sure which. I hear it's very good. She's the great Abbey Theatre actress." A vote was instantly taken and passed unopposed, to invite Dairin McGivern. Yeats and Dairin together being a safe choice and made in Ireland, so to speak.

Eddie Fox who had been whispering with Liz Atkins now piped up. "Has anybody on the Committee read Tomas O'Sullivan's poem?" There was a heavy silence. Nobody had, it seemed, except "the damned Englishman" Colin and the absent Canon, read the work of their native son. "What about asking Myles Murtagh down from Dublin to give a reading of the poem? He is a well-known personality on TV, an actor off and on stage and I may say always in trouble which is in itself a draw?"

Everyone applauded this, but the obsessed priest muttered, "We do need some form of censorship."

It was Fallon's turn now to shut him up; he showed the teeth again and it was not a smile. "Father, the more uncensored a Festival, the more visitors it will attract, and we want to make money for Ballyfungus, don't we?" Father Hannigan thought of the much needed repairs to his church and presbytery and kept silent.

"I think your drama group should put on something noble, something classical, Father Kevin." Liz Atkins spoke up for the first time. Indeed everyone was wondering why she had been silent for so long; she was usually in the forefront of every social activity, but then, of course, the Festival had been her idea in the first place. "Shakespeare perhaps? You are welcome to the mill house garden." Clapping followed mostly from the Hodge Podge Players and Father Kevin bowed delightedly.

"I say, good people, I say." Lady de Bracey took the floor with a tremendous rattle of bracelets and geegaws. "I am frightfully sorry my nephew Tottenham won't be here. He being a poet himself would have been glad to assist in any way but he's going to be in Mexico next spring, I don't quite know why, but incidentally if it's to be a poetry festival we jolly well need more poets, don't you know?" Auntie Al still used the slang of the twenties. "We dash well need about a dozen. I say, Colin, you read a lot, I vote you go up to Dublin and engage half a dozen of the best you can get. There's a good chap." She plumped herself down and a fearful rending sound followed, part of a handwoven jacket had come away!

Meanwhile John Fallon was preparing to leave. He was putting away papers in his brief case, as much to hide his yawns as anything else. The great man was bored to death. He had more things on his mind than the tiresome residents of a small country town. He addressed Eddie who was in the front row of seats. "Let me know when you're having another meeting and I'll send someone down. 'Fraid I'll be in New York myself. You need a good PR man working on this. I'll see to that. Let him have the programme of events as soon as possible." He moved towards the door.

"Stop. Fallon. One moment." Mabs rose having first pinched the Doctor and the General into life; they had slept throughout the proceedings. Indeed the Doctor's snores had been most disturbing. Fallon paused surprised.

"Fallon." Mabs, again the Governor's lady; even Fallon was somewhat awed. "There is a rumour, Fallon, that plans are being laid for some sort of," she hesitated, "some industrial development which might affect Balooly Woods?" There was a heavy silence while the audience waited for the answer; everyone leaned forward as if listening for the oracle to utter at Delphi. "Speak man," abjured her ladyship.

"I will be frank," replied Fallon, choosing his words with care. "There are certain plans being formulated towards an industrial complex which might require a road adjacent to the Woods. But I must impress this on you, our plans are not in the near future."

"Fallon, if you cut down one tree in Balooly you will regret it. The Woods, Fallon, will make you pay dearly." She sat down and a burst of cheering followed. Fallon shook his head pityingly and walked out smiling.

"I can't understand Fallon's interest in a poetry festival." Eddie sank into a comfortable chair and lifted the Siamese cat onto his knees. Liz and the boys were enjoying a postmortem accompanied by nightcaps, back at the thatched ranch. "I'm sure he's never read a line of poetry in his life and there's no money in it for him."

"I think it's to divert attention from his other activities."

Colin threw a log on the fire; a November gale was starting up outside; they could hear the rain lashing against the windows.

"While he's posing as a patron of the arts and a benefactor to the town he'll be laying plans for countrywide devastation."

"I'm sure you're right, Colin. How clever of you! That's just it. We must organise against him — after the Festival. Poor Mabs, if they do lay Balooly to waste it will be fatal for her. Ferncourt is right on the edge of the danger zone. However, Mabs is a powerful lady. She won't give in without a struggle." Liz knelt crouched beside the fire and looked into the flames.

And you're a pretty powerful lady yourself thought Eddie watching her. Now in her fifties, Liz had achieved great success with her painting, had discarded four husbands and enjoyed many loves. The current man in her life was Tom Nolan, nephew of Jamesy Nolan the dishevelled lodge-keeper at Ferncourt. Tom was a splendidly handsome man in his middle years with a bed-ridden wife; his two sons had emigrated to Canada so Tom was able to devote his days, and some coarse persons said his nights, to Miss Atkins. Ostensibly he functioned as gardener and handyman to the Old Mill. An aged cousin took care of the invalid wife who was a bit gone in the head, God help her.

"Another thing. Why is Mairin O'Kelly, the ghoulish postmistress, interested in poetry? She has never read any-

16

thing in her life except other people's mail and the *Sunday World*."

"I can only guess, Colin dear, it's a home product made in Ireland and she's a patriot. Did you hear the bitch's remarks about no English need apply, and next to Fallon we're the biggest subscribers to the Festival. Tom tells me that her nephew is very high up in the Provos, a high-class teenage bomber, and her other nephew, Ignatius, is one of the Hodge Podge Players and is the apple of that jaundiced eye."

"You do learn a lot from Tom." Eddie mischievously sniggered.

"Not so much as I learn from Emerald Walsh," she retorted.

"Ah yes, Emerald Walsh."

They all burst into laughter. Mrs. Walsh cleaned for everyone within twenty miles of Ballyfungus. She was a talented gossip and news purveyor.

"I must be going." Liz rose and wrapped herself in a floating grey tweed cloak.

"I'll walk to the door with you." Eddie followed her into the hall. "There might be a murderer lurking in the bushes."

"Don't bother, dear. Tom is there; he'll be watching out." Liz, wearing a deadpan expression, waved to him and stepped out into the darkness. Eddie burst into laughter and returned to the living room.

"She's shameless, absolutely shameless! Tom is sitting up for her, or rather lying down for her. Now I better call this strange Committee together. First I must list them." He sat down at the charming little eighteenth-century escritoire (belonged to Madame Récamier, dear) and began scribbling and talking to himself, "First Liz Atkins; the Canon; the General; the Old Doc, the young one's too busy and his wife's too grand. Then there's Auntie Al and Mabs and Albie and Father Hannigan, oh, God, *he* is a drag! and the adorable curates, the prolific Rector. He looks quite broken. How many babies do they have?"

17

"Six I think and another any minute. That's why he missed the meeting; she was having pains."

"So was I. And think of the poor Archdeacon with no bairns at all. I presume Muriel, that chubby little lady, won't open her legs for him." Eddie laughed again; he was enjoying himself. "There is no justice is there? Mairin the postmistress who smells, but does not wash. The grease on her hair reminds me of the grease on top of cold beef gravy. And we must ask poor Oliver MacCrea, that walking ruin. Colin, we'll have to run up to Dublin and shop for poets."

Colin began putting out the lights and pushing chairs into place; his neatness was maniacal. "God, that means a round of pubs. I'm going up to bed. Coming?"

"Yes, this promises to be a macabre experience."

Publicity began appearing in the newspapers around Christmas, continued right into March and burst into full flower around April. Fallon's PR man was relentlessly thorough and disturbingly hungry for intimate news about the Committee and indeed the whole area around Ballyfungus was screened. Every bit of information that could be scraped up about the wandering poet was used over and over again. The papers dwelt long and lovingly on the earthiness of his poetry. "Just another name for dirt," remarked Father Hannigan bitterly. Myles Murtagh consented to give a public reading of the Poet's Work and the theme of the Festival was to be LOVE. "There is nothing abnormal or suggestive in this great epic which is a hymn to Joy," wrote Myles in his Sunday column. "I simply do not believe in the innuendos relating to the poet's sexual proclivity. The poem as I read it celebrates normal love between boy and girl. Phelim the young fiddler who accompanied him on his wanderings was a cousin — nothing more." Immediately the gay clubs in Dublin were up in arms. Why shouldn't Tomas O'Sullivan be one of their own? What are you going to do? Cut out half the gay Elizabethans? Father Hannigan's soul was a battlefield especially when he was drawn into the musical side of the festival. However, he did get a letter off to the Dublin dailies warning that the Irish people would be voting themselves into hell if they allowed the Government to put forward any form of legislation legalizing birth control.

In Ballyfungus things were booming. Auntie Al was setting up a special exhibition of her weavers' work in the Town Hall. The Hodge Podge Players were rehearsing for an open air performance of *Midsummer Night's Dream* in the Old Mill garden. Some odd little wooden structures resembling the temporary latrines set up on building sites were being assembled around the hotel. They were described as chalets and were designed for extra visitors. Posters advertising the Dairin McGivern reading were plastered all over the town and even decorated Fungusport. "The Women of Yeats." A Terrible Beauty is Born. Eddie said mournfully, "It amounts to this, she was once a beauty and now she's simply terrible."

A TV crew was coming down to record the Murtagh reading. Daisy Lodge, a refined guest house run by the Miss Croziers and usually the haven of middle-aged gentlemanly anglers from England, was now taken over as a refuge for Myles and a gigantic Welsh soprano who was giving a Wagnerian recital. An old sad forgotten English poet Giles something was pushed in there with her and a non-English speaking string quartet from Yugoslavia. Five rather minor poets had been located in the Dublin pubs and had signed on to attend and give readings. They also gave an undertaking to stay sober during the readings; they could do what they liked afterwards.

The great day of the official opening arrived and by the mercy of God it was fine. The actual ceremony took place in the street just outside the Town Hall with a brass band brought in from Fungusport. The whole town was ablaze with plastic floral arrangements, coloured lights were strung across the street and tropical flora (plastic) was set up in pots around the hotel. The Festival was declared open by the President of Ireland, two Catholic Bishops and one Protestant, and John Fallon assisted by the influential Committee. During the blessing Mabs Vigors' new dress was liberally splashed by carelessly thrown holy water (the Bishop was very old and shaky and not quite right, d'you know, but just wouldn't resign). The blessed fluid went right down the back of her neck. The General had to come to the rescue with his handkerchief. "Of course he knew I was a Protestant," fumed Mabs loudly. "It's the Inquisition all over again." Meanwhile Liz took the opportunity to whisper in Eddie's ear, "Did you hear about Father Hannigan's sermon last Sunday? Our newsworthy cleaning lady was there. She always goes to Mass in Kinealy; it's more exciting. Well, he said *The Celebration of Spring* English version was disgusting and immoral and that all Catholic Youth was to keep away from the Murtagh reading. He's reading the Irish version in the hotel on Sunday night, the last day of the Festival." Eddie moaned, "I knew he'd do something like that. What's this for God's sake?" He stared down into the street.

A Demonstration led by Mairin O'Kelly and other concerned citizens appeared carrying placards which read "Balooly Threatened"; "Save Balooly Woods"; "Balooly belongs to the People." Eddie could hardly believe his eyes. The General, the Doctor and the widows of Ferncourt had joined the demonstration, and was it possible — it was — the Canon had left the grandees on the stand and had joined them also carrying a placard, "Save Our National Heritage." Eddie looked around to speak to Liz, but she had disappeared. She was out there with the demo. They surged round John Fallon's car booing and hissing. John Fallon looked at them scornfully. "If his eyes were bullets we'd be dead men," remarked Tom Nolan who was standing protectively beside Liz. And as if things weren't bad enough, Mairin had substituted her Balooly poster for "Release Republican Prisoners. Stop the Torture" which she was waving provocatively at the President's Mercedes. At last the Gardai, who were also hissed, cleared a space for the presidential procession which drove majestically towards Fungusport where a small select lunch had been arranged. "Why did I do this?" sighed Eddie. "And tonight is sure to be a crucifixion."

It was. For the Murtagh reading the hotel banqueting hall usually used for weddings had been gradually renovated; a small stage had been installed with curtains and seating for a hundred at least had been hopefully set up. As the Committee filed virtuously past the bar they were deafened by a roar of voices and laughter. It was jam packed with drinkers, so was the lounge and the TV room. The Committee it seemed comprised the entire audience for the reading. Eddie urged the pitiful group to move up to the front which they did slowly and sadly. "I can't get anyone out of the bar." Eddie was almost in tears. "I wonder if we paid them ..."

Meanwhile the hall was a welter of cameras, cables, lights and cynical TV engineers preparing for the great Murtagh's reading which was to get nationwide coverage.

"Father Hannigan has arrived; he's sitting at the back," said Colin warningly. "Look out for squalls."

"Ah, here comes Murtagh, we must clap him. Clap! Clap! Clap!" Colin looked at Eddie anxiously. His partner was on the brink of hysteria.

Then did Myles Murtagh, a colourful vision of middle-aged boyishness, stride onto the stage. He was in full costume as of a nineteenth-century Aran Islander. "An Irish gondolier?" whispered Colin reducing Liz to nervous shakes. With the nonchalance of long experience Myles adjusted the reading lamp to his liking and then flashed his pixie smile over the nation. The lights having temporarily blinded them the sparse audience now focused on him.

"As ye all know I am about to read excerpts from Tomas O'Sullivan's epic *The Celebration of Spring*." He began using that roguish lilt which went down so well with college audiences in the USA. "Cantos which I consider the most delightfully humorous of this folk song to love." He paused dramatically. "And here we go ...

The Harlot's Lament
Travelling footsore from fair to fair
I would ply my trade in the market square
As evening came with its lowering sky
Flaunting my bosom and swaying my thigh

You see friends," Myles leaned forward and addressed the audience confidentially, "stripped of its cosmetic overtones we hit on something deeply primeval in Tomas O'Sullivan." (At this point Father Hannigan remarked quite audibly, "Slime.") Eddie was then aware that some people were entering rather noisily from the bar and seating themselves at the back. Myles ignored the racket.

> *"But the lusty fellows would not come near*
> *Edging away to their games and beer."*

More people were crowding in now. Also tinker faces were pressed against the windows. The combined smell of drink and smoke and unwashed bodies was overwhelming. Albie said she felt faint; the General was shaken by mysterious and uncontrollable hiccups, but the Doctor was alert and interested.

> *"Young priests would pass with a hasty glance*
> *But their vows would hold though their pulses dance*
> *But many there are who more strongly warm*
> *To a slender cad than a woman's form*
> *On such they would look with lusting eyes*
> *And find their pleasure t'ween boyish thighs."*

"Stop," shouted someone from the back of the room. Everyone turned as did the cameras. A large tow-headed farmer had tottered to his feet. "That's dirty so it is. This is a Christian country."

"Hear! Hear!" shouted his uncouth companions.

"Hush! Hush!" whispered the Committee. The noise was now deafening but Myles, unperturbed, read on. The TV crew remained detached. They were, alas, used to this sort of thing and it made the job more interesting.

> *"And the old men's limbs are weak and slow*
> *With cocks that have long since ceased to crow*
> *And I thought of the silly maid in trouble*
> *With belly that's swollen to nearly double*
> *And I let her grease the wise woman's palms*
> *And the ancient hag used all her charms*
> *In haste and speed at dead of night*
> *To remove the trouble and set things right."*

"Good man! I'd have done the same myself," shouted the Old Doctor but his approbation was drowned in the uproar. All the drunks were on their feet now bellowing crudities which Tomas in his most abandoned moments would not have dreamed up. Myles closed the book. The Committee could not but admire his self-possession. "You clods," he shouted, "you don't appreciate one of your own great poets when you hear him. You don't know any goddam thing except the price of a bullock. What are you doing here anyway? Get back to your cowsheds. Clods! Peasants!"

The tow-headed farmer was rolling up the sleeves of his dirty sweater. Meanwhile Eddie had slipped away to summon the Gardai and Auntie Al was urging the General to stand on his head — it was the only way, she said, to stop the hiccups. Mabs with her sister's and the Doctor's help was standing upon a chair. "You disgusting drunken brutes," she shouted, "get out of here. I say, somebody throw them out. Father Hannigan throw those wretches out."

Father Hannigan did nothing of the sort. Everything was working according to plan — his plan. Myles leaped off the platform. In spite of the corroding years he was in pretty good trim and before you could say Jack Robinson, the tow-headed one was flat on the ground and Myles was standing over him laughing. The cameras had been levelled on them throughout. What a nation-wide opportunity. At that moment when all seemed lost and the hiccuping General was having his neck pulled and slapped by Liz (her cure for this affliction), the Gardai arrived and took over for the second time that day. Amid applause from all establishment members, except Father Hannigan, the drunks were evicted, the hall was cleared and the lout was carried out by his friends. The Gardai, of course, came in for a string of abuse, most of it politically motivated and the lout was distinctly heard shouting, "Turn me back to them boys. I refuse to recognize the fuckin' court."

Then Father Hannigan shouted above the din, "Good people, I'm reading the Irish version of the poem in this very hall next Sunday at eight P.M. and I want all good Christians to attend, and what's more I have something will surprise you." He disappeared into the night leaving everyone in a state of wild surmise and apprehension. So ended the first round of the Poetry Festival. Smilin' Myles departed for Dublin by helicopter followed by the TV crew in their conveyances, a merry lot they were! It was not the last they would see of Ballyfungus.

The influential Committee trooped back to the thatched mansion where drinks awaited them. The postmortem on the night's proceedings was stormy while Colin dispensed drinks aided by Father Kevin and a helpful actor from the Hodge Podge, a Goggins of course, but nobody knew which Goggins there were so many and all looked alike. He was playing a clown in *The Dream*.

"May I ask why the devil none of you told me about the Balooly protest? I was completely taken by surprise." Eddie choked down two aspirin as he spoke.

Liz patted his arm. "You had enough on your mind already, ducky. I thought it was marvellous except for Mairin's dirty switch with her placards."

"Yes, and I suppose you heard as I did through — who do you think?" Eddie raised his voice, "Who?"

Everyone answered him; "Emerald Walsh!"

Eddie laughed bitterly. "Right. Mairin's Provo nephew has been seen in town and Mairin boycotted the reading tonight

24

because it was not in Irish and she's backing Father Hannigan all the way home. You can't do anything in this country without politics creeping in."

"I was fearfully tempted to beat those brutes up myself tonight," said the Archdeacon who was warming his bottom at the fire. It was a chilly April evening. "But thank God I restrained myself."

Colin pressed a drink into the respected cleric's willing hand. "They were incited to it by Father Hannigan. You should have beaten him up, George."

"By jove, most unecumenical, Colin. Incidentally, I suppose you heard, poor Green had twins. That makes it six."

"Why does he do it?" Colin shook his head sadly.

"Absence of mind," sighed the Archdeacon. "Poor fellow! He tries so hard."

Mabs tittered and Albie whispered, "What does he mean?"

Mabs dug into her enormous handbag in which she carried at all times a complete cosmetic outfit: medicinal restoratives, including brandy, a small roll of toilet tissue, a cheque book, car keys, and family correspondence. "What is on tomorrow night? I'm so confused."

"So am I." Liz consulted her programme of events. "Dairin McGivern's one-woman show in the Convent of the Heavenly Angels at eight o'clock. They have a nice little theatre and no bar which should ensure some order. We may do well on this, Eddie."

"Don't be funny," snapped Eddie. "We've had to draft a captive audience from the school itself and another thing, I've been warned that once Dairin starts it's hard to stop her."

"Oh dear, how I wish Tott, my nephew, was here," cried Auntie Al whose love for her nephew bordered on idolatry. "He's so worried about the Woods. He thinks we should go after the county council and our T.D. and have more demonstrations . . ."

"Protests are no good," growled the Doctor who had been competing with the Archdeacon for backwarming. The

Archdeacon being twice the size of the Doctor naturally won. "Assassination is the only answer. Kill them."

"Darling Josh, this is not Ulster." Albie took his gnarled old hand and pressed it affectionately. She was greatly addicted to petting and pressing accompanied by cooing. Colin called her "pigeon lady," but not to her face.

"Do you all realize we have six more days of this ghastly so-called Festival," moaned Eddie. He was on his second brandy.

"Eddie dear, it's going to be a great success. Don't worry. And I'm sure *Midsummer Night's Dream* is going to be a great success." Liz was moving around comforting the wounded, Florence Nightingale in person with a glasss of whiskey in her hand instead of the lamp. She hovered over Father Kevin who was seated with a bottle of stout before him, looking very pale and sad. "Isn't it, Father Kevin?"

"I should have been rehearsing tonight," he answered, "but there was nowhere to rehearse except possibly on the town dump."

"And Puck has an ingrown toenail," added the Goggins character mournfully.

"Don't you think it will be a success, Mabs?" Liz sat down beside Lady V who was again searching through the handbag, this time for her car keys.

"I don't know what you think, Liz, but I do know that Jamesy Nolan ran into the kitchen this morning crossing himself in a terrible state. He said he'd heard a terrible death cry and a warning coming to him on the wind from the direction of Daisy Lodge. He had to be given a cup of strong tea. It turned out to be that huge Welsh soprano practising swine maidens' cries, at least I think that's what it was, for her recital. I rang Daisy Lodge to find out. Imagine, it's nearly a mile down the road from us. The Croziers are absolutely browned off because that old English poet goes wandering off into the Woods and search parties have to be sent out for him. I think I've lost my car keys."

"We must all go home." Albie rose. "We must all go home because Eddie needs a rest, we all do. Josh, shouldn't we

phone up and find out how Artie is? He drove home hiccuping."

"If he still has them by morning I'll give him a hot sago
enema," said Josh calmly. They all took the hint and trailed
home, after a search for Mab's car keys, which were eventually found in her pocket.

Alas, it rained heavily all the next day and into the following night. *Midsummer Night's Dream* had to be postponed.
It was decided at an emergency meeting to move the Welsh
singer and the English poet into Ballyfungus Protestant
Church, St. Botolph's, and give the Fungusport Theatre to
Midsummer Night's Dream. Father Kevin was at his wits
end. The young man who played Bottom was a Gardai in real
life and had been assaulted while arresting a drunken poet.
His right arm was in a sling and his left eye bandaged. The
poets, for whom this Festival had been planned, had lost the
battle against the demon rum and were thoroughly disgusted
with the empty houses for their readings. After an extremely
business-like conference with Eddie, now suicidal, they saw
nothing for it but to move right into the pubs with their
guitars and forget about the hall.

Punctually at eight o'clock Dairin McGivern, the world
famous Irish actress, strode out on the stage of the convent
school's little theatre. She was swathed in black as the first of
Yeats' Ladies — Madame Maud Gonne. The bulk of the
audience was made up of fifty giggling schoolgirls, a couple of
teaching nuns and the Reverend Mother. Father Hannigan
was not present, neither was the Rector, but the Old Mill
mob were there en masse and this included the widowers.
Also present was the postmistress and two of her nephews,
fierce looking lads wearing dark glasses and black berets
which they courteously removed on entering the convent.
"They're here for no good," commented Eddie who now had
an advanced case of persecution mania.

When Dairin turned into the more legendary ladies she
threw a green shawl over her shoulders and ruffled up her

hair which was dyed a deep red and hung to her shoulders. She then, as they say, "acted out" *The Land of Hearts Desire* with frequent recourse to the book and, being a large lady well over seventy, was not convincing lolloping around as the Faery Child. At nine-thirty there was a blessed interval when tea and instant coffee and digestive biscuits were handed out, courtesy of the Heavenly Angels. At ten everyone dragged themselves back into the theatre and Dairin began graciously reading from *The Plays for Dancers* then went on into *The King of the Great Clock Tower*. Eventually she moved into *Purgatory* where the audience joined her in spirit and at eleven o'clock the Reverend Mother whispered to Eddie that it was very late for the young ones; in fact, it was past their bedtime and when was Miss McGivern going to close down? Eddie whispered despairingly, "What am I to do?" The Reverend Mother who feared neither man nor beast only God, and that occasionally, whispered back, "I'll take the girls out, don't you bother. Blame me." The noise occasioned by fifty young girls clambering over chairs, giggling and pushing did not bother Dairin at all. She just went right on into *The Cat and the Moon*. Colin who now feared for Eddie's reason sidled out after them. Just as Dairin was intoning "Minnalushe creeps through the grass, alone important and wise and lifts to the changing moon his changing eyes," the lights went out and the theatre was plunged in deep darkness. In a few minutes Colin suddenly appeared with a flashlight and shouted, "Good people remain calm! I fear we must bring the curtain down on this fascinating evening but there has been a blowout in the main, and it cannot be rectified for some time." The words were hardly out of his mouth before the theatre was cleared. As soon as everyone was safely outside the building, the great actress included, the lights suddenly went on again. The General who had slept throughout the evening took Miss McGivern by the arm and almost threw her into his car. "Dear lady, a memorable evening. Not easily forgotten. I will drop you off at Daisy Lodge." He started up the engine before the dazed actress could remonstrate. "Not a word. It's on my way."

"You pulled the switch," Eddie sternly faced his partner, when they reached home.

"No, the Reverend Mother did. She said God moves in a mysterious way and pulled it herself."

"A great woman," said Eddie brokenly. "Would that she could do the same for the whole Festival."

Sunday came, the last day of the Festival. There were those who thought it would never come. The poor girl at the desk in the De Bracey Arms told Eddie she hadn't closed an eye since the Festival started, "what with the drunken brawls, smashed bottles, glasses and the Gardai say they'd had it. Ten arrests and two riots. Never again, Mr. Fox, never again. 'Tis too much." One thing could not be avoided and that was Father Hannigan's rendering of the *Celebration of Spring* which was to be read in the hotel at eight P.M. No one could imagine how he could bring in contraception or abortion and they were all too exhausted to care. It was the lack of the artist's approach to the Festival which disturbed the Committee. "We haven't cleaned up on anything except drink and all the money is in the hotel bar and goes to John Fallon. The people from all over the southeast have been taking advantage of the relaxed drinking laws for the Festival, and have been drinking here into the small hours. Poetry, it's a laugh!" groaned Eddie.

As was to be expected the bar and lounge of the De Bracey Arms was filled with drinkers, but surprisingly enough the banqueting hall was also full, this time the audience was comprised of devout old ladies mostly unmarried and the senior class from the convent with male escorts from Darragh Abbey School. They were chaperoned by two young liberated nuns in short skirts who looked as if they too could do with chaperons. Eddie couldn't help smiling in spite of his depressed mental condition when he saw the handsome Father Dermot giggling with them. Mairin was seated in the front row this time without her nephews. She was wearing a large badge with "Remember Bloody Sunday" on it. There was something specially menacing about this, Eddie felt. Today being Sunday and the Festival obviously building to a disastrous climax. At eight o'clock Father Hannigan stepped onto the stage beaming, all smiles and good cheer. It was very hard to believe in that strain of madness. On the little table in front of him he placed what appeared to be a goldfish bowl covered with a white cloth.

"He can't be going to celebrate communion," whispered Liz apprehensively.

"I say, how frightful," whispered Auntie Al nervously clanking her Celtic jewelry.

A blackboard was then carried in by a small boy and placed behind the priest. Eddie clutched Colin's arm; something awful was coming. The priest turned to the blackboard and chalked out boldly in Irish and English *The Celebration of Spring,* and underneath this he wrote "God and the Family." The Rector who had just seated himself behind The Boys whispered, "He can't get after me." He looked exhausted. "I've done my best."

"Tomas O'Sullivan," thundered the Father, "in spite of all the dirty drivel the translators have written of him was a pure minded god-fearing man. There is no reason to believe he was not married. Young Phelim the fiddler who accompanied him on his wanderings was a fine lad who honored his father and his mother and this was the only way he could earn money to send home to his good mother. All we know about this great poet was that he wrote in the true Irish, God bless him, and that he said his prayers and loved nature." He repeated "nature" three times and amidst subdued applause launched into his reading. The Father's rendering of the poem in Irish sounded more like prayers for the dead than sexual orgies. After fifteen minutes he suddenly closed the book and broke out into English. "The public, my friends, deserves an answer to many questions. I will do my best. People, especially the Irish, should see more easily the malice, I repeat the malice, of contraception when it takes human life. Abortion," he rumbled oblivious of nervous sniggers from the audience and lost in his own womb-world, "is murder." With a dramatic flourish he now uncovered the object on the table which appeared to be a specimen jar with something floating in it. "Inside this homely jar, you may step up anyone who cares, and look upon an eight-week foetus — this perfect little creature — this human being was murdered . . ."

At this there were muffled screams from the girls, one of whom slumped to the floor in a dead faint. The embarrassed nuns rushed to her assistance. Father Dermot, red in the face and inwardly raging, helped to carry out the casualty, while three of the other girls announced they were going to vomit and Auntie Al stood up and shouted, "Disgraceful! This is revolting!" Several of the Darragh Abbey boys surged eagerly towards the exhibit. At that moment when all seemed lost, there were sounds of commotion outside and Old Mick tottered into the hall. He was trembling and distraught.

"The safe's gone. The money's all gone. We're ruined! It's been took, Father."

"What's been took?" demanded Father Hannigan angrily, forgetting his grammar.

"The money. The take from the Festival. The drink money. Ten thousand pound. Three lads with guns and stockins' over their faces took it, safe and all, and a car waitin' for them outside. It went off heading North. It's no use your goin' after them. Father Dermot, they're gone. Mercy on us that young lady is took bad! 'Tis the comet! I told you, Mr. Fox, t'would have us all ruined."

He tottered out again and disappeared into the confusion and dismay in the foyer. The audience inside the hall was undecided whether to join the throng outside or wait for more horrors inside.

"Ten thousand pounds. That's a big sum." Mairin O'Kelly sidled towards the door; she was smiling.

Father Hannigan seized the specimen jar and shouted, "In view of the tragic happenings, I declare this meeting adjourned and the Ballyfungus Poetry Festival closed." Without waiting for anyone to second the motion he disappeared into the wings with his precious burden.

This time they all drove back to Ferncourt for the postmortem. A light rain was falling and a cold wind was blowing, but colder still were the hearts of the Festival Committee. Inside the cozy Victorian mansion bodily comfort at least was awaiting them. Betty had a huge fire going in the drawing room; a drink trolley was drawn up near the fire offering promise of alcoholic rehabilitation. As the sad company swept into the house, the grandfather's clock in the hall boomed out eleven and all the other clocks followed suit. Everyone talked at once and nobody really listened, so it was impossible to evolve any sort of real reassessment. The noble bloodhound Dolphie spread out on the hearth rug, occasionally barked, growled and incessantly slobbered.

"Well Eddie, I never thought it would end in crime. Boredom, yes, but not crime."

"My dear Colin, it was not crime it was the IRA."

"I don't see the difference."

"Artie Petsy, do look after the drinks. You must, or I'll slap you! Father Dermot darling, help the General."

"The whole thing was a bloody disgrace!"

"Eddie, do you actually think there was a foetus in that jar?"

"If it's any comfort, Auntie Al, I heard one of the Darragh Abbey boys say it was a shrimp."

"By George! How did he know?"

"The march of science, Archdeacon, haven't you heard that goosestep?"

"But . . ."

"Be careful, Auntie Al, we mustn't embarrass Father Dermot."

"Doctor, do you really think Father Hannigan was putting it over on us with a shellfish?"

"Of course, Colin. I've had enough experience over fifty years to know a foetus when I see one."

"What I can't understand — Scotch please, no ice — what I can't understand is why Father Hannigan is so passionately anxious to re-populate the world and does nothing about it himself."

"Quite right Mabs — do you need a refill? — look at the Rector with six and he isn't yelling about contraception though I must say — Good God, is he here?"

"No mercifully, he had to give one of his infants the bottle."

"Well he certainly can't give it the breast."

"Don't be disgusting, Artie. Give poor Auntie Al the bottle. Do you think the Festival was a failure, Colin, frankly everybody, was it a failure? No Eddie, calm down. It was a success. It put Ballyfungus in the public eye."

"Darling sweet Colin, I can't see why being in the public eye helps anyone. It's just an exchange of motes."

"A teeny drop more, Artie."

"I agree with you, Albinia. The public eye only leads to indecent exposure and worse. We were all very happy as we are; nothing has been changed in this house since the Crimean War and I like it. Betty, bring us some cheese and biscuits and some plum cake. Don't stand there staring, girl. Doesn't Father Hannigan understand that he's making all those girls frigid? That he's possibly cheating them of a healthy relaxed attitude to sex?"

"Liz dear, it's hopeless. We can't all be like you, dear."

"Colin, what do you mean?"

"Fifty years as a country doctor . . ."

"I feel very guilty about poor Oliver MacCrea. He was at both readings. Didn't you see him, Mabs?"

"No I didn't, Colin. No wonder, he's got so dim now you need a flashlight to find him. Nobody asked him to read his poetry and there he sits in poor broken-down Racketstown writing, forever writing, the unreadable."

"You can't look after everyone, Eddie. MacCrea has a very pretty daughter whatshername — I ought to know her name, I christened her."

"You certainly should, Archdeacon. She's working in Blood's stables I hear. Does anyone know how *Midsummer Night's Dream* did? Father Dermot, how did it do?"

"Well poor old Kev is rather cast down I think."

"He is? But I think it was a mistake to cast a Titania seven months pregnant, and so does he, now."

"Nothing's been heard of Midas, I mean Fallon?"

"My dear Liz, he only came for the opening with the President."

"Tott my nephew is coming over here soon for a few months. He'll keep an eye on that cad Fallon. Incidentally, Doctor, Attracta Mulcahy my best weaver is pregnant again."

"Good God, Al, that will be her third. I delivered her of the first before I retired. My son delivered her second. I don't mind actually — no Father Dermot not even an eensy drop more. What did you say, Auntie Al?"

"I said Attracta works up to the very last minute and she adores her children. My dear, the mother looks after them and adores them too."

"What does Father Hannigan say about her?"

"Well, Liz, now you mention it he likes her and them because she didn't abort. She didn't desert them and she's adding to the population which is all he seems to want."

"Father Dermot, Father Dermot, why do you Catholics want to populate the earth? It's grossly overcrowded already."

"It's God's will, Miss Atkins. We cannot question it."

"Come Eddie, you're too tired to drink any more. We must go home. Thank you, thank you, thank you. Lovely, Lovely, lovely. It's raining again."

"By jove I've just remembered it."

"Remembered what, Archdeacon?"

34

"That girl's name, the MacCrea girl. Felicity — that's it — Felicity."

They were going; they were gone. They streamed out into the moist chilly April night and the grandfather's clock struck twelve o'clock.

In the penthouse of the Grand Hotel Fungusport, used exclusively by John Fallon, four men were seated round a table poring over a map. The quorum consisted of a large smiling Canadian, a small unsmiling Japanese, a square faced solemn West-German and John Fallon himself.

He was speaking. "You can see from the map, as compared with our initial planning, it will be necessary to cut a road through Balooly Woods to the factory site which will be here. It is a wild strip of country, used to have good duck shooting, and the site should not in case of accident, which God forbid —" he looked sternly at his listeners and they looked right back at him — "should not provide a hazard to the surrounding villages. We may run into some opposition, gentlemen, but I think we can overcome it." He finished speaking and rolled up the map. There was a silence and then the bells of the Franciscan Priory across the road struck twelve. The sound of the bells faded away and far off in the bay the waves could be heard beating ceaselessly, forever and ever against the breakwater. And now there came a mysterious rustling through the trees in the enchanted Woods. Balooly was waking when others slept. Now the pagan creatures emerged; they were preparing for their celebration of spring. Twelve midnight. The Woods were alive, arming, ready.

Chronicle Two

THE HORRORS OF the Ballyfungus Spring Poetry Festival took some time to fade from people's memories, but gradually they ceased to talk in whispers about Father Hannigan's bottled foetus and life resumed its usual sleepy ah-sure-it-will-do rhythm. But towards the end of the following June, the wettest in living memory, a fresh scandal shook the Community.

"Mummy, I'm sorry to bother you, but I'm going to have a baby."
"You're what?"
"I'm pregnant."
"But — but you're not married."
"I know, Mummy, but nevertheless I am pregnant."
"Felicity, how can you stand there calmly and tell me such a dreadful thing? Are you sure?"
"Don't scream, Mummy. I am sure. Dr. Browne says so."
"Dr. Browne! Then all Ballyfungus will know."
"Who cares about Ballyfungus? I will go to London and have it. I will be an unwed mother. Mummy, everybody is doing it."
"Disgusting! Who is the father?"
"Paddy Roche. He works in Colonel Blood's stud. That's how I met him. He's married already. Two children. So that's that."
"I'm going mad. Mad!"
This poignant conversation was taking place in the library of Racketstown House, postal address Ballyfungus, Co. Wexlow, a decayed Georgian mansion inhabited by an equally decayed Georgian family, the MacCreas. Mrs. Elinor Mac-

Crea, a vague, incompetent lady, was seated at her writing desk, engaged in a task described as going through her bills. Her daughter, Felicity, the erring girl, had just come in from the garden, and though it was June she looked frozen. No wonder! It was an Irish summer day, which meant a keen northwest wind was blowing and a light cold rain was falling. Felicity was not more than twenty-three and, in spite of a red nose, damp clinging hair, and sloppy clothing, was in a ghostly way charming. Now she stood shivering in front of the empty fireplace, rubbing her blue hands together and sniffing.

"You will have to support the child yourself. We can't pay our bills and the new taxes have just about finished us. Unless you put it out for adoption."

"No, no," cried Felicity, "nobody does that anymore. They bring the child up themselves. It's much more interesting and rewarding. Really, I know. Meg Crawford just had one and she's never had a better time and always in a job."

"I never heard of anything more repulsive. What, oh what will I tell your father," moaned Mrs. MacCrea. She cried noisily and her tears dropped on the Victorian blotting pad.

"Daddy won't mind. He isn't in this world anyway." This was true, the mother could not deny it. Oliver MacCrea was a failed poet and spent all his days in a summer house, known as Father's Folly, scribbling. The estate had been sold bit by bit until all that was left was the house, a hopeless walled garden, a holy well which could cure warts, and an interesting dolmen. Luckily his wife had inherited a trust fund from her father which kept things going, or rather staggering. There were two sons: Alexis, who was studying to be an art dealer, and Ian, who was hoping to be a professional jockey. They were both older but, I fear, not basically wiser than their sister.

Felicity sat down beside her mother; she mopped up the poor broken woman's tears with a crumpled tissue. "You see, Mummy, I got into the habit of sleeping with Paddy

Roche when I was working in the stables, though I never went out with him socially, and things sort of caught up with us."

"How do you propose to keep this — this incubus?"

"Polly Craig runs a children's boutique in Chelsea and she's offered me a job as a salesgirl. I can sleep over the shop. She always employs unwed mothers. I keep the baby beside me in the shop, and look sorrowful, and people buy out of admiration for Polly's kindness and pity for poor me."

"Dreadful! It's like some sort of traffic in human flesh."

"What's that?" Felicity started up. "I thought I heard someone outside the door."

"You did. It's Mrs. Walsh's day. She's out there cleaning the brasses."

"The fly on the wall." Felicity laughed bitterly. "We might as well have told the Town Crier."

She was right. Next day, working full speed, Mrs. Walsh spread the news of Felicity's dilemma, as it came to be called, all over Ballyfungus. This intrepid character, who cleaned for everyone, sped from house to house on her motor scooter, helmeted and goggled, with a midwife's black bag strapped to her shoulders. Amongst other things, she carried in the black bag at least half a dozen latchkeys entrusted to her by employers so that she could enter at all times freely with due authority. She was a small thin active woman in her fifties, with such a bad squint (glasses did little to help) that it was impossible to gauge in which direction she was staring. One thing you could be sure of: nothing escaped those gimlety eyes. This affliction, combined with a continuous flow of conversation, made her visits, though functionally useful, somewhat exhausting. Mrs. Walsh was a born espionage agent; not for political reasons, simply for the pleasure of knowing everyone's business and conveying hot news from house to house. Her husband was a bus driver and there were no children. Once a year she and her mate went off on a package tour to some exotic foreign resort. They neither

41

swam nor enjoyed beach life, so they sat all day in the hotel sending postcards to their friends. She had been christened Emerald but was known to friend and foe alike as "Mrs. W."

Colonel St. John Blood, the successful Irish trainer and owner of the stud farm on which this lamentable affair originated, had a sharp talk with Paddy Roche, which came, as might be expected, to nothing. Paddy was a powerful-looking fellow with red hair and a pair of menacing grey eyes. He was a sharp man with the horses and greatly valued by the Colonel. The interview took place in the stables, which were centrally heated, luxuriously upholstered, no expense spared for the fortunate occupants.

"What's this about you and Miss MacCrea?" blurted the Colonel, never one to beat about the bush.

"What's what, sir?" grinned Paddy, showing little respect.

"You know damn well the girl's in foal and it's your doing."

"That's between me and Miss MacCrea," retorted Paddy, still grinning.

"All very well, but what about your wife? Dammit, man, haven't you any feelings? You got this poor girl in trouble and oh hell I know the family."

"My wife don't mind so long as I bring home the cash. Felicity is independent-like. She's asking for nothing. Sure, Colonel, aren't we all in the same boat, now and then?" He looked very hard at his employer, who wilted and moved away. He had just come through a highly publicized nasty divorce and was now living openly with the lady in the case.

"Let's look at Little Nell," the Colonel murmured and moved down the stalls. The grey filly, Little Nell, was second in the National Stakes at the Curragh and was favored for the Irish One Thousand Guineas. She ranked far above the human filly Felicity MacCrea in worldly and indeed emotional importance. "What did the vet say?"

"One of them common hoof disorders."

"Thank God."

"He recommended Absorbine Hooflex. So we applied it. It's okay now."

"Good man." Ah, indeed, Paddy was invaluable.

Oliver MacCrea cried a little when told the news. He was a tall thin man with a bald egg-shaped head ending in a long melancholy face. A cigarette was placed perpetually on his lower lip, from which he puffed feebly. He did not inhale, it took too much energy. He spoke with a hereditary speech impediment.

"How could she fall so low?" he moaned. "A stable lad smelling of the stables."

"Jesus was born in a stable, Daddy," retorted the daughter.

"Sure you do not wish to convey the impwession that you are cawwying the Second Coming?"

"Oh, Daddy, really. What about Aunt Violet?"

"That was wape. Legal wape." He paused and with a great effort went on: "He can't mawwy you of course, not that I would cheer for it."

The MacCrea family was seated in the library drinking cheap sherry before dinner. Gin or whiskey was out of the question. It was in the nature of a family conference, the subject being Felicity's dilemma. The two brothers were present. Alexis the art dealer was sprawled on the sagging sofa, the father was perched sadly on a chair with no back, and Mrs. MacCrea was darning some withered socks for her husband and of course weeping gently. The paper was peeling off the walls, the curtains hung in curious brown tatters, and there was a heavy smell of dog emanating from two unhealthy-looking bassets. Really, thought Felicity, it couldn't be more dreary. She longed for escape. The more she thought about it, the more desirable the prospects of glamorous unwed motherhood in London seemed to be.

Alexis the art dealer was tall, golden-haired, and blue-eyed. He wore his hair like his sister's, flowing to the shoulders. As part of his profession he was extremely excitable and restless. Art dealers invariably feel that they are missing some extraordinary find if they don't keep moving. Alexis already had a nervous habit of turning teacups upside down to evaluate their markings and weighing flat silver ruminatively in his hands. Ian the jockey was also blue-eyed and yellow-haired, but he was small and rather bandy-legged. Now he was lying flat on the hearthrug deep in sleep. Occasionally he twitched as if going over the jumps in his dreams.

"It's really too bad, Felicity," said Alexis irritably, "sleeping around like this. You might catch something."

"She caught a baby." The jockey opened one eye.

"None of you think of the moral side," cried the mother hysterically, "and you needn't turn that bowl upside down, Alexis. You know it's Coalport and cracked."

"As a matter of fact I do care about the moral issues," replied the art dealer. "If the man had loads of money I wouldn't mind, but having a bastard by a penniless peasant *is* immoral, to my way of thinking." He rose abruptly. "Anyway, I must go now. I have to get to Shannon." He looked at his watch.

"Shannon." Mrs. MacCrea looked at him in amazement. "But I thought you were here for dinner. I made a shepherd's pie."

"Sorry, Mother, but I'm catching a plane to New York. I'm taking over an important Holy Family — we have a potential buyer there. My driver will be here in a few minutes. Don't worry, I'm packed; I'm always packed. You'll have to look after the child yourself, Felly, somewhere else. And I earnestly hope the Colonel fires your paramour."

Ian sat up. "He won't; he's promoted him, actually. Paddy's head man round the stud."

Alexis laughed sardonically and tossed his golden mane; he was not queer but didn't mind being thought so. "I should think he's proved his worth all right. Felly can testify to that."

"You're all so coarse," whimpered the mother. "I can't understand it. You've had every advantage."

"What I can't understand, Felicity, is — haven't you heard of the Pill?" Alexis eyed his sister accusingly.

"Of course. I meant to go to Dr. Browne, but it all happened so suddenly."

"It usually does, those rolls in the hay. They shouldn't have girls like you around the stables."

"It was not a roll in the hay. It was — it was — a Grand Passion."

Her brothers burst into cruel laughter. The mother sobbed afresh and the father rose to his feet. "May I go now?" Oliver shambled towards the door. "I'm in the middle of something." He had contributed nothing to the conference except cigarette smoke.

"Father's been in the middle of nothing for years," remarked Ian.

There was more rude laughter in which even Felicity joined.

"You heard about poor little Felicity MacCrea?" Muriel, the wife of Archdeacon Musgrave, addressed her husband. The fat little woman was lying on the sofa reading a Gothic romance novel. There was something wrong with her legs, never properly diagnosed, which prevented her moving around much except in search of food. It certainly ruled out all parish work. "Mrs. Walsh was telling me about it. You ought to go and see them, darling. The girl is pregnant by a stable lad who's married already. The MacCreas are heartbroken."

"Surely the Rector can deal with that?"

"Mr. Green? Dearest, he doesn't know how babies come."

"He must have some idea. There are now six little Greens."

"I mean outside wedlock. Unpleasant things like that."

"It's rather delicate, isn't it?" queried the Archdeacon irritably. He was a powerfully built man who had in years gone by captained the Irish rugby football team and was prone to tackle parish matters according to rugby football rules. Nevertheless, he was greatly liked and respected, and though he had no children himself — possibly because of Muriel's legs — the young adored him. The Musgraves were seated in the pleasant sunny library, the windows of which opened out on the gardens. The gardens stretched down to the heavily polluted River Fung, which meandered past the small cathedral town on its way to the sea. The Archdeacon sighed. He would have preferred to spend the morning at his desk composing next Sunday's sermon, but duty, that stern and boring daughter of the voice of God, called. Grumbling and muttering he drove toward Racketstown House full of misgivings. What could he say? What line should he adopt? The hall door was open. Except during winter storms, nobody bothered to close it. All Ballyfungus, even the itinerants, knew there was nothing left to steal.

"Yoohoo," hooted the Archdeacon as he tiptoed through the hall. Nobody answered. He opened the drawing room door and peeped in; he was lucky. The fallen girl was seated near the fireplace, knitting something white, one presumed for the baby. She was enveloped in what looked like a balloon, but was in fact a smock designed to conceal her condition.

"My dear," the Archdeacon approached her as if walking on eggs, "what's this I hear? You are in trouble?" He sat down beside her and was immediately seized with a nervous fit of coughing. Felicity looked at him sweetly, pityingly.

"Yes, but it's all right, Archdeacon, really. Everything is organized. I am going to London and I will bring up the baby myself."

"Very laudable. Most courageous." Again he coughed. "The child, alas, will be nameless."

Felicity stared at him in genuine surprise. "Oh no, dear Archdeacon. If it's a girl I'll call her Sabrina after my great aunt who had a child, they *think*, by Edward the Seventh, and if a boy, Patrick Roche."

"Yes, yes, of course." Words failed him. What should come next? he pondered. Reprimand? Shock? Not anymore. Those days were gone. "The man, I understand, cannot marry you. The child is therefore illegitimate."

"Of course," was the calm reply.

"That will be hard, my dear; you will face comment, even censure."

"No, I won't. You should hear Liz Atkins. You know the famous artist in the Old Mill? The minute Mrs. Walsh told her she drove over to see me. She said it was a beautiful thing, that I was to be congratulated, instead of censured, for taking such a courageous stand. She is in fact giving a party for me — and for the baby."

"What?" Words again failed the Archdeacon.

"She says it's a blow struck for the liberation of women from the ridiculous old-fashioned sex codes. She says Ballyfungus must march with the times. She's asking you; she's asking everyone to the party."

The Archdeacon looked stunned; he was stunned. "A party."

"Yes, do come, dear Archdeacon. We all love you." She leaned forward and kissed him on his cheek. The Archdeacon closed his eyes. The thought, a pleasant one, crossed his mind: The kiss of youth was it always perfumed with violets? He rose to his feet. This girl was not in need of consolation, spiritual or otherwise. "Thank you my dear," he murmured. "Your father is . . . ?"

"In the Folly, as usual, translating some Bulgarian poet." She accompanied him to the door.

They stood there bathed in the amber sunshine. A dove suddenly flapped over their heads. The Archdeacon pressed her arm. "Good-bye, my dear. If you need help or advice, come to me."

As he drove home the Archdeacon's thoughts took a curious turn. How had this thing happened? he pondered. Where and how did it come about? Where did the fragile golden-haired nymph embrace that brutish satyr Paddy Roche? The stables? The hayloft? The thought was titillating, and his favourite lines of poetry flashed through his mind:

47

There on beds of violets blue
And fresh blown roses washed in dew,
Filled her with thee a daughter fair
So buxom blithe and debonair.

Good old Milton! That was the real Milton, not the gloomy metaphysican of *Paradise Lost*. Thank God I have no children, murmured the Archdeacon to himself. I could never have coped with this generation. Never.

Mrs. Emerald Walsh was helping out at the presbytery. The Canon's housekeeper was off seeing a sick brother who was "took bad in the privates," and Mrs. Walsh's help was enlisted in giving the Canon and his two curates their supper.

"Ye heard about Miss MacCrea?" she remarked in an off-hand manner as she plumped down an enormous pot of tea on the table. The curates looked up at her questioningly. Felicity worked for the Hodge Podge. She was Father Kevin's most valued stage manager. Naturally he pricked up his ears.

"What's wrong with Miss MacCrea?"

"She's havin' a baby."

"A baby? When did she get married?"

"She's not married, Father Kevin, that's the trouble."

"Good God." In his agitation Father Sheedy knocked over the milk jug. "You mean . . ."

"I do, then. Don't mind about the milk, Father dear, I'll get a cloth."

"Who is the man, Mrs. W.?"

"Paddy Roche at Blood's Stables."

"Paddy Roche — but he's married.. The dirty scoundrel. I'll tell him off. I'll get the Canon on to him. I will."

"She's goin' to London to live."

"London. But she can't. She's stage-managing our next production. She can't."

"Kevin, are you crazy? Sit." Father Dermot pulled the smaller man down. Mrs. Walsh meanwhile was mopping up

48

the milk, alert to possible scandal. "You can't concern your-self with these things, Kevin. As a matter of fact I meant to tell you, I bumped into that Atkins woman in the post office and she asked me to a party for Miss MacCrea. She said some people might think it was a sad occasion but she thought it was joyful. She told me then what had happened. Poor Felic-ity. I think we should go to the party. She needs Christian sympathy and concern."

Father Kevin dejectedly sighed out, "What will the Canon say?"

"I don't care. We're not living in the Middle Ages."

"No, but the Canon is."

No denying that. He walked in at that moment covered with medieval dust and avid for twentieth-century sustenance. Mrs. Walsh, with a look of perfect understanding, placed a huge dish of ham and eggs in front of the holy man. He said grace, as if in his sleep, and food was handed out to the hungry. Towards the end of the meal Father Kevin repeated the story of the fallen Felicity to the Canon.

"I know what they would have done to her seven hundred years ago." The Canon turned his cavernous eyes on the young priest. Possibly because of his life in the ruins he had begun to look like a carving on an ancient tomb.

"What, Canon?"

"Walled her up alive. That's what they did with erring nuns."

Father Kevin paled. "Would you care for some toast, Canon?" he murmured.

"Toast," responded the Canon smiling grimly; "that's it. She would have been burned at the stake."

"But she's not a witch, Canon."

"All women are witches," was the terse reply.

At this interesting point Mrs. Walsh poked her head around the door and announced her departure. She was wear-ing her cycling helmet and goggles, the black bag strapped to her shoulders.

49

"That woman's a witch if ever I saw one," remarked Father Dermot when the hall door banged. "On a broomstick, flying from house to house, laden with mischief."

"I don't think we should bring up the party," whispered Father Kevin. "Not quite the moment."

"No. He won't go, but we will. Leave it to me. I can always bring up Mary Magdalene at the foot of the cross. You know?"

"Everyone's coming regardless of race, creed, or colour." Liz handed out drinks. It was evening and they were seated round the fire in her studio.

"Reel off your list," demanded Eddie.

"Let me see. Well, the two Catholic curates; the Protestant Rector, and the Archdeacon, with Muriel, of course."

"Of course. Let's keep it clean."

"Let me see. General Ironside, the old and the young doctors Browne, Mabel Vigors and Albinia. Alicia de Bracey, thank God, is ill. Mrs. Walsh's account of her symptom is appalling. She keeps belchin' and belchin' and the bile risin' and risin'."

Colin rose to make himself a drink. In passing he patted Eddie's shoulder. "Incidentally, Liz, incidentally, have you heard the hideous rumours about Johnny Fallon's newest enterprise? He's to tear down Balooly Woods and make a development around some factory."

"Good God! We must alert everybody. He can't do this." Liz rose true to form and paced the floor. "He must be stopped."

"Darling Liz, calm down. The case of Felicity MacCrea is first on the agenda. *Reposez-vous.*" Colin pushed her into a chair.

"I feel this party should be a salute to the future." Liz looked at them with fearful earnestness. "You've no idea how everyone has responded. Offers of help have poured in . . ."

"Liz, dear," Colin took her hand, "some women are born liberated, some achieve liberty, and others have it thrust upon them. *You* were certainly born liberated, but be careful not to thrust it upon those who are unequal to carrying the burden. Because, darling, liberty *is* a burden. Liberty is for the strong. I feel that Felicity would be happier under restraint and discipline. She is a feeble little thing and would be very happy with a respectable bank clerk in a new housing development."

"No, no. You're wrong. Felicity is on her way to a wider life and a braver world."

Colin patted her hand. "We'll see, darling. We'll see. Meanwhile she's going to have a slap-up party, thanks to you."

The day of the party arrived. Liz had planned to have it partially outdoors — the garden round the millpond was so charming — but unfortunately a strong wind was blowing from the southeast and the sun stayed behind heavy clouds. All day Mrs. Walsh had been scrubbing and cleaning and, needless to say, talking. All day Tom had been setting out glasses, polishing them, arranging bottles, and seeing to the fires. He also mowed the lawn and did a bit of hasty weeding. Liz herself worked on hors d'oeuvres and arranged flowers.

"I know what I'd do to that Felishitty," snarled Mrs. Walsh over a cup of tea snatched at zero hour. "I'd have beaten the hide off her and sent her to the informatory."

Tom smirked. He lived in a very comfortable glass house and was not going to throw any stones. "Ah, she's a nice little girl and it takes two to make a babby, Mrs. W., don't forget that."

Liz, haggardly handsome in a grey velvet pantsuit, surveyed the studio with reasonable pride. Never had it looked more seductively, luminously inviting. Through the open windows you could see the limpid waters of the millpond and far off hear the splashing of the weir rivalling the flood of verbal comment from the crowd. Mrs. Walsh, a human tape recorder, moved amongst the guests proffering delicacies. "Them's fish; them's their eggs."

"Caviar, how wonderful!"

"Better you than me." She was wearing a white uniform over the jumper and trousers, had applied lipstick, combed the grey locks away from the bony forehead, but the bedroom slippers were still evident.

The Archdeacon and Muriel were the first to arrive. Those legs always got her to a party. They were closely followed by the entire MacCrea family with the maid of dishonor between them. Felicity looked very touching and innocent in a long white dress cut low to reveal swell of bosom, a white shawl draped across the stomach which still seemed very flat. Tears stung the Archdeacon's eyes as he looked at her. So young, so sweet. Mrs. MacCrea was draped in black as if for a funeral, which was just how she felt, and her husband was wearing a business suit built for him in the thirties by a Savile Row tailor. It was now, alas, green with age. "All right for St. Patrick's Day," sniffed Mrs. W., giving him the once-over. Drinks were handed round by Tom who took occasional sips just to make sure they were all right. Father Sheedy, on arriving, made straight for Felicity, threw himself at her feet, and begged her in an impassioned whisper not to go to London. His sister had worked in an Abbey production right up to the birth of her baby. In fact there was some fear she might give birth on the stage.

Everyone brought little offerings for the baby, which were presented in a furtive manner to Liz: "For you know who!" The parents of the fallen girl sat like two shabby old mourning doves on a distant sofa sighing in unison. The Old Doctor was in great form, shouting medicinal folklore at everyone. "Old wives' tales always accurate. This for instance: 'If the fart be loud and the piss be clear, the trot of the doctor you'll never hear.' Ha! ha! Absolutely right."

("Did you hear that?" groaned Mrs. W. "Disgusting.")

Felicity was the centre of attention. Surrounded by rattles, bootees, and christening mugs, she sat curled up on the sofa. The shawl had slipped off; so had her shoes; she tossed back martinis, devoured caviar, and laughed and talked uproariously. Father Sheedy and several other young men surrounded her.

"The next production is *An Enemy of the People*," whispered the curate. "It presents considerable problems in casting and staging. I'll be up to see you in the morning with the script."

"Not too early, Father Kevin. I'm apt to be sickish in the mornings."

("Did yer hear that? — no shame!")

Loud cheering broke out. Colin had arrived from Fungusport with a load of fresh prawns, shelled, washed, and ready for eating. He had also brought a tasty dip.

Liz threw her arms round him. "Prawns. Colin, you're a pet. Felicity must have the first prawn. Here, guest of honor. It's all yours."

("One rotten prawn and a death follows. Me husband's first cousin went black and died in twenty minutes from one of them," whispered Mrs. W., but nobody heeded her.)

Mabs clutched Colin. "Colin, dear, who is the father of this famous child?"

"A stable lad, I believe. He's not here of course."

"Archdeacon, ducky," cried Muriel approaching her husband, "time to go home." She tried to stifle a yawn. No wonder. She had been seated beside Mrs. MacCrea for what seemed hours. The poor lady had the effect of instant sedation on her listeners.

"Good heavens." The Archdeacon consulted his watch. "Nine o'clock, time to go."

It was then it happened. Liz gasped, clutched Colin's arm, and pointed towards the door. No words came from her; she was too stunned. Suddenly the conversation died down and a great silence filled the studio. Paddy Roche was standing in the door. He was wearing a golden-brown tweed suit patched with leather at the elbows, a white polo sweater, brown suede shoes. A small deerstalker was pulled down over his eyes which added to the menacing quality of his personality. He looked like every gentlemanly horse-dealer.

Strange, thought Colin, the moment the parvenu gets money or power he takes on the colour of the erstwhile hated oppressors. My God, the insolence of the man! Paddy took off the hat and walked into the room displaying no embarrassment, no shame. He walked towards Felicity, who stared at him as if mesmerized.

Father Sheedy stood up and confronted him: "You've no right to come here, sir. No right at all."

"I've all the right in the world. Mind your own business, Father, and I'll mind mine." He took a sealed envelope out of his pocket and tossed it into Felicity's lap. Then, before anyone could interfere, he stooped down and kissed her long and hard on the lips.

("You could have counted sixty. I was near faintin'. The heart racin', me armpits drenched.")

"For the baby," he said coolly. "And if you need more, let me know." He put on the hat, looked at everyone as if daring them to say a word, and strode out of the room.

There was silence. Mrs. Walsh dropped the prawns and screamed. A roar of conversation broke out. Regardless of the floor being strewn with shellfish, people rushed at each other exchanging comments on the scene: "Better than a play," said Albinia. "Tasteless," said her sister. "The infernal brute," Ian shouted. "We should have kicked him through the window."

Felicity stood up; she glared at her brother. "He's not a brute. Why didn't you kick him? I know, you know damn well that Paddy is going places and you better not be on bad terms with him or you won't get a mount. I love Paddy. I know I'll never see him again." She ripped open the envelope. "A check for two hundred pounds. He does care." She began to weep then. Oh how hard it is at that age to accept finality. She ached for those ruffianly arms around her once again, but it could never be. She had, in a sense, been paid off.

"Chalk it up to experience," whispered Liz. Having laid eyes on the villainous Paddy, she recognized his charm. He

54

was that fatal thing — the male sexpot. He needn't lift a finger, women came to him.

"It was wonderful while it lasted. But now it's over. It was a good-bye kiss," sobbed Felicity.

The Archdeacon pressed her arm. "Be brave; endure: we are all with you." Somehow he couldn't bring himself to mention God. I know lust when I see it, he thought. That man lusts after women. Oddly, Father Sheedy was thinking the very same thing. Some things are inevitably ecumenical.

"I would have stopped him," Tom explained, "but he was in the door before I knew it."

Mrs. Walsh, in tears, was sweeping up prawns. ("Never see the like even on the pixtures I never seen the like.")

Felicity's parents held a hasty conversation and decided to leave for home. The two priests hurried off. They were earnestly hoping that no details of the party would reach the Canon's ears. Felicity held on to Liz, the only one, she felt, with an ounce of understanding or sympathy. "Thank you," she whispered, "I'll come and see you soon."

Gradually all the guests disappeared, streamed out into the summer twilight, and made their way home. Mrs. Walsh took off the uniform, put on the helmet and goggles, poured heaps of prawns, cheese, and hard-boiled eggs into the black bag, and stormed off on the scooter. She had to be at De Braceys' at nine the next morning; between then and now the news had to be given out.

She did not reach De Braceys' luxury bungalow until ten the next morning. She was panting and hoarse when she arrived. "What I have to tell don't bear repeatin'. Holy God, nothing like it ever known before in Ballyfungus and there have been people here since the flood. Tie yourself to a string now. I was passin' the Doctor's house on me way here when I saw the Old Doctor comin' out to go fishin'. He signaled me to stop. For a moment I thought he wanted a lift because he's been goin' a bit soft-like. When he told me the news I took such a turn me stomach went churnin' and churnin'. The

55

young doctor was up all night at MacCreas'. Miss Felishitty took bad in the night. At two o'clock it was all over. She'd lost the baby. Now 'tis no surprise to me, when I saw her stuffin' down them prawns, tossin' back the gin, sittin' on the soffy bold as brass; the Queen of Sheba bargin' up the Nile, I said to meself, you're doing yourself no good, me lady. And wasn't I right? I'll get you a sup of tea now. You don't look so yaller today as I seen you last. Honest now I thought the breath was left you and you was took be death. I'll draw up the blind now so you can see the morning light. Ye never know when it's the last time. But keep the ball rollin', I says, up to the end. Sit be the window, dear, while I change the bed. Tis lovely outside, lashin' rain. The party, well you wouldn't believe. I never seen the like and never will again. Who do you think come but the devil himself, Paddy Roche! Paddy Roche, the father of the lost baby! God rest its little soul. She was only four months gone. I don't know what the Archdeacon will say when he hears about Miss Felishitty, but bein' a Protestant he don't take them things as hard. Pardon me, Madam, I didn't mean to be defensive in me speakin', but the Canon now is different. Told poor Father Sheedy who was cryin' with pity for her that she should be bricked up live with a serpent. As for Father Hannigan, he wants us all to be virgins. It's the highest thing to be, he says, nothin' better. And what was wrong with your mother, Father? asks Father Dermot boldlike. No answer to that one."

Felicity returned the money to Paddy Roche with a short note saying he was under no obligation to her from now on and she never wanted to see him again. She fled to Dublin and got a job as a waitress in the Silver Platter, a chic basement restaurant run by a pair of charming highway robbers. The restaurant opened only late at night when the patrons were drunk and in no condition to count the change or check the bill. The reactions to her tragedy were peculiar and would have delighted Dean Swift. Previously under a cloud for having an illicit pregnancy she was now under a darker cloud for not having it. As Liz Atkins put it, "Something rather fine, rather wonderful has petered out into a sordid little miscarriage."

The morning after the party Albie accompanied by Jamesy Nolan was doing a tour of the garden. The gardens were her affair. Mabs looked after the household. It was a cold wet morning. Albie was shrouded in a nun's waterproof cape with hood purchased in Dublin and Jamesy was wearing an old coat of the late Colonel Bing's which reached to his heels. He was in a lamenting mood, the cold wet summer was getting him down. "Not a bit of kindness in the earth yet. No good weedin', ma'am, sure they answer you back. I tell ye pull them up; five minutes after they're up again and laughin' at ye. Wait, till I tell you ma'am I was sittin' yesterday afternoon on the wall near the front gates when a car as big and black as Goggins hearse from the undertakers stopped at the gate and out lept a foreign fella. There was a little yaller man sittin' in the car and a yank driver. Well he asked a flood o' questions about you and the house and the Woods. Declare to God I took fright thinkin' it might be a special squad goin' after Provos, but then I thought, sure he's a foreigner and no harm. Lovely country, sez he, aye sez me, sure I grewed up in it and there's none like it anywheres. You'll see great changes soon, he sez. How so? I sez. We're building a road right where you're sittin', he sez, to a factory the other side of the Woods and yous will all be gettin' plenty of work and lovely money. Is that true, ma'am? Wouldn't that be a terrible thing?"

"It would, Jamesy, but don't worry, we won't allow it. If you're talking about it to anyone just be sure and tell them it won't happen here. Remember that, Jamesy, it won't happen here."

But the underground conspiracy to destroy Ballyfungus was already in full swing.

Chronicle Three

Over the next eight months Ballyfungus remained more or less at peace; the inhabitants pursued their usual torpid way of life and death. True there was a bus strike (an inspector accidentally kicked a conductor; he said his foot slipped) so the town was for some weeks cut off from civilization. Unless you had a car, and then the price of petrol precluded much driving except for the sternest necessities. The telephones were frequently out of order (the operators were demanding longer tea breaks); added to these nuisances a series of electric power cuts kept plunging the country into spasmodic periods of unexpected darkness. Under cover of blackouts Goggins assistants in the supermarket (most of them young girls who should have been at school) ran round the store changing the labels and upping the prices. There were also sinister rumours about another bank strike frightening the wits out of people who had suffered in the previous strike and causing a hysterical run on post office savings. A West German industrialist, one Herr Krause, occupied the penthouse in the Grand Hotel and spent great deal of time driving round Ballyfungus and environs staring and making notes.

One evening towards the end of February the fearsome foursome was seated in the drawing room of Ferncourt playing, what do you think, bridge. The huge wood fire crackled pleasantly and the stomachs of the gentlemen rumbled noisily, the plain truth being they were hungry. Owing to the various strikes it was increasingly difficult to shop in Fungusport and Goggins supermarket was obviously taking advantage of the situation and robbing everyone right, left and centre. The Ferncourt ladies always bought their meat in Fungusport, but the old car had been giving trouble and they were doing without meat as much as possible. They were therefore unable to offer the usual hospitality to the gentlemen. However, sandwiches and hot soup were promised later with the drinks. The bridge game was proceeding at the usual pace and whether it was hunger or old age everyone seemed more muddled than usual.

"Two clubs," announced the General determinedly. As he spoke he sneezed liberally, spraying the cards on the table. The ladies sighed and Mabs flicked her handkerchief across the table.

"Two diamonds darlings," came from Albie. This evening she wore a red wig; not a good sign.

Mabs passed. "No bid." The General sneezed again; this time he sprayed her Ladyship who groaned and said, "I should have worn a shower cap."

"There's no cure for the common cold," announced the Doctor. "Strange. Not even the herb doctors were on to that. They used seven herbs of great value and power and they are still used. Two no trumps. Ground ivy, vervain, eyebright, groundsel, foxglove, the bark of the elder tree and the young shoots of the hawthorn. Mint was . . ."

"Josh, please do pay attention, sweetest." Albie pinched his wrist sharply; the Doctor yelped. At last the game scattered on to a dishevelled finale, the General making countless adding mistakes.

"Liz Atkins phoned this morning; she's in trouble," remarked Albie brightly. "It always cheers me up when someone else is in trouble. Makes my day."

"You never told me," grumbled her sister.

"You were out shouting at Jamesy. Yes Liz is in trouble."

"She can't be at her age," jeered the Doctor; "not even Tom Nolan can perform that miracle."

"Josh, you're a dirty old man." Albie giggled and slapped his wrist. At the end of an evening he was generally covered with slaps, pinch marks and on one or two memorable occasions — bites.

"Course I am; always was. My profession was hardly cleansing. Well, what's her trouble for God's sakes?"

"Some odd young American has turned up here. A protégé of Liz's sisters. I'm not sure it isn't a relation. This young chap is living in Daisy Lodge for a few months while he finishes a book."

"What's wrong with that? Daisy Lodge is damn comfortable. Wouldn't mind staying there myself." The General sneezed again and pulled out, rather belatedly, a ragged handkerchief.

"This young man is very peculiar. Liz thinks he's having a breakdown. She doesn't know what to do about him."

"Sounds fishy. I'd like to know more," said her sister.

"You will — she's asked us to dinner with him and The Boys."

"How silly. How can a lot of old people help with an insane young man? We can't give him anything . . ."

The General burst into song: "I can't give you anything but love baby, I can't give you anything but love." He had forty years ago, ere this story opens, wooed unsuccessfully one of London's most beautiful chorus girls.

"Artie, spare us," Mabs put her hands over her ears.

"Too bad Tott isn't here. Auntie Al says he's now involved with a West Indian dancer," sighed Albie; she pulled her wig into place.

"Male or female?" queried the General.

"Neither. Belly."

The welcome sound of the food trolley was heard outside the door and in came Betty wheeling the precious load followed by Dolphie the accursed bloodhound.

"There now," chanted Betty. "You'll love this. Ham, egg, cheese sandwiches, lentil soup very fillin' and to follow, macaroons. Coffee for them that likes it. Blessed mother, it's gone up to three pounds a pound. The drinks do follow."

"Leave it over there, boy." Boy was a term of address which Mabs used absentmindedly; it was of course a hangover from Government House days. "Thanks mum," was the humble response.

On her way out the half-witted retainer whispered to Mabs, "Dolphie's been out and done his business. It seems a bit loose d'ye know?" Mabs frowned. This was disquieting news.

A few minutes later Betty wheeled in the drink trolley and this time addressed the company as if they were a group of mentally deficient persons on the same wavelength as herself. "Eat up God help yees, before the next strike hits us. I hear tell in the village every mortal man in the county will be out on strike; and the dead not to be buried. God help Ireland!" Very pleased with herself she meandered out of the room and banged the door.

"I hope Dolphie doesn't really have diarrhea," whispered Albie apprehensively.

"Nonsense." Mabs poured the soup out of the thermos flask into the cups provided for the purpose. "Albie, stop fussing and hand out the sandwiches."

For the next half hour nothing was heard but lapping sounds as the soup went down; the chewing of sandwiches and scrunching of macaroons for which the Ferncourt cuisine was noted. Disjointed sentences between bites made little sense.

"Did you see a bishop was questioned on morals charges?"

"Can't be an Irish bishop and certainly not a Catholic bishop. Must be USA."

"No Albie, East Africa."

"Thank God, that makes more sense. Did you read about the Mayo farmer who had two children by his own daughter, Josh?"

"Doesn't surprise me, a farmer called Foley in Balratty was responsible for several curious looking lambs, one had red hair and a lisp."

64

"Auntie Al has gone into pottery; do you think she's wise? They're all in pottery now; the last Morgan girl's getting married to a carpenter from Kinealy ten years younger than she is."

"Albie, Albie, the poor girl was desperate they'd shut her up in that Norman tower."

"Rapunzel, Rapunzel let down your hair."

"My dear Artie, you're so romantic. He could have let *his* hair down; it is I'm told a rope ladder to his waist and he plays the guitar. Poor girl so plain; doom was written on her nose."

Suddenly there was an appalling sound from the Doctor: mixture of a gulp, a sob, and a vomit. The other three looked at him startled. He had been up to the moment happily involved with a macaroon but now disaster had struck; his dentures were imbedded in the sticky mass!

"Can I help you, old chap?" The General rose gallantly to his feet, not that they usually responded happily to him. "I think the ladies better leave the room."

"Blah! blah! blop!" was the only response from the Doctor. Dolphie began growling. The Doctor now dead to all sense of decency pulled out the mass of half-crunched macaroon to which his dentures were visibly adhering.

"Good God!" exclaimed the General. Not since Dunkirk had he been up against such a challenge.

"Josh, leave the room at once," cried Mabs. "How dare you."

"I can't get the damn things out," shouted the Doctor frantically.

"A screwdriver might do it," said the General taking command. "You must have a toolbox somewhere, Mabs."

"In the pantry. Oh Josh, you're not fit for human consumption." Albie covered her face with her handkerchief.

"Come, Josh." The General led the Doctor out. "This is men's work!"

The ladies left alone stared at each other. "What next?" sighed Albie.

"I'm going to tell his son. Something must be done." Mabs rose and paced the room.

"We must never have macaroons again. They are chancy, Mabs."

In fifteen minutes the gentlemen returned. "Betty did it," announced the General triumphantly. "Boiling water, a tin opener and a fork." The Doctor though shaken was unrepentant. He demanded a shot of whiskey for his nerves. It was most grudgingly handed to him by Albie.

"This must not happen again, Josh" said Mabs sternly; it was her royal command voice. "If the Waddington-Henns or the St. George-Mahoneys had been here it would have been most embarrassing!"

"Good God, Mabs, I didn't do it on purpose. You talk as if my trousers had fallen down."

"It would have been pleasanter, Josh!" Albie pinched him again.

"No it wouldn't, not at my age. Aha! eleven o'clock." He cupped a hand to his ear; clocks indeed were striking all over the house. The gentlemen rose to their ruined feet. "We must be off." It was then that the Doctor chose to strike — with the clocks — a warning note. "Fallon's on the warpath again. The Castle's to come down, and I quote, 'twenty-four stately Georgian mansions' built in its place."

Everyone exclaimed in horror, "Are you sure, Josh? Who told you, it may be a rumour," demanded Mabs.

"It's far more than a rumour. I heard it from Rooney. I hear all things good and bad from Rooney."

"Does poor Alicia know? It will break her heart."

"Yes she knows, but what use is it to her now?"

"Rooney also told me Fallon's marriage has broken up. He has a lady friend." He wound a long grey woolen scarf around his neck. "I did not weep for him."

"When these parvenus get rich their morals go out of the window," said Mabs. "The bedroom window," she added.

"You better go fast friends," exclaimed Albie. "Dolphie I'm afraid *has* diarrhea!" She pulled a bell rope frantically, it

66

was the last house in the county to have bell ropes. "We must get Betty."

The gentlemen went fast, faster than light.

The same evening Eddie Fox was visiting Liz Atkins in the Old Mill. He had been summoned to a conference regarding the eccentric visitor from the USA. Colin couldn't come, he was in the throes of a new Tierney. Tom greeted Eddie at the door.

"Terrible night, Mr. Fox. You walked up? Let me take your coat. Would you like coffee or whiskey?"

He's the host now, thought Eddie, amused. Poor fellow, he better make the most of it. Any moment, like Catherine the Great — Liz could find another lover. She was easily bored and Tom, though handsome, was not exactly stimulating mentally.

"I'll take a little whiskey, Tom. Thanks. She's in there?"

"In the studio, Mr. Fox. There's a roaring fire. I'll bring the drinks in."

Liz was lying on a sofa near the fire. She was wearing a white caftan and looked, as Eddie put it to himself, exquisitely sated.

"Sit down, darling Eddie. Listen to this . . . it's from my sister Grace, from Cambridge, Mass. Her husband teaches comparative literature there — Harvard."

"Thanks, Tom. No ice. Soda. Splendid. Proceed, Liza."

" 'Alan Plodd comes of the most normal American household you can imagine. Father a Hartford Insurance Executive, a golfer. Two sisters married to Junior Hartford Insurance executives. Alan went to a good prep school, then Yale. Lightweight boxer. Normally sexed.' " Eddie broke into laughter and murmured, "How boring." Liz continued reading, " 'The poor boy is in graduate school here writing his thesis on Samuel Beckett — we have the great Beckett man here but Alan has gone steadily downhill into a depression. We have never seen such complete identification with subject. It only goes to show that the detached cynical supermarket approach to the academic life is the safest. Now horror, horror, horror, he has gone to Ireland to finish his thesis. And he's in a guest house near you. For heaven's sake, for his parent's sake, (incidentally his mother is my sister-in-law so he's a nephew of mine!) cure him.' " Liz with a desperate expression folded up the letter and looked at Eddie.

"Cure him of what?" Eddie moved nearer the fire and put his feet up on the fender. "And why is he coming here? Beckett lives in Paris and was born and brought up in Dublin."

"I suppose he wants to get away from it all. My wretched sister must have mentioned Ballyfungus. She says he's only twenty-five. Who in God's name can I ask to meet him? Felicity MacCrea has fled to Dublin, her brothers are impossible and Father Kevin's up to his eyes in *The Lower Depths*."

"What do you mean?"

"Gorki. The Hodge Podge, you know. Father Dermot is too athletic. There's no one under fifty anywhere."

"If he's mad why bother? You're not a psychiatrist."

"I have to bother at least once for my sister's sake."

"What guest house is he in? I presume the one and only Daisy Lodge."

"Yes, and the poor Miss Croziers are so baffled by him."

"No wonder. Innocent creatures. You have asked him to dinner I suppose?"

"Tomorrow evening, and I want you both too. I also asked the Ferncourt widows."

"Good God! Poor fellow! It will be like a carnival in an Old Folks Home. You haven't asked the Miss Croziers I trust, because I simply could not face an evening with Clara and Maud *and* a deranged youth."

"No, I didn't. They've had enough. Please Eddie, do come. Help me. I'd help you."

"I can't answer for Colin; he's now Tierney but I will come; loyal, faithful, and true. I must get home now and prepare a midnight supper for my ink-stained partner." Tom saw him out, full of solicitude and good cheer. Eddie shook his head as he walked down the road. "If I went back to the Mill on some pretext, I'd find them in each other's arms," he thought, "but who am I to judge?"

When The Boys arrived the following evening they were intrigued by the sight of a racing bicycle against the front steps. "Must be Plodd's," remarked Colin. "Well, at least he can move his legs. Most Beckett characters are crippled."

Emerald Walsh opened the door to him. She had been summoned to help. Tom it seemed was not enough. She was wearing her uniform. White overall over dark green pantsuit and exceptionally large bedroom slippers. Her hair was in curlers under a green net.

"Janey Mr. Evans, Mr. Fox you never seen the like," she hissed at them. "He's like somebody's pet white rat left out in the rain. They don't know what to make of him at the Lodge. Go in. Miss Atkins is with him. Lovely bit of roast lamb tonight brought in from Fungusport."

It was with understandable trepidation the two men entered the studio. Liz was standing by the fireplace; tonight wearing a black velvet pantsuit and earrings which seemed to hang to her navel. Her expression could only be described as hunted. She hastened to meet them, Eddie remarked afterwards, "as if we were ambulance men."

"Welcome darlings, welcome. Isn't it a hideous night? Tom, you might bring in the ice. And here is Alan Plodd. Alan, this is Colin Evans and Eddie Fox. The Ferncourt ladies can't come. Their horrible dog has diarrhea. Hope it dies."

They saw before them a small dusty young man; his shoulders carried an avalanche of dandruff; his face was pale; his eyes were pink-rimmed and lifeless. His clothes were grey and crumpled.

"Good to meet you." He flapped a pale hand in their direction and sank back into his chair.

"Well." Colin sat down and put on an air of fatherly concern. "Tell us all about yourself, Alan."

69

There was a heavy pause; everyone waited breathless. Even Tom stood stock still holding the ice bucket, staring.

"I'm writing my thesis on Samuel Beckett's lack of superlatives; taking a graduate course under Eckstein, the Beckett man at Harvard. I'm from Hartford actually. Got my degree at Yale." He spoke in a monotonous tone as if reporting to a police interrogator and then took a swallow of whiskey.

"What do you think of Ballyfungus? Are you happy at Daisy Lodge?" It was Eddie's turn to interrogate.

Another pause; the words came out slowly. "It's very quiet, except for the wood pigeons."

"The wood pigeons?"

"Yes I believe that's what they're called. Moaning and cooing. Sometimes both."

"That should tie in with Beckett."

Plodd lifted his head. "Nothing ties in with Beckett." He laughed scornfully; "Beckett is alone. Around Beckett — nothing. Regard me as the non-hero —" The head went down again. He appeared to be studying the floor.

Eddie and Colin exchanged glances; it was worse than they expected. Liz looked as if she was about to burst out crying. A heavy silence fell upon the room. Everyone furtively helped themselves to more whiskey.

In the kitchen Emerald Walsh was handing out her bulletins to Tom. "As God is my witness he lies in bed half the day with the curtains drawn and the blinds down. Sleeps naked as his mother bore him."

"How do you know he was naked?" Tom, who was carving the lamb, looked up at her grinning.

"Not a sign anywhere of nightwear, pyjamas or the like. Miss Maud said she nearly passed away the other day when he came out of his room without a stitch on."

"Bet that ould one had never seen that before."

"God forgive you, Tom Nolan. Well, as I says he gets up at twelve-thirty, takes his lunch and goes off to the Protestant churchyard in Kineally where he spends the day. True as

God. Then he comes back at four when it's darkening and is given supper at seven. He writes half the evening sitting in the toilet. I tell you the Miss Croziers never gets to the upstairs toilet no more. Good thing it's out of season and he's the only guest. If you took a bath itself you wouldn't mind but he's maggoty dirty. Soup's goin' in, Tom, mind your meat. Keep carvin'. She opened the door with a flourish. "Dinner is served, Miss Atkins."

The party by the fireplace appeared to be in a trance, the word dinner roused them and they moved gratefully towards the table.

"Hm very good soup," murmured Eddie who was a magnificent cook himself and praise from Eddie was praise indeed. He kissed his hostess's hand. "Madame Bovary, I congratulate you."

Plodd raised his head suddenly and then paused and listened as if he heard distant firing. "Bovary! Gosh! Flaubert! You can't deny Mr. — er — Evans that *Murphy* is Beckett's sole exercise and an anomalous one at that in the workmanlike use of Flaubert's symbolism. I think I'm quoting accurately from Professor Kenner's study. Or was it Kenner?" He frowned.

"Don't ask me," replied Colin frigidly. "I'm only a poor best-seller crime man. I've never read a line of Kenner and never intend to."

"Mr. Evans sir," Plodd solemnly pointed a dripping spoon at Colin. "I'm deeply sorry for you."

"The Hodge Podge did a very good production of *Waiting for Godot* a few years ago. You must meet the drama club, young people," said Liz quickly. "We have an up-and-coming young priest — Father Kevin Sheedy — you must meet him. Incidentally how is your latest whodunit going, Colin?"

"Very well. There are feelers out already for the film rights."

"That's splendid." She did not dare look at Eddie who was concealing his laughter behind his dinner napkin. Plodd's head was now right back in his soup plate. "You have sisters, Alan?" Liz addressed the pallid guest who was noisily gulping down the last of his soup.

"Sisters?" Plodd frowned. "Sisters. I think so. Yes. Two. I never see them."

"Your mother is the sister of my brother-in-law, Jim Plumb. My brother-in-law is your advisor." She spoke loudly and clearly as if to the deaf.

"Professor Plumb? I never see him now."

"Who do you see?"

"Well ma'am, I guess I live within the skull."

There was no answer to this. In desperation Liz opened up the subject of Auntie Al's weaving industry, which had now gone into pottery.

"Everyone's gone into pottery now," said Eddie. "Frightful objects are being turned out. They did better in the Stone Age."

"Auntie Al, God bless her," Colin shook his head, "presented me with something which looked like a soup bowl for a dinosaur the other day."

"Poor Auntie Al. She does her best. Is Tott coming over soon? Alan would like Tott." A silence followed this. The unspoken thought was — would Tott like Alan? The silent vote was taken and carried NO. "Shall we drink our coffee around the fire?" Liz rose and the others followed her, Plodd bringing up the rear. He quickly sank into a chair and remained in reverie. Heaven knows what nightmare visions were pulsing through his skull.

"The curse of the Ravens is on that boyoh," remarked Mrs. Walsh as she bore the coffee tray back into the living room. "It's my belief he needs a priest."

"It's my opinion he needs a woman," Tom replied, his mouth full of roast lamb.

"If anyone ought to know it's you, Tom," was on the tip of Mrs. Walsh's tongue but she suppressed it. As she said often to her friend the postmistress, "Never let your tongue cut your throat."

"That new motel over at Fungusport is appalling," remarked Eddie chattily. "Rooney built it; he told me proudly 'It's Swiss Tudor.' It's a twentieth-century abortion I said . . ."

Plodd at the word abortion showed signs of life. "Why not?" he mused dreamily. "All life is an abortion. Have we really progressed beyond the foetus except in size? All we are given beyond the condition of suspended animation which is life and the dangerous state of suspended animation autopsy — death — is a question mark, a name on a tombstone."

It would be impossible to describe the depression which fell upon the company that evening. Colin afterwards declared that though the clock ticked loudly the hands never moved. Mrs. Walsh looking in to collect her wages told Tom they looked like the living dead. "Stricken like when they saw the apparition at Kinealy." At ten-thirty Plodd consulted his own watch, pulled himself to his feet and murmured it was time to go. Eddie and Colin also rose.

"May we give you a lift?" asked Colin yawning.

"No thanks, I came on my bike. Beckett you know was a cyclist in his formative years."

Liz signed to The Boys to stay on and then followed Plodd into the hall. The student pulled on an old raincoat much too large for him and placed a battered grey hat on his head. "Are you getting good work done?" she asked the scholar.

"I work in a graveyard — in Kinealy Protestant churchyard. It has the right answers. Thank you for an arcane but interesting evening." He mounted the bicycle with some difficulty. All that whiskey, thought Liz anxiously.

"Be careful," called Colin who had joined them in the hall. "The driving's terrible here especially at night. They mow you down and grind you up into fertilizer."

They watched Plodd cycle rather unsteadily into the night and then slowly and sadly returned to the studio.

"What have I done," moaned Liz, "to deserve this?"

"He's very ill." Eddie poured himself a drink. "Do you mind, dear? Just a nightcap. I need it. Colin?" He held up the bottle suggestively.

73

"No thanks. I must work tonight." Colin flung himself on the sofa and closed his eyes. "What a frightful youth," he sighed. "What can we do about him? Shouldn't he see a doctor? He might get violent."

"I don't think, Liz dear, that Alan Plodd will murder any one. He will more likely be found hanging."

Liz gave a little scream. "I never thought of that. I'll go over to Daisy Lodge tomorrow and consult the sisters."

The telephone rang causing them all three to start violently. The nervous strain of the last two hours had weakened their nervous systems. Liz gingerly lifted the receiver. "Who? Oh, Mabs, it's you? Yes, this is me. I'm here. Sorry you didn't come to dinner but maybe it was just as well. No darling, he was gloomy and boring. What? Oh, I'm so glad. No dear, of course not. I'll be in touch." She put down the receiver and faced them.

"What's wrong?" asked Eddie startled. "You look stricken."

"You gathered it was Mabs. Dolphie is better. The symptoms have eased off and he's sleeping peacefully." There was a chorus of groans. "I had hoped for news of his death. I know Josh has been in close touch with Molloy the vet about poisons and he was playing bridge there last night so I thought this might be the result. Alas not so."

"We must go." Eddie tapped Colin's head. "Time, gentlemen, time. Never mind Dolphie, Liz, it's Plodd you must concentrate on." He patted her shoulder. "We'll all help."

Ballyfungus' reaction to Plodd was what one might expect from the varied personalities. Liz appealed to the two curates for help with her problem but Father Kevin had Alan pointed out to him in Goggins supermarket (the student was buying prunes) and decided he would be too depressing a figure around the Hodge Podge Players. They were depressed enough as they were presenting Gorki's *Lower Depths*. Father Dermot said the man was hopelessly out of training and the famous Tottenham — Auntie Al's beloved — was in Lon-

74

don. The postmistress told Mrs. Walsh he reminded her of poor Michael ni Houlihan on the sixteenth day of his hunger strike. The final word as usual came from Mrs. Walsh. " 'Tis my belief it's a tapeworm eatin' him alive and nothing but the back tooth of a mare in foal can save him."

Clara and Maud Crozier were the daughters of the last rector of Kinealy; they were both in their early sixties and beyond occasional trips to Dublin, usually for the flower show, and two memorable visits to London, they had seen nothing of the world outside Ballyfungus. Maud cooked and Clara did the housework. Mrs. Walsh came in one morning a week, polished the brasses and washed the floors. Daisy Lodge had once been the rectory but the Croziers (in some odd manner nobody could explain it, not even the Archdeacon) had acquired it. The church and the graveyard were only a few yards down the road and it was here the problem paying-guest spent most of his waking hours. Both sisters were plain but kind, Maud being small and chinless with pop eyes and Clara being big and mannish with a baritone voice. Daisy Lodge contained two double and three single bedrooms. The rectors always had very large families (Mr. Green over in Ballyfungus only followed in a tradition), a drawing room with TV, a large dining room and a small room known as the library, though there was only one bookcase containing the novels of Walter Scott, Dickens, Thackeray and George Eliot. There were also two volumes of *Punch* 1896–98. This comprised the main quarters. The garden was walled and in its dishevelled way beautiful. It was full of old-fashioned musk roses, clumps of geraniums, and lavender mingled with currant and gooseberry bushes. Beyond the wall loomed the tall trees of Balooly Woods. It was only a step down the road to where there was an entrance to a trail. The birds were delightful in the spring mornings and summer evenings when the house was full of guests — possibly because the ladies fed them as well as the guests. In February, however, all was grey

75

and still, except for an occasional windstorm, but now March had stormed in, there was hope.

Liz delayed calling for a few days but eventually she did drive over to Daisy Lodge. She found the ladies in the kitchen. Maud was rolling pastry and Clara was polishing silver. Liz being in an anxious mood was wearing a black cloak and black sombrero.

"Sit down, Liz dear, we always have a cup of instant coffee at this time."

Mrs. Walsh had just arrived on her motor scooter and was removing her helmet and boots and replacing the last with the well-known bedroom slippers.

"Terrible wild morning. How's the little fella?" She pointed ceilingwards to denote Plodd.

"He had quite a fall on his way home from your dinner party, Liz. Might have been killed but he didn't seem to notice. He doesn't notice anything much, poor boy." Maud sighed. She began preparing coffee.

"He jolly well smashed up the bike though," commented Clara.

"Oh dear too bad, but he's rich I think. He can afford it."

Liz removed her cloak and tossed the sombrero into a chair; she sat down at the table and lighted a cigarette.

"I've come to consult you about him. You see I do feel responsible. In a way he's a connection by marriage." She shook her head and pointed significantly at Mrs. Walsh who with her back turned to them was buttoning on the historic white overall.

Maud got the message instantly. "Mrs. Walsh dear, you might take Mr. Plodd's breakfast up to him. There's a cup of cold tea in the fridge and you'll see three water biscuits. That's what he requires. Ugh."

"It's murder," commented Mrs. Walsh arranging a small tray. "And still in bed," she sniffed, "and he only in his

76

twenties. Me Granny always said them that doesn't scatter the morning dew will never comb grey hairs." Much to their relief she stumped off with the nauseous breakfast.

"The poor boy does seem to me mentally ill," moaned Liz. "I feel we should consult somebody, but who? The Archdeacon is so hearty and he only reads Milton! I don't think he's heard of Beckett. Mr. Green is enfeebled by child care and The Boys are so selfish. They never do anything that doesn't amuse them. Oliver MacCrea is barely alive and the General just snorts and blows . . ."

Maud clasped her hands agitatedly and said, "What about the Old Doctor Josh Browne? I know he's old, but he's so wise. Besides now he's retired he has plenty of time."

Liz beamed at her. "You're right, Maudie. Old Josh is the man. I'll drop in on him now. We could arrange for him to call here accidentally on purpose and just observe the young man."

"The poor boy seems to be possessed," sighed Maud again; she was given to prolonged sighing.

"It's the sort of thing Our Lord would have tackled and made a good job of it. 'Take up your bed and walk,' he would have said quite sharply, and no more nonsense! But the Old Doctor is the next best thing to the Saviour," Clara added reverently.

"Meanwhile, not a word." Liz rose and put on the cloak. All three looked at each other and nodded.

Mrs. Walsh, the woman with her ear to the ground, had returned. She shook her head. "If he were my son I'd say he'd be going out of this house feet first. Aye, begin with a cough and end with a coffin . . ."

"Sit down, Mrs. Walsh, and have your elevenses." Clara and indeed the rest of the County had abandoned all class distinctions long ago with the possible exception of Mabs Vigors, but then she was a relic of the splendid British Colonial past.

Mrs. Walsh sat down and poured herself a cup of black

strong tea, tossed four lumps of sugar into it, followed up with a douche of milk. "Mr. Plodd, as I see it, has gone mad on some writin' fella of the name of Beckett. I thought he might be one of the Becketts owned the fish shop over to Fungusport. Two of them went off the pier at full moon. Drownded. Ran in the family. They was eaten by shellfish. I couldn't look at a crab since." She bit deeply into a slice of bread and jam.

"Well I'm on my way and thanks for the advice." Liz winked at the Miss Croziers, then pulled on the sombrero and tied it under her chin. Looks as if she's off to fight a bull, thought Mrs. Walsh, eyeing her over the rim of her cup.

The Old Doctor was out bird-watching she was told by his daughter-in-law when she called at the house. "In the Woods as usual," said Mrs. Browne junior. She was a six-foot English girl from Tasmania with a choked voice and the adjective "super" was frequently on her lips. "Isn't it a super day?"

"You might ask him to phone me this evening; it's very important."

"I certainly will. Super!"

He did phone that evening and Liz poured out her tale of woe. "What do you suggest I should do?" she asked. "I'm no head shrinker."

"Just observe him and see if it's serious, then we might have to call in a psychiatrist or send him home."

"The Croziers are so worried. Josh, he just isn't in this world."

The Doctor chuckled. "And who'd blame him? You know the saying a good laugh and a long sleep is the best cure in the doctor's book. I'll drop over tomorrow morning. You say he takes his lunch to the graveyard. I'll offer to accompany him. I can do a bit of bird-watching."

"Thank you, Josh. You're a pet and a love. I'll tell the old girls you'll be there tomorrow around midday."

Being a man of his word the Doctor appeared the next day at the guest house at the time arranged and was greeted warmly though in whispers by the two ladies. They behaved as if taking part in a production of *Macbeth*, placing their withered fingers on their lips and pointing upwards. The Doctor was wearing his bird-watching outfit — a black rain-proof cape at least forty years old over tweed jacket and knickerbockers, deerstalker hat with red feathers. His bird glasses slung over his shoulder, he also carried a stout ash-plant.

"Where is he?" he roared. The ladies shivered and looked behind them apprehensively.

"Here comes Mr. Plodd," whispered Maud. "Alan dear, Dr. Browne."

"Glad to meet you," sighed Plodd, who appeared as usual to be walking in his sleep. "You have my lunch, Miss Maud?"

"Yes dear, I do wish you'd eat something healthy." She reluctantly handed Plodd a small lunch box. "It's dreadful, Doctor Josh, this lad eats nothing but cold fried eel and a bottle of stout with it."

"Eel," exclaimed the Doctor. "Fried. Cold. How horrible."

"I know, Josh, I know. But it seems some character in a book which Alan admires liked cold eel."

The Doctor now had an opportunity to look more closely at Plodd who was rummaging round for his hat and raincoat. He certainly seemed below par. Grey skin, matted hair, a running nose and every evidence of eye strain. He shook his head and could barely restrain himself from demanding to feel the pulse.

"Oh, Josh dear, I wonder if you would take this little parcel along with you. Chicken and ham sandwich and in this little flask a drop of Irish whiskey." She winked at him, the medicine man grinned and if Plodd hadn't been deep in his skull world he would surely have smelled an outsize rat.

"I'm walking down the road to the churchyard. Some interesting birds there. A rare type of buzzard." The Doctor winked at Maud who had to retreat to the kitchen in order to hide her laughter.

"I eat my lunch there every day," Plodd explained. "I think better amongst the dead."

"Do you write on a tombstone?" asked the Doctor curiously as they walked down the road.

"No, I write in the lavatory during periods of constipation!"

(Constipation. No wonder on that diet. He's worse than I thought.) Aloud the Doctor remarked, showing professional interest, "What's wrong with your gait? It's halting."

"I have," said Plodd with simple pride, "a boil forming between crotch and thigh. Pus also. Lots of pus."

"Pus. That could be serious," exclaimed Josh. "You should consult my son, the young doctor."

"I've no use for doctors, if you will forgive me. Besides I choose to be septic in my approach to this predicament called Life." A cackling laugh followed. (Did he say septic or sceptic? Let it pass.) At this point they were compelled to push their way through a flock of sheep which was slowly crossing the road from one field to another.

"If it isn't sheep it's cows," said the Doctor, "and they're all orphaned and allowed to wander oe'er hill and dale."

Despite the honking of a school bus and the vociferous curses from a motorcyclist the animals, evidently deep in meditation, ambled towards safety. The sky was lowering and the distant mountains half wreathed in mist assumed menacing shapes on the horizon. Occasionally there came a disillusioned piping from some bird simulating carefree happiness in the heather. Plodd sighed contentedly. It was pure Beckett. As they neared the gaunt, deserted church a truck drove alongside them and came to a standstill. The driver, a fellow with a blazing red face, poked his head out of the window and asked in a thick voice, "Would you know where the Heavenly Angels is?"

Plodd started. Was the man mad? The Doctor remained calm. He pointed southwards with the ashplant. "The Convent School? Ah, yes. Keep going and when you come to the signpost at the cross-roads turn right. The school is on the right. The odor of sanctity should guide you. Alas, the signpost is turned, the wrong way. Some prankster, but follow my instructions. Bye." He turned to Plodd when the truck was out of sight. "It's a girl's boarding school and I can tell you they are no angels."

They were now passing a ruined cottage; the roof had fallen in and the windows were glassless. A black goat stared out at them from one of the windows. The Doctor leaned on the wall and pointed the stick at the gaping door. "See this cottage. The woman threw four of her thirteen children down the well before anyone cottoned on to it. Listen ma'am I said, when I was waiting for the Guards, Two's company, three's none, but four's a damn sight too many. . . ."

Plodd nodded approvingly. "Drowned them. Quite right."

They had now reached the graveyard. The doctor followed his limping companion through nettles, long grass and festering weeds. Most of the inscriptions on the tombstones were illegible because of the assaults of time, weather and neglect. Plodd flung himself down on one which was comparatively recent and free at least of nettles.

"It's my favourite grave," he explained. "The occupant, lucky little fellow, died in infancy."

"Better have some lunch." The Doctor sat on a raised slab near him. He gratefully took a swig from the flask and began eating his sandwiches; they were very good. Maudie's cooking was infallible.

Plodd sat up, opened his lunch box, muttering to himself. "This cloacal disgust of self from which I suffer points in one direction — rebirth. Doctor, you have committed the crime of being born; we all have. We all must creep back into the womb." (By George, the fellow's in very poor shape! Something must be done at once, but what?) A silence followed between the strange couple. The wind sighed mournfully through the cypresses; rooks cawed round the belfry. The church loomed up beside them locked, empty, rotting.

Anonymous dripping sounds could be heard. In the distance a cow mourned endlessly for its calf, even now being processed into veal. Horrid thought!

The Doctor stood up suddenly and lifted his binoculars towards the sky. "B'jove there's a hawk! See him. It's a sparrow hawk. Look at it hovering!"

But Plodd did not look up. Those living within the skull world actually prefer to look down (I can't get through to this fellow; he's three quarters dead). Rain suddenly began pattering down on the leaves. "We better move out of this, m'boy. You seem to have a cold already and this won't help." The Doctor staggered to his feet; arthritis was hitting him hard.

Plodd stared up at the old man without moving. "When you enter the Beckett world you're never the same again." He sneezed violently. (I can certainly believe that. This fellow is tucking himself up in his own shroud.) Plodd continued in a low moan. "You move around in a thick miasma of misery. There is no hope and the worst sin — Doctor — the worst sin is procreation."

This drew a hearty response from old Josh. "Procreation has always been a sin. The sooner the human race blows itself off this unlucky planet the better and it looks like it might happen any day. If you go on lying there, m'lad, you'll get piles on top of your crotch boil."

Plodd rose heavily to his feet; he moved like a very old man; in fact the pixie Doctor moved faster.

"Doctor, I begin to think that you and I see things the same way." (God forbid!) He tapped his forehead. "Somehow I didn't get inside the skull world today." He slapped his forehead this time. (Strange, the tapping seemed to have a hollow ring. Shall I ask him to do it again? Better not.) They had now reached the road and were heading back towards Daisy Lodge. The Doctor felt his hopes fading; the man was impossible; nothing could be done. Suddenly they were conscious of the authoritative hooting of a motor horn; the car drew up alongside them. It was a very old Morris.

Mabel, who was driving, leaned out of the window. Albie was seated beside her. Both ladies were wearing dark glasses and huge black fur hats of the type worn by the cossacks under the Czar. Dolphie was spread across the back seat, his tongue lolling out and the saliva dripping into a shopping basket filled with vegetables.

"Where are you going? Who's that?" snapped Mabs, as if on border patrol.

"I'm taking my constitutional and this is a young visitor to Ireland, Alan Plodd."

Plodd tentatively moved towards the car and inclined his head politely. "Glad to meet you Mrs. — er."

The Doctor repeated the ladies' names and nudged the addled youth.

"We can't give you a lift?" Albie leaned across her sister.

"No thanks." Alan started back as the huge face of Dolphie suddenly appeared at the window and those terrifying bloodshot eyes gazed menacingly out at him.

"Down, Dolphie dearest." Albie smiled sweetly at Alan. "He won't hurt you, darling boy, bye."

"The two weird sisters," said the Doctor as they pursued their way along the road, "and the hound of the Baskervilles." He launched into a life history of the Ferncourt ladies to which Alan paid no attention. "See Balooly Woods in the distance." He pointed his ashplant towards the horizon. "There are the Woods, our natural paradise." He stopped and looked towards the hedge. "There's a robin redbreast. Hi, little fella! There is a nice legend about the robin redbreast. It's unlucky you know to kill one. The county people say that the robin redbreast plucked out the sharpest thorn that was piercing Christ's brow on the cross; and the precious blood spattered the little bird's breast and it has ever since worn the sacred sign. Holy Balls of course. Here we are at the gates of Ferncourt. Nice avenue of limes isn't it? And here is the entrance to a trail through the Woods which winds for two miles and then you come out on a piece of wild moorland." He pulled out a huge silver watch and studied it.

"This repeater belonged to my grandfather. He carried it through the Zulu Wars. By George, we can't go in the Woods today. I will have to wend my way back to Ballyfungus. Do you mind? It's getting late."

"You seem to like living," observed Plodd wonderingly.

"Well, me boy, I've seen so much of death, of cruelty, and pain and injustice that I'm grateful for the simple fact that I'm alive and well except for the hearing. An old fellow I was treating said to me once, 'Doctor, I've seen in my lifetime the three most delightful things: a garden of potatoes covered with white blossoms, a ship under sail, and my woman after childbirth and I'm dying a happy man.' And I never forgot it for that man was lying in a workhouse bed with none to mourn him." Josh stopped suddenly and waved the old ashplant. A girl was coming towards them riding a bicycle. She was wearing a green raincoat and her long yellow hair was streaming behind her. As she came nearer Plodd could see that she was pretty, almost beautiful and obviously beaming with life and happiness. She jumped off and wheeled the bicycle towards them.

"Doctor Josh, and how's *yourself?*"

"Attracta Mulcahy and how's *yourself?* I needn't ask, you're looking like whatshername, the girl who brings in the spring."

"Persephone?" suggested the highly educated Plodd, "or Proserpine?" Oddly enough the sun had suddenly emerged from behind the clouds and a blackbird was singing away in the hedge beside them. The sickly student absolutely raised his head and the shadow of a smile crossed his sallow face.

"The little fella has a throat so I left work a bit early. You're looking well, Doctor, thanks be to God." She mounted the bicycle. "Must get home. Ta now." She was off in a flash of green and gold.

"Lovely girl." The Doctor laughed. "I brought her into the world and let me tell you I delivered her first baby and my son the second."

"She's married?" (Was there a slight note of disappoint-ment in that disembodied nasal twang?)

"Married how-are-you? Not at all. She had one son by a Christian brother — he's now in Australia — and another by a sailor off a Russian freighter came into Fungusport. Great girl. Supports the children with the help of her Da and Ma who don't care a damn what people think and nobody does think anymore. Attracta has a job in Alicia de Bracey's weav-ing what-you-may-call-it. Aha, there's a very rare little fella." The Doctor raised his bird glasses and peered across the ditch. "A yellow breasted flycatcher. Thought they'd all gone with this bloody drainage."

"She's pretty," remarked Plodd deep in thought, or rather skull.

"The flycatcher?"

"No, that girl. Attracta. She will marry somebody."

"No. She hates men. Loves children."

"Gosh. That's strange."

The Doctor looked at him sharply. A thought crossed his mind. (Could sex be the answer? Would Attracta take him on?) "Another superstition here I like," continued Josh — some more sheep were crossing the road — "they say it is good to meet a white lamb in the early morning with the sun on its face." They had reached the gates of Daisy Lodge; they moved slowly up the modest driveway. Maud was peeping out of the bow windows to the side of the hall door. She rushed out to greet them. The Doctor patted Plodd's shoul-der. "You drop around to my son's surgery. Thursday around two. He'll give you something for the boil. . . . Wait. No. Friday afternoon around four-thirty and then I'll meet you for a pint in Rooney's afterwards. Right?"

Plodd managed a tired smile. "Thanks." He waved his hand as if flapping away a fly. "Plodd *meurt*. Eh?" He tot-tered upstairs. They heard a door bang.

"He's in the lavatory and he'll be there for hours." Maud clutched the Doctor's arm. "What do you think? Is it fatal?"

85

The Doctor laughed. "No. He needs the full treatment for addiction. Don't worry, Maudie. Tell Clara to relax. I must be off."

Josh's relationship with his daughter-in-law could only be described as wary. That evening he waited until they had driven off to a dinner party in Fungusport to phone Liz. Liz was in and avid for news.

"You've seen him? What do you think?"

"Just serious minded. Deeply involved with his subject. He can, I hope, be cured." He spoke with quiet confidence.

"How? Shock treatment?"

"In a manner of speaking — yes."

"You're a good man, Josh."

The Doctor shuddered. "Never that. I start treatments this Friday. Give me a few weeks. Basically he's a decent enough little fella. Incidentally I was walking near the Woods yesterday and there were a couple of foreigners and John Fallon walking along the trail. I hid behind some trees and watched them. They're up to no good and when I came out on the road there they were staring up the avenue of Ferncourt. That damn swine Fallon! God bless us to think that I delivered him by candlelight. It would have been only too easy to make an honest mistake. Oh, for the gift of prophecy."

"Thank you, Josh. I can't wait to hear more. And I'm mad with curiosity to know how."

Two days later on the Wednesday to be exact the Doctor paid a surprise visit to the Ballyfungus Arts & Craft Centre. The musty old basement rooms were freezing cold and very dark. In fact the girls were trying to work by candlelight. The Doctor could barely grope his way through the looms to the little office where Auntie Al was seated crying over her tax returns. "Josh, sit down."

"What's going on here? How can you see? And indeed how can you feel?" He lifted her poor red hand and studied it. "No signs of frostbite yet."

"It's an Electricity Strike. Happened just as we opened up.

No warning. It's what's called a lightning strike." She looked pitifully at him, trying to smile. "Hardly apt, is it?"

"I see Goggins has put his prices up again. That's another lightning strike on his part. Auntie Al, I want a little information from you. How old is Attracta's last child?"

"What an odd question. You don't think she's . . ."

"No, no. When was the last — the Russian one?"

"Two years ago at least. Then last year you may remember she had a miscarriage, poor thing. Nearly the same time as poor Felicity. She said poor Attracta, it's because she met a lame woman — a magpie — and a white cat, all on the same morning. That is said to be a sure sign of disaster. I think the father was one of the Gardai at Kinealy. But one can never be sure with Attracta."

"May I have a word with her? I need her cooperation. But Auntie Al, I don't want anyone to talk about anything. You understand?"

"Josh, you're not being foolish." Lady de Bracey looked at him sternly.

"Lady de Bracey. How dare you! Good God! At my age!" The Doctor rose appalled.

"Sorry I didn't mean it really. There she is. Over there."

The Doctor made his way through the artistic debris and finally located Attracta who was weaving vigorously. She looked up at him surprised.

"Doctor Josh, what are you doing here? You're not taking up the weaving?" She looked up at him with her ravishing smile. A smile which promised the earth but oh how deceptive it was! Attracta gave nothing and asked for nothing, except impregnation in her own time and on her own terms.

The Doctor sat down beside her. "I want your help." He went on whispering and she nodded occasionally and laughed. Auntie Al watching them through her little window was blazing with curiosity. Finally she saw the Doctor rise to go. He tapped Attracta's shoulder and she nodded again. Then the old man made his exit slowly through the looms. As Josh ascended the stairs to the hall the lights suddenly went on;

the lightning strike was over. He heard cheers from the basement. It was like feeble cries from a famine ship, he thought.

At five-thirty on the Friday the Doctor entered the lounge of Rooney's pub — the biggest one that is — The Norman's Head. It had once been an old fashioned dirty pub with sawdust on the floor mixed with spit but now it was all tarted up with red sofas and marble topped tables and Georgian prints on the walls. Rooney like everyone else had gone Georgian. Plodd was already there seated, with a glass of stout in front of him, wearing as usual an expression of bleak despair. His appearance had not changed for the better.

The Doctor greeted him and sat down. He threw the ashplant down on the seat beside him and placed the bird glasses on the table and then unbuttoned his jacket. "How's the boil son?"

"Better. Your son gave me an antibiotic. The side effects were most unpleasant. Diarrhea and vertigo. I'd rather have the boil."

Josh nodded. "They all say that. Mixed reactions. Isn't that life —"

Plodd leaned his elbows on the table and faced the old man. "Doctor, you've entered or rather you're entering the life within the skull which is reward for all human despair. Let me congratulate you. You think you're looking into a sandy expanse. You are but it is a sandy expanse strewn with human excrement." He stopped suddenly in mid-expanse as it were. Attracta had entered the lounge and was moving towards their table.

The Doctor rose and greeted her warmly, displaying carefully simulated surprise. "Sit down, my dear. You've met Alan Plodd."

"I saw him with you that afternoon. Thanks, I'll just have an orange squash." Like most healthy contented people she didn't need stimulants; she was a stimulant herself. "Lovely evening outside. Did you notice the evenings is getting

88

lighter and the daffodils is budding in the Woods." She was casting furtive glances at Plodd, sizing him up and wondering if the Doctor had asked her to perform an impossibility. The few Americans she had met were clean, upstanding, magnificently healthy hikers, bearded, yes — smelly feet because of the walking — but this little fellow looked sick and decayed. Needless to say she had not read the works of Samuel Beckett.

Plodd, sneaking glances at her, thought she was painfully pleasing to the eye. Before entering the skull world he had liked girls, indeed enjoyed several liaisons at college. Attracta meanwhile had removed her coat, displaying full contours of breasts under a tight sweater. It was obvious she wore no bra.

"How's work at the chamberpottery?" asked the Doctor genially.

"Oh Doctor, you're terrible," she laughed heartily and even Plodd managed a twisted smile. "Do you like Daisy Lodge?" She addressed the student.

"I think so. I don't enjoy anything really. And they try to make me eat, which I find unpleasant."

"Have you met any of the young ones here?" She sighed. "Not that there are many. Most of them have gone to England or America. Sad. Sure there's nothing for them here." She drank her orange squash.

Plodd shuddered. "I don't want to meet anyone. I'm here to think and work."

"That's silly, so it is. All work and no play makes Jack a dull boy. Don't it, Doctor?" Her grammar Plodd couldn't help noticing was haphazard. Ah well, she was a child of the people. The Doctor meanwhile looking at Plodd in his present form saw a strong resemblance to a stuffed bat.

"Yes, of course he must play. Joe bring two more pints and another orange squash."

"And put lots of ice in it love," implored the enchantress looking up at the bartender.

Plodd inspected her again. Those breasts were remarkable. Mustn't think about them. Think instead about the human cesspool; the Dead Sea; ulcers, boils, a child with two heads. She was an extraordinary girl bringing up two bastards in an Irish Catholic country town. She was, let's put it this way, worth talking to if only to learn about the social structure especially when the physical structure was so appealing.

"Do you dance, Alan?" She smiled up at him displaying her beautiful teeth. Plodd's own teeth up to the Beckett period had been excellent but now they were slowly rotting under the exigencies of the skull diet.

"I used to," he confessed. "But I don't anymore, because of this predicament." She was about to ask what the predicament meant but they were conscious that the people at the bar had stopped talking and everyone in the lounge had as it were sprung to attention. A big fattish man had entered from the back of the pub. He was bald; his expression was jovial but his small grey eyes were keen and watchful.

"Rooney," bellowed the Doctor. The big man, who was in his shirtsleeves, came towards their table. He shook hands with the Doctor and nodded to Attracta. "Well how's yourself?" The Doctor eyed him keenly. (Overweight, asking for a coronary.)

"Great, thanks be to God. And yourself?"

"I'm into injury time, Rooney, but the game was rough so maybe I have a few years yet. I hear you and Fallon are planning great things?" He eyed the publican keenly.

"Never, Doctor, never. Sure I'm not in the same world with Johnny Fallon. He's a millionaire, I'm only a poor tradesman. Isn't that so, Attracta Mulcahy?"

"Well I don't know, Mr. Rooney. Sure I'm only a poor weaver."

"And this is Alan Plodd, an American writer," the Doctor indicated Plodd who was staring at the tablecloth.

"A Yank is it?" Rooney smelt money. He smiled roguishly at Alan. "Writin', ah, that's the thing. My son is up in Dublin studying law. He's great for the writing." He lowered his voice. "Sure I'll be frank with you, Doctor, I always was. The

Castle's coming down and a housing estate going up. Fallon did mention this to me."

"The Castle. Too bad. I thought Fallon was going to rebuild it and live there himself. When is this happening?"

"I don't rightly know but not far off. Thank God I say. Think of the employment 'twill give."

"I've seen foreigners prowling around Balooly, what would they be up to now?" The Doctor eyed Rooney keenly over the rim of his glass. Well he knew his man: slippery, very slippery.

"It's an international combine or conglomerate — Alpha-Omega is the name. Japs, Canadians and Germans is at the back of it. I think they're putting up a factory between Kinealy and Fungusport. They have a sort of an office in the Grand, but the HQ is in Dublin. God bless!" Rooney moved over to a couple of strong farmers who were whispering together about the price of cattle and the hellish EEC.

"Villain!" murmured the Doctor. He looked at his watch and stood up. "Must be on my way. I'm due at Ferncourt for dinner at six-thirty and Mabs Vigors will have my life if I'm late. I'll leave you two youngsters together now." He winked at Attracta and collected his belongings. She smiled back at him, but shook her head as much as to say he's impossible.

The General was parked outside waiting for Josh in his battered old station wagon. "What the devil are you up to? Surely you haven't taken to the bottle at your age?" growled Artie.

"I was just doing a little rescue work. I've news for you." He retailed his conversation with Rooney. The General listened to it, groaning at intervals.

"Don't tell the girls until we're absolutely sure," Josh implored him; "it's no use putting the wind up." He added with a mixture of snort and laugh, "We'll leave that to Dolphie."

"And we want to enjoy our meal. The first in a month," said the General as they rounded the gates of Ferncourt. "It's steak and kidney pie. Mabs bullied Goggins into bringing down the price; threatened to horsewhip him with a rhino lash. And she would, by jove!"

Back at the pub Attracta took control. "He's a darling old pet is the Doctor. Everyone does love him around here. Half the patients never paid him. I must be off." She stood up. "Are you on your bike or what?"

Plodd said he was on his bike.

"I'll ride back with you as far as the Lodge; it's on the way to my home; it's just a little further on." She led the way out into the street. "I hear you eat your lunch in the graveyard every day. Don't you get depressed down there amongst the dead?"

"It's part of my work," he answered. "My thesis you see is written around this death in life."

It was a quiet windless evening towards the middle of March when the birds were rehearsing their love songs and the trees were already burgeoning and there were little lambs tottering around in the fields. Cherry trees wore a blazing pink and there was the faint outline of a new moon. "Thanks be to God I didn't see it through glass," remarked Attracta raising her eyes to the heavens. "It's bad luck if you do." She greeted an old man who was driving two recalcitrant cows along the road. "Good evening to you, Mick. Isn't it a gorgeous evening thanks be to God." She waved at a group of children who were seated on the roadside. "Open your eyes ducky." She tapped a little boy on the head who was making a dart across the road in front of her. Plodd pedalling after her felt extremely disturbed. He was suddenly conscious of a dangerous, a most unspeakable happiness. She sped along in front of him, the long yellow hair streaming on the breeze. Occasionally she waited till he came alongside and smiled that merry seductive smile at him. "Here's your place." They had arrived at the gates of Daisy Lodge. I'm further on near Kinealy."

"I'll go with you," said Plodd madly, "as far as your gate."

When they reached the little farmhouse which was her home he jumped off his bike and said pantingly, "Good-bye. Thank you."

"Thank you for what?" She looked at him sideways; her eyes he saw were green. A disgraceful thought punctured the skull universe. Without her clothes she would be Botticelli's "Venus" to the life.

"I might drop in on you some day at the graveyard. I always go home for lunch to see the little fellas. Would you like that?" Plodd nodded speechlessly. "You need a bit of cheering up boy." She waved her hand to him and wheeled her bicycle into the farmyard. Plodd pedalled back to Daisy Lodge in the half light; fearful doubts back were assailing him. His thesis only just outlined, and then the skull world. Was he able for it? After all Beckett did not require celibacy from his followers.

Three days later the non-hero was lying on his favourite tombstone in the churchyard half asleep. A light rustling sound disturbed him. He opened his eyes and looked up. Attracta was there standing between him and the sky laughing down at him. She was wearing blue jeans and a pink sweater; for once it was not raining.

"I brought my own lunch. Move over, love, I'm going to sit beside you. I brought some for you. Me Mammy made some homemade bread and I got some cheese."

"Thank you." Bewitched he moved over and made room for her.

"God it's warm today." She removed the jacket. Those breasts! He averted his eyes.

"Thought I heard the cuckoo yesterday when I was passing by the Woods. It's a bit early yet though. Alan, I'll take you into the Woods next time. They're magic, Alan, you never seen the like. The trees reach to the skies and it's so quiet, so quiet, you can hear yourself breathing." She drew her finger down his cheek: "You're a funny fella."

"Am I?" Her green eyes held him in a web of enchantment.

"You should take care of yourself."

"Should I?"

"Yes." She smiled coaxingly at him. Plodd closed his eyes, surrendered, went under.

Three weeks passed and no word from Daisy Lodge. The Doctor was growing anxious. At last on the morning of the twenty-first day he found a note addressed to him on the hall table. It was from Maud. "Josh dear, you're a wizard; the reformation has started. He takes a bath every morning, is eating much better. Takes enough lunch with him for two. He's not yet what I'd call a cheery lad, but at least he's not in a decline. Thanks, Josh dear. P.S. Do drop around and see for yourself." The Doctor smiled to himself. It sounded very promising but he wanted to know more. He waited two days then walked over to Daisy Lodge. (Out of mercy for the countryside the Doctor's driving license had been refused two years ago. Eight miles an hour in the centre of the road and bird-watching at the same time was too risky, even for Ireland.) The only person he feared, the only wrecker, was Mrs. Walsh whose powers of deduction rivalled Sherlock Holmes. Any widespread gossip would destroy what he guessed by now must be an idyll in a country churchyard.

Maud and Clara received him in the drawing room, where between two-thirty and four-thirty they relaxed and, as Maud put it, became artistic. Clara was knitting something serpentine and grey which the Doctor on first glance decided must be long underwear for a gorilla. Maud was embroidering a chair cover. He was greeted with cries of pleasure and offers of refreshment. There was no sign of Mrs. Walsh, which was encouraging, and no sign of Alan, which was not encouraging.

"Alan is quite changed," fluted Maud. "Sure you won't have a cup of tea, Josh dear?"

"No thanks. So Plodd is changed for the better?"

"Yes. Isn't it delightful. He's quite a good-looking fellow

now. The boil has quite gone and so is the dandruff. He's interested in everything. Did some weeding in the garden for us." Clara agreed.

"But I wish he wouldn't work in the churchyard at night." Maud was the nervous type. "I'm so afraid he'll be murdered."

"Works at night you say?" The Doctor looked thoughtful.

"At least three nights a week and he's taken to wandering in Balooly Woods. When he works at night he borrows two of Father's old carriage rugs and a pillow." Maud sighed. "He comes back tired but cheerful and demands cocoa."

"Two carriage rugs you say?" The Doctor smiled. "That's very sensible. Comes home rather late? Doesn't stay out all night."

"Heavens no," exclaimed Clara in shock at the very idea.

"He actually came home singing the other night. I was afraid he'd been drinking but he hadn't, poor boy. He said he'd been communing with nature and it always made him sing."

"Very interesting." The Doctor rose to go but at that moment Alan walked into the room. The Doctor sat down; he could hardly believe his eyes. All he could think of at that stunned moment was the fairy tale about the toad coming up out of a well and changing into a fairy prince. He had been reading a fairy tale dwelling on that theme to his youngest grand-daughter. What a transformation! A handsome rather low-sized but well-built young man in blue jeans and aran sweater stood in front of him and shook him warmly by the hand. A firm grasp this time not like the wet flap of other days.

"Well Doc, good to see you. Say I'm sorry I didn't look you up but I've — I've been working."

"How's the thesis?" asked the Doctor. Last time he had said how's the boil?

"That. Oh I think I'm on top of that at last," replied the student.

(He's been on top of more than the thesis reflected the

95

Doctor cynically.) The ladies meanwhile were shrilly demanding Josh should stay for tea but he resisted their blandishments and escaped, pleading another engagement. Alan walked to the gate with him talking vociferously about the beauties of the Irish countryside, the wonderful warmth and kindness of the Irish people, the healing peacefulness of the Woods and the glorious birdcalls especially at dawn. He sounds like an Irish tourist-board brochure thought the Doctor barely able to restrain his laughter. He had to keep snorting into his handkerchief. "Did you ever run into Attracta Mulcahy again?" he asked when they reached the gate.

There was a pause. Plodd blushed deeply and looked away into the middle distance. "Well as a matter of fact — yes. She cycles along this road in the evenings and I sometimes run into her. She's — she's most unusual." He shifted his feet; it was obvious that he did not dare face the old man.

"She's a wonderful girl," said the Doctor and meant it. The young man raised his head and smiled. The Doctor recognized it and a sad pang went through his heart. It was the smile of a lover who was dwelling upon the beauties of his beloved. Sixty years ago the Doctor had smiled like that too, but she who had inspired it was long since dead.

Josh phoned Liz that evening. His inquisitive daughter-in-law was safely out of the house. "Good news. I've seen Plodd. He's greatly improved. In fact, I don't think you would recognize him."

"But how, Josh," breathed Liz. "Tell me, are you giving him some kind of medicine?"

"Yes it's some kind of medicine, but I'm not at liberty to divulge it — yet."

"I hope it isn't one of those awful new things with side effects."

"No, it's not new, but it could have side effects. *Good* side effects."

"Josh, you're a miracle worker."

"Mind you he's not out of the wood yet." (I should have

made it plural when you think of those evenings in Balooly.)

"I'll get an air-mail off to my sister now," said Liz. "Do you think Alan should be asked here again? I might get a few younger ones like the curates and that dreary Irish-speaking Goggins girl who plays the penny whistle; and those St. George-Mahoney twins with the acne . . ."

"I wouldn't go too fast. Wait a few more weeks."

"Perhaps I should. I'm working so hard for my London show . . ."

Dear Grace,

I'm doing all I can about your nephew. He *is* a problem. Do they all take their thesis so hard? I hate to think what he'd be like if he was concentrating on the Marquis de Sade. I've called in the aid of an old friend and neighbour Dr. Joshua Browne, a medical practitioner as was his father before him. He's keeping an eye on Alan. The guest house is very well run by two elderly ladies and they do all they can to make him eat healthy food though I must say the price of food here is appalling. A great many people are subsisting on canned dog food which they say you can make into a tasty shepherd's pie though at the rate we're going we'll soon be eating the shepherds. Not much news except always at our backs we hear the tax collector drawing near. There are horrid rumours of "a development" and a poisonous factory going up here. And the beautiful Fung River has suddenly gone black with pollution, dead fish floating down in thousands. They say it's an unknown virus but it's common knowledge it's a pig processing factory discharging effluence. We're appealing to the local TD's and the County Council and the health board, but they all bleat about unemployment and the tremendous benefits we will receive from whatever the poison is and we all know that very one is paid off. However, apart from the taxes I'm glad I moved here. You get to know the few people around so intimately, like a Jane Austen novel, and as most of them are extremely eccentric you're never bored. We all meet at each other's houses once or twice a week and everyone knows every one else's business.

97

I left this letter open so that I might add a further bulletin about Alan. Dr. Browne reports an improvement. He's been in touch with Daisy Lodge personally, has seen Alan recently and says he is much more normal. So that's an advance. Mrs. Walsh, my cleaning lady, has given me appalling reports of my gardener Tom Nolan's wife who's in extremis. She's been anointed and her legs keep jerking and jerking and "terrible incompetence"; this turns out to be lack of urinary control so any minute the grim reaper. . . . They just adore a hideous and prolonged death here. I sent you some hand-woven tablemats and a carriage rug from the Ballyfungus arts and crafts industry. Beautiful colours, handle them gently they do tend to ravel. Do, both of you, come over this summer. You know I'd love to have you and it would do you good to get away from all that crime. I never will forget my last visit to New York. I couldn't open the many pro-digious locks on the apartment doors. Once I went out I could never get back unless someone was in and then you have to utter cries for help, identify yourself through a peep-hole and show your passport. Nothing happens here. A local farmer ran down and killed his wife's lover and a man who molested several little girls got off with a warning because he was marrying a widow woman who promised to reform him. The worst was a young Gardai blown up by a booby trap mine by — one presumes the IRA — for no apparent reason. The itinerants only beat each other up but rob us inces-santly without violence. Otherwise it's the Garden of Eden. The little blue anemones are out and my cherry trees are in bloom and the daffodils along the banks of the river are really dancing.

The evenings were now light up to eight o'clock and Plodd begged the Miss Croziers to leave him something on a tray when he got home. "I found a darn nice little spot in the Woods," he explained, "so quiet you wouldn't believe and the bird songs pure poetry. I find it more inspiring really than the graveyard."

"My dear boy, I'm delighted," Maud patted his shoulder.

"I was really worried about you lying on that tombstone. We will leave you sandwiches and soup and you will only have to heat up the soup yourself. Clara and I like to watch our TV or play Scrabble after dinner."

"I understand. Of course, you should be off duty then." Often in the evenings when Alan returned to the lodge he would be startled and unnerved by the sounds coming from the TV room. Shots, explosions, screams, curses, death rattles, sound of heavy blows on human flesh. Once or twice he peeped and saw the two ladies sitting there in front of appalling scenes of carnage entranced and absorbed. "By the way," he bit into his sandwich, "I heard some commotion here last night. You had visitors?"

"Yes. Mabs Vigors and her sister for Scrabble. Mabs gets so fierce if she doesn't win. She shot lions in Africa you know."

Alan laughed. "Dear Miss Maud, I'd let her win if I were you. My mother knew a woman who shot her husband at the bridge table."

"I say how dreadful. I honestly don't think Mabs would do that. But she does come of a long line of military men. Her grandfather owned a horse called Balaclava who won the Derby and when the animal died he wanted it buried in the churchyard and a memorial put up in the church. Didn't he, Clara?"

"Quite a frightful man," Clara agreed. "The horse was not buried in the graveyard, people made such a fuss, but there is a memorial. He threatened the Rector's life. The Archbishop was furious. By the way, Maud, poor Mrs. Nolan died last night. A jolly good thing; she was in frightful shape according to Mrs. Walsh. The funeral is on Wednesday. And oh dear, Alan, Miss Atkins phoned. She wants you to phone her."

"Really. Gosh, I haven't seen Ms. Atkins since I had dinner there. Remind me."

"Maud, old girl, 'Manhunt' is on now. Sorry Alan." Crash,

bang. An explosion shook the room. It was the old children's hour.

Mrs. Nolan's funeral obsequies involved the whole village. The population of Ballyfungus being so small and so closely knit any death, even poor unimportant Mrs. Nolan's, drew them together. Goggins was reluctantly closed the morning of the service but any loss entailed was made up by the young assistants charging round the night before putting up the prices fifteen percent on the tinned goods. Because of her delicate situation (everyone knew about the liaison with her handyman), Liz did not attend the service but she sent flowers and went up to Dublin for two nights. After the service was over and the graveside ceremonies completed Mrs. Walsh sped back with Miss O'Kelly for a cup of tea. Her account of Mrs. Nolan's last hours was harrowing. "I dropped in — d'you know — to see what I could do. Poor old Katie Gahan who spent the last ten years of her life helpin' out with Aggie Nolan was run off her two feet. Poor Aggie, God help her, lay there for a week with the eyes turned back on her, if you'll pardon me — rottin'. Sprayin' with the Jeyes did nothin' to help. And that brute Tom sittin' there with crocodile smiles on his face and slippin' slyly back to the Mill under the pretext of keepin' the heat going. Heat is right! Thanks be to God poor Aggie died innocent of the black doings around her. She was anointed five times, the two curates were kept runnin' back and forth but the evening of the sixth day we knew it was comin'; a hen crowed at dawn in Halloran's yard next door but one, McGraw's whippet hound howled all night and the fire turned blue and only lit on one side and them's sure signs that death is hooverin'."

Miss O'Kelly nodded affirmatively. "Me Granny who was from Sligo said before the death there is a rushing of wind through the house yet nothing is broken or disturbed but 'tis the death blast!" Mrs. Walsh was not to be outdone.

"And they do say that when Colonel Bing died at Ferncourt — that was the ladies' grandfather — the sound of a galloping horse was heard under the windows and they do say the great racehorse Balaclava came back to claim his master."

The cemetery being so near, the mourners walked behind the hearse to the graveside, then everyone returned to Tom's small council house for refreshments. Out of respect for the dead Tom did not show up for night work in the Old Mill for nearly a week.

All this time since the fateful meeting in Rooney's the lovers Alan and Attracta had been meeting each evening. First she would speed home from the Weavers to give the little fellas their supper and put them to bed, then meet her lover at the entrance to Balooly Woods. They would wheel their bicycles along the main trail and then make a diversion into the more remote part of the forest. It was action rather than words, Attracta being simple, direct and non-intellectual. Alan soon found her ignorance of Beckett's work was bottomless so no communication was possible on that subject. She was very interesting however on folklore and provided him with varied and unusual nature notes. The ritual was simple; two rugs were spread on the ground, a pillow placed under the head of each and though the evenings were far from balmy the garments were removed one by one.

"We were closed all morning because of poor old Aggie Nolan's funeral. I didn't go. I do hate funerals. Tom her husband was much younger than Aggie and they say he was a gorgeous lookin' fella in his time. He works for Miss Atkins and they say he does most of his work in bed. Will you stop hauling and dragging? Can't we lie still for a moment like Christians? Whisht. I thought I heard a cuckoo. They say if you hear it on the fifteenth April it's a lucky year for you and if you hear it in company of a lad you'll conceive and have a child with the first snow in January."

"Good idea. Let's try now."

"Stop it or I'll slap you. It is a cuckoo. Listen."

"Sort of monotonous isn't it? I mean once is enough don't you think? You really have beautiful breasts."

"That's what they all say."

"Hey, what do you mean? All say?"

"You needn't get in a rage. I had a life before I met you."

"Oh Hell! hell! hell!"

"Alan you're a great big babby. I'll tell you about it. Well I looked around me a few years ago when I was barely twenty and what I seen I didn't like. All those wives having sex once a week, as if it was going under an operation, usually Saturday night when the husband was drunk or half drunk and having children forced upon them, whether they liked it or not and I says to myself, marriage is not for you, Attracta, but I'll have children when I like and by whom I like. Do you hear that outrageous cuckoo? My first love I met in Fungusport; he taught school there and he was planning to go into the priesthood. He was very learned like and gentle. Yes, he was a very loving lad. He's in New Zealand now farming for an uncle. It was a sad day when I kissed him good-bye." She sighed deeply.

"I can't understand you. If you really love somebody you want to be with him always. You had a child by him?"

"Yes. Colm. He looks like his Daddy. My second one Anton is fair. His Daddy was a Russian sailor. They're both brainy. They speak Irish and English to the cat."

"To the cat? Are you serious?"

"Oh yes cats know what we're saying. The little fellas talked with the cat before they talked to us. Haven't you ever noticed a cat knows the hours? We have a tabby that comes in for breakfast eight o'clock on the dot, at one for dinner and at six for her tea. They have clocks in their heads."

Alan was beginning to like this simple chatter. It was more restful than academic long-winded discussions about a life after death; ethnic problems; the population explosion; is there a God? He sat up suddenly. "That reminds me. I think there are some developers plotting against the Woods."

"Not our Woods. Not this Wood." She also sat up. "Holy Saint Anthony what do you mean, Alan Plodd?"

"I was waiting for you the other night and some men were below me, down in the glade there. They couldn't see me. I know some German so I could follow it. They're going to cut a road through the Woods because they're setting up a factory on the other side."

"Mary Mother we'll have to stop it. The Old Doctor will be out of his mind."

She jumped up regardless of her nakedness and stood beside the primeval oak nearest them. I was right, thought the lover, staring up at her bemused. She is Primevera, one hand modestly guarding her pudendum, the long yellow ringlets streaking to her shoulders and those curious slanting green eyes. She was so beautiful he felt a sharp pain go through his heart because she was unattainable. He wondered if the others ever dreamed of her as something beautiful which for a few pulsing moments had illuminated their lives and which could never be experienced again. "You're not going yet?" He looked at her in dismay.

"I must. It's going on to eight and it's near the half light when the dead walk. My little fella is out in a rash. No, Alan, I must get back. Will you stop pulling me. There, be quiet now. Tell you what, love, I wouldn't mind having a little boy or a little woman, by you."

"Let's try now. I adore you. Lie down."

"Will you stop pulling me."

"Do you love me? Please be serious. Marry me."

"No. Never. You wouldn't want me to tell a lie. You'll go back to the States now and marry a nice well-educated girl. You'd get tired of me and I wouldn't want your world. Besides I could never leave my two boys."

"Oh God." He kissed her passionately. "How can I leave you? I feel as if I'm kissing the world. Do you know, Attracta, for the first time I understand what a daughter of joy is — it's you."

"Zip me up, you silly lad."

When Alan returned to Daisy Lodge that evening he was greeted as usual by the sound of gunfire from the TV room. He crept in and there were the two ladies enrapt by "Kojak." The programme was due to end so he waited until he could get their attention. "Retracing the Old Testament" was to follow but it was contemptuously turned off.

"Alan dear, there is some hearty vegetable soup for you on the stove. Oh, my dear boy, you're absolutely covered with leaves and pine needles! Miss Atkins phoned. She wants you for a party on Saturday evening."

"I suppose I should go. I'll phone her. Incidentally, why I came in here was to tell you I'm booked to fly to New York a week from today." He sighed as if his heart was breaking. How could he leave Attracta? He felt sick to his stomach at the very thought.

"Oh dear, so soon. We did enjoy having you, Alan dear. Indeed Ballyfungus has done a great deal for you. You were quite sickly when you arrived and now you look, if I may put it so strongly, in fighting trim."

"Thank you, Miss Clara. Gosh, I feel like that myself. I think it's your excellent food and the comfortable bed and the view from the window. I can look into the Woods . . . yes, I'm going to miss it all."

"And how's your thesis going?"

"I'm a bit worried about it, I seem to have bogged down but it's always like that with a thesis. I've known guys work on a thesis for up to ten years!"

Meanwhile plans were going ahead at the Old Mill for the party of the year. Everyone had been asked old and young, alas mostly old.

Twenty people had been invited, everyone accepted with eagerness; the Old Mill parties were notoriously exciting. Even the Archdeacon's ailing wife Muriel agreed to attend. "I'll go, George," she said bravely, "in spite of my legs. Do you remember the last time we were there Felicity MacCrea's seducer turned up and there was quite a scene. I did so enjoy it." The Archdeacon winced: he did not enjoy it. His feelings towards Felicity were somewhat ambivalent. Even the Miss Croziers were coming, accompanied by the guest of honor. The Doctor had painted such a glowing picture of Alan's recovery (without revealing the treatment used) he had Liz and The Boys on tenterhooks of excitement for his arrival, so that they could see for themselves. Mrs. Walsh was helping. She'd had a new hairdo which she described as "me honeycomb."

"I think she means beehive, but I'm not sure," Liz murmured to Colin. Eddie had arrived early with a heap of smoked salmon which was received with cries of pleasure by the hostess. Tom was now moving around wearing a solemn expression as befitted one recently bereaved. Everyone in Ballyfungus was wondering if Liz would be mad enough to make an honest man of him.

"Tott is coming the end of August and will stay through September," announced Auntie Al exultantly on arriving. "By the way, Attracta Mulcahy told me there were sinister men talking German in the Woods lately."

"How does she know they were talking German?" demanded Mabs Vigors true to form. "She's only an uneducated peasant."

"She's my best weaver," retorted Auntie Al indignantly, "and she works right up to the last moment of her pregnancies, I love her. I was a bit worried that Tott might be foolish about her, but she didn't fancy him, thank goodness."

"Where is this Plodd?" asked the General impatiently. He was echoed by the rest of the company and at that very moment the Miss Croziers walked in with the hero of the evening behind them. Both ladies had been worried about what to wear, so to be on the safe side they decided on what they described as their "low necks." This time Alan literally sprang into the room, wrung Liz's hand, wrung everybody's hand in turn and greeted them warmly. His hair was a golden brown; his complexion was clear and his body looked splendidly muscular. The Boys and Liz remembering that dreadful dinner barely two months ago couldn't believe their eyes! Those who hadn't known the Beckett student previously just thought here's another healthy prosperous Yankee. In the kitchen Mrs. Walsh remarked to Tom in awestruck tones,

"It's my belief he drank a pint of water from the holy well at Kinealy."

"Begob, I think it's a woman," said Tom. "He has the look d'you know as he'd eaten a good meal."

Mrs. Walsh snarled back, "Don't talk dirty, Tom, and poor Aggie only dead ten days."

"Ballocks!" was the brief response. "I'm bringin' the chicken salad in; you follow with the praties, my good woman."

Inarticulate with rage Mrs. Walsh followed. "Thinks he's married to her already."

Meanwhile Alan happily joined the group described by Mabs as "the Youngs."

"I hear you're a Beckett scholar," said Father Kevin. "Would you think of giving a little talk to our drama group on Beckett the dramatist?"

"I'm afraid I'm leaving next week but otherwise I'd like it immensely," replied Alan. At that moment, he felt a strange reluctance to return to Beckett.

"What are the Hodge Podge up to next, Father Kevin?" Liz joined them for a moment. "I thought the Gorki was splendid but depressing."

"I have a new script by an Irish dramatist in the offing but I'm not allowed to say who or what at the moment."

"How exciting!" Liz was tapped on the shoulder in rather a proprietary manner by her handyman. "Supper's in. It's on the table, pet." Liz frowned and moved over towards the fireplace. Tom, she said to herself, better not get ideas.

"What's your sport?" asked Father Dermot.

"I boxed for Yale. Lightweight."

"Great! I'd like to get you down to the Boys Club and give them a few pointers."

"Too bad I'm afraid I'm leaving next week. A friend tells me you run the local football club, Father."

"I do with the Archdeacon. He used to play for Ireland."

Hearing the word football the Archdeacon was over in a flash. They all plunged into a discussion about training methods in the United States and Alan felt quite at home and enjoying himself in a normal way. Not that he didn't enjoy himself in a normal way with Attracta; he thought of her then with mingled pain and pleasure, the thought of putting three thousand miles between himself and his lover caused him to emit a heartbreaking sigh which was overheard by Tom who handed him a stiff whiskey. "Drink up, lad, that will put a smile on your face."

The older people meanwhile had withdrawn into a group round the fire. The Doctor was one big grin. Never had he achieved such a complete and lasting cure.

"I wish you'd tell us how you did it, Josh," asked Albie coaxingly.

"I will in good time," replied the Doctor.

Now, another of the Youngs, Ms. Una Goggins, was a keen traditionalist and spoke nothing but Irish. She had rather a gloomy time because only the curates could talk back to her so she sat in a corner near the fireplace and played traditional tunes on a penny whistle.

"Who is that strange girl?" asked Mabs pointing rudely at her.

"Una Goggins, an Irish speaker," whispered Liz.

"Most unfortunate-looking girl, looks like a sandpiper in an oil spill," was the Doctor's comment. They all continued to look at the poor girl as if she were an interesting exhibit in the zoo.

Now in planning this gathering Liz made one fatal error. She had invited Ian MacCrea the gentleman jockey simply because he was young. In fact, she couldn't abide him because he was stupid, snobbish and mean. He arrived late and rather drunk with Linda Blood, the daughter of Colonel Blood who owned the stud farm where his sister Felicity had worked with such unfortunate results. Linda had her right arm in a sling; she always was in a sling, or on crutches, because of her numerous falls while training her father's horses. Besides being constantly crippled she had a very low IQ and her vocabulary was limited to two words — "shit" and "fuck"; occasionally she experimented with a longer word such as bugger. She had hardly ever been known to formulate a sentence. This nymph was not loved or admired by the citizens of Ballyfungus and neither indeed was her escort.

"I never asked that horrible girl," Liz said in a low throbbing aside to Mabs.

"Order her out," was the prompt reply.

A cloud settled down on the proceedings when this obnoxious couple arrived. Alan Plodd looked them over once and decided they were not his type. MacCrea looked at Alan and made some insulting and laughing aside to his companion. He then turned and addressed Plodd.

"You ride?"

"No as a matter of fact I don't know one end of a horse from another."

"What do you do then?"

"I'm trying to get my Ph.D." The thought occurred to Alan at that moment — what would Beckett have done about this S.O.B.? The answer came swiftly — put him in a garbage can, close the lid and put a stone on top of it so the horse's arse couldn't get out of it in a lifetime.

Muriel and the Archdeacon were seated with the Ferncourt ladies enjoying their supper. Colin and Eddie were beside Auntie Al, who was, of course, discoursing on her dearest Tottenham's genius, when everything blew up. The sequence of events which led up to the explosion was innocent enough. Liz moved over to "the Youngs" carrying her plate and sat down beside Father Kevin. "May I sit here?"

"Of course, Miss Atkins. This is a splendid party but your parties are always great."

"Thank you. How is your administrative council now on Hodge Podge?" (She herself was one of the advisors which simply meant agreeing with the curate on all points.)

"We're doing very well really, though we do miss Felicity MacCrea." The minute the words were out of his mouth he regretted them. Obviously embarrassed, he continued, "I have a good stage manager in her place, but of course Felicity went to Dublin and we —"

"Good thing too," interposed Felicity's loving brother. "She's got a good job instead of playing around with fucking amateur theatricals." Father Kevin flushed up with rage and he prayed to heaven for polite restraint.

"You've got Attracta Mulcahy now, haven't you?" Father Dermot broke in hoping to keep the conversation on an even keel.

At the sound of the adored name Plodd raised his head and looked sharply at Father Dermot. Poor Father Dermot. Little did he know that he was treading on even more dangerous ground.

Ian broke into a roar of laughter. "Very competent, Father," he hooted. "Isn't she the town whore!"

Alan Plodd rose to his feet first handing his plate of chicken salad to the astonished Liz. He stood in front of Ian. "Repeat what you just said."

"The town whore," Ian repeated very slowly, staring insolently at Alan. "Why, have you retained her services?"

The only way to describe Alan's reaction was in the form of a news bulletin: "the marines have landed and are moving into action." Plodd shouted in loud ringing New England tones, "You goddam son of a bitch," lifted the jockey up and dragged him kicking and struggling out in the hall.

Tom who followed him threw open the hall door. "Shall we put him in the millpond, Mr. Plodd?" he asked.

"By all means," said Alan who seemed to have no difficulty in handling Ian.

But the rest of the assemblage had now excitedly poured into the hall. Father Dermot and the Archdeacon begged Plodd to restrain himself though both of them had itched to follow Plodd's example.

"Just throw him out," suggested Mabs from the background.

It was done. Ian was deposited outside on the grass and the door was closed on him. Panting, red-faced and dishevelled,

Alan addressed the shocked assembly, "Attracta Mulcahy is the most beautiful, wonderful girl I've ever known or probably will ever know. I asked her to marry me but she won't."

Lady de Bracey pushed forward and shook Alan's hand. "Good fellow. She is a great girl."

"So that was the cure." Liz turned to the Doctor who had been hopping around enjoying every minute of the painful scene.

The poor Miss Croziers were horror-struck. They didn't know what to think. "It was those evenings in the Woods," whispered Maud brokenly.

Suddenly Linda Blood shoved her way through the onlookers, kicking people right and left; she reached the hall door and opened it, turned and shouted, "Buggers!"

"You too," said Tom as he closed the door on her.

Then everybody trooped back into the studio where Mrs. Walsh was clearing debris and thinking up news bulletins to be handed out in the village the next morning. Albie held on to the Doctor's arm. "We always have such a good time at Liz's parties."

"Yes, like a public execution," remarked Colin drily.

"Nonsense Colin," giggled Eddie, "it was like a beautiful satisfyingVictorian novel."

Suddenly another sensation burst upon them. Ms. Goggins, who had been imbibing, took the floor and began dancing to the penny whistle. Whatever she was doing, it was deeply traditional, but it was also to put it mildly, embarrassing. Nobody knew where to look.

"She can't go on very long, or can she?" Liz clutched Eddie.

"She'll pass out soon," said Eddie comfortingly. The Archdeacon urged Muriel to rise; it was time to go home, but suddenly Ms. Goggins danced right up to him and took his arm whirled him round, shouting what sounded like challenging war cries. Barely had the frightened Archdeacon struggled free of the strange girl, before she had laid rude hands on Mabs Vigors and pushed the daughter of a hundred colonels around the room clutching her round the waist and screaming.

"Rescue her, Artie!" screamed Albie, "she'll have a heart attack." The General, like most generals, was too cowardly to do anything, but the two curates, assisted by Alan and Tom, eventually intervened and Ms. Goggins was driven home in a confused state of mind. Alan was afraid to go home with the Miss Croziers; it was only delaying the painful scene which inevitably had to follow, but he just couldn't face explanations that night. So he went back to the presbytery with the two curates, had a bottle of stout with them and when he eventually got back to Daisy Lodge the two ladies were safely in bed.

The following Monday Mrs. Walsh on her way to The Boys dropped in at the Post Office. "Do you know what it was like?" she began. Miss O'Kelly was making a show of filling in forms. "It was like the time Father Heron choked givin' the holy sacrament and fell foaming on the altar steps. Everything went by me like a flash. I was handin' out the chicken salad and the next minute they was rollin' on the floor."

"Threw him out did he?" Miss O'Kelly leaned forward expectantly, hungry for horrors and you certainly never went hungry when Mrs. Walsh was around. "Tell us."

"Like a baby he lifted him. In course young MacCrea is next to a dwarft; them jockeys have to be, but the Yank isn't that big neither. That Linda Blood is dirt, plain dirt."

Miss O'Kelly sniffed loudly. "So's Attracta Mulcahy — dirt."

"Ah, but she's good clean Irish dirt and that makes a difference."

"So the Yank's been going with her all this time." Some wretch had come in to buy stamps. Miss O'Kelly waved the intruder away and continued talking. "That will be a shock to the two Miss Croziers. Them poor omadhauns wouldn't know what he was up to. The poor creatures think a baby

111

comes in a head of cabbage." She turned to the customer grudgingly. "Now you have to wait your turn."

Liz felt it was her duty to put the Miss Croziers wise as to what led up to Plodd's public avowal of his relationship with Attracta. "So you see. I admire that girl. She's so proud and independent and takes care of her children beautifully."

"Children," Maud moaned. "Do you think . . . Oh." Her voice trailed away. "Do you think?"

"I do think so," answered Liz firmly. "Look at her record."

"This is truly frightful."

"She refused to marry him but I've no doubt that their relationship was fruitful, in every way. Has he come down to breakfast?"

"Not yet. Thank you for the interesting evening however. You give such delightful parties. That Ms. Goggins is an odd girl. Thank you for phoning, dear Liz."

Maud tremulously joined Clara in "the breakfast nook" which used to be a pantry off the kitchen, but "nooks" were all the thing now. "That was Liz on the phone. She was wondering about Alan."

"Nothing to wonder at now. We know how he spent those evenings in the Woods," said Clara grimly. "I've hidden father's carriage rugs. I cannot bear to think of them being used for — for such a purpose. Hush! here he comes."

Alan walked slowly into the kitchen. He had not yet talked with the ladies since the events of the previous evening. They both looked at him stonily. "I thought, Miss Clara and Miss Maud, that I should return home earlier than I intended. I did not intend that anything like this should happen, so I think I better go into Fungusport now and change my flight. I did not intend . . ." He repeated himself and began to sound like a record player running down, which was rather how he felt. He looked at them so wretchedly that the two ladies who were noted for their softness of heart (in fact they were indignantly accused by their friends of encouraging tinkers) began to melt. Alan turned and moved towards the door. "I guess I better go now. Only, Miss Crozier, you wouldn't wish any lady of your acquaintence called that."

"Alan, dear chap," Clara rose and moved towards the sinner. "You acted like a gentleman, but I wish — I wish — well you know what I mean."

"That horrible little Ian MacCrea! I never could stand him," cried Maud. "Sit down; your coffee is ready."

Alan tried to smile. "Nature is nature," he shook his head, "and I'm no better than anyone else."

"Alan, old chap," said Clara, she clapped him on the back, "you mustn't go any earlier. Stay until the date you arranged. We've grown so fond of you. Sit down, old boy. Your rashers and eggs are all set out on the hot plate."

The last meeting was, as one might expect, heart rending. It was a wonderful evening, mellow, calm and the birds were in full song.

"Our last night and no rugs," the lover groaned. "They hid them but they've been very good really. I brought along my old raincoat and a couple of sweaters."

Attracta was more silent than usual. She stood very still leaning against their favourite oak tree and stared into space. "You know, Alan, I'm sure I've conceived. I don't know for certain, but I just sense it."

"That's done it." Alan flung himself down on his knees and clasped his mistress round the waist. "I can't go. You have to marry me. I won't have my child a bastard."

She thrust him angrily away from her. "How dare you, Alan Plodd. None of my children are bastards. They're love children and let me tell you they're the best."

"I'm sorry. You're right." He sighed and moaned and caught hold of her again; this time she did not repulse him. "I can't leave you."

"You must," she said gently stroking his hair. "We've had all we need of each other. You will go back home and work and be a teacher and marry. But promise me you won't read any more of those dirty books."

Alan drew back in amazement. "I don't read dirty books!"

"That man, whatshisname, you're writing about . . ." she murmured.

"Beckett! Good God, Attracta, he's not dirty. He's the greatest writer of our time."

"He didn't seem to be very good for you."

"Insane girl!" A long lingering kiss followed. Alan rolled over on his back and stared thoughtfully up into the greenness above him. "I think what it is, now that I look back on it, we American scholars (not that I'm one yet) tend to delve too deeply into things. We identify too much with the subject. We go footnoting around in a maze of details and then somehow we get lost, or worse still, boring. I knew a guy who was writing his thesis on Byron, shot himself in the foot so that he could *feel* club-footed. You know I'm thinking of changing to Byron myself."

"Alan, don't cut any more capers, promise, love."

"I promise. Promise to let me know what happens dearest." Though he could only dimly sense it he was a fortunate youth who had been loved in passing by a goddess. The old old trees arching overhead, the evening twitter of small birds, the sound of doves in the branches and the sweet smell of crushed bracken were all part of a radiant experience which he would cherish for the rest of his life and look back on only with the most tender happiness.

"Two months later Attracta informed her employer, Lady de Bracey, that she was pregnant.

"Oh dear, is it wise?"

"No," Attracta laughed merrily. "Sure I've never been wise and never will be."

"But, my dear, what will you do about money?"

"Alan's father sent Miss Atkins a cheque for her favourite charity because of what she did for Alan. So I'm her favourite charity." The goddess smiled happily and returned to her loom.

Chronicle Four

I T WAS EARLY in June when the affair which went down in history as the Fungusport Fiasco first raised its ugly head.

One morning the telephone rang in the studio. Sighing, Liz lifted the receiver. She was trying to get a show ready for a London gallery and any interruption jarred.

"Oh, it's you, Father Kevin."

"Forgive me disturbing you, but you're on the Advisory Board of the Hodge Podge so I took the liberty of calling you."

"Go ahead."

"Well, Peader Rooney has just won a big prize in Dublin for his play. You know him?"

"I don't but no matter. Is he the son of that villainous publican and property developer Rooney?"

"Yes. Young Peader was sent up to National University to study law but he sort of went on the skids. Plays the banjo, wears his hair in braids and is some sort of Socialist."

"He sounds better than his father."

"He's not talking to his father. None of them are now-adays. Anyway it's a big prize, so the play must be good. My sister who acts with the National Theatre says they have it under consideration but that takes two to three years and then it's usually negative."

"So what is your problem?"

"Peader wants us to do it. He used to act with the Hodge. He would like us to give it its première. He has sent me some scripts. I haven't had time to read it yet. Do you think it's a good idea?"

"Of course I do."

"I felt you would. I can pass them round to the Advisory

117

Board at once. That comprises Lady de Bracey, Mr. Evans, Mr. Fox, Mairin O'Kelly, John Fallon, the Archdeacon," he paused, "and Father Hannigan."

"Oh dear, Father Hannigan won't pass it unless it's something like *Peg O' My Heart*. You know him and sex."

Father Kevin groaned. "The script may be too avant-garde. Ballyfungus is a bit of a backwater."

Liz Atkins laughed. "A holy backwater! Well, Father Kevin, get scripts out and around and ask for a quick reading. Then you can call a meeting here."

"Oh thank you, Miss Atkins," she could hear him sigh, a sigh of relief. "You never let us down. It was a great day for Ballyfungus when you came here and converted the Old Mill."

Liz laughed heartily; she liked Father Kevin; everyone liked him. "But you never converted me, did you?"

Wish I could convert her, thought Father Kevin as he put down the receiver. She reminds me of Teresa D'Avila. That gaunt strength of hers and the way she gets things done. Then again he thought of Miss Atkins' four discarded husbands and her odd relationship with her handsome handyman and put the thought away from him as slightly impious. Alas Miss Atkins was no saint, but Father Kevin was that wonderfully rare thing, a selfless enthusiast. His whole heart and I fear a great deal of his soul was wrapped up in the drama group. When the Canon occasionally remonstrated, he would say respectfully, "But think of the hundreds I've kept out of the pubs the last few years," and then he would relieve the old man of some tiresome parish duties, leaving him freer to pursue his archeological researches and nothing more would be said.

On the other hand, the vociferously puritanical Father Hannigan, parish priest of the neighbouring Kinealy, lived in a chilly looking presbytery. His housekeeper to whom Father Kevin handed the play was a dwarf with a huge wart on her nose. The young priest could not help reflecting on poetic justice as he greeted the gnome with what he trusted was a pleasing smile. He was rewarded with a mixture of snarl and grunt. Caliban's sister, thought the Father, as he sped away on his motor bike (he was a terror on the roads), "and serve Father Hannigan right."

That evening Colin Evans phoned Liz. "My dear, I've read the play Father Kevin so thoughtfully left on my doorstep. It centres around masturbation."

"What!"

"You heard me. Known in good King Arthur's day as self-abuse."

"How boring."

"Not boring, dear. Sensational. The plot concerns a simple-minded farmer's son dominated by a deeply religious wid-owed mother. Of course, she keeps him away from normal sex and then catches him masturbating. She calls in the priest and they both read a hell-fire sermon to him on this nasty practice and the poor fellow goes off and cuts his throat. The title is *Under the Blanket*. Get it?"

"They can never do it here. Never."

"Why not? The dialogue is powerful and the idea is sound. Think of Father Hannigan. Not a play passes without a letter to the *Times* from him about the evils of sex."

"I'm going to read it this minute. I'll phone you tomorrow morning."

Liz read the play in bed. She read it through twice. On the second reading she was inclined to agree with Colin. The more she thought about Rooney senior and Rooney junior and their modes of life the more she thought it should be done. She often felt that Ballyfungus was ready for a Second Coming and now Rooney junior might turn out to be — well — at least — John the Baptist. Also if one wished to use one's own body for pleasure, why not? It was the only untaxed territory left to a citizen of Earth. People could no longer

119

afford prostitutes. Their prices had gone up like everyone else's. What was left? Home products? Like growing your own vegetables organically. . . . Liz fell asleep.

Father Kevin also read the play in bed. At first he couldn't believe what he was reading. As he read on a light sweat pricked out on his forehead. It would have to be turned down immediately! He read it again and then it began to take hold of him. It was believable. He knew what the problem was . . . who didn't? No doubt it was powerfully written and the judges were all intelligent and knowing. The poor fellow lay palpitating in bed (he hardly dared go under the blanket); he was certain if he didn't do the play he might lose power. The young talented members of the club would think him craven, old fashioned, a Holy Creep. They were all liberated and thinking for themselves; he knew several of them were on the Pill. They laughed at Father Hannigan.

The excitement amongst the Ballyfungus intellectual community was intense. News of the play spread like wildfire and the turmoil was greatly helped by Mrs. Walsh, who carried the news from house to house. "Terrible dirty stuff about a fella handlin' himself, d'you know, and then gettin' old mick for it. I wouldn't let any child of mine go within a mile o' that filth." Luckily Mrs. Walsh was childless.

A meeting was called for the following Tuesday night in the Old Mill, "kind permission of Miss Atkins." The sherry to be supplied by the Hodge Podge. As might be expected everyone turned up. Packed into the big studio were the Hodge Podge Players in toto and the Advisory Committee. Aisling Geraghty, secretary and often leading lady of the drama group (by day a bank clerk), moved gracefully around offering what might fairly be described as cooking sherry.

Father Kevin opened the proceedings. He was extremely nervous and the sight of Father Hannigan, a menacing figure in the background, was not encouraging. "Friends," he began, "you've no doubt heard of young Peader Rooney's success in Dublin. His play, *Under the Blanket,* has won an important prize and we, at least some of us, feel that it ought to get its first production in Peader's home town. I've been in touch with the author and he is all for it. The Advisory Committee has had an opportunity of reading the play so I await their decision." He sat down.

Father Hannigan rose. A ripple of laughter could be heard from the younger people; it was immediately suppressed. "I have read this disgusting play," thundered the priest (he was a consistent thunderer). "It is filthy! Obscene! It deals with a subject in a manner which glorifies sin. This play must not go on!"

Colin jumped up. "Nobody wants to glorify masturbation which is in itself a confession of failure. All the author points out is that it should not be punished as a sin."

Auntie Al clapped her hands. "Heah! Heah! Jolly good Colin. It's a very sad thing really, but it's part of nature, actually after all innocent dogs do it."

"Dogs," roared the priest. "Are you implying, my Lady, that we are brute beasts? Isn't that with the help of God and His Holy Mother what we're trying to rise above?"

"If it comes to that," retorted Auntie Al, "I'd rather have a nice kind spaniel bitch any day than you, Father Hannigan."

"Good people," the Archdeacon desperately tried to make his voice heard above the laughter. "Freedom of thought, freedom of speech we must support at all costs. To be frank I didn't like the play. Not a laugh anywhere . . ."

Mairin O'Kelly, who had been fiercely knitting near Father Hannigan, to whom she was devoted, now spoke up or as Colin said, spat up. "I think we should take a vote on it." Now Mairin came of a long line of patriots. Beginning with cattle maimers, going on to Fenians, then the "out in sixteen lads" and finally the Provos. Her old Pappy had shot a record number of persons in his time and would certainly get a bang-up funeral with a military IRA Guard of Honor. She had a nephew, a general they said, in the Provos up North, but on the other hand, a favourite nephew Ignatius worked in a garage in Ballyfungus and was only interested in acting with the Hodge Podge. Her loyalties were therefore dangerously split between Father Hannigan and her beloved Iggy, who was present, and watchful.

"Very sensible," shouted the Archdeacon. By this time everyone was shouting. "We should take a vote on this now. All those for production raise your hands." All hands were raised, except Father Hannigan's. The vote was carried. Production won.

Father Hannigan rose to his feet and made for the door. He hissed at Father Kevin in passing. "I'll see the Canon tomorrow and what's more the Bishop must be told." He banged out, much to everyone's relief.

"Incidentally, Father Kevin, where do you propose to put on this play?" asked Liz.

He answered nervously. "Up to this as you know we have been graciously lent the little theatre in the Convent of the Heavenly Angels. This production would not be suitable there, but the little theatre in Fungusport is available and with the money we made from *Peer Gynt* we can afford to rent it."

"You will direct the production, Father Kevin?" asked Liz, trying to comfort the poor curate. He looked so cast down.

"No indeed," said he wretchedly. "You can understand after the Canon has read it I won't be able to do much at all. However, I consulted with my sister who works in the Abbey Theatre and she's sending down a director from Dublin, a professional, Lesley Butler, who wants seventy pounds and bed and board for three weeks."

"I'll be glad to put him up," said Liz patting his shoulder. "No trouble at all. Now we'll all have a little whiskey. Eddie darling, you know where I keep the hard stuff. Bring it out." The meeting broke up and became disorderly from then on.

"And when you come to think of it," commented Eddie Fox, "everything is under the blanket in this country. Bribery, corruption, political jobbery, (cheers followed) we know there is something sinister going on about Balooly Woods. This play is only a tiny segment of what's wrong. Irish or Scotch?"

"Too bad! Not a laugh anywhere," mused the Archdeacon.

"Irish! Not too much thanks. Wish they'd do some Gilbert and Sullivan . . ."

"Well, here's to *Under the Blanket.*" Liz lifted her glass.

Incoherent cheers followed, even Father Kevin was smiling.

Suprisingly the Canon after a visit from Father Hannigan made little fuss. The truth was Father Hannigan bored him. The man knew nothing about twelfth-century Ireland and had shown little interest in the restoration of the twelfth-century Cistercian Abbey, which was the Canon's absorbing interest. As for the Bishop he was senile and had forgotten his own name.

"Mind you, Kevin," said the Canon, "you're only in there as an observer. No more."

"Of course, Canon," Father Kevin replied. "Nothing more."

The director from Dublin was due to arrive on the bus on Saturday morning. Auditions for casting were to be held in the hotel that very evening. Liz Atkins had her guest room prepared and was full of interest, as indeed was Mrs. Walsh, who had been called in to do some hard cleaning. Father Kevin borrowed the presbytery car. He was desperately trying to subdue his total commitment and to act merely as observer.

Full of excitement he entered the hotel. "There is a young man waiting for me?" he asked at the reception desk. The lady clerk happened to be a member of the Hodge Podge so her interest was intensified.

"No Father," she smiled and winked. "There is a young lady waiting for you."

Father Kevin started. "A young lady?"

"She's come be the bus. She's in the lounge waiting for you. And she's got a poodle with her and a parrot in a cage and a case."

"She can't be for me." The curate paled.

"She is so. Her name's Butler."

Father Kevin walked nervously into the lounge. There sure enough seated near the window was a tall beautiful young woman, wearing a grey pantsuit and a large black hat tied under her chin. Her hair was long and golden and floated to her shoulder. When she removed the dark glasses he could see her eyes were dark blue. Sure enough there was a birdcage beside her on the floor and a white poodle sat at her feet.

"Miss Butler?" stammered Father Kevin approaching her. It would be hard to say which was redder, his face or his hair.

"Lesley." She rose gracefully and held out her hand. "Your sister probably told you all about me."

(She did not, thought Father Kevin, and I'll give her hell.) "Yes indeed she did," he lied. "Let me take your suitcase. I've got a car outside."

"Thank you. I'm to direct the play with your help. You I understand are the producer." She spoke softly, calmly and was entirely in command of the situation. "You don't mind my sweet macaw Captain Hook and my poodle Winnie. They're part of my life, my scene. Am I to live in this horrid dump?"

"No indeed. Miss Atkins, the artist at the Old Mill, has offered you hospitality."

"I was hoping I might stay with you. We must confer so often and alone." They were moving through the hall now towards the door. Father Kevin was unpleasantly conscious that staff and visitors had emerged from the bar and the dining room and were eyeing the interesting visitor with admiration and amusement.

"I'm afraid that would be impossible. I live in the presbytery with my fellow priests."

"That's too bad. What a sweet old car! I would love to

have moved in with you for conference purposes. I adore priests. My uncle is a Monsignor. Is this Miss Atkins the painter? She knew my mother. I think they were both married to the same man once."

To say that Father Kevin was stunned would be an understatement. He was beginning to wish he'd never heard of Peader Rooney's play. Was this girl any good? Not morally of course, professionally, but even that looked dubious. She didn't seem at all his idea of a professional director. Much more like a visiting film star. And then that wretched parrot, not to mention the poodle.

Liz was waiting for them. Mrs. Walsh in uniform — bedroom slippers, apron over pantsuit, hair in curlers — was behind her. Her jaw dropped when she saw the beautiful visitor. (Blessed God the presperation burst out all over me. The shock went through me, down to me varkis veins.)

Liz could only stare and made no attempt to conceal her astonishment. Miss Butler however remained perfectly calm. Having survived an exceptionally macabre childhood she was ready for any emergency.

"Very good of you to have me, Miss Atkins. I love your work. I hope you don't mind my children coming with me. I feel disembodied without them. Dear Father Kevin, we must talk, talk, talk . . ."

Liz regained her composure. She addressed the visitor politely. "Let me show you your room. I hope you brought bird seed and dog food. I have none."

"There is little else in my suitcase, dear Miss Atkins. I think you know my ex-step-father, Denis Hale."

"Denis! Yes, I was married to him once." Liz stared.

"So was Mummy. She could only take it for one year and then — Out. I spent my childhood between a castle in Mayo and London's East End. Sad. I'll put Captain Hook here on this table and poor little Winnie sleeps with me." She moved to the window, threw back the curtains and gazed out on the millpond.

"Oh the sound and the look of water is so soothing and beautiful. I'm highly nervous you know!"

"You don't look it," rejoined Liz drily. "I'll leave you to unpack. Early supper at six. I believe you have to work this evening."

Out in the studio Liz and Father Kevin faced each other speechlessly. Then she burst into laughter. "Mrs. Walsh, for God's sake make some strong coffee. Father Kevin needs it."

"I need it myself. Even me toes is tingling." Mrs. Walsh rushed into the kitchen.

"I took it for granted Lesley was a man. I never thought," stammered the young man. "My sister never said . . ."

"Never mind, Father Kevin. She's certainly beautiful if eccentric and it will be quite an experience working closely with her." She laughed again. Father Kevin blushed. His face merged into his hair so to speak. "It's terrible!" he whispered.

If Liz and Father Kevin were stunned, the same could be said for the assembled players in the hotel. Miss Butler had changed into a black velvet pantsuit, a white scarf round her head. Her make-up was as Mrs. Walsh put it "the colour of a corpse long dead." Her eyes were heavily framed in green. Father Kevin tried to, but could not, take his eyes off her. The profile was the nearest thing to a goddess since Ancient Greece. The poodle accompanied her; mercifully not the parrot.

She took the floor at once and addressed the players. "Well, I take over from now. The author will be here in a couple of days. *Mes enfants,* I've studied the play thoroughly. It only needs four superlatively good actors, four or five supporting cast, excellent staging and lighting. Otherwise let's forget it. Father Kevin I believe is my lighting man. Aren't you, darling?" Father Kevin again turned red and nodded speechlessly. There were a few titters from the company. "I must see the theatre as soon as possible. Have you the drawings for the set there? Ah yes. Put them beside me, Kev, we'll look at them together. I can't call you Father it's too unprofessional.

Now let's get on with the auditions." The casting swallowed up two evenings and was conducted in an icily professional manner.

Rather to Father Kevin's secret perturbation Ignatius O'Kelly was not cast at all. Like most of the Ballyfungus natives the Father was slightly afraid of Ignatius O'Kelly's auntie. "He's too knowing. He would never have cut his throat. He would have defied his Mum," Lesley whispered in Father Kevin's ear. Her mouth was often close to his ear. She chose for the lead a spotty timid-looking clerk who worked in the hotel, Tim Foley, by name. "This Foley darling gives one the feeling of a masturbator living under a blanket and doing little else."

"He has a wife and three children," answered Father Kevin rather crossly, "and up to this he has only played minor roles."

"Wait and see, dear Kev, Lesley can bring out the best in people *and* the worst."

Father Kevin started. Was that a threat?

"Did you get the part, Iggy?" Miss O'Kelly addressed her nephew who had dropped in at the Post Office on his way home from the final auditions.

"I did not," he snapped, "that shitty Foley got it. I'm to do props. It's my turn." He mimicked or tried to mimic Lesley's Old Vic accent. "I look too normal, darling. That's a bitch if ever there was one."

" 'Tis a filthy play anyhows," snapped Auntie, "and should never have been put on. And it's my opinion it won't come off at all."

"Oh yes it will. That woman could raise the dead."

"There are others who can raise things, lovey. Leave it to Auntie."

"Well don't go fuckin' around with the Bishop or Father bloody Hannigan," retorted the nephew irreverently. "I don't go along with the holy stuff."

"Mind your own business, Iggy, and I'll mind mine."

That evening Miss O'Kelly made a couple of long distance calls, the result of which seemed most satisfactory. She was quite gentle and kind with her old Pappy and gave the cat a saucerful of chicken livers.

Peader the author arrived the next day. He was large, fair-haired, wore a red caftan and yellow sandals which exactly matched his toe nails. Though he was scheduled to stay in Ballyfungus three weeks he brought little else with him except his banjo and a portable typewriter. He was accompanied by a girl friend, who wore a blue caftan, had greasy black hair, brown teeth, and hated her parents, who were rich. The happy couple shared a tent which they set up in a field on the way to Kinealy. Peader wouldn't go near his family. "A bunch of shit," he said. He was knocked all of a heap by Lesley; nobody had warned him. Before he could utter a word she went up to him, placed her hands on his shoulders and looked deeply into his eyes.

"Darling, it's a very powerful play and I believe in it. But leave everything to me. You know I rather agree with Hilton Edwards, the Dublin director, who says I prefer my authors dead. Now what I want you to do, dear Peader, is to stay very quiet and *act* dead. We'll work on cuts together and alone." Father Kevin did not like the sound of this, neither did the girl friend. "Don't you agree with me, Nuala darling?" she addressed the girl friend who was biting her nails. "Peader is a potential genius. Give him lots and lots of yogurt and warm milk. I do recommend rhubarb soup."

Peader bemused, like everyone else, humbly agreed to act dead and also agreed on cuts. He sat very quietly at rehearsals beside the girl friend with eyes closed, but occasionally he opened them and made some heartbroken notes on a torn envelope.

Two days passed. "Kev darling," murmured Lesley one evening at rehearsal, the lips as usual close to his ear. He was becoming addicted to this form of communication. "I made some more cuts. Poor Peader suffers so, but I soothe him down."

"I can imagine that." The young priest answered rather drily. He had noticed the soothing methods and so had Peader's girl friend, the pimply Nuala, and she, like Father Kevin, did not like it at all. Father Dermot, too, had taken to hanging round the theatre offering to do odd jobs. He usually despised Hodge Podge activities but now some magnet seemed to draw him. Once Kevin had seen Lesley running her fingers through Father Dermot's crisp brown curls. He reproved her for this when they were driving home to the Old Mill one night after rehearsal. "People might misconstrue it. We are in a very delicate position."

Lesley laughed gently; her head was almost resting on his shoulder. "Darling Kev, it was absence of mind combined with exhaustion. I might have been patting my poodle. I get so involved in the play I don't know what I'm doing."

"I understand," said Kevin immediately won over. "I was just giving you a little warning. There are some fearful gossips in this town." He thought of Mrs. Walsh and the postmistress and shuddered. It must be said Lesley was doing a splendid job. Never had the players worked harder, never had they been more enthusiastic. Truth to tell the play was not that good but she infused it with vitality and credibility because she believed in it herself.

She had her critics. Liz for instance. She had taken to phoning The Boys for sympathy. "I never see my own car. She blandly uses it for transportation, not only for humans but for furniture bits and pieces they call props. I'm sick of the squawking parrot and the horrible poodle who bites people in the bottom for no reason. It's worse than Dolphie. She is a relentless egotist absolutely humourless, uses everyone, man and woman and child to her own advantage." On reporting this conversation to Colin, Eddie giggled, "For a while I thought Liz was describing herself!"

Colin raised his eyebrows. "It's as if Elizabeth One and

Mary Queen of Scots had been shut up together for three memorable weeks."

However most of the Ballyfungus citizens capitulated to that silky smooth sweetness. Ignatius O'Kelly had fallen a victim. He had even consented to do props, regarded as a despicable job, but all Hodge Podge Players had to go through "props." It was a form of initiation. One evening Iggy arrived at rehearsal breathing triumph. "I found a Victorian bedside commode," he shouted pointing at his precious load. "Oh Iggy, you're wonderful! Miracle man! Lesley loves you." She did indeed kiss him gently on each cheek. Iggy looked as if he might faint. Then he revived and opened the lid of the commode. "For you," he said reverently.

There were other critics. Aisling Geraghty asserted to anyone who might listen that Lesley had bad breath and Bride Murphy (pronounced Breede) said Lesley's fingers were like a string of Goggins sausages "gone off" she added. Nuala, Peader's girl friend, packed up and left at the end of the second week. She complained that Peader kept calling out "Lesley, Lesley," in his sleep. "It's my opinion she's a witch and needs exorcism. That Father Kevin will be in trouble yet." Peader hardly seemed to mind her defection. For him there was nothing now but the play and the director of that play. Father Dermot called Lesley the White Goddess and said jokingly of course that Kevin was under her spell: Father Kevin angrily disclaimed such an uncouth accusation. It was lucky for them that the Canon was back in the twelfth century and extremely busy at the moment. The excavators had just uncovered a whole score of skeletons which seemed to indicate the plague had reached Ballyfungus around 1385. "It's my opinion it's reached it again," quipped the bitter Aisling who was watching Lesley putting "the leads" through their paces.

Needless to say Mrs. Walsh was the most eloquent on the subject. She usually dropped into the Post Office on the way home when Seamus was on evening duty. It was the ideal time to retail the day's doing or misdoings. This evening the office was closed and Miss O'Kelly was upstairs in the parlor, modishly called the lounge, feeding her aged parent his tea. The one-time fighting patriot was confined to a wheelchair. At some point in his tumultuous history he had been shot in the kneecaps by a colleague and for the rest of his life was immobilized on a pension. The lounge was kept at fever temperature; the walls were hung with holy pictures and there were many receptacles for holy water placed at strategic points. In one corner there was a life-size statue of the Blessed Virgin with a red light non-stop burning below it.

Mrs. Walsh removed the cycling helmet, loosened her coat and sat down. "Well, Holy God, I pity poor Miss Atkins with that jade Butler under her feet most of the day. You never seen the like. In the mornin' she sits with her legs twisted and knotted, starin' madlike at the wall; eats nothin' but bananas and raisins and what you call yoggy."

"Blessed mother." Miss O'Kelly paused cup in hand. "Here Pappy, drink this. Chicken soup dontcherlike it?" The aged patriot nodded violently; a cascade of chicken soup plummeted down his chin.

Mrs. Walsh continued: "Miss Atkins asked me if I'd twist the parrot's neck. The jade brought a parrot with her. Holy God, Miss Atkins, says I, sure that would bring bad luck. Now you won't believe what I'm goin' to tell you." She paused. Miss O'Kelly pushed another spoonful of soup down her aged parent's throat almost choking him this time. She turned eagerly to Mrs. Walsh. "Miss Butler, Lesley Butler that's the Christian name, Christian moyah — tells fortunes be the navel. Now choke that down."

"Be the — you mean?" Miss O'Kelly pointed wordlessly towards her stomach.

Mrs. Walsh nodded. "The same. She done it be the ambivalent cord which hands out messages. All ye do is press in the navel like you was defrostin' the fridge and viberations does the rest."

"I never heard the like. Filth."

"And wait keep your ears unbuttoned. Father Kevin's with her mornin' noon and night. Night." Miss O'Kelly tittered. Mrs. Walsh continued. "If Father Hannigan heard tell there'd be a givin' out I can tell you. Oh the collar means nothin' anymore."

Miss O'Kelly's brow darkened, the dentures descended, the Dracula look took over. "Father Hannigan doesn't want this play to go on at all. He'll find a way to stop it. I tell you there's dirt all round us, Emerald. Dirt! Dirt! Dirt! And he don't find a way there's those that will."

Mrs. Walsh was beginning to wish she'd never opened her mouth. Sometimes the postmistress frightened the wits out of her. Miss O'Kelly droned fiercely on. "And Iggy there is mad about her. Came looking for props and took away part of the back bedroom. Declare to God I thought he'd take Pappy with it. He was strippin' the place and for a filthy disgustin' stinkin' heathen play. Iggy won't hear a word against it or her. Here Pappy, that's the end of it." She wiped the aged man's mouth with a piece of tissue, his head fell to one side and she smacked it back again into position. Mrs. Walsh put on the cycling helmet and made her getaway.

Meanwhile great preparations were going ahead for the opening night of the play. The Grand advertised cordon bleu after-theatre suppers and Mayor Goggins was to open the proceedings. Critics were coming down from Dublin and up from Cork and a couple of watchful producers were expected from London. The RTE crew was also scheduled to attend the opening night ceremonies. They hoped for some sensational happening, which, on the record, seemed more than likely. One morning a boy on a bicycle arrived at the presbytery with a note for Father Kevin.

Dear Father Sheedy,
    I'm taking the liberty of sending over a few cases of gin and whiskey with the soft stuff also, for the opening night

of my son's play. Don't mention it to anyone, least of all to that stupid fool Peader. The proceeds can go towards expenses. Mind you not a word. Yrs. P. Rooney.

The young priest struggled with his conscience. Should he take anything from that villain Rooney who was hand in glove with Fallon? Still the drink could make a nice sum for Hodge Podge and the expenses had been heavy. Out of evil comes good. Yes, think of it that way. Out of evil comes good. Hang on to that, Kevin. Accordingly he phoned Rooney and thanked him for his offer which would be kept a secret until the night.

The following afternoon Lesley phoned him from the Old Mill. "Kevin dearest, I've nothing to do for an hour or so; would you take Lesley for a drive? Everybody tells me about beautiful Balooly and Lesley wants to see it. I met the Old Doctor, he was here last night and he's a sweetie. He told me the Woods were haunted; that it was a pagan stronghold and Lesley is a confirmed pagan."

Could he? Would he? Should he? What harm could it do anyone? And maybe he might improve the shining hour by instilling some form of faith into her; she must at least forego her paganism. "Yes. If I can get the car. I'll phone you back if I get it."

By a mad stroke of luck the presbytery car was available. "I just have to go over a few details with Miss Butler before the dress rehearsal," he explained and his look, Father Dermot noted, could only be described as shifty.

"Okay Kev, the Archdeacon's giving me a lift to the playing field and you needn't mind about the Canon; he's knee-deep in medieval skeletons. Better look out for yourself though." He laughed and bounded up the stairs before Father Kevin could reply.

Lesley, of course, was wearing a white pantsuit with a white kerchief binding up her blonde hair. "Before we go into the Woods," she said seating herself cozily beside him, "I would love to go up that little mountain you can see from the Old Mill."

"Knockmeldon. Yes, there's a beautiful view from there. You can see the whole of the Wexlow coast." He answered trying to subdue his delight in her company.

"Lesley is so happy." She pressed his arm. It was unfortunate that they passed Mrs. Walsh speeding homewards on her scooter from her half day at Daisy Lodge. Father Kevin groaned in spirit. That woman permeated everyone's lives. She seemed to be everywhere at once.

It was the rarest of things in Ireland, a magic summer's day. No wind, no rain, a cloudless sky. The country spread out on either side of them seemed to be basking as they were in the golden warmth. Kevin took the road to Kinealy; the same road on which Alan Plodd first met Attracta Mulcahy. After they passed Daisy Lodge and the desolate Protestant Church and graveyard he took a sharp turn up a narrow winding road which climbed so steeply that Lesley complained of her ears crackling. Presently the fields gave way to heather, broken stony ground, then rocks. The air here was sharper, cooler, and infinitely pure. He parked the car in the layabout and they got out and walked a little further up where he told her the view was best.

"Thalassa, the sea," cried Lesley. "One should always see the sea from the top of a mountain. How perfect."

Kevin stood beside her pointing out the various land marks. "There's Fungusport. And there's Ballyfungus itself. You can see the church spires rising above the trees and there to your left are the Woods of Balooly, kingdom of the birds. And the house beside the Woods is Ferncourt."

"Why it looks like a little pink doll's house from here," she sighed.

Kevin moved closer to her: "And there's the River Fung winding its way to the sea. It does look like a silver ribbon doesn't it?" He gazed lovingly down on the familiar landscape. It was extraordinarily still up there. Only the twitter of small birds, a farm dog barking below them and the gentle baaing of sheep broke the stillness. And away in the distance the sea shimmered, dazzling the eyes.

"So lovely. So lovely; nothing must change it. It's photographed on my mind forever. Oh Kevin, thank you." She pressed his arm gently. He remained silent. Poor fellow, he only knew that he was happy, that it was an exquisite moment in his life and it would float away so soon, a leaf on the wind, and be only a memory.

"Come let's go down into the Woods." He sighed and turned away. Once they were in Balooly Lesley walked ahead of him stopping now and then to exclaim about the majesty of the primeval oaks and arching splendour of the beeches, the delicious smell of the pines and then suddenly she stood stock-still and waited for him to catch up with her.

"Doves," she exclaimed, "doves, I hear them crooning to each other." Father Kevin looked at her bewitched. She whirled around suddenly and faced him. "I didn't tell you but I had a miserable childhood. Nobody wanted me. When my mother got tired of me she shipped me off to my father and when he got tired of me he would palm me off on an aunt and then she would throw me into boarding school and I'd be forgotten. I was batted around like a tennis ball. I know you think I'm phoney and affected and that I put on an act. Well I do. It's no use your trying to convert me, Kev; I lost my faith when I was six years old. My funny faces are my defense against a brutal world." He looked at her wordlessly and saw her face change, it had become strangely wan and pinched. In that revealing moment the face of a maltreated little girl who had been damaged for life looked at him. His heart was wrung for her, but there was nothing he could do.

"I think we better be getting back," he said gently and took her hand. "Dress rehearsal tomorrow night. And I have parish duties this evening."

Driving home he told her all about the threats of development, the factory and the evil Fallon. Lesley listened in horror. "Never let it happen. Promise me. Fight it."

"You never win against greed." Kevin shook his head sadly. "Greed and money. Now it's the greed for minerals, for oil, for all the fruits of the earth. Morals play no role in this mad pursuit."

"I agree, Kev, and to quote the Protestant collect, 'and there is no health in us but thou Oh Lord have mercy on us miserable sinners.' " She burst into laughter and patted his hand. "I wish you might have been my brother, Kev. I don't say this because you're a priest vowed to celibacy and might have been my lover. I always longed for a brother to share my loneliness."

"You'll get married some day." He tried to smile but he didn't like the idea at all.

"I don't even crave lovers. I'm not even a nun, the bride of Christ. What nonsense that is! Consolation prize. Everything was spoiled for me long ago. Well Father Kevin, we understand each other." He looked at her and saw one forlorn tear roll down her cheek. At that moment he would have given up the world, his faith, everything he strived for, to kiss that tear away and offer her his love. But she turned quickly away, got out of the car and ran into the Old Mill.

During the summer months the ladies of Ferncourt opened up their conservatory for entertaining which meant the bi-weekly bridge evenings. The hothouse flora consisted largely of climbing geraniums and a sickly vine (planted during the Boer War) which yielded no grapes and never seemed to prosper but then neither did the Boer War. Scattered around were some rickety straw furniture and a profusion of empty flowerpots. It did retain a little heat however from intermittent solar energy though the insistent pattering of rain on glass was often somewhat discouraging.

"Like native drums, by George," observed the General on an evening when it was even more thunderous than usual. "Don't you think so, Mabs? Two hearts."

"One did not hear native drums in Government House, Artie," was the haughty reply. "Four diamonds."

136

"The sun shone today for almost two hours," observed Albie, all brightness, "and that makes it quite tropical in here." The wig, this evening, was a rich brown; both ladies were wearing their summer dresses, white crochet with short sleeves and low necks and both were wearing for no obvious reason dark glasses.

"Have you heard anything about that play they're putting on in Fungusport? Hodge Podge I mean. I hear it's filthy," said the Doctor chattily after a sharp round of recrimination had followed on the previous game. "Mrs. Walsh was helping with dinner at our place and she said everyone's trousers were down as bold as brass. I intend to go. There's an extraordinary girl producing it, a mad girl from Dublin. Poor Liz is on tranquillizers. The girl has been foisted on her."

"I met the girl in Goggins; she was buying bananas. Her mother was a De Vere," said Albie. "Liz introduced me and I knew at once who she was. De Vere."

"De Vere? Lady Clara of course." Josh quoted with relish, "Oh teach the orphan boy to read or teach the orphan girl to sew. / Pray Heaven for a human heart and let the foolish curate go."

"Why curate?" asked Mabs looking at him over the top of her glasses. "Tennyson said yeoman."

"Because, my dear girl, the young curate Sheedy is in attendance according to Liz. De Vere!" He teeheed again.

"Her name was not Clara it was Doris." Albie leaned forward and pinched the Doctor's wrist. "Your bid, Josh."

"Four spades. I cannot believe a De Vere could be called Doris." The Doctor shook his head. "This girl is called Lesley."

Albie addressed her sister who was looking frighteningly stern this evening. "The girl's mother, if it's the same, *was* striking looking. Do you remember her, Mabs? She married several times with horrid results and is now living in seclusion with a plumber. I pass."

"No plumbers are secluded, Albie. Plumbers are the most wanted men on earth." Mabs was really very snarly this evening. The Doctor studied her. Possibly a touch of liver!

"Which of these husbands of Doris De Vere fathered this girl?" asked the General. He was shuffling and dealing and dropping cards on the floor much to the other players' scorn. His gout was at him.

"A Butler from Kilkenny I think." Albie smacked the General's wrist this time. He uttered a yelp of pain.

"Goddammit, Albie, that was my bad wrist," he shouted.

"All Butlers come from Kilkenny." The Doctor shook his head and looked at his cards and murmured without reverence, "Gentle Jesus!"

"A butler? I thought you said he was a plumber." The General looked and was addled.

"That was another one." Albie laughed delightedly. "You silly old man."

"What did the butler do besides getting Doris with child?" the General implored them. "Not that I care a damn. Two spades."

"Then you shouldn't ask." Albie shrieked with laughter; she was holding good cards. "Anyway this girl is a lady though strange. Liz says the curate Sheedy is in love with her."

"He can't be; he's a Catholic curate," retorted Mabs looking grimly at her sister.

The Doctor gave her a sly look. "Nonsense Mabs. Catholic curates and parish priests and even bishops travel widely with young ladies who are known as their nieces."

"How do you know Father Sheedy is sinning." Mabs rapped her tropical fan on the side of her chair; in a moment it might rap somebody's head. "You have no evidence. The girl is staying in the Old Mill and Father Sheedy is in the presbytery entirely surrounded by his fellow priests."

"Love will find a way," sang the irrepressible Doctor.

"Trump that if you can. Hark, do I hear Betty and the trolley?" It was indeed Betty and the trolley and what a sight she presented. Both gentlemen looked at her in horror. She was wearing a white shower cap and a hospital mask and this combined with her usual dirty white overalls caused her to resemble some dreadful apparition from an operating theatre wheeling out a corpse.

"Good evening, Betty m'dear." The Doctor rose and looked at her with professional interest. "What are your symptoms?"

"I do hab a cold ib by head." She approached the Doctor who backed hastily away. Where the common cold is concerned even the bravest shrinks from contact.

"Jamesy Nolan told me to tie a bunch of fresh mint to me wrist and my dose would clear."

"And has it?"

"To be trootful it hab not. And be ladies bade be wear dis horrid ting." She pointed to the mask.

"I must make a note of that." The Doctor was a great believer in herb lore. "Mint. Interesting." He looked sadly at the trolley. No food alas. The rocketing inflation had sadly restricted Ferncourt hospitality. Nothing was offered now but drinks. Meanwhile Dolphie the noble but unpopular bloodhound had as usual followed the trolley and had chosen to slump down at the feet of the man who hated him most — Artie Ironside.

"Help yourself, men," Mabs commanded, "and while you're about it, I'll take a Scotch and soda. You may go, boy." She addressed Betty who was sneezing violently behind the mask. The poor broken servitor shambled out of the conservatory.

"I'll get four seats for the opening night," said the General after swallowing down some whiskey, "and I'll give you ladies supper in the Grand afterwards."

"I'll go halves with you," Josh looked at the others questioningly. "Does anybody know the name of this play?" Nobody seemed to know the name of the play or what it was about except that it was risqué.

"Wish to God," sighed the General, "Hodge Podge would do something jolly like you know what — maybe *Rose Marie*. That Russian play was appalling. I slept all through it."

"You sleep through everything, Artie," Mabs sneered. "I

don't know how you kept awake during the war or indeed how you got to be a general."

"I didn't sleep when I was young, Mabs," replied the General sadly. "This dropping off is a fact of old age. There's nothing funny about being old, is there Josh?"

The Doctor considered for a moment. "No. However, you have the last laugh. Whatever or whoever you are about to meet in the next world must be an improvement on this one." He pulled an envelope out of his pocket. "I had a letter the other day from the young American fella who was here in the spring. He thanks me for the happiest days of his life." The Doctor held the letter up to his nose so that he could see better and spelled it out, slowly. " 'I've changed my thesis to Ernest Hemingway. Beckett didn't seem quite right to me.' Who's Hemingway?" He looked questioningly at the others.

Mabs put her finger to her lips and considered. "I connect him with Africa, don't you, Albie? Wasn't he a big game man?"

"I connect him with castration," said Albie frowning.

"I say," the General laughed, "that's more like disconnection." He laughed heartily at his own joke in which he was joined by snorts from the Doctor but the ladies looked disapproving.

"By Jove," the Doctor pulled out his watch, "it's getting late; night and the rain both falling. My daughter-in-law always has something cutting to say about old men and late hours."

"Your daughter-in-law is so good, so competent and so boring." Albie laughed softly. "You don't mind about my being frank?"

"You voice my own sentiments exactly." The Doctor shook his head sadly. "My other daughter-in-law does everything wrong but I love her." He rose to his feet and did a little dance to get the circulation going. "She's a rather silly dove and the other's a squawking crow."

"You see everyone as a bird, Josh." Albie rose also and put her arm around the Doctor's shoulder. "Now what sort of bird is this Lesley whatshername — the theatre girl I mean?"

The Doctor brooded for a moment. "A white blackbird," he said at last.

"There's no such thing," sniffed Mabs.

"Yes there is but they're very rare. So is she."

Driving home, the General, between yawns, remarked, "Mabs is very edgy lately. Have you noticed? Nothing's right and I wouldn't be surprised if she took a swipe at Betty occasionally. In Africa they swiped at everyone."

"She's brooding on this threat to the Woods and the rumoured road going through Ferncourt. I told my son to prescribe Valium."

"I didn't mind their eccentricities so much when we were given dinner but now it's not so rewarding. It's the wrist slapping."

"We might cut down our visits," suggested the Doctor.

"Tell the truth," said Artie ruefully, "it's loneliness with me. I'd rather be snarled at by Mabs than sit alone staring at TV or falling asleep over the newspaper. After a while you can hear the silence, don't you know —"

"Heyho," groaned the Doctor, "they'd like to get me out of the house and into some infernal old folks home run by holy Marys, but I'm sticking it out. Ferncourt is a damn sight better than having my daughter-in-law staring at me and obviously wishing I was dead."

Then came the dress rehearsal: it was a living nightmare. Three important lighting cues were missed, causing Father Kevin to cry out upon the Lord. Part of the bedroom wall fell across the bed just as the leading man was about to deliver the famous soliloquy beginning, "Shit the world." He got off with a slight concussion. The leading lady had a sore throat, they always do, and a dead rat was found in the gent's dressing room. The author sat throughout the proceedings with his head in his hands softly crying and wishing to God he'd never put pen to paper. Lesley, of course, remained calm. She moved gracefully around whispering words of comfort and encouragement; she caressed the lighting man who was threatening suicide; showed people how to move, to forget their hands, and remember the deaf man at the back of the theatre and project, above all project. It was two o'clock in the morning before the rehearsal staggered to a conclusion. Lesley called a word rehearsal for the following evening. "To encourage you darling Kev, Iggy's father had to go and be sick in the lav he was so moved by the play."

"He was drunk," said Father Kevin drily. "Iggy didn't want him there at all. He got in by mistake."

The following morning, Sunday, Father Hannigan broke the long silence. At twelve o'clock Mass he delivered a ferocious sermon on permissive sex in general and masturbation in particular.

"When sex is made cheap, marriage is made cheap," he positively roared. "Unchastity is at the root of broken marriages. History also shows that it is at the root of the decay of people. Great unhappiness has been caused in wide circles of families and friends by pregnancies outside marriage and the crime of abortion. Aiding and abetting this dreadful situation is dirt. Dirty writing, filthy movies, lascivious plays. Tomorrow night, yes tomorrow night you are invited to attend a performance of an immoral filthy play in Fungusport written, alas, by a young fellow from these parts who ought to have known better." He paused. There seemed to be quite a commotion at the back of the church. A group of persons was stamping out and talking angrily. The priest recognized Peader Rooney senior and family. Let them go, thought the angry crusader. True, Peader senior is a generous contributor to Catholic Charities but first things first and with Father Hannigan sex was first. He continued raising his voice to a shout. "This filthy play deals with a sin. The sin of masturbation. Now, my friends, masturbation is always objectively wrong in that it involves the abuse of one's sexual appetite in seeking to enjoy a pleasure alone (ipsation) which in our Catholic Church was ordained by God for the enrichment of husband and wife in marriage. Those who watch disgusting plays and films," he paused again. Was that laughter he heard? Yes it was. Some young fellows and girls were openly laughing at the back of the church. But the old people especially the women were most attentive and leaned forward eagerly to hear more. He caught sight of Miss O'Kelly's upturned face just under the pulpit. The front dentures had been lowered, she looked like a laughing death's head. Even Father Hannigan shuddered and paused in the midst of his diatribe. Could she and those like her be the only true believers, the only audience left to him? Why wasn't she in Ballyfungus parish anyway?

The sermon caused a minor sensation. The departure of the Rooney family from the church and the fact that the two curates over in Ballyfungus were involved in the production named by Father Hannigan were eagerly commented upon. What would the Canon do? What the Canon did or didn't do will remain forever unanswered for a much worse thing happened and pushed the sermon out of everyone's mind.

On the Monday morning a Mrs. Bridie O'Leary, a widow in reduced circumstances, arrived at the theatre to do the cleaning. It had been left in a shocking state after the dress rehearsal. She was accompanied by a slightly retarded orphan from the Little Sisters who helped her. "You go after the toilets, Rosie," she snapped, "while I do the hooverin'." Rosie obeyed reluctantly. She was always hoping for promotion and do out the offices, maybe, but it never came. So she obediently went down into the depths.

Presently above the roar of the Hoover Mrs. O'Leary heard the phone ring in the ticket office which was not yet occupied. Miss Draper who officiated never got in before eleven but then neither did Mrs. O'Leary. Nobody in Ireland thinks of arriving at work before ten or eleven o'clock, except doctors and farmers. Sighing and groaning Mrs. O'Leary picked up the receiver. A male voice with, as she put it afterwards, "a terrible foreign accent" answered.

"There's a bomb in your theatre, lady."

"A what?" asked Mrs. O'Leary who was a bit hard of hearing.

"A bomb," shouted the voice, "and it's timed to go off in ten minutes, so get out now." He repeated it again. Mrs. O'Leary dropped the receiver. She was shaking from head to foot and all sense had left her. She rushed out into the street to look for help and made for the traffic intersection in High Street where there was usually a Gardai. There was one, thanks be to God. She dropped at the feet of Gardai Murphy gasping out "a bomb in the theatre." The words were hardly out of her mouth before there was a tremendous explosion, people began running and shouting. They could see smoke was pouring out of the theatre. It was only when she came to that Mrs. O'Leary remembered poor Rosie and fainted again.

The theatre was a shambles; they dug poor Rosie out of the toilets and carried what was left of her away in a blanket. Otherwise there was no loss of life.

The anger was widespread. The loss of the beautiful little theatre, it could never be restored, and the tragic death of poor innocent Rosie evoked a storm of indignation. "A foundling, born apparently in a toilet and died in one," commented Colin Evans. "Of such is the Kingdom of Heaven." The Hodge Podge Players were knocked out after all their efforts, after all the heartscaldings, the hard grinding work to end like this — in nothing. Letters and telegrams poured in from all over the country offering them help and other accommodation for production but all to no avail. The main drawback being that Lesley had to honour her commitment in Wigan. Also most of the actors were locally employed and would find it impossible to travel afield. The Canon was outraged by the loss of the theatre. "Think of it, an Angelica Kaufman ceiling perfectly preserved gone forever!" he moaned. The loss of Rosie was as nothing compared with the loss of an eighteenth-century theatre. There was an impressive funeral for Rosie; hundreds of school children who had never heard of her before and never would again marched behind the coffin carrying white wreaths, the white was for innocence. Prominent among the mourners was Miss O'Kelly swathed in black, carrying a wreath in the national colours. A fund was set up for a promising orphan to be given a scholarship to the Heavenly Angels. All terrorist organizations denied complicity in the bombing, though there were hints at some communist splinter group. Whenever there was a particularly vicious bombing it was said to be communist inspired. Peader Rooney shut himself up in his tent, like Achilles, and refused to come out. Those were black days for Ballyfungus, but blackest of all for Father Kevin.

He drove Lesley to the train. Father Dermot was not encouraged to accompany them. "I'll never forget this, darling. It was such an ennobling experience working for you." Father Kevin couldn't answer; he was afraid he might break down. Should he tear off his collar, abjure his vows and follow the enchantress to the ends of the earth? Even to Wigan? Far down in the depths of the covered cage in the back seat he heard the parrot squawk, "It won't work. It won't work."

"Damn you," exclaimed the priest. He turned to Lesley. "It's the bird. I don't like his message; it's too negative."

"Darling Kev. Captain Hook knows everything. He has strange powers. He knows." He looked at her and saw now the mask was off, the face of a withered child. This time the tears stung his eyes and it was she who put forth a hand and wiped his away. "Fra Kevin, fare thee well."

He carried the suitcase and the birdcage and she followed with the poodle. Protesting loudly the poodle was put in the luggage van and the squawking parrot accompanied her on the train. Then she bent down and kissed Father Kevin and whispered, *"Frater ave atque vale,"* and disappeared. He stood on the platform in a trance of misery until the train was out of sight.

Most people blamed Father Hannigan for the Fungusport fiasco, but they were somewhat unjust to him. He loved the little Fungusport theatre. He was devoted to classical music and had spent many happy evenings in the theatre listening

145

to chamber music. He was sad about the orphan Rosie to whom an unkind world had dealt the final blow; he did not really deserve the dwarf housekeeper who, with an evil smile, was placing a supper before him, consisting of two unpleasant looking kippers on burnt toast with rice pudding to follow. Diet can do strange things to a man.

The evening of Lesley's departure Father Kevin sat in his monastic bedroom locked in a deep depression. The destruction of the theatre, the abortive production of the Rooney opus were unimportant compared with the loss of the seductive director. Next door he could hear Father Dermot's thumps and poundings as he went through his usual nightly physical jerks. The Canon was already in bed and the housekeeper Ms. Josie Halloran was enjoying her late night pastime setting up mouse traps. The cat was so overfed he let the mice play round his feet. Father Kevin's room was of course deeply celibate. It was painted a sickly sexless green and the horrendous holy pictures on the walls did little to cheer one up. His bed was narrow and very hard and one felt might even include nails. On the little bedside table was a crucifix and alarm clock and a prayer book. The grate was empty and masked by a fan of pink paper. True, the bookcase was bursting with plays in paperback and a photograph of his beloved sister in an Abbey Theatre production did something to humanize the surroundings but on the whole it was — well — monastic. The church bell tolled eleven and Father Dermot bounded into the room clad only in shorts. He was panting and breathless from the jerks.

"Aren't you going to bed, man?"

"Oh I suppose so." He rose stiffly from his hardbacked chair and stretched. "Dermot how do you get a woman out of your mind?"

"Prayers, physical jerks, and jogging," was the reply given without the slightest hesitation.

"I feel as if I'm lost. There is nothing for me anymore."

"Bosh, get busy on your next production. Prayers, man,

prayers." Out went the happy Father Dermot and into his comfortable — well, not exactly comfortable, but certainly well-adjusted — bed.

"Is it worth it? Is it worth it?" Father Kevin addressed the Sacred Heart.

Three weeks later he found a letter, with an English stamp waiting for him on the hall table. His heart leaped up. Was it? Could it be? It was.

Fra Kev,
   Wigan is uncompromising, my darling, except for someone who invented an artificial hip. Pinter is relentless but a genius. The man manages to say so much with so few words. He sends out telegrams to the world. I miss darling Ballyfungus and you most of all. The tragedy of the theatre lingers with me still. Don't let developers into your little town, keep out industry! The ugliness here is unbelievable. The company is sad and I am sad. Captain Hook is in a clinic with an infected bill. Winnie yawns incessantly. Oh that you could come over this instant and take over sound effects and lighting. The creature here who is supposed to be working in that capacity is a mentally disturbed cockroach. I yearn to stamp on him but he's too big. Lesley is wistful. Lesley needs her Fra Kev. Write to me at once, but I know you won't. I'll never hear from you and never see you again. We might meet in the next world but I have strong doubts about a next world. How is Iggy and how is his auntie? That's a wicked old puss. I wonder if she didn't have something to do with the bombing. And the adorable Canon and Liz, whom I did *not* like. Much too powerful. The sort of woman who arches over you, takes the light away and you can't see the sky when you're with her. Remember me to poor Rooney. Darling, why don't you do *A Month in the Country*? Turgenev. You have the cast. Incidentally I'm off to Canada after Wigan. Been offered a job directing a small rep in Winnipeg. Two years. Send up hundreds of Hail Marys and novenas for Lesley. *Frater Ave Atque Vale.*

Father Kevin kissed the letter and then tore it into shreds. Canada. She was right, he'd never see her again and it was all for the bloody best! Better not reply. Forget. That evening he walked five miles through and around the Woods and returned to the presbytery exhausted, but purged. He ate a huge tea and when Father Dermot remarked on his improved spirits he said, "I'm thinking of our next production."

"Oh! What is it to be?"

"*A Month in the Country*. A friend recommended it."

"It sounds great. Nothing like work. Pass the jam."

"Hand over the butter. Yes, work does it, and," Kevin added hastily, "prayers of course." Sometimes it seemed there was an element of cliffhanging about his Faith.

Chronicle Five

BALLYFUNGUS HAD BARELY recovered from the Fungusport fiasco before the township, as the Archdeacon put it, was shaken by another convulsion. At one point it seemed as if nobody was working anywhere and the whole Republic was on strike and those who were not on strike were redundant. Redundant, the very word was like a knell. It meant you were useless, not wanted. Out. A drought persisted during the summer months and rumours of a water shortage frightened everyone. Also the activities of the Alpha-Omega Multi-International Conglomerate continued to alarm the residents and need one say, behind every fresh cloud of rumour was heard the voice of Mrs. Walsh?

"Aye black doins', black doins'. Did I say black? Take that away and choke youself. Yellow's more like it. Thousands and thousands of them little Japs comin' to work the poison factory. If it was Yanks you wouldn't mind but Blessed Mother 'tis like stirrin' up an ants nest with your foot and all the little yeller fellas scurryerin' around. And if that isn't all, the road a jooel carriageway is to go smashing through the Woods and first — as Saint Joseph is me witness — right through the droring room of Ferncourt. And Satan himself, John Fallon, behind it all. But let me tell you ma'am and any as who's listening the curse of Balooly has struck John Fallon, so let him look to it. The wife in the asylum with drink and drugs, the daughter run off and the boys won't talk to their Daddy at all. And Fallon himself has took up with a model, only another name for a whore and there you have it. Devil's work! What can you do? Seamus, me husband, says there'll be a line of buses runnin' between here and the factory and he'll put in for an inspector's job. Sure, you have to live and

151

look at the prices! Goggins gone out of his mind changin' the labels on the tins and givin' out different prices to the girls. 'Twenty-three pee for a tin of cat food' says one and 'twenty-nine pee' says another and coffee only to be drunk be kings. It's the end of the world and good luck to it!" Not only was Cassandra wailing along the walls but the Greek chorus was in full cry.

One evening in August the Ferncourt Foursome was seated in the conservatory playing bridge. The conservatory presented a more colourful appearance than when last seen in June. The ancestral geranium was in massive bloom and the heat was almost tropical. The gentlemen were in their shirtsleeves and very sweaty they were too and the ladies were using fans.

On their way over the two old men had discussed the problem of heat. "Why the devil can't we play in the drawing room?" groaned the General.

"It's Mabs. She likes to think she's still in Africa, Queen of the British Colonial Protectorate," sighed the Doctor. "I think I'll warn her of the danger of strokes, that might do it."

"The Earl is over from London," bawled the Doctor suddenly. "I had a pint yesterday with him in Rooney's."

The General nodded. "I met him in the supermarket. Frightful sight. He's grown a black beard and wears orange pyjamas."

"He's over the eczema," remarked the Doctor. He sighed gustily as he looked at his cards.

"I didn't notice the eczema. Mainly because I was blinded by the pyjamas. What a colour! God bless us! Eton and Oxford. You'd never know it. Amazing. Two hearts."

"My dear Artie." Mabs rapped the General's wrist with her fan. "Tottenham is an Earl in name only. And what a name! It goes on for miles. Charles Henry — blah — blah — blah — blah Crosby. No seat, no land, no money. All his low friends call him 'Nopenny.' I should think he'd drop the silly title."

"A title pays off Mabs," answered her sister. "The English are incurably class conscious. Look at all those socialist Labour M.P. Lords. Laughable!"

At that moment Dolphie gave forth an almost human belch. "Remind me to get something for Dolphie's flatulence," remarked the Old Doctor. "Molloy the vet has a new thing, Windjam, which is also used in humans with very good results. It's strange the way we doctors and vets are working together nowadays. T'would surprise you! The pills they give for gout are used for racehorses."

"We'll ask Tott for dinner. Albie, remind me to phone poor Alicia." Mabs slapped down a card. "Two no trumps. It's the one good meal he gets here. Alicia can't boil an egg. Her mind is on the arts and crafts and the crafts it seems do not include cooking. Tott is a well-meaning boy, but he read some of his poetry to us the last time he was here. Couldn't understood a word of it. Tott, I said, let's get back to reality; read me Wordsworth's 'Daffodils.' "

Between rubbers Albinia revived the subject. "Too bad there isn't a girl to ask with Tott. Since poor Felicity Mac-Crea went up to Dublin there's no acceptable female here under seventy. Anyway after her lamentable affair with the stable lad I wouldn't dangle her in front of Tott."

"He's certainly not a pansy," remarked the Doctor as he groped his way through Victorian bric-a-brac to the drinks trolley.

"Get me one too, Josh, Scotch. Not much water," commanded the hostess. "Tottie has plenty of affairs. Alicia tells me all. Mostly with suicidal female poets and black dancers. There was also that sculptress whose face would turn anyone to stone."

"What does he live on though?" asked Albinia vaguely.

"He has a teeny tiny income. Poor Alicia is frightfully hard up."

"Tott," said the Doctor, "tells me he's getting away from the London crowd; he's also finishing a book of poems."

Everyone moaned "poems" as if it meant leprosy. The General spluttered, "Why the blazes doesn't he drive a taxi; earn an honest living?" It seemed there was no answer to this.

Albinia looked around her, puzzled. "I can't remember whose deal it is. I don't think the cards were left on the right side."

"How did that happen?" Her sister stared angrily at the Doctor. "Somebody must have shuffled the cards and put them on the wrong side."

"Possibly the dog." The Old Doctor grinned and winked at the General.

"Dolphie has not yet attempted to play bridge," was the haughty reply.

"Give him time," retorted the General.

"I'll shuffle," said Albinia firmly, "and deal. Two hearts," she announced when all was ready. The demented game proceeded for a while in silence except for groans from the General and clicking sounds from the Doctor. Dolphie rose at one point, waddled towards the table and drooled half a pint of saliva on the General's pants. (A couple of shots at night might do it, pondered the old warrior, barely controlling his rage.)

"John Fallon is up to mischief I hear," remarked the Doctor.

"Our native born multimillionaire," sneered the General and when he sneered it was the charge of the light brigade. "With his Georgian mansion in Dublin, his goddam villa in Spain, his stud farm in Meath, his little pad in New York, but thank God, blackballed by the Kildare Street Club."

Everyone chanted "Amen" to this.

"You can't be serious, Josh," exclaimed Mabs. She turned pale under the rouge. "Balooly is practically at our front gates."

"I am serious," the Doctor spoke in melancholy voice. "I

hear they're going to cut down the trees, and oh Mabs, think of the birds. It hit me right between the eyes." He demonstrated.

"I wish to God someone would hit John Fallon between the legs," exclaimed the General coarsely.

"In case of rape kick 'em in the crotch my husband used to say and he being a doctor should know." Albinia laughed, she was a match for the General.

"Talking of the crotch," mused the General, "I saw in the paper the other day that Fallon had got an annulment and was marrying someone else. How did he do that, Josh? He's a Catholic and had five children by his first wife. I thought you had to be frigid or impotent to get an annulment."

The Doctor jeered. "It's the new Catholic form of divorce. You have to pay through the nose for it."

"Through the pope's nose, eh Josh?" Albinia pinched the Doctor's arm and giggled.

"What's wrong with his poor wife?" queried Mabs shuffling and dealing.

"They say drink. Those Jonnycomeups all grow out of their first wives and have the poor devils put down like old horses. Four hearts." The Doctor groaned as he looked at his cards.

"Saw those two gay dogs Colin and Eddie in the supermarket."

"You can't use that word gay anymore, Artie." Again he was slapped with the fan.

"I used it advisedly. Do you think I don't read the papers?" The General grinned. "They are gay — gay as hell — and who cares? They give good dinners and their cellar is second only to yours, Mabs. My God that dog!" The General held his nose.

"Windjam!" said the Doctor. "I'll bring some next Wednesday."

"Tott! Tott!" squeaked Auntie Al. She was clearing away the breakfast things before leaving for the Art Centre.

"Where is the lad?" She had already donned her handwoven tweed cloak and tweed cap with vizor. She paused. No answer. Oh, of course, he was in the bathroom. "Tott," she knocked on the bathroom door and spoke loudly and slowly as if to the deaf, "Tott, Mabs Vigors wants us for dinner on Saturday night." Her nephew, who read for hours on the toilet seat, emerged from the bathroom, reluctantly. His costume as of today was eighteenth century. Jacket and knee britches of some seedy black material with dirty ruffles at neck and wrists. The Earl was tall, thin and pale, and looked as if he might easily break in two. His black hair straggled to his shoulders and between that and the beard the face was hardly visible.

"I can't go, Auntie Al," replied the nephew plaintively. "Too sad. Too dreary. All that Victorian Gothic and the smelly dog."

"Tott dear," exclaimed Auntie, "they're such toppers and their cook is first rate. Best food in the County. Oh Tott." She looked at him beseechingly.

"I'm on such a tight schedule, Auntie. I have to polish up my cycle of sonnets for the *London Review*. It's a deadline."

"Cycle." Lady de Bracey slapped her side. "That reminds me, I have a puncture; can't go on the old bike. I'll have to take the mini. Damn, the petrol has gone up again. Tottsy boy, why don't you get something in the city and make a fortune. Be a company director. They could use your name, everybody's doing it."

"And end up in prison. No thanks, Auntie Al. I don't like the rich; they're evil. I prefer decent poverty. Incidentally what is that foul character John Fallon going to do with our Castle now that he owns it?"

"They say it's to be entirely rebuilt and made into a country club with ski slope."

The nephew burst out laughing. "He'll have to import the snow." He jammed a Scotch bonnet on his head which looked odd with the rest of his costume and moved towards the door.

"I'm going for a walk in Balooly Woods. See you this evening I presume."

She followed him to the door. "There are frightful rumours about the Woods, Totty. They say a factory and a lot of dreadful little houses are to be built in them."

The Earl positively jumped. "Auntie Al, you don't mean it. That's frightful. We must fight this. It can't be allowed."

"How can we stop it, Tott? Men like Fallon own this country. They're destroying it and we're powerless to fight them."

"Watch me," replied the Earl. He waved to her and made for Balooly.

Tottenham had always loved the Woods. There was something so deeply soothing about its murmurous solitude. He loved walking under the leafy canopy when one seemed to tread along a soft path of turfy green, cut off from the world, so tenderly, peacefully healed of one's wounds. As a little boy he used to walk in Balooly with his old great-uncle De Bracey who could name every wild flower and identify every bird song. He used to tell the little boy how old the trees were; he would lovingly press his hand against the trunk of a primeval oak. "The Elizabethans cut down the Munster forests, Tott, to build their damn ships of war, but they never got Balooly." But will they escape greedy opportunists like Fallon? pondered Tott ruefully. . . . When he was two years old both Tott's parents had been killed in an air crash; he had been brought up by the De Braceys but now the Castle was sold and poor Auntie de Bracey was reduced to living in a jerry-built "luxury bungalow" on a quarter of an acre of gorse and heather. The bungalow was barely fifteen years old, but already there were cracks in the walls and fungus was spouting in the built-in cupboards of the guest room. Still Auntie Al seemed happy. Tottenham put the thought of happiness away from him with a shudder. He existed in a gentlemanly way on two thousand a year, from a trust fund, and he had no expectations; everyone connected with him was ruined; taxed out of existence. The sun glinted through the branches and painted the grass around the trunks a most sparkling green. Far off he heard the wood pigeons calling to each other. Love calls? His lips curved in a sneer; his last affair had just broken up; she was a beautiful black dancer and had caused him much agony. Not all bad though; she had inspired a remarkable group of hate sonnets. Goodness; who was coming through the trees towards him? Was there no peace? It was a young girl wearing a long grey cloak, hooded. She seemed to be deep in meditation, and what was more peculiar barefoot. Risky thought Tott with all those brambles, nettles and sharp stones. He wouldn't do it himself.

"Good morning. Beautiful day." He removed the bonnet with a flourish. (She couldn't be a tinker girl; much too clean. What was she then?)

The girl started and came out of her dream world. "Yes. Lovely," she said shortly and shot a resentful look at him. (Maybe she's a mental patient? There was a clinic for slightly disturbed rich persons half a mile away. Could be.)

"It's so lonely here," said the Earl loud, "I find it healing."

"That's why I come here. I like to be alone," she replied. (He must be a mental case. Those clothes so strange and dirty. Could he be a mad tinker?) The thought made her nervous. She quickened her pace in order to pass him and then stumbled and squealed sharply.

"Gracious!" exclaimed Tott (he made a point of never using strong language). "What's happened? Oh, I see you've hurt your foot. You shouldn't walk in the Woods barefoot."

"It's bleeding," she cried. "It was a bit of glass."

"Good Heavens, so it is. Have you a handkerchief? I could bind it."

"No, only a tissue," she sighed.

"I have a handkerchief," Tott said, "though I'm afraid it's rather dirty. You better sit down on that tree stump. I'll bandage it." Kneeling down in front of her Tottenham took a filthy handkerchief out of his pocket.

Amongst other things she glimpsed egg stains. If anything would give her tetanus it would be that handkerchief. "No

158

thank you," she said hastily and sprang to her feet. "It's stopped bleeding. It was nothing really." She had a gentle Anglo-Irish accent and now that she had thrown back the hood she saw she was pretty. It was that fatal combination, golden brown hair and brown eyes with incredible dark lashes.

"May I ask where you live?" Tott rose and put away the handkerchief.

"I'm staying in Daisy Lodge, the guest house; it's quite near." She had noted his muted Oxbridge accent. Mad possibly, but not a tinker.

"Aha with Miss Crozier's hostelry; I know it well. Let me walk there with you. Your foot might start bleeding again. Are you staying there alone?"

"Yes I like to be alone, very much."

"I do too. I am by nature a recluse."

"I am too." She smiled sadly. "The rest of my family is gregarious. I am a great disappointment to my parents."

"We all are. I don't know anyone who isn't a disappointment to their parents; except of course myself. I am an orphan."

"Oh dear. I'm sorry."

"It happened years ago. I never knew them. I'm a most contented orphan."

"Sometimes," she hesitated, looked down, "I'd like to be an orphan."

"Don't you like your parents?"

"I don't approve of my father and my mother is rather difficult."

Tott laughed gently. "Funny you should say that. All the girls I know find their mothers difficult. It's a bad relationship." He shook his head knowingly.

They walked along in silence for a while, each pondering the identity of the other.

"Are you here on a visit?" asked Tott at last.

She sighed again, she seemed to be full of sighs. "I'm just here by myself, thinking things out."

159

It must be a love affair thought Tott. Some Dublin oaf, no doubt; distasteful thought.

"Actually," the girl stood still and looked at him; the brown eyes were enormous, "I'm considering entering a convent, taking the vows."

Tottenham started and looked at her in amazement. A nun? Not possible. Was she joking? No, she seemed very serious. "I'd think twice about that if I were you," he said gently.

"I have thought about it many times." She looked up into the branches of a beech tree and smiled. "Listen to that lovely bird singing his heart away."

"It's a song thrush."

"How do you know?"

"An old uncle used to tell me about the birds. He and the Doctor, the Old Doctor, would take me for walks here when I was a little boy; they knew every dashed bird's name. Good old Doctor Josh."

"Don't you like the sound of the Woods? It sounds like the distant sea — a busy murmur."

"That's called soughing. Splendid word."

The girl regarded him thoughtfully. "Do you write? I feel you write. You're a poet, aren't you?"

"How did you know?" He looked at her surprised.

"I just knew. You look — well — like a poet." They both laughed.

"I don't think you should enter a convent," remarked Tottenham when they reached the gates of Daisy Lodge. There was something so wistful and charming about her; he longed to know more.

"I'm not sure yet but when I'm absolutely certain of a vocation I must follow it. It's a call to higher service."

Tottenham couldn't help thinking of other services she might render. This girl was too human, too, well, let's face it, desirable, to shut herself up in a convent. It would be a crime against nature to see her creeping around in black robes, wearing on that charming face a holy scrubbed look. Even the short skirted liberated nuns were depressing. The two loners walked very slowly up the short avenue, the gravel being hard on bare feet. Daisy Lodge was a comfortable square yellow Victorian house very neat and very well cared for. It was early September and the pink, the blue and white hydrangeas surrounding the croquet lawn were already beginning to fade. The chestnut trees were turning an orange brown but the Miss Croziers' dahlias, of which they were very proud, were in full splendour. The hall door was open and Mrs. Walsh was polishing the brasses. She was wearing a blue apron over a trouser suit; her hair was done up in curlers under a scarlet kerchief. Elastic stockings protected her varicose veins. She glimpsed the curious couple approaching the house and called out to them. "Janey, is it yourself Mr. Tott? You're lookin' great. I heard you was come from London. Very close day."

"Hi, Mrs. Walsh." Tottenham flapped his hand at her. By the afternoon he reflected ruefully the gossipy old hag will have my meeting with the Interesting Unknown all over Ballyfungus.

"Well, good-bye." Off came the bonnet.

He held out his hand. "Good-bye."

She touched his hand lightly. "Thank you for seeing me back." She smiled. "Next time I'll wear shoes."

Tott hesitated (he was fully aware of Mrs. Walsh's twin search-lights focused on him), "Do you walk in the Woods a lot?"

"Most mornings," she replied.

"We'll meet again I hope?" For diplomatic reasons he now approached Mrs. Walsh and the small grey eyes, those search-lights, were glinting at him threateningly through the steel spectacles.

"How are you, Mrs. Walsh, and how's your husband?"

"Thanks be to God and his Blessed Mother, well." She lowered her voice. "He has had trouble with his possertites, but sure that comes to us all."

"Too bad. See you." She cleaned Fridays for his aunt so he knew right well he would see the dreadful woman again.

The mystery girl entered the hall. Mrs. Walsh sniffed as she passed. "That fella you was walkin' with is a Lord," said she, still going through the motions of rubbing the door knocker.

"I only met him by accident," the girl looked coldly at Mrs. Walsh and Mrs. Walsh looked right back at her. "I don't even know his name. He was kind enough to walk me home when I cut my foot."

Mrs. Walsh's blue lips widened somewhat, it was the well-known Walsh smile. "Moyah, your foot, is it? You need boots in them Woods. Well that fella's the seventh Lord Tottenham. He's nephew of poor old Lady de Bracey. A lot 'o class, but no brass. Nice enough, but gone in the head, so's his auntie."

"Oh, really," said the girl icily, "he seemed sane enough to me." She ran up the stairs to her room and banged the door.

As Tottenham walked home he suddenly recollected he didn't even know the name of the woodland nymph. No, no a dryad. She was one of those glimmering silvery spirits who lived in trees. The tree trunk opened suddenly and tippety tappity out stepped the dryad with her floating golden hair, yes; her shyness, her elusiveness, even her voice was delicate and remote. She was the spirit of the Woods. "Come unto these enchanted Woods," he quoted to himself. And he didn't even know her name. What was she doing in Daisy Lodge alone, or in Daisy Lodge at all, for that matter? The guests there being retired elderly persons from London or Dublin enjoying a quiet inexpensive holiday. Some of them fished on the Fung for trout and enjoyed talking about it even more. There was no sign of a lover and then there was this nun business. He sighed. Tott came of Protestant stock. At one point, under the influence of Gerard Manley Hopkins, he had inclined towards Catholicism but it was only a passing phase. Now he was happily nothing. The bungalow was empty, Auntie Alicia always snatched a bite in the Art Centre, so Tott made himself a cheese sandwich, removed a beer from the fridge and lay down on the once beautiful but now battered Victorian sofa. Auntie Al had crammed the bungalow with remnants snatched from the "sale of Castle and contents." The Hepplewhite chairs, all six of them; the small hunting table to seat six drink-sodden gentlemen; the corner cupboard, filled with cracked eighteenth-century *objets d'art*, seemed strangely alien against the shoddy late twentieth-century background. The two enormous family portraits "after Lawrence" took up all available wall space and a bust of Dr. Johnson frowned at you from an aperture in the tiny hall. Tott sighed as he chewed on his dreary sandwich. It was all so mistaken; the past was past and let it pass. Then he fell to brooding upon the morning's happenings: that odd encounter with that odd girl. Tomorrow morning he planned to walk again in Balooly, just in case. His cogitations were interrupted by the noise of a motor bike stopping outside and a moment later, the door being open, Father Kevin Sheedy walked in. "I heard you were here, Tott, and I want your advice." He removed the cycling helmet revealing the luxuriant flaming hair. "May I sit down a moment?"

"Certainly. Get yourself a beer out of the fridge."

"Thanks a lot." The curate sat down bottle in hand. "So you're here?"

"That would seem to be the case," said Tottenham drily. "What's the local news, Father Kevin?"

"You heard about the Fungusport fiasco?"

"The bombing of the little theatre. Yes, and the death of the poor girl. Disgusting."

Father Kevin winced; it still hurt him to remember that horror.

"What's your next project?" asked Tott.

"What do you think about this: *Love's Labour's Lost* in modern dress with rock music? I had thought of *A Month in the Country* but I changed my mind."

"Good idea! I love the play. On the other hand why not the *Duchess of Malfi* with shameless emphasis on the incest motivation behind the brothers."

"Thanks, that's just what I want to avoid. We did *Under*

the Blanket with emphasis on masturbation and it certainly blew us to blazes."

"Good Lord." Tott jumped up. They both stared. Someone was tapping at the window. It was Doctor Josh winking and becking and signing to be let in.

"Dash it. I left the front door open. Come in, Doctor. How's yourself?"

"Never better." The visitor hung his deerstalker on Dr. Johnson and entered the living room rubbing his ancient hands. "I was just passing on my way to the Woods. Thought I'd have a word with you, Tott. How are you, Father Kevin?"

"Grand! Grand!"

"Care for a beer, Josh?" asked the Earl.

"Wouldn't mind." The Doctor threw himself into a small Sheraton chair. The back immediately fell off. It had been badly repaired by Tott.

"Sorry, Josh. Sit on the piano stool. Here's your beer."

"Tell the truth, fellas, I'm worried about Balooly Woods."

"I'd like to have a word with that brute John Fallon," said the Earl. "He never comes down here anymore does he?"

"No except on mischief. He did come to the Poetry Festival but he only stayed for the President's speech," said Father Kevin.

"We've got to stop this threatened horror about the Woods." Tott began pacing up and down. "But how?" He stopped in front of the Doctor and bellowed, "We've got to stop Fallon. Down with Fallonism. Hey, there's your slogan."

The priest laughed and the Doctor covered his ears. "That's a most unacceptable sound level, Tott." He wagged a finger at the irate peer. "But it certainly should arouse the country. Tell you what, young fella, better get Liz Atkins and Mabs Vigors on to this. Mabs will certainly fight hard. They're threatening to build a road right through her property. But let me tell you they'll have to build a road right through Mabs Vigors."

"Miss Atkins is splendid at this sort of thing," suggested

164

Father Kevin, "she's always been a great help to me. Get her to call a meeting of concerned citizens. She's a great lady." At this dramatic moment came a thunderous knocking on the front door.

"Gracious," exclaimed the Earl, "this is like *Macbeth*. Who can it be?" He opened the door. "Tom Nolan! What a coincidence. We were just talking about the Old Mill. Come in, get yourself a beer if there is one. Fridge."

Tottenham was utterly without snobbery. Class barriers meant nothing to him. He vaulted over them happily and the lower down the social scale he descended the happier he seemed to be.

"Thanks, Mr. Tott." The newcomer stalked into the hall. "I brought a note from Miss Atkins. She wants you for dinner next Saturday. Eight o'clock. Her phone does be out of order. That's why I came be the ould bike."

"How are things with Miss Atkins?"

"Good! Good!" Tom sat down bottle in hand and nodded to the other two. "Your health, Doctor, and you, Father. Miss Atkins does be in fightin' form."

"Fighting form. That's just the way we want her," exclaimed Tott. "Tom, did you hear anything about the planned destruction of the Woods at Balooly?"

"I did, Mr. Tott. John Fallon is at back of it. There was a Jap and a German stayin' in the hotel last week. Sez I to the porter Paddy Scanlan, Paddy what's goin' on at all. What are them foreigners up to. No good at all, sez he. It's some sort of a factory they're buildin' up in the Woods with a thousand houses around it and Fallon himself is expected down here in a coupler weeks. Rooney the publican says it's great, 'twill bring money in sez he and employment d'ye know. But do you know what I said, Mr. Tott, I said there's a curse on anyone who cuts down a livin' tree in Balooly Woods. Sure as God they'll die themselves in great agony. I remember me ould grandfather tellin' us that. A curse is on them." He drained off the bottle and wiped his mouth.

"I heard the same." The Doctor leaned forward. "Anyway there's a curse on the whole damn country at the moment." He rose to his feet with some difficulty.

The curate jumped up and put on his helmet. "I must be pushing along. Glad you approve of *Love's Labour's*, Tott. As far as Balooly is concerned count me in. I'll work for you."

"I'm off too." Tom followed them. "See you Saturday, Mr. Tott, and your auntie. Jesus! There's the note, I nearly forgot."

"We'll be there. Tell Liz Atkins I intend to get a committee set up immediately to stop Fallon."

"Play up the curse business, Tom," said the Doctor. "That sort of suggestion soaks in eventually. Phone me, Tott, as soon as you get going."

"Auntie Al," said Tott that evening, "ring Mabs Vigors and tell her I will accompany you to dinner there tomorrow night."

"Oh Tott," Alicia de Bracey clasped her hands and beamed at her nephew, "how charming of you. They will be delighted and, my dear, I met Mrs. Walsh in Goggins and she told me Mabs had ordered veal from Fungusport to be delivered tomorrow. Delicious!"

"I want to get Mabs and her sister roused against this scheme of John Fallon's. There's no time to be lost. It's my duty."

"And you'll get a very good dinner too, darling; they haven't been giving dinners for ages because of inflation — this is all for you."

The next morning Tottenham skipped two centuries and donned his blue jeans with blue shirt and denim jacket. Around eleven he decided to take a walk in the Woods where he could think things out and map out his strategies against the marauders and maybe even meet with the mysterious dryad. Rain came down just before eleven, but nothing daunted, carrying a red umbrella Tottenham set forth. The

166

grass squelched beneath his feet and the rain pattered down upon the leaves. It was not encouraging, but suddenly the dryad appeared clad in yellow oilskins.

"Hi," Tottenham greeted her, "you look as if you're going to launch the lifeboat."

"I was thinking," replied the girl, who seemed much more cheerful and on to herself, "that you should shave your beard. You'd look more Byronic then."

"Do you want me to grow a club-foot?"

She laughed. "Well Shelley then. Did you know that Shelley came to Dublin once with poor Harriet and threw revolutionary pamphlets into the street from his hotel window?"

"Better than throwing bombs."

"Anything's better than that."

It seemed the most natural thing in the world for him to be walking in the Woods beside her. "I'm rousing the populace here against a villainous dictator," he said after a pause.

"Oh, who is he?"

"You wouldn't know him. One John Fallon; he was born here, left here, and made a pile of money."

There came a sharp yelp from the dryad. She seemed to stumble. Instinctively Tottenham put out his hand to steady her. "Is it that foot again?" He looked at her. The brown eyes looked unutterably sad.

"No, thank you," she murmured and looked away from him. After a moment she whispered, "Why is John Fallon so bad?"

"He's a destroyer. A monster. He's one of those disgusting gombeen men who are tearing down the Republic."

"I've heard of him," the girl said hesitatingly, "but I believe he buys pictures and sculpture and gives to the arts. He can't be all bad."

The Earl snorted. "Tax evasion, my dear innocent one. Oh, by the way, may I ask your name?"

"Fiona Smith," she replied, "and I know yours. It's Tottenham."

"Call me Tott, everyone does." He burst into laughter. "I bet Mrs. Walsh etched in a short but telling biography of me."

"She did. But you got off lightly. You should hear what she said about the rest of the Community."

"I have," said the Earl grimly. "I bet she said I'm a penniless bum and I am." He stopped in his tracks and closed the red umbrella. "The rain's stopped and there's the sun. I'll help you off with your coat."

"Yes, isn't it lovely. There's your song thrush again." She had removed the rain hat and her hair which was a light brown with gold highlights floated to her shoulders. But why was she so sad, his enchanting dryad? Tott gazed at her wonderingly. A girl who looked like that should be happy; he longed to know more about her. Smith? It sounded bogus somehow. And why on earth Daisy Lodge? They continued walking in silence and a shadow of something, he knew not what, walked between them.

"Do you live in Dublin?" asked Tott gently.

"Yes. I went to school there but I also went to boarding school in England. I decided against college and instead studied art. Then things happened and I don't know what next."

"You have a family? Siblings I mean."

"Four brothers. They're still at school. I'm the eldest."

"You have difficulties in the home as who doesn't." (I'm beginning to sound like a psychiatrist, thought Tott nervously.)

"Yes. I have. My mother has breakdowns and my father married again lately. So, we're all rather confused."

"Confusion reigns supreme in every gracious home. Goodness listen to the doves calling to each other. Rather charming isn't it? The Balooly love call."

"Love. Ugh." Fiona shuddered delicately.

"I agree with you," he replied gravely. "It's only for the birds, but I must say they seem to enjoy it. I've done with the whole wretched business."

"So have I. Nothing goes right for me." She looked at her

watch. He couldn't help noticing it was a small diamond affair and must have cost plenty. She saw his glance and laughed. "From Daddy. Hush money, or wait, propitiation. It's nearly lunch time and the gong goes strictly on time."

"But why Ballyfungus? Why Daisy Lodge? It's for the old."

"By mere chance," she answered and he knew it was an evasion. They had reached the gates now. Fiona giggled suddenly and said, "Thank God Mrs. Walsh isn't here today."

Dinner at Ferncourt was just as good as they anticipated. The group round the table included Liz and The Boys. The old men had been brutally excluded. "We can't feed the county," said Mabs severely. Albie nodded agreement. "Artie and Josh guzzle like starving Indians and then Artie begins to hiccup and Josh will talk about keeping the bowels open." She added, "We need a rest."

However, it was a pity that Tott waited until after dinner to launch his Save Balooly schemes. Strong cocktails first; wine flowing at table and brandy with the coffee did not leave the diners with crystal clear intellectual power. Enthusiasm yes, but not organized thought. As the evening wore on the conversation became more and more confused. Dolphie too contributed his usual quota of noise from belching to a sudden startling howling.

"It must be robbers," exclaimed Albie peering out of the window. "You know, Mabs, he only howls when there are robbers or spiders." She turned to the room and addressed her sister. "Another thing. I can't take Dolphie around the garden anymore. He relieves himself on the spinach."

Now this was an untimely statement of fact. Spinach had been served at dinner this very evening. Colin and Eddie looked at each other. The same thought occurred to them. Is a dog's urine poisonous? It's too late now to put a finger down the throat. Just at that dangerous moment Betty arrived with the drink trolley. "Whiskey," whispered Eddie to his friend. "It's an antidote to poison. Get it down fast."

"A beautiful dinner, Betty. Many congratulations," said

Auntie Al who was the soul of kindness especially to the underprivileged. Like the Miss Croziers she infuriated her friends and neighbours by handing out aid and comfort to the most dishevelled tinkers.

Betty was delighted. "Thank you, ma'am me Lady. Does you find now the taters is dreadful wormy this time o' year? Declare to God I was scrapin' and scrapin' this morning, but ye didn't find any, did ye?"

Worms, thought Colin, on top of dog's urine. What next?

"You may go, Brady," commanded Mabs. Mabs called underlings by their surnames as if they had none other; it was a hangover from Colonialism. "But I must say the food was good."

Tott was wearing an attractive black velvet suit with ruffles at neck and wrists. Partaking of pea soup while wearing ruffles is a risky business. For the rest of the meal the ruffles were dripping. He was now trying to dry them at the fireplace without rousing comment. "Wring your ruffles out on Dolphie's head," suggested Eddie kindly. He had noticed Tott's predicament.

"Ladies and gentlemen," Tott opened fire (for a while there he had forgotten his mission). "May I interest you in the rape of Balooly?"

"Who? What? Somebody raped? How amusing." Albie fluttered back from the window and joined the group near the fire. "How old world and delightful. Like the Bishop of Devonshire in our conservatory. Do you remember Oliver MacCrea's sister accused him? She was found with her dress hanging off her and her shoes in the fountain." Albie burst into laughter in which she was joined by Mabs. Everyone else laughed though they couldn't quite see the point.

Tott persevered. "I mean the developers are after Bolooly Woods. This ghastly fellow Fallon and some other ghastly chap from foreign lands want to build some ghastly factory and they want to drive a ghastly road through our beautiful Woods."

Albie clapped her hands together. "Ah yes, Jamesy told me

about it. He's been watching from the wall and he says queer looking men have been round measuring and photographing . . ."

"Somebody should arrest them." Mabs stamped her foot.

"I'm afraid they're within the law," responded Tott.

"If Emerald Walsh is the public tape recorder, Jamesy is the camera. He's never off that wall," remarked Eddie.

Liz now rose glass in hand and addressed an imaginary audience. Strange, she too was wearing a black velvet suit with white ruffles but the wrist ruffles were still dry. "Friends of Ballyfungus, be on the alert. Danger is all around us. To your guns. We must form a committee of concerned citizens and begin our campaign now." Everyone applauded except Dolphie, who howled.

"Tomorrow," Tott announced, "I will set forth. I will conduct a house-to-house campaign. I will use Auntie Al's mini."

"Petrol is so expensive," sighed Auntie Al. "Never mind, it's cheaper than stamps. They're up again."

"I will pay for the petrol, Auntie Al, don't worry," said Tott grandly. At the moment he was seriously overdrawn and was planning to borrow the immediate cash from his aunt.

"I will give you a cheque, dear boy, for the initial expense." Mabs moved towards her writing desk. "This is a national emergency." She sat down and began fumbling and rustling through a welter of papers. "Where *is* that damn cheque book?"

"We'll write a cheque tomorrow." Eddie and Colin spoke together. They frequently did. It was not parapsychological, it was just Tweedledum and Tweedledee. Very different.

Albie moved to the piano and slowly lifted the lid. "Last time I opened this a mouse hopped out. I will sing to you all," she announced warningly. "Do you remember, Mabs, poor Mamma used to play Chopin in her night dress."

Mabs looked up crossly. She was dashing off a cheque. "Your wig's crooked." She was always very snippety when writing cheques and even more so when giving to charity.

Albie good humouredly adjusted the wig, it was gold to-night, and then her fingers wandered over the keys, producing strange sounds, but stranger still was the sound of her singing voice. "Come back Paddy Reilly to Ballyjamesduff, come back Paddy Reilly to me," she entreated vocally.

The piano was frightfully out of tune and so was Albie and the intolerable bloodhound howled along with her. It was too much, the company broke up in every sense, made their adieus and left.

When he reached home Tott examined the cheque which Mabs had thrust into his hand. "Gracious," he exclaimed, "she's made it out to herself and it's one of her sister's cheques." He learned his lesson; never launch a campaign after dinner, it must be done in daylight and cold sober.

That was no idle threat. Not only Ballyfungus but the whole county heard from Tott. The following three weeks proved to be furiously busy ones for the Earl. All day and every day he was tearing round the country in the mini, talking to people at cottage doors, in country houses, in market places, in pubs about the Balooly menace. He was loyally supported. The Archdeacon preached a sermon on "human locusts" and the Canon followed up with one during Sunday Mass with an attack on the criminal destruction of national monuments by ignorant men; Father Hannigan in Kinealy contributed a blisterer on the brutalization of nature. Of course, he did manage to introduce a few words about abortion. The newspapers were flooded with indignant letters. It might be said the whole county was in a ferment. Meanwhile Tott's woodland sessions with Fiona continued; he managed to squeeze them in somehow. He read her his new poems; the hate sonnets had been abandoned, the new ones were more hopeful and concerned with nature. He had told Fiona the whole story of his affair with the black dancer and she had related to him her amorous experiences which, it seemed, had been few but bitter. "You're only a child. Just twenty," remarked the Earl who was an elderly twenty-seven. "You must forget the past — that actor fellow sounds like a giant rat.

Live in the present." He was braiding and unbraiding her hair as he spoke. "The shower of gold," he murmured reverently. She had even agreed to meet Aunt Alicia. "Midday lunch Sunday. The food will be frightful. My aunt is a disaster in the kitchen. She had an Edwardian youth you know. Ring a bell. Somebody comes."

Dinner at the Old Mill was always agreeable. And the conversation spicy and intelligent. Eddie Fox and Colin Evans were there (a strong bond of tax evasion bound these neighbours together) and Mrs. Walsh was also in evidence darting in and out between kitchen and studio. The head had been released from curlers and resembled coils of brassy barbed wire, increasing, as Eddie remarked, its extraordinary resemblance to the Gorgon's head. Mrs. Walsh herself peering through the kitchen door whispered to Tom, "Don't they look as if they was at one of them fancy dress balls?"

"Balls, is right!" replied Tom briefly; though of course devoted to Liz he was not enthusiastic about her visitors. "Buggers one and all," he added, "except Mister Tott." The persons grouped around the dinner table did present rather a macabre appearance. When the mood took her, and it took her this evening, Liz would allow nothing but candlelight. The curtains were not drawn across the great window which looked out on the millstream. This evening it was blowing hard and raining so one stared into sombre darkness and shuddered. True a huge turf fire blazed away in the enormous grate, the wine flowed freely and the candlelight was charming, still there was always that damn window, a reminder that there was a black world outside. Lady de Bracey, redder in the face than ever, was wearing a green flowing robe handwoven and handmade and cascades of handbeaten jewelry dangled from ears and wrists. Something resembling a holy soup-plate dangled between her breasts. Tottenham had chosen to wear an old military uniform worn by his great-great-uncle who had been killed at Balaclava. It was colourful if moth-eaten. Eddie Fox who was small and fat wore what seemed to be garb of a chubby gondolier and Colin in black presented a sinister clerical appearance. The hostess was draped in grey priestess robes with a huge silver cross swinging from a chain round her neck.

"I'm sorry no girl for you, Tott," remarked Liz, puffing on a small cigar. "There isn't a virgin left in Ballyfungus."

"Heavens, Liz," exclaimed the Earl, "it sounds as if you had some satanic ritual planned."

"I saw a very beautiful creature floating out of Daisy Lodge the other day," Colin remarked putting on his dark glasses for no reason whatever, "wearing a voluminous grey cloak. Hippy type, but strangely beautiful."

"That must be the girl Totty's bringing to lunch tomorrow," cried Aunt Alicia innocently.

Tottenham could have shot his dear aunt. He murmured in a sheepish manner, "Yes. I met her in the Woods by accident. She seemed rather pathetic and lost. In fact she's thinking of becoming a nun." (All I can say is, said Mrs. Walsh to herself, she was removing dessert plates, if she's a nun — I'm the blessed Infant of Prague!)

"A nun!" Eddie yelped, and Colin giggled.

The Earl shrugged his shoulders; part of the tattered uniform sleeve came away. "I was interested in talking to her from a theological point of view."

"I never knew you were on to religions," cried Liz. "Maybe I can interest you in the worship of Isis. Some friends of mine near here have half convinced me."

"I don't know a thing abut the girl," said the Earl angrily, "and care less." He drank off his wine and choked.

He's in love, thought Liz. We better change the subject, so she refilled the glasses and said tactfully, "Now Tott, what's all this about your crusade against John Fallon?"

The Earl rose to the bait. "I need your help, everybody's help. We're holding a protest meeting in the Town Hall second week in October to protest against the rape of Balooly Woods. The Mayor of Fungusport has promised to take the chair. The Archdeacon will be on the platform and also the old Catholic Bishop, if he's still alive. We've also got a promise from the Fianna Fail T.D. Goggins. The Fine Gael chap is in Brussels."

"I thought Goggins T.D. was dead or dying," Colin interposed.

"And I presume you have the fearsome foursome from Ferncourt."

"Certainly." Tott pulled a tattered notebook out of his pocket. "And I want you, Liz Atkins, to head the Ballyfungus committee. You're right, Colin, Goggins is on his last legs but his wife does everything for him and will be elected in his place when he passes on to a higher life."

"It will have to be higher," remarked Eddie acidly, "because it couldn't be lower." He added, "I think, Tott, if you removed that sleeve now entirely you would be more comfortable."

Liz immediately consented to do all she could; everyone thought it was a splendid cause and everyone vowed assistance.

"Being a brutal Saxon invader," Eddie took out his cheque book, "I will here and now help to save Dark Rosaleen from herself."

The rest of the evening was spent planning the demonstration and though the planning became rather foggy as the evening, and the drink, wore on it was felt when midnight came that real progress had been made.

In the kitchen Mrs. Walsh whose ear had been to the ground was holding forth to Tom: "There'll be bad work out of this yet. Fallon will have Mr. Tott cut up and put down a drain head first that's the way they're doin' it up North and what they do up North, Tom Nolan, comes down South."

Tom who was cracking out ice for the after-dinner drinks laughed. "It's Fallon will die. The Balooly curse will take care of him!"

"There's somethin' dirty goin' on between Mr. Tott and

the holy bitch at Daisy Lodge Miss Smith. Moyah!" hissed Mrs. Walsh. "She tells the Miss Croziers she's bird watchin'. Sez I, it's formication pure *and* simple."

After the Sunday lunch at the bungalow, which was rather strained, Auntie Al pronounced Fiona "a jolly nice girl, a sterling good sport, she didn't seem to mind the scrambled eggs being watery, a topper."

"I did," snapped Tott; he was a bit on the snarly side. Auntie he felt had been patronizing to Fiona, positively demanding that she help at the Fung Art Centre — start making pottery or give a hand with the quilting. And also asking which Smith family did she come from. Was it Smythe or just plain Smith. After dinner Tott saw Fiona back to Daisy Lodge. They walked very slowly; the return trips to the Lodge were taken at a snail's pace.

"Tell me more about your great-uncle, your aunt's husband?" Fiona questioned him.

Tott smiled. "Well he read *Ivanhoe* twice a year because there was a De Bracey in it and he looked, I'm sorry to say, like Edward the Seventh. Now you tell me more about your forebears."

She looked up at him smiling. "Serfs. Peasants. My father were born here — a barefoot boy. My mother," she paused, sighed and continued, "was a barefoot typist."

Born here? The Earl frowned. He'd never heard of a peasant called Smith around these parts. Strange! "I do wish, Fiona, you'd come clean with me. It does one good to talk things out." He took her arm and pressed it to his side. "Sorry about the awful lunch. Some evening I'll take you to the Grand in Fungusport and give you a slap-up dinner."

Fiona giggled. "That will give Mrs. Walsh food for thought. Not to mention the Miss Croziers who are beginning to look what is described as askance at me." Once more she faced him smiling. Her teeth he noted were very good. His were rather bad. Ancestral dental problems had always tormented the Tottenhams.

"You must be very lonely in the evenings, Fiona, with all those creepy retired civil servants muttering in corners. Maybe you can help me with my project." He launched at once into an account of the coming demonstration in the Town Hall concluding with his slogan "Down with Fallonism — Out with the Fallonists." "Don't you think those are frightfully good slogans?"

Fiona removed her arm from his side and shook her head. "No thank you," was the cold reply, "I don't wish to get involved in those things." Tott stopped and looked at her in surprise. "But darling, I thought you loved the Woods and the bird songs," the "darling" slipped out unawares.

"I do. I do." She sighed and he saw one tear roll down her cheek. Tott was horrified. What sensitive nerve had he touched? His nature was so thoroughly gentle and kind he could not bear to hurt anyone and certainly not his dryad. "I respect your feelings," he said hastily. "I won't press you."

"It's not that I don't think you're right." She looked at him piteously. "But there are difficulties. I *know* you're right, Tott." She caught his hand and pressed it to her cheek.

It was such an innocent, spontaneous gesture Tottenham felt the tears spring to his eyes. In that moment he knew he was committed; he loved her. He caught both her hands in his and tenderly kissed them. "Dearest Fiona, I'll see you tomorrow morning. Let's hope it doesn't rain. Goodness there are the Miss Croziers watching us from the window. Don't be lonely. You've only to lift the phone and call me."

"It's out of order," she said brokenly.

"So's mine. It's hardly ever in order and that could be said for the whole rotten world."

Over the following weeks right into October the Balooly Woods affair blew up into an issue of national importance. There were leader articles in the Irish newspapers; even the English and American media gave it coverage. The *Fungusport Guardian*, which was one of the few things not owned by Fallon and had a radical editor, kept up a relentless bombardment against the developers. *Hibernia*, the weekly muck-raker in Dublin, issued the most sinister statements about the multi-international conglomerate, naming names, prominent amongst them being Fallon, and immediately a libel action was slapped on them. A further sensation was caused by Fallon threatening an action for slander against the Earl and his associates; he also announced that he was coming down to Ballyfungus and would be on the platform during the meeting and present his own case.

"If Fallon does take an action against me and wins it, I'll have to go to prison," Tott told Fiona. "I couldn't possibly pay damages. I'd have to be jailed, possibly for years."

"Don't talk like that." Fiona turned pale and trembled.

It was the morning of the meeting, which was scheduled to open at eight P.M. in the Town Hall. Fiona and Tott were of course in the Woods; it was a fine morning and she was seated on a fallen tree trunk and he was squatting on the ground beside her, his head resting against her knees. Within the last few days the Earl's outward appearance and indeed his whole personality had undergone a remarkable change. It was, he stated, for the Cause. Not only had he shaved the beard and cut the hair to a reasonable length, he had also donned a business suit in order to impress the bourgeoisie in the audience with his conformity, sound thinking, and total reliability. Fiona however was not impressed. She was glad the beard had gone because now she could evaluate the face, but she did not like the business suit; it revived too many painful memories.

"If only you were coming tonight," groaned Tott clutching her hand, "I wouldn't feel so nervous. Everything has mushroomed horribly. They're sending down a TV crew from RTE and journalists are already piling into the hotel. I hope it doesn't end like the Poetry Festival or poor old *Under the Blanket* in Fungusport."

"Of course it won't," she said tenderly. "This is very different. It's much more important."

"They're going to have loudspeakers outside for those who

can't get into the Town Hall and they've got special security set up for Fallon. He's already at the Grand in Fungusport with the rest of the conglomerate marauders."

Fiona shivered and withdrew her hand. "Fallon is there! Oh Tott! I'm afraid."

"Who's afraid of the Big Bad Wolf?" Tott groped for her hand again.

"I am," said Fiona.

"But you don't know him."

She paused and clasped her hands. He looked at her surprised; her face was flushed a deep crimson. "Was he a lover, Fiona?" he asked nervously.

"No. No." She almost shouted at him. "I hate the man. He ruined someone — someone close to me. No."

"Then why, if you hate him, won't you help in the campaign to save our Woods? I can't understand you, Fiona."

She suddenly burst into tears. Tott, distraught by now, knelt at her feet and tried to draw her to him but she resisted.

"Fiona," he groaned, "I love you. Marry me. Darling, I haven't anything to offer you except a perfectly nice three-room flat overlooking Clapham Common or if you like we could live in Connemara in a native hut."

Fiona stopped crying, she smiled through her tears and sniffed. "But you don't know anything about me really."

"What does it matter? What do you know about me? Nobody knows about anyone until they've lived together and it's always a toss-up."

Fiona broke into laughter. "Anyway, Tott, I know I haven't a vocation. Maybe my vocation is you. Maybe we should just live together and find out." She tweaked his black hair and leaning forward tenderly kissed his forehead. "I do love you, Tott." And it was at that idyllic moment they were startled by male voices just behind them, the crackling of twigs underfoot and three men swung into view. The leader was middle sized, rather paunchy, with reddish face, balding with keen brown eyes. He was wearing well cut and obviously expensive tweeds. Following him was a grey-faced man in a grey suit wearing dark glasses; last and certainly smallest came a Far Eastern type carrying camera and binoculars. The lovers were completely taken by surprise, and remained frozen in each other's arms, until Fiona looked up and caught sight of the leader. She screamed and sprang to her feet. "Daddy!" she cried.

The man she addressed as Daddy gasped. "Fiona, what the hell are you doing here?"

"Who are you?" demanded the Earl rising to his feet.

"John Fallon, and who, may I ask, are you?"

"Tottenham." He glared at Fallon. So this was the enemy and he was Fiona's father.

Fallon laughed. The German murmured "Mein Gott" and the Japanese character gurgled.

"The last I heard of my daughter she was about to enter a sisterhood; a silent order. By God it doesn't look like that now." Again he laughed.

Fiona went up to her father and stared coldly in his face: "I hate you, Daddy. I hate what you stand for and what you've done to Mummy. I hope they humiliate you tonight."

"Fiona is going to marry me, Mr. Fallon," announced the Earl literally through clenched teeth; he was shaking with rage.

"No Tott," Fiona turned to the Earl. "You can't compromise your campaign. Good luck for tonight, darling. I'm going back to Dublin, to home. They need me. Daddy abandoned us, you see."

Tottenham tried to hold her but she eluded him and walked rapidly away.

"This won't do your cause much good." Fallon addressed the Earl who was standing rooted to the ground as if under a spell. "She ought to have told you who she was."

Tottenham regained his composure. "Maybe she was ashamed," he said coldly and he too walked away, but he did not follow his lost dryad.

Fallon looked after him for a moment and then turned to

the other two men. "Come on, let's go. We've wasted enough time and there's another mile of woodland to survey."

All three players in this drama did some hard thinking that afternoon. Back at the bungalow Tott was the most tortured. If it came out that he was, to put it crudely, courting Fallon's daughter his motivations would be under suspicion. Who would believe he had made love to the girl not knowing she was Fiona Fallon. Any association with a man like Fallon carried a suspicion of venal doings. What a father-in-law! The thought revolted Tott. He would never under any circumstances take a penny from the brute. Never. He groaned aloud when he thought of his sad beautiful dryad alone at this moment and probably weeping. How could he bear to lose her? Would Fallon make use of the scene in the Wood and his connection with Fiona? He feared it was possible. On the record Fallon was a cruel and ruthless man. If he does I will have to resign from the committee, he thought. Oh God my speech! I must study my speech! Strong language for once!

Fiona was hurriedly packing her suitcase; she had given the Miss Croziers notice, explaining urgent family business necessitated her return to Dublin. The dear ladies, however, did not believe a word of it. They immediately scented a love quarrel and whispered colloquies were held in pantry, kitchen and bedroom. Mercifully for all concerned it was not Mrs. Walsh's day. Miss Clara the more forceful of the sisters ventured to approach Fiona. "Too bad dear. The weather is improving and you seemed much calmer here lately. We were hoping you would accompany us to the meeting tonight. Mabs Vigors said she would keep two seats for us near her, and I'm sure she wouldn't mind if you squashed in between us all; they're only benches and you can do anything on benches," she added vaguely. In all matters except cooking Maud was vague.

"I'll think about it, Miss Maud." Fiona stifled a sob. "May

I tell you later?" She could only remember as she hurled things into her suitcase the expression of disgust on Tott's face when he looked at her father. Oh it was shameful! Never again would she meet anyone like Tottenham, so gentle, so kind, so truly loving. He was, she knew, in matters of the world ineffectual, and except for the Balooly Woods affair would never make a stir. His poetry was minor but his honesty was major; he would never be bought.

"Miss Maud," she said having spent the afternoon crying, "I will go to the meeting but I think you ought to know that I am John Fallon's daughter, but," she added hastily as Miss Maud recoiled, "I don't approve of him. I never have and if he says anything bad this evening I'll boo him. I'm not afraid of him. I only came down here incognito to think things out and I thought it would complicate things more if I came as Fiona Fallon. Forgive me." Needless to say she was forgiven and made to swallow two aspirin, drink a glass of milk and lie down. The question of love was never raised, because the Miss Croziers, daughters of the last Rector, were brought up never to probe below the surface, unless invited to do so.

The third character, John Fallon, attended a business luncheon in the Grand at Fungusport in the company of some provincial moguls but his mind was on other things than fertilizer mergers. What was he to do about that idiotic Earl and his own idiotic daughter? If they weren't such fools, both of them, he might have made a big deal out of it. He could for instance rebuild Ballyfungus Castle, install them in it, quiet the Earl's nonsense about the Woods, give them a good allowance and talk about "the Earl, my son-in-law," but now it was a mess. He wondered if he should call the fool Tottenham and make a deal. What a merger that would be! After lunch he tried to put through a call to the bungalow but the number was out of order and even the operator had not, it seemed, returned from lunch. I'll destroy the Minister for Post and Telegraphs he promised himself quietly. It was a heartening thought and took his mind off other things. As for the meeting that evening it didn't bother him; he knew he could take care of it, take care in fact of everyone.

By seven o'clock that evening, which fortunately was fine, the hall was already packed with concerned citizens and several hundred others less fortunate were milling around outside. They had most of them come in special buses from Fungusport and a great many others from the adjoining parish of Kinealy. Father Hannigan the ubiquitous parish priest of Kinealy was already there; his sights were usually trained on extramarital sex and the evils of contraception, but this time and on this issue he was wholly behind the cause. Tottenham every inch the young executive was mingling with the crowd, handing out ecological pamphlets and anti-Fallonism leaflets, and giving interviews to the press. Inside the hall people were tripping over TV cables and the camera crew was suddenly blinding people experimenting with lighting angles. The reporters from Dublin and Cork were already reasonably drunk and the speakers were nervously gathered in a room at the back of the stage discussing the programme. They comprised Canon Morragh and Father Kevin Sheedy; the Archdeacon of Moyaglen and Kilvert the venerable George Musgrave (the Archdeacon's diocese embraced Ballyfungus); the Rector Mr. Green (everything had to be ecumenical); Seamus Goggins, who owned a chain of supermarkets and was Mayor of Fungusport. He was for this occasion wearing the gold chain of office. Seamus was a tiny man and the chain hung to his crotch and at times one felt it might even drag him to the floor. The Catholic Bishop was present, Most Reverend Dr. Magill, who was old and failing. Sean Goggins, the Fianna Fail T.D., was being pushed around in a wheelchair and pushed around in every sense by his wife, who everyone knew planned to inherit his constituency. (The Irish Government was full of widows who took on their deceased husbands' seats.) The Goggins were brothers, which helped a lot in every way. Fallon came last, arriving in an impressive Rolls with chauffeur and special branch man. The Gardai in large numbers were also present, inside and outside the hall, everyone being very nervous and tense after the Fungusport Fiasco.

Tottenham joined the speakers as the witching hour approached and found to his rage Fallon already in full command, planning the order of speakers and dominating the proceedings in the most irritating manner. There was no question about his personal power and his ability to crush opposition. Tottenham nodded coldly to him when the introduction had been gone through by the Mayor. He was disgusted by the servility of the other speakers towards Fallon. Only the Archdeacon and the Canon remained cool; the Archdeacon, being part of a fast dwindling minority group, stood to gain nothing from the Fallon types and the Canon was a passionate conservationist. Meanwhile in the front seats, or rather benches, below the stage, sat what was known as the Old Mill mob: Colin Evans, Eddie Fox, Liz Atkins, Lady Vigors, her sister, Mrs. Travers, General Ironside, Dr. Josh Browne, and beside them the Miss Croziers with Fiona squashed between them. The dryad held a magazine *Woman's Own* in front of her face and pretended to be absorbed. She did not, for obvious reasons, wish to be recognized by her father.

The Mayor opened the proceedings and introduced each speaker in turn. There was to be a question time, he added, when the final speaker had finished and John Fallon was there to answer questions. There were some boos and hisses at this. Fallon smiled gently and contemptuously, one hand across his chest (Napoleon surveying the field of Austerlitz) derisive of the penniless persons around him, all of whom he knew, or guessed, could be bought. Tottenham as leader of the Cause spoke first. Fiona peeping around *Woman's Own* could see the pages of notes shaking in his hand. Her heart bled for him. Poor love! He never looked robust at the best of times, tonight he looked positively ravaged. In trembling tones he spoke about the primeval oaks, the rare birds and the wild flowers and what all this meant for the people of Wexlow and indeed for Ireland, not only for this generation but for generations to come. "Come unto these enchanted Woods," he quoted. He told how people came from far and near to walk in Balooly and he added emotionally, "I have enjoyed the happiest times of my life in Balooly Woods." Then he sat down to deafening applause. The Mill House mob rose to their feet and the General could be heard roaring "Bravo, Bravo, Tott! Good fella." The other speakers spoke of the dangerous traffic problems which would be caused by an influx of population. What about sewage? Water supplies already were dangerously low. The Canon said there were the remains of a twelfth-century Abbey in the Woods which were crying out for excavation and restoration. What about that? Father Hannigan spoke of sinister foreign industrialists eating up the country like locusts which was true.

Then came Fallon's turn. There were boos and hisses when the great financier rose to his feet, but he didn't turn a hair, not that there were many to turn. He spoke well and fluently (having had lessons in public speaking) and of course had all the facts at his finger tips. He said there would be at least seven hundred well-paid jobs ensured; money would come pouring into Ballyfungus and Fungusport. They already had water and sewage promised and they were hopeful of permission from the Minister. There was clapping on the job issue and more on the money. Then came a pause and Fallon added with a horribly roguish smile; "I noted my opponent the Earl of Tottenham, my son-in-law to-be, who I am proud to sit on the same platform with, even if we don't see eye to eye on this occasion. . . ."

It would be impossible to describe the sensation this caused except with the opening cliché, all hell broke loose. First of all there was a low murmur which gradually swelled to a roar which the unfortunate Mayor was unable to control and finally came the thunderstorm. Then indeed history was written by flashes of lightning. Tottenham trembling with rage jumped to his feet, opened his mouth, but nobody could hear what he was saying. Finally he took a couple of steps towards Fallon as if to strike him, but was restrained by the Archdeacon and the Canon imploring him to be cool.

Meanwhile Fiona to the horror of the Miss Croziers had risen from her seat and pushed her way towards the platform. She looked up at her father and screamed, "He's not your son-in-law, Daddy, and never will be and what's more you know it. Don't listen to him people." For once Fallon hadn't a word to say, he simply gaped at his daughter.

The Earl however was not wordless. He bawled down at his dryad now taking on the appearance of a fury. "Shut up, Fiona! You know we're going to be married."

"I'm not," Fiona screamed back at him. "I couldn't marry anyone, with a father like that." She shook her fist at the great financier who actually quailed.

Again Tottenham tried to jump off the platform but again the Archdeacon restrained him. "What's that to you?" roared Tott. "I'm not marrying your father. Don't be an ass, Fiona."

"I'm not going to marry anyone, I'm going into a convent tomorrow and never coming out," Fiona screamed back at him.

By now, a small, but deeply interested group surrounded the lovers, some of them on the platform, others below offering advice, commenting coarsely on the situation and taking sides. The Mill House mob were expressing their horror to each other at the revelations and poor Auntie de Bracey now standing on her bench was vehemently defending her nephew. "Never told a lie in his life — the girl's name was Smith she told us — I tell you it's all a lie." Nobody listened to her; finally she lapsed into tears.

The back of the hall was in a state of pandemonium. Mairin O'Kelly had become entangled in her own knitting (like Madame Defarge she took it to all public meetings). She was willing and able however to make shrill abusive comments. "Oppressors! Bloodsucking Landlord! Sassenach, Land Grabbers. Fools you've left us our Fenian Dead. God Save Ireland from you Fallon." Until her famous upper den-

tures descended, clouding her speech. Members of the Hodge
Podge, who had been ordered to attend by Father Kevin, were
acting up in every sense. During the run of Gorki's *Lower
Depths* they had been accused of communism and they were
having their revenge. "Fascist Fallon! Fascist! Exploiter of
the Poor! Bloodsucker! The Woods Belong to the People.
Out with Foreign Speculators." And then all together they
roared "Down with Fallonism." Father Kevin smiled; "just
in case" he had given them a few rehearsals. The most frightening was Mrs. Emerald Walsh who rushed up to the platform brandishing an umbrella and screamed at Fallon,
"Dirty old Turk — you. We knows about your harem! White
slaver!"

In one corner of the hall Tom Nolan was standing on a
bench shouting about the Balooly curse and the death toll it
had exacted from marauders over the years. Meanwhile
never had the TV crew enjoyed such a heaven-sent opportunity for sensationalism. "Not since the fuckin' Poetry
Festival was there anything like it." They had now focused
the cameras on the platform where Mrs. Goggins had seized
the opportunity to make a speech on behalf of Fianna Fail
but as nobody was listening it made little impact. "This sort
of thing could never happen under Fianna Fail," she addressed the Bishop who awakening from sleep asked everyone
what was the lady's name and where was he, at all, at all!
    At last Tottenham did leap from the platform and try to
seize Fiona. "Listen, listen," he panted, but she eluded him
amidst cheers and escaped into the crowd outside the Town
Hall.
    John Fallon shook his head pityingly, looked at his watch,
murmured something to the Mayor who was trying to remove his chain of office and quietly departed. The Rolls was
waiting for him outside and a crowd of exceptionally dirty
tinkers with two mildly interested ponies and several yapping
dogs were looking for handouts. Fallon ignored them,
stepped into the car, thanked the Gardai for their efforts,

leaned forward, murmured, "The Grand," and was driven away.

Poor Alicia de Bracey departed in the mini alone, overcome with shame, hoping that Tott might be in the bungalow already with evidence of vindication. Not that she doubted him for a moment. Alas, the bungalow was empty.

In the Old Mill things were humming. Drinks were being served to the mob by Tom who had already lighted a fire and the conversation like the fire roared up into white heat.

"I can't believe that Tott deceived us. Do you suppose Fallon means to buy him off through the daughter?" Liz moved around like an uneasy stewardess. She was overwhelmed with outbursts for the defense from Father Kevin, the Old Doctor and Tom. The latter who had helped himself to several drinks was the most vociferous.

"Ah for Godsakes, she told him her name was Smith and he took it as God's truth. Mr. Tott is that innocent he couldn't lie to a fox. He's real gentry."

"Hear! Hear!" shouted the General.

"He'd be no match for Fallon," remarked the Doctor.

"But Tott does need money," said Albinia doubtfully.

"He looks richer since he shaved the beard," remarked her sister.

Eddie scratched his head and looked thoughtful. "Where is he now? You might have thought he would have shown up to explain."

"But you all miss one hard fact." Colin accepted a large Scotch from Tom. "You heard her say she was not going to marry Tott because of her father."

"Fallon never looked more evil," sighed Liz.

"Aye Pet," agreed Tom who was bending over her in the most familiar manner. The excitement was so intense nobody noticed it. "The Earl of Hell himself!"

Suddenly the telephone rang, startling them all into silence. "It's midnight," exclaimed Liz jumping up. "Who can be phoning at this hour? I'll take it in my bedroom." She returned two minutes later. "Associated Press trying to trace Tott. Where can he be?"

"He'll have a hard time explaining to the media." Colin looked grim.

"And what about Balooly Woods?" asked the General, coming down to hard tacks. He was a great one for hard tacks.

Father Kevin put down his glass and prepared to leave. The Canon had only allowed him to attend the autopsy as an observer. "I'd say it was a lost cause."

"If you take a look around you Father," snorted the old Doctor, "so was the crucifixion."

The telephone rang again. This time Tom lifted the receiver; he held it out to Liz. "Holy God," he breathed, "Holy God!" Everyone held their breath. Naturally they thought it was the Earl. "Who is it?" asked Liz in a trembling voice.

"This John Fallon." Liz squeaked in astonishment. Father Sheedy who had put on his cycling helmet, took it off again. "May I speak to Lord Tottenham?"

"This is Liz Atkins. We don't know where he is, Mr. Fallon."

"He's not at home and he's not at Daisy Lodge. You may tell him if he does appear that the Balooly Development scheme is postponed. That is to say it's in abeyance."

"Thank you, Mr. Fallon. That *is* good news. Just a moment, did Tott, I mean the Earl of Tottenham, know that Miss Smith was Miss Fallon?"

"No, Miss Atkins, he did not and somebody should give that damn fool daughter of mine a good hiding. If Tottenham has any sense he'll do just that." There was a pause. The listeners were all seated as if turned to stone, straining to hear, their mouths slightly open, breathless. "Miss Atkins is your telephone in good working order?"

"About fifty percent of the time — yes."

"That's all I wanted to know. Thank you." He rang off.

Trembling with excitement Liz put down the receiver and faced the company. "That was Fallon himself. And he says silly little Fiona *was* masquerading and that poor Tott didn't know she was Fallon." There was applause from her listeners and a roaring "Bravo!" from the General. Liz raised her hand for silence. "And he says the Balooly Development is postponed." More cheers.

"Glory be to God we've won," said Tom reverently.

Mabs Vigors frowned. "Postponed. I don't like that."

"What actually is abeyance?" queried her sister.

"It means," remarked Colin thoughtfully, "more money must pass."

"I don't like it," repeated Mabs Vigors.

"But where is Tott and where is Fallon's erring daughter?" Liz sat down exhausted. "And why did Fallon ask me if my phone is working? Am I tapped?"

"No, you're pooped, darling." Eddie stroked her hair. "Mr. Fallon is out to get somebody and I would guess it's the Minister for Posts and Telegraphs. We must creep to our places of rest. Come Colin."

"That Fiona would make a powerful nun." Once more Father Kevin put on the cycling helmet. "But I'm afraid she's lost to the sisterhoods. Night all."

The lovers were at that moment clasped in each other's arms in their own enchanted Woods. It was very chilly, the moon was behind clouds and Tott said he heard a barn owl hooting nearby but all misunderstandings and worldly interruptions had been cast off they hoped forever. They are married; the ceremony took place in a registry office and Fiona is now described by Mrs. Walsh as a collapsed Catholic. They live in the flat overlooking Clapham Common and they do not accept a penny from John Fallon.

But Mabs Vigors was right to be mistrustful. The Battle of Balooly Woods had only just begun.

Chronicle Six

O̲NCE AGAIN BLEAK winter closed in on Ballyfungus. The excitement engendered by the threat to the Woods slowly died down and the Committee of Concerned Citizens became increasingly unconcerned. It was generally believed that for the time being the Woods were safe and that plans for the setting up of the "poison factory" had been abandoned. Everyone and everything resumed the usual sleepy ah well — it'll do — daily round. Towards the end of a vicious January Mairin O'Kelly's old "Pappy" died and was buried with full military honours. He was over ninety and one of the last survivors of the Volunteers who fought in that seriously over-crowded General Post Office, Easter 1916. "It was a simple and touching ceremony," reported the *Fungusport Herald*. However it was not everyone's idea of simple and touching. Faceless men, or rather lads, wearing black berets and dark glasses fired a volley over the grave. The Last Post was rather quaveringly delivered (the bugler being somewhat under the weather) and an inaudible oration was shouted out in Irish. Scuffles broke out between the various splinter groups. As the coffin was being lowered, a shot was fired and the police charged anything that moved. Sinister characters from the North appeared and disappeared, one of them was Miss O'Kelly's nephew, last seen in Ballyfungus during the robbery of the Poetry Festival money. Everyone put two and two together and arrived at fifteen, though this time the lad was wearing a false beard. Miss O'Kelly, uttering banshee cries, was supported by the nephews at the graveside and the Post Office was closed for the day. The most sensational incident occurred after the funeral and subsequent riots and it was recounted by Mrs. Walsh in her own inimitable style when she arrived at the Old Mill the next morning.

"Father Dermot was drivin' back to the presbytery for his dinner. God help him the housekeeper Josie's cooking would scar the stomach of a goat, when his car was stopped by a squad car and the Father was hauled out. Well hang on to your uppers and wait till I tell you wasn't Father Dermot driven off to Wexlow Police Station, stripped to the bone, finger-printed and his clothes took away and Blessed Saint Rita didn't they start to intoorogate him. Ah sure you know and I know that's only another name for torture. Mairin O'Kelly says they gev them boilin' enemas. Then I'm tellin' you they picked the wrong man for those capers. Father Dermot knocked two of the intoorogaters senseless and gev another a black eye but you oughter see the Father's own face, it's all colours. I tell you the President will hear about this. Then didn't a Gardai from Ballyfungus, Paddy Lucey with the squinty eyes, happened to look in and to his horror didn't he recognize the priest. He identified him. Oh Miss Atkins, he said he felt like retchin' up his dinner with the shame of it! Didn't he play on Father Dermot's own football team. The Canon was sent for; they had to pull him out of the Abbey dungeons and he borrowed Lady de Bracey's car and drove to Wexlow. He gev them all hell in the station. Mairin says they were kneelin' at his feet beggin' for forgiveness. They couldn't find Father Dermot's clothes and he had to druv back naked as the day he was born exceptin' for an old rug. Josie said she burst out cryin' when she saw the Father's face. As far as I can unravel the knots, a Provo from the North came down to the funeral disguised as a priest and the specials from Dublin thought they had nabbed him. I tell you they're sorry men this day."

"How terrible. There's sure to be trouble about this," said Liz. Trying to stem the flow she suggested a cup of tea.

"Thank you I might have a sup o'tea. Wait Miss Atkins, here's another egg from the goose but, it isn't a gold one. Attracta Mulcahy had her baby yesterday. I seen her Mammy in Goggins. A boy. She's callin' it Carter after the Yankee president. I told Mr. Evans I met him on the way here and he says that girl's a league of nations in herself. Laugh, I thought I'd wet me drawers."

"That's very nice. I must send Attracta something." Liz moved towards the kitchen, Mrs. Walsh and Hoover trailing after. She thought, I better drop a line to the USA. Alan will be interested.

"Hold on now, Miss Atkins, there's worse to follow. Fallon's at it again. A German laddo called Kross or Krass has been drivin' round the eeriah lookin' for a house to buy. He's a director of that Alpha-Omegger development company. Now what does he want with a house if he isn't goin' to dig his two feet into the ground and grow a tail? And if he digs in the feet, somethin' grows up into the head and up from under the hat."

"Thank you, Mrs. Walsh. You're right." Liz phoned Mabs that evening and gave her the news. It was received with consternation.

A week after the O'Kelly funeral the foursome met in Ferncourt. Both ladies were wearing black. Albie's wig was red and an atmosphere of tenseness hung heavy in the air.

"Artie," said Mabs waving a jeweled yellow hand at the General, "sit down. Something has to be done."

"Done m'dear, what has to be done?" the General seated himself beside her; he was noting with appreciation the crackling fire and the loaded drink tray alongside.

"That frightful Hun called on us. Krause. Artie, Josh, they *are* going to develop Balooly. He was quite frank about it. The Alpha-Omega Multi-International Conglomerate — sounds like a herd of elephants — is moving in. Ferncourt will be surrounded. Liz phoned me, gave me the news."

"Sacrilege," shouted the Doctor. "They can't do it. It's a bird sanctuary."

"It's also a human sanctuary, Josh, for wild flowers, love-making and picnics. I adore to walk there," sighed Albie. "Three quarters of the population of county Wexlow was conceived in the Woods. They have some pagan aphrodisiac

195

quality." The Doctor rose and paced the room. He always paced when seriously agitated.

Mabs clasped her hands and leaned forward towards the General. "Artie, Josh. What can we do? He's going to run a road through the Woods and right through us. I almost thought of joining the IRA."

The General rose to his feet, twenty years ago he would have jumped. "The IRA! My dear Mabs, a frightful crowd. They only bomb pubs where people are enjoying themselves. Other people's pleasure seems to infuriate them."

"The indiscriminate shedding of blood has taken the place of religious worship. It's always other people's blood," said the Doctor thoughtfully. "The young used to go into the Salvation Army and blow a trumpet or beat a drum, now they throw bombs or kidnap elderly persons."

"But Artie, what can we do about this Krause and it's not only Krause, behind him are at least two other villians, a Canadian, and a Jap and of course that arch-wretch Johnny Fallon. The German says it will be a modern town around the factory. In time you will see rising from what were woods — beautiful but non-functional woods — a busy town with shops. . . . Oh, I can't go on."

"Non-functional, what is that?" asked the General.

"An outside privvy," answered the Doctor smartly.

"The Woods at one time were part of the De Bracey demesne, but that was all sold to Fallon. You see people, the Woods I fear do belong, in part at least, to Fallon." Albie rose and stood by the drink trolley. "Whiskey Artie? Whiskey Josh? Help yourselves."

"I think you understand there will be no bridge tonight," Mabs rooted around in her evening bag. The contents of which were just as varied and unusual as those in her day bag. She now drew forth a small notebook and a fountain pen. "We have graver things to think about."

The Doctor returned to his place by the fire, glass in hand. "Nature sometimes wins when you least expect it. Who knows, Krause might die suddenly. Overwork. Tension. Heart."

"Sudden death!" Mabs sat up.

"We might drop a hint to the IRA," murmured Albie. "Just a hint, in passing."

"They wouldn't be interested." The Doctor took a gulp of his drink and choked. If he wasn't choking he was coughing, often both combined. "Useful constructive assassination is not in their line," he croaked as soon as he could get the words out.

"Yes, but think Josh; it would set an example to other foreign speculators who come here to ravage our country. They'll think twice," she added.

"Mabel," the General looked his hostess fair and square in the face, "are you suggesting murder?"

"Justified removal," said she quietly.

"Nothing justifies the taking of human life."

"Then you shouldn't have been a general," came from Albie. "Even if you didn't take one personally you urged others to do it."

The General sat down. "You have me there, Albie."

"You don't either of you," continued their dreadfully calm and resolute hostess, "have a leg to stand on. Josh here must have killed a lot of people in his fifty years' practice."

The Doctor smiled and shook his head. "It's the ones I didn't kill I regret . . ."

"John Fallon's hand in glove or rather pocket with Krause . . . you should have been here and heard that creature Krause. Liz says Mrs. Walsh told her that Krause told someone in her hearing that he'd make life impossible for us."

"And Mrs. Walsh is the pulse of the nation." The Doctor rose and renewed his neurotic pacing. Occasionally he gave a little skip and a jump. "What will we do?"

"Kill him," answered Mabs Vigors without hesitation.

The General shook his head. "I don't want to spend the last few years of my life in prison. It's too high a price."

"We won't be found out." Albie had obviously been giving serious thought to the problem. "The way things are now every one will think it's somebody else. And who in the world would suspect us? We're above reproach and suspicion."

"What about Tott, wouldn't he want to be in on this and Liz, and The Boys, not to forget the curates?" The Doctor absent-mindedly poured himself another Scotch.

"Certainly not. Tott would be suspected immediately. He's in bomber age-group and eccentric, besides Fiona is pregnant. Liz and The Boys have their lives in front of them. We don't. We have nothing to lose and terrible is he who has nothing to lose."

The Doctor skipped around and stood in front of Mabs. "I think you're right, girls. But how do we go about this grim business?"

"We'll ask him to dinner. He's dying to meet the county families. He told us he wants to keep horses to hunt."

"What do we do then?"

"We dispose of him in such a manner that nobody will ever find the body."

"Wait a minute," the General sat down heavily; he needed another drink but hadn't the strength to get it. "How?"

"Poison," snapped Albie and looked hard at the Doctor. "Poison," the Doctor started and returned the look, "which Josh can get for us."

"What we need," announced the General, "is an incinerator."

"Which we don't have," Mabs smiled a cryptic smile and looked at her sister.

"What we do have," said Albie, "is a well."

"A well?" The two men looked at her wonderingly.

"Yes, we have an unused and what is reputed to be a bottomless well in our equally unused stable yard. There would be no trouble disposing of the body."

"Let me get this clear." The General might have been

back at HQ where he spent most of World War II pointing to strategic positions on a huge map. "You ask this man to dinner. You slip poison in his drink and then put his body down the well under cover of darkness. How do you answer any questions as to who was the last to see him alive?"

Albie laughed gently. "It's so easy. The car will be driven by you, Artie, up to Balooly Woods and there abandoned. There will be bloodstains in the car and a note from some terrorist organization saying they're responsible. Josh can follow you in his car and drive you back here."

"You've taken lessons from Colin's Tierney." The Doctor looked admiringly at Albie. "I hope he doesn't recognize his own work."

"While we're busy murdering Krause what about Betty?" asked the General.

"Betty." Albie laughed and Mabs smiled. "Nobody believes poor Betty. She's known to be half crazy."

"Brain damage. I delivered her," said the Doctor brazenly. "She was born in the orphanage — Our Lady's Nest — and the mother decamped shortly afterwards. . . . But I think we might give her a sedative just to be on the safe side."

Albie who had been consulting a notebook looked up. "Krause is low-sized and quite thin. We do need a stretcher."

"No problem," said the General quickly. "I can make one."

"What about your housekeeper?" Albie frowned at him. "Won't she question you making a stretcher?"

"Her sight is almost gone, Albie, and her hearing is practically nil. I found my bedroom slippers in the bread bin the other day. No problem there."

"We must move fast, faster than Krause." Mabs consulted her calendar. "A week from today. What about that. You two come at seven. I'll ask him for seven-thirty; gives us time for a dress rehearsal. I'll phone the beastly man tomorrow morning."

"Time for the rubber." Albie shuffled the cards suggestively.

"Too much on my mind." The General frowned and rose with a groan. "God my arthritis. I'll take myself off. Josh, you coming?"

"Oh yes certainly."

"And, boys, all of us," interjected Mabs, "I'm talking to myself as well, don't go near Emerald Walsh or be in any house when Emerald Walsh is operating. That woman was born a bloodhound bitch. Wasn't she, Dolphie?" Dolphie growled.

When the men had gone Mabs stood up and poked the fire. "I hope they don't get cold feet. Trouble is Josh hasn't got much motivation, neither does Artie. Their home, their very existence is not threatened like ours."

"Josh has motivation. You know how he feels about the birds. And the whole of Ballyfungus adores the Woods. We all have motivation."

"He's coming; he's coming." Mabs was cozily in bed, her breakfast tray beside her and her mouth to the phone. "And I don't mean Our Lord. Krause is coming to dinner."

"I say," the Doctor chuckled. "Goodoh!"

"Did you get the stuff, Josh?"

The Doctor hesitated; his phone was in the hall and his daughter-in-law was disturbingly inquisitive. "Yes." He cupped his hands round the receiver. "Yes, it's a new thing called Toegreen, used mainly for foot rot in sheep."

"Good God, Josh! The man's not a sheep."

"Got it at the vet's. It's used as a spray but taken internally it's lethal. Tasteless, colourless and instantaneous. He was telling me about it. Some wretched stable boy took it by mistake and died. I snitched some while he was out looking at a barren mare."

"Good. Don't forget the pills for Brady."

"Betty? Yes, I'll bring them along too. How are things?"

"A lot of men have been up at Balooly. They were measuring and taking notes."

"That's as far as they'll get." The Doctor laughed again.

"Bye for the present." Mabs replaced the phone. "What will I give Krause for dinner," she pondered. "It seems such a waste when he's going to be . . . better get a nice leg of lamb, though," she giggled. "I suppose it should be a foot. Toe-green!" She laughed again. She couldn't wait to tell Albie.

The two fellow conspirators arrived punctually at seven. The drawing room was beautifully warm and comfortable. Both ladies wore black as befitted the occasion. Albinia in a curious tea gown with wig to match and Lady Vigors in a swinging bead outfit (1939 Nairobi) with a black feather boa. Dolphie was snoring away on the tiger-skin rug, occasionally breaking wind.

"Where's the stretcher?" asked Albie anxiously.

"I left it in your hall cupboard. You don't usually bring a stretcher to a dinner party, Albie, unless you plan to be carried out dead drunk."

"That's true. Have you brought the — er — potion, Josh?"

The Doctor slowly removed from his pocket a small blue bottle marked Holy Water. "Aggie Feehan got several of these at Lourdes," he explained. "She presented me with a couple for treating her entrails. The stuff is in this. Who's looking after the drinks?"

"Artie," Mabs pointed at the General, who winced. "He will actually administer the poison in the guest's after-dinner brandy. Come here darlings." She beckoned them over to the drink tray. "There are four snifters for us and one small brandy glass for him. No room for error. Now follow me. We also have four flashlights, on this bookcase." They followed her as if being shown round a museum. "We'll need them to get to the well. That's going to be the trickiest part of it."

"Splendid." The General was greatly reassured everything was falling into place. "Now are we all ready? Remember, Josh, we have to draw some blood from him. Have you brought your apparatus?"

The Doctor pointed wordlessly to his old black bag which was placed beside his chair.

"I say, Mabel," continued the General, "what condition is the well in?"

"Very good or at least very bad. Twenty feet deep and full of disgusting water. The cover is easy to remove. The nettles are the worst part of it."

"There's a car coming up the avenue, it must be he," cried Albie sneaking aside the curtains. "It is."

"Incidentally, what does he drive?" asked the General.

"A Mercedes-Benz I believe. They all do."

"I just wanted to know if I have to drive the damn thing."

"What about a quick one, Albie?" suggested the Doctor nervously.

"Good idea," the General obligingly splashed out some strong drinks and they had hardly gulped them down before Betty flung open the door and announced, "Mr. Crust."

A small pale-faced man with a square clean-shaven face confronted them. He was wearing a tailored grey suit and exuded neatness, cleanliness and after-shave lotion. His eyes were concealed behind square dark glasses. The company, including Dolphie who snarled, rose to greet him, and Lady Vigors graciously went through the introductions with much waving of the boa.

"Sherry, Herr Krause?" the General questioned him, "or maybe something stronger?"

"Sherry will be good." The visitor sat down; his English was perfect, almost BBC. He glanced at the table beside him on which was lying a page from Albie's sketchbook. "Aha, someone paints around here?"

Albie removed it hastily. "So sorry. It's just a little study of the umbrella stand in the hall. Watercolours are my pastime." Lady Vigors seated herself beside him. "My great-grandfather built this house in eighteen twenty."

There was an awkward silence while the visitor sipped his sherry. The Doctor and the General stared at him. They were both thinking the same thing. Weight? Could they manage the body physically? Their eyes, though they did not know it, were those of a butcher assessing a bullock. Suddenly a perfect fusillade of natural gas emanated from the noble bloodhound. Everyone started.

Herr Krause found his voice first. "Very wet weather," he remarked, "but never have I seen such greenness."

"Yes," answered the Doctor dryly, "Irish people are very green."

At that point Betty put her head round the door and announced dinner, as if it were an invitation to a hanging, which in a sense it was.

"Mr. Krause, follow me," Lady Vigors waved the boa at him. As they passed along the passage to the dining room the guest had time to note many dim portraits of violent-looking military men.

"The wrong side of the blanket all of them," she murmured.

The visitor bowed agreeably. He was totally at sea. "Very good," he murmured.

The dining room was large and very cold. "Too bad your wife is not here, Mr. Krause," remarked the hostess as soon as they were seated.

"I return to Stuttgart every two weeks. Of course I won't bring the family here until we are settled and have a house. I brought some snapshots with me. You might care to see them after dinner."

"That will be very nice." Albinia clinked her bracelets. "Our children are all grown up and so are the grandchildren. Two of mine are in prison already." Krause stared. Could she be serious? She was.

"Personally I loathe children," said Lady Vigors, "always have."

The General rose, not with alacrity. His arthritis was troubling him and also the Ferncourt wine was terrible. The Doctor used to say it was the vintage they used for gargling during the Black Death.

The dinner was good and the doomed man obviously enjoyed it. The retarded Betty instinctively was a first-rate cook the way some dim-witted persons are first-rate card players.

"I have not tasted such gourmet food since I came here," beamed Krause helping himself to blue Stilton. The two ladies tried to put thoughts of the Last Supper out of their minds while the gentlemen hoped he wasn't putting on too much weight.

"Tell us more about your plans, Mr. Krause?" Albie leaned forward and moved a candlestick (George II 1750) out of the way, so that she could observe the villain in action as it were.

"My plans. *Our* plans rather. Ah they are very thorough. I plan in Balooly a model town around the works. About eight hundred houses. (The General emitted a low whistle.) These will, in time, enclose a square or rather park with playground for children and a swimming pool. The houses will by necessity be to one design and the amenities come later. In time of course we shall require more land. No more wine, thank you. In time," continued Krause all innocence, "with Johnny Fallon we plan a resort in the west, one thousand holiday chalets. We also plan, but this is secret, a restaurant — glass — suspended from the cliffs of Moher seven hundred feet above the sea."

Lady Vigors rose, one finger pressed to her forehead; it was her defense against vomiting. "We will take our coffee in the drawing room, Brady."

Krause followed and as he followed he made a quick inventory of the pictures, furniture, and *objets d'art*; he intended purchasing cheaply — when the time came.

"Do show us the photographs of your dear wife and children," pleaded Albinia. "I adore looking at photographs. Mine are such a chamber of horrors."

"Thank you. Two lumps please, no cream. That is my wife," he passed the photographs round. "She was an airline hostess when I met her. They are chosen for their beauty. That is my son. Fifteen. He will go to school here. His English is very good." He started and broke off. Albinia was placing a cup of coffee beside the dog. Mad people, no doubt of that! He continued. "That is my daughter. She is twelve."

"Damn pretty girl," remarked the General, "some lucky Irish boy will grab her."

"He would, dear sir, have to be noble. I would not wish for her to be married — for her advantages." He smiled patronizingly. Poison's too good for him, thought the hostess, we should have killed him, slowly. Krause meanwhile had removed the dark glasses. His eyes were pale grey and as the Doctor noted with interest, red-rimmed like a vulture's.

Meanwhile the victim was studying those whom he considered his victims with particular regard to their health and longevity. He was discouraged on the whole. They are all four depressingly alert, vigorous, and on their toes. At the moment they were standing in the path of progress, but time was on his side and everyone can be bought. People seemed extraordinarily easy to buy in Ireland.

"What I would wish to discuss in a friendly manner," Krause finished off his coffee, "is the road. The road to Balooly, the new road will I fear have to go through your property."

Lady Vigors rose. "No, no, pleasure before business. Artie dear, *you* take care of the brandy." The two old men made their way to the drinks and Albie poked the fire. Dolphie as if scenting blood already sniffed horribly and growled. "And now," continued her Ladyship joining the men at the bar, "now I will take Brady her little glass of sherry. We allow her this little treat while she is washing the dishes." At this point Krause alarmed them by rising and making a gesture as if to get his own brandy, but he was restrained in a peremptory manner by his hostess. "No, no, you are the guest." She vanished.

"Your brandy sir," the General courteously placed the small glass beside the visitor. He drained his own down remarkably fast.

Lady Vigors returned from the kitchen, the feather boa in full action. "Betty is doing very well," she announced smiling at the Doctor.

The visitor lifted the brandy glass to his lips, while every one watched him, then put it down again.

"Your health, Mr. Krause," Albinia lifted her glass and smiled at him, "and success to your undertakings."

The doomed man rose to his feet, clicked his heels, raised his glass. "Your very good health, dear ladies," he took a large sip, sat down and took another sip. There was an audible sigh of relief. The moment had come. The Doctor blatantly pulled a chair over beside Krause and began staring at him intently. Meanwhile the company seemed to take on a sinister air, the room was so dimly lighted and even the fire had died down. The bloodhound rose slowly from the tiger skin and looked at Krause, saliva dripping from his jowls. Those eyes! Krause shuddered. Bloodshot, and Mein Gott, they are crooked; they are crossed. The cold was beginning to creep up around his feet. He hastily finished the brandy and then everything seemed madly funny. He laughed, it was the last laugh. Suddenly his whole body stiffened, he fell sideways in the chair.

The Doctor darted forward. Assisted by the General he tried to raise Herr Krause. They pulled and tugged to no avail. The man had stiffened into a piece of sculptured iron.

The Doctor removed his coat and rolled up his shirtsleeves. "Hand me my black bag, Albie." As he worked he talked, everyone else tried to think about beautiful things. "Better draw the blood, no time to lose. As you said the other night, Artie, we've nothing to lose. Just a few years in jail, taken care of by the State. As for disgrace, forget it. There's no disgrace in murdering people anymore. It's all done from the highest motives, the highest of course being liberation of someone or something. Ours is for preservation. Preservation of Nature? Preservation of privacy, and preservation ultimately of the goddamn planet. I'm doing it for the birds. I lost my faith in humanity fifty years ago." He handed the General another of the blue Lourdes bottles. "Here's the blood. Aha, the Toegreen is working." Suddenly the body loosened up, rolled off the chair and onto the floor. "That's better, boy! Now get the stretcher, Artie. By the way search his pockets, Mabel old girl, we need his car keys. Everything else goes down the well with him." Shudderingly Albie obeyed; in silence she handed the keys to the General who had returned with the stretcher.

"Nice piece of work," he remarked happily. "I had to do it at night in case my housekeeper asked questions."

Snorting, gasping and cursing (never had the ladies heard such language) they loaded the body onto the stretcher and the slow funeral procession made its way to the underworld. The ladies carried the flashlights. As they passed the kitchen door they caught sight of Betty seated in the kitchen stupefied, but not unconscious.

"You didn't give her enough," groaned the Doctor, "she's a witness. We'll have to put her down too."

There was a muffled scream from the ladies. "No, no, no," cried Mabs, "we'll never get another cook. We'll have to risk it. Besides she's in a sort of torpor." She smacked Betty sharply on the side of her head. There was no reaction. "See?"

At last they reached the well. It was a pitch black night, a light rain was falling and things were oozing all round them. Albie twice screamed "bats" and Mabs lost a shoe. They put the stretcher down and the General raised the lid of the well. The Doctor flashed the lights and they all peered down and saw nothing but blackness. The General dropped a stone and far, far below they heard it splash. The body was then hoisted off the stretcher and thrown head first down the well. There was a bloodcurdling splash. The General hastily replaced the lid.

Lady Vigors lifted her hand in benediction. They all bent their heads. "The peace of God which passeth all understanding be with you now Gunther Krause and forever more."

"Amen," they all murmured.

"That was a nice thought, Mabs," observed the General greatly moved.

"He'll have a development going up there in no time," remarked the Doctor cynically. "What about a hot cup of tea?" Indeed they were all shivering.

The General stopped suddenly one foot in a puddle. "A thought crossed my mind. What about Jamesy? Doesn't he work around the yard? Doesn't he know about the goddamn well?"

"Darling Artie," whispered Albinia reassuringly, "he doesn't know about anything. He just brings in the wood and polishes the brasses and has his dinner with Betty."

Thankfully they entered the house. Betty was sitting exactly where they had left her. Except that occasionally she emitted a sort of whinnying sound.

"What *was* in that pill?" asked Albinia curiously.

"Don't really know. I had a lot of them mixed up in my pocket."

"Artie, what on earth are you doing?" asked Lady Vigors crossly. The General was taking off his shoes and replacing them with a pair of old plaid bedroom slippers.

"Footprints. They'll be looking for footprints. I'll burn these old shoes when I get back. You haven't forgotten I have to drive the bloody fellow's car up into the Woods. Josh, you follow me in your car as far as Cahin's bridge. Wait for me there." He slowly drew on a pair of white cotton gloves, the type clowns wear. "Bring the blood along, Josh. Oh Mabel, have you got our message ready?"

Mabs blushing like a girl simperingly held up a square piece of white cardboard on which was written:

WARNING TO FOREIGNERS
THIS LAND BELONGS TO THE
PEOPLE
FIRST BLOOD '77

"It took me ages," she said, "but it's rather sweet. And first blood is so threatening. A warning of more to come."

"Absolutely brilliant," exclaimed the General and he was echoed by the others. "Well we're off. Come Josh."

"We'll have tea for you on your return," Albinia called after them. She hurried to the window and peeped between the curtains. "He's having trouble starting up the car. Ah there he goes and Josh following him."

Half an hour passed; it was like a lifetime. At last their vigil was broken by what seemed like the clattering of hooves. The door opened without the heralding respectful knock and Betty entered at full gallop with the tea tray. She came to a full stop in front of Lady Vigors and stood there snorting and tossing her grey locks.

"Oh Missis, Oh me Lady! Oh the things that I did be seein'! Oh you wouldn't believe . . ." another whinny followed.

"I certainly wouldn't believe anything you said, Brady," said her mistress coldly. "Put the tray down, Brady, and compose yourself." But Betty could not be quenched; she was in full spate.

"I fell asleep like with the dish towel in me hand standin' up, and I seen true as God, four terrible lookin' creatures pass the door with a dead man on a stretcher and Madam me Lady they never did come back."

Albie laughed merrily and Lady Vigors snapped, "Really Brady, this is going too far. I'll have to have the head doctor to see you."

"There's nothin' in me head ma'am, me Lady," said Betty piteously.

"That's the trouble, Brady, I'm afraid. Go downstairs now and finish the dishes. Look at the time."

"I seen what I seen," neighed Betty as she galloped out.

"Thank God, here is Josh's car," cried Albinia, who was as usual like sister Anne at the window. "Mabs, I think Betty thinks she's a horse!"

The General entered first carrying the bedroom slippers in one hand. He removed the cotton gloves and sank into a chair; "Albie, be an angel and throw those confounded slippers in the fire." Albinia obeyed him and the fire blazed up merrily. "Mission accomplished," the warrior continued. "The Mercedes is now in the Woods blood-bespattered and I left your note, Mabs, on the front seat. My heart was in my mouth that I'd run into another car. It's a lovers lane up there you know. Give me a dash of whiskey, sweets, I'm feeling my age."

The General kissed Albina's hand. "Bless you. Remember everyone, we all tell the same story. Krause left us at nine-thirty to drive back to his hotel. We know nothing more. Nothing. I'll leave the stretcher in your closet if you don't mind. I can pick it up later."

The Doctor rose stiffly to his feet. "I've got to get home or my damnable daughter-in-law will be asking questions. Everything worked perfectly, ladies. You've every reason to be proud of yourselves."

"Just a minute, Josh," Lady Vigors stopped him. "Just what did you give Betty, or what did you give *me* to give Betty?"

"She's behaving so oddly," Albinia echoed her sister. "She came in here just like a mad horse. Neighing and tossing her mane."

"As a matter of fact I realize now there was a little mix-up in those pills. It was a snitch of something they give barren mares to bring them into heat. She may gallop round a while tonight, looking for a mate, but it will pass."

"Josh, how could you? Why *don't* you stay away from the vet. And now you see she wasn't unconscious; she did see everything."

"No, she had a sedative too, something they give restive cows. Don't worry. Come Artie. Home, sweet, home."

The disappearance of the wealthy German industrialist who was going to do so much for Ireland provoked a hue and cry which would take the pen of a De Quincey to describe. Reporters appeared in droves. Police roamed the county with dogs, beating bushes, dragging the Fung, searching all ruins and empty cottages, interrogating the inhabitants of Bally-fungus, Kinealy and Fungusport until everyone thought they themselves were suspects and so fell into a state of intolerable confusion and fear. The headlines in the Dublin evening papers were most disturbing: Strange Rumors of a Curse! Does an Elemental Stalk Balooly? Baronet's Widow Inter-viewed: Says Krause was nervous. Find the Body or . . . says Minister. IRA Issues Statement on Ballyfungus Mystery. Sub-Human Footprints Found Near Car. Mystery Footprints! Are They Human? ("Artie's feet of course," said Albie. "They're barely human." She was enjoying it all immensely. "Thank God we burned the slippers.") Mrs. Walsh was incensed be-cause she seemed to be the one person the police did not interrogate. "And there's plenty of dirt I could have told them," she sniffed. The nose twitching was almost continu-ous during this trying period. Auntie Al had several conver-sations with Tott on the hot line to London. "He'll turn up in Australia with his secretary," said Tott, "or in South America. They always do. This ought to frighten Fallon though. Fiona is in fine shape. Don't worry." Colin Evans felt there was a strange air of *déjà vu* about the whole affair. "As if I'd read it all before." Liz thought it was hard on the ladies of Ferncourt — "They're practically in a state of siege; the media keeps pestering them. They refused to go on 'The Late Late Show,' which can be a form of interrogation." The Post Office was humming with rumours. "The body was sliced up of course." Miss O'Kelly's uppers were down and the Dracula look was evident. "Do you remember old Tommy Gilfoyle killed his brother with a meat axe it was all over who owned the farm and the body was strewn I'm tellin' you, strewn, across the county. A leg here an arm there and the stomach, liver and whatnot turned up in a bin behind Goggins Butchers Shop in Fungusport. At first they thought it was a sheep but the police found it was Gilfoyle's. Mary and

Joseph they nearly put it on the counter." Goggins super-market on Friday mornings became a madhouse of conjecture and rumour. Customers leaned on their trolleys shouting at each other, which gave Goggins an excellent opportunity to falsify their bills and change price tags. The Catholic Boy Scouts volunteered to help the police on their cross county searches but the Protestant Scouts remained aloof. It was a time of extraordinary tension. Quesions were asked in the Dail which remain to this day unanswered.

A week after the event, as yet one hardly dared to call it murder, the sisters had a visit from two Special Branch officers. They were a couple of hard-faced middle-aged men very neatly dressed with very short haircuts. They had eyes that Betty said afterwards went right through you and out the other side like bullets. She showed them into the drawing room salivating with excitement, a symptom she shared with Dolphie.

Mabs motioned them to sit down and Albie asked them if they'd care for a glass of sherry which they declined.

"I've already told the local sergeant, such a nice man, we've always known him, that Mr. Krause came to dinner and left early. He said he had work to do at home."

"Did he seem in good spirit?" asked the bigger and more intimidating of the interrogators.

Mabs smiled reminiscently. "He showed us pictures of his wife and children, poor fellow, he was full of plans for the future."

"Yes," Albie took up the tale. "He seemed very happy about coming here to live and all the beautiful things he was going to do for us. I wonder what happened. I see that all the terrorist organizations have disclaimed responsibility."

"Would you say, did he drink much, indulge, you might say?" asked the smaller man delicately.

Both ladies hooted with laughter. "Gracious! No," cried Mabs, "he had one glass of sherry before dinner, half a glass of wine and a teeny drop of brandy afterwards with his coffee. Sober as a judge."

Albie leaned forward eagerly. "Do you think they'll ever find the body — if there is one?"

The big Special Branch man shook his head. "The way things are going he might turn up in Libya; it's all international now. Well good day to you, ladies. We won't take up any more of your time." Obviously there was nothing to be gained by further interrogation; the ladies radiated well-bred innocence.

Three months passed; it was coming into summer and poor Krause, such is human nature, was almost forgotten, though the search for the body continued in rather a perfunctory manner. There was silence from Alpha-Omega and no work as yet had started on the threatened development. However, there was some banging and blasting going on around the Castle. In private the Ferncourt Foursome began to congratulate themselves on their victory, though Mabs did nag on about Fallon and advise liquidation of that villain. The others demurred. They simply didn't have the energy. "Besides," said the General shudderingly, "would he fit on top of the other load?"

"Do you think, Josh?" asked Albie wincingly, "that the other has risen to the top?"

"He's not a soufflé, Albie," replied the sister severely.

"The well is bottomless isn't it?" The Doctor looked at his cards disgusted. "I pass."

It might have remained a mystery for ever if Colin had not suddenly remembered why the Disappearance seemed so familiar. Of course; it was one of his own mysteries (*The Widows' Well*, 1967) and one morning he happened to meet Sergeant Moriarty in the Post Office. They both engaged in conversation about the postage. Stamps like everything else were up again. "Incidentally," said Colin, "you should have called me in on the Krause mystery."

"Why so, Mr. Evans? It does seem as if we've explored every avenue."

"It's not an avenue you need, Sergeant, it's a well. Of course an avenue might lead to a well." The sergeant stared at him. He was not very bright or he wouldn't have been stationed in Ballyfungus. "Why so, Mr. Evans? You're larkin'."

"Some years ago I wrote a book about two elderly ladies, who assisted by two old gentlemen put their embezzling solicitor down a well. I'm not implying that the ladies of Ferncourt put anyone down a well; that would be laughable."

It was laughable. The sergeant absolutely roared. "Them ladies wouldn't hurt a fly if it jeered at them."

"But of course," said Colin thoughtfully as he followed the sergeant out into the street, "there are other wells. I don't even know if Ferncourt has one, but there is a holy well which cures warts in the Castle. Good day to you."

Still chuckling the sergeant drove off in the squad car but slowly the smile faded from his face. Had they searched all the wells? Ponds and rivers yes, but wells he wasn't sure. If not, why not?

Largely owing to the instigation of the Ferncourt ladies the ecumenical memorial service for the late Gunther Krause was held in the little cathedral. Frau Krause notified she was too grief-stricken to attend and also too frightened which was understandable.

Prominent amongst the mourners at the service were Dr. Josh Browne and General Arthur Ironside both wearing dark suits and black ties. The Ferncourt ladies wore black suits and black mantillas. The Miss Croziers arranged the flowers, they always did perform that service. "I think of white," Maud coughed gently, "considering there is no body. A few blue delphiniums might add a note of hope. Mrs. Walsh says he's been seen in Australia." Mabs and her sister had chosen the hymns. First a rather ominous one beginning, "Christian seek not yet repose, hear thy guardian angel say, thou are in

214

the midst of foes. Watch and pray." The Archdeacon who had liked nothing about the late Krause delivered a short insincere eulogy. He did dwell rather lovingly on the human locusts who are now eating up the earth and transforming it into a desert, implying the late Krause was in fact an unlamented locust. He was followed by the Canon who said he was sad about the loss of employment if the schemes were not put through but the threat to ancient monuments was even more serious if the schemes did go through. Then they all filed out into the June sunshine to the sound of Chopin's funeral march played by the blind son of a Protestant carpenter. Mabs Vigors and her sister flanked by the Canon and the Archdeacon stood outside the cathedral and shook hands with the congregation as they filed past. Muriel was not present. The rumour being that she hardly moved at all now, except for intake of food. The two male assassins hovered respectfully in the background. Liz, who was present with The Boys, kissed Mabs and Albie tearfully; like a great many hard-hearted ruthless persons she was highly emotional at funerals. A head-on confrontation with the grim reaper often floored them. "That was a sweet thing to do. There's something so lonely about poor Krause."

"Do you know," exclaimed Eddie, "I had the shudders during the service when I thought Krause might walk into his own funeral, a dripping spectre."

"Did you hear my theory?" Mabs overheard Colin addressing the Archdeacon. "It's all like a plot I devised some years ago for a book called *The Widows' Well*. They found the body in a well." Mabs stiffened. She forced herself to look at the General who she fancied had turned pale.

Albie rushed into the breach. "You must all come back to Ferncourt for a little bit of a wake. We have soup and sandwiches and drinks all set out. Please." Everyone in the little group thankfully accepted. "We must hurry back, Mabs. Artie, we're going with you." She hustled them all off.

"Did you hear Colin?" hissed Mabs.

"I did," groaned the General.

When they drew up in front of Ferncourt a dreadful and alarming sight met their eyes. No less than two Gardai squad cars, an evil looking black van and two more official vehicles were drawn up in front of the hall door.

"What can this be?" cried Mabs. Filled with foreboding she entered the house, the male assassins bringing up the rear. In the dining room where the funeral baked meats were so tastefully arranged were the two infernal Special Branch men, the sergeant and a couple of other official characters. Betty and Jamesy, white-faced and trembling, were holding Dolphie. "What does this mean?" demanded Mabs. In moments of danger she became the governor's lady. "Speak boy." She addressed the larger Special Branch man who was all of fifty.

"Acting on a tip," replied the detective coldly, "Lady Vigors, we searched all wells in the neighbourhood and we did yours as a matter of routine. I'm sorry to say we recovered the body of the late Herr Krause in your well. So we would appreciate it if all four of you, because the gentlemen were both present that evening, would accompany us to the station and assist us with our enquiries."

"We better go, Mabs," whispered the General. "The game's up."

Lady Vigors took her handbag off the table, adjusted her hat, put on her black gloves and moved towards the door. "Tell them," she said, "that I died for Ireland." She stopped in front of the Special Branch men. "And *you*, if you'd been patriots, you would have left well alone." As the squad car containing the assassins moved out of the gates of Ferncourt the cars containing the invited guests from the memorial service drove in and little did they suspect the shocking news that awaited them.

The arrest of the foursome created a sensation which went far beyond Wexlow, beyond the Republic, it was worldwide. Four respectable old people whose combined ages amounted to three hundred and twenty years had plotted and carried out a dreadful assassination. Even Mrs. Emerald Walsh's powers of description failed her. It was too much, too overwhelming. For the trial the four Accused were advised by counsel to put on an act of drivelling senility, which might help to bring in a verdict of diminished responsibility or of unsound mind. Accordingly the General appeared to be totally illiterate and couldn't sign his own name to anything, nor indeed was he at all sure what his real name was. The Doctor hopped and flapped around, explaining to all that he was a persecuted sea-gull. He was piteous in court asking people to remove the oil from his wings and blaming mankind for the obliteration of his species. "I am a sea-gull," he moaned, "I am a sea-gull. (Echoes of Chekhov, sighed Eddie who was present at the trial.)

Mabs sat with her head in her hands, she had apparently lost the power of speech and she was dressed like some forlorn figure out of a Beckett play (they should have put her in an urn remarked Colin, who was also present in the courtroom). Albie was the worst: Defense counsel was very pleased with her. It seemed she thought she was Ophelia, threw flowers and bits of parsley and lettuce at the jury. She wore three hats over a long gold wig and begged them to let her float quietly down the Fung. Outside the courthouse there were picket lines of concerned citizens, led by the Earl, who had flown over from London to lend support. They were all dressed in black, carried placards reading: "They Know Not What They Do, Forgive Them, They Are But Human, The Motivation Was Pure if the Deed Was Doubtful." On the third day of the trial to counsel's horror the Doctor stood up and made a speech saying amongst other things that Ireland was a nation of talented small farmers, fishermen and horse dealers and should stay that way. Where industry was concerned they were babes in the wood. (The wood evoked a chant from the spectators, "Save Balooly Woods"); Ireland, continued the horribly sane Doctor, "should be a small but valuable bread basket for Europe and keep out foreign investors who would lift every penny off the naïve government in control" (loud cheers followed). The defense counsel buried his head in his hands and several people were ejected from the courtroom. Mercifully the Doctor quickly relapsed into senilty and began crying out, "I am a sea-gull." A verdict of guilty but of unsound mind was quickly brought in and the foursome were ordered to be detained at the President's pleasure. They were committed to a luxurious mental hospital just outside Dublin where they seem on the whole to be reasonably content. The bridge games continue; they are kept well supplied with books, watch television and correspond with their friends in Ballyfungus. They are allowed visitors; it became quite the thing to make a holy pilgrimage to Dublin to see the environmentalist martyrs and bring offerings. Of course they will never be freed; but as the Doctor keeps murmuring, "Think of our age, it won't be long now. Death unlocks all doors. I am a sea-gull!" Then he guffaws.

There was silence from Alpha-Omega, but everyone knew that a fight was still on their hands. One tragic note was struck. Dolphie had to be put down. The hospital refused to accept him. On Mab's instructions he is buried in the Ferncourt garden with a simple inscription on the tombstone: "Gone With The Wind."

Chronicle Seven

A YEAR PASSED and the shock of the Ferncourt murder faded gradually from everyone's mind. Ballyfungus indeed could be compared to a sleeping beauty who was wakened every year or so by a tremendous explosion and then dozed off again. Of course the ordinary events took place; people were born, married and died. Jimmy Carter Mulcahy was thirteen months old and already talked to the cats in Irish and English. The Tottenham baby was younger and immensely vigorous. The infusion of peasant blood into the weak blue Norman fluid was proving beneficial. Ferncourt had been sold, none of the heirs wanted it, and bought, to everyone's consternation, by John Fallon. He also acquired "Batty Betty" the famous cook. A great many people were after her; the poor thing had been more or less put up for auction. Rumour had it that Liz was tiring of Tom and interested in someone else and sadly rumour in this case was right. It is hardly necessary to add that Emerald Walsh was "business as usual" flying around on the motor scooter. Mairin O'Kelly though ostensibly in mourning for Pappy was still engaged in underground political activity. A phone call here and a phone call there, (provided the phone was working) and instructions were carried out. The distinguished tax dodgers were doing well. Colin had produced another Tierney which won the Crime Fiction Award and Liz had a record success with her London show. Nearer home things were also booming. The Hodge Podge won the National Award for their production of *Love's Labour's Lost*. Ah, but it was the calm before the storm; the last blooming of the last rose before the petals began to fall one by one. We are now entering the year of the Mushroom . . .

It was Friday and the first week in April when one dreamed of primroses, bluebells, and coming of the cuckoo. Alas rain mixed with snow was falling on Ballyfungus and the temperature was way below normal. Friday was the day when those persons who dwelt on the banks of the Fung converged on the village for their weekend shopping. Saturday was considered rather vulgar for this operation and the more refined persons could be seen in Goggins supermarket wheeling the shopping carriages and exchanging pleasantries.

Colin and Eddie were there that morning. Eddie was doing the shopping, he being the cook, and Colin was standing at the window which looked out on the main street. He suddenly exclaimed loudly and called to Eddie.

"Eddie! Come here. Quick!"

"What's up?"

"Look. There's a fellow walking down the street who's the dead spit of Our Lord. There. See."

"So he is! And he's carrying a cross! Mr. Goggins, do you see that fellow going by, dressed as Jesus Christ? Is it a joke?"

Mr. Goggins, owner and manager of the supermarket, joined the two bachelors at the window. "Oh, that one! That's poor Bejasus. He's gone in the head. Harmless. Once a year, just around Easter, he makes a pilgrimage from Dublin to Cork. He always goes through Ballyfungus."

Bejasus was wearing a dirty white caftan, with shawl pinned across it and brown sandals on his bare feet; his red hair flowed wildly down his back and his beard almost obscured the face. The eyes were blue, red-rimmed, sad and wildly innocent. Goggins ran out of the shop and tapped the zany pilgrim on his arm. "Would you step in for a minute Bejasus and partake of a cup of hot coffee or tea maybe? 'Tis powerful chilly today."

Bejasus lowered the rough-hewn cross for a moment and stared at Goggins, bemused, then recognition dawned. He knew everyone on his route. "Ah, Mr. Goggins. God bless you. I can't stop; I have to be in Calvary tomorrow. John and

Peter, you know, will be expecting me!" Surprisingly he had a pleasant educated voice.

Goggins pushed a pound note into the poor fellow's dirty red hand. "You'll need that, son, for a bite of food on the way."

"Thank you, Mr. Goggins. My father who is in Heaven will reward you." He shouldered the cross and hurried on . . .

Shaking his head Goggins returned to his mart. He was not given to charity, except for keeping on good terms with the Church, but the thought nagged at the back of his mind, supposing Bejasus turned out to be the real thing? Honest to God you never know. . . . It might just turn out to be a good investment if it came to a Second Coming.

"What beats me is," remarked Colin who was perturbed by this apparition, "that nobody seems to be surprised. He's taken for granted."

"Comes of a good family too. Had a breakdown at college. Too much learnin'. Now Mr. Fox, what can I do for you. That's a nice line in soups. Game. Very tasty." Goggins revered The Boys; they were amongst his best customers. "I suppose you heard Archdeacon Musgrave's wife was took bad."

"I didn't. She was always complaining of her legs. Wasn't she, Colin?"

"Dr. Browne has given her up."

"So did the Archdeacon years ago," Eddie tittered and Mr. Goggins winked; it was a salacious wink hinting at dreadful things. "I suppose we must inquire. Colin we'll make a detour around to the Rectory. I say, Colin, could we get away with tinned prawns in the bouillabaisse?"

"Why not?" Colin yawned. "Your tinned prawns are good, aren't they Mr. Goggins?"

"Mr. Evans," the shopkeeper looked injured, "you know the best is not good enough for me. As God is my witness."

"That's a pretty powerful witness, Mr. G. I'll take three tins." Eddie threw them into the trolley.

"Can I help you, Mrs. MacCrea ma'am? What can I do for you now? And how are you? I needn't ask. You look as fresh as a morning in May." The elderly lady Goggins addressed looked much more like November.

She smiled faintly and pointed at some withered cabbages. "Thank you, Mr. Goggins. I'll take that and half a pound of margarine. Oh, and do you have a loaf of your own brown bread left?" She turned to Eddie. "Good morning Eddie; good morning Colin. I suppose you heard about Muriel Musgrave?"

"Yes, Mr. Goggins has just told us. Heart I suppose?"

"I think a clot. She never took any exercise. It's very serious. Oh, Mr. Goggins, four bananas please, not too ripe. Felicity is coming home for a rest. She's quite worn out working in that dreadful basement restaurant in Dublin." She lowered her voice and tapped Goggins on the arm. "Where is the toilet paper, I never can find it. Four white rolls please. My husband doesn't like the coloured."

"Yes we saw Felicity there a few weeks ago. The Silver Platter run by a country gentleman with two wives. A dreadful place, like an unlighted public lavatory. I don't know how poor Felicity stuck it so long." He smiled at Mrs. MacCrea who was smelling a bunch of withered parsley. "And how is Alexis?" That beloved name brought a smile to Mrs. MacCrea's defeated face. Alexis was her eldest son and favourite child. His pursuit of art was to him like the Holy Grail — the little old senile lady with an attic full of George II silver.

"Lexy's in Prague; he heard of a wonderful icon. By the way, Felicity dropped in to see Mabs Vigors and the others in the Asylum." Mrs. MacCrea hesitated. "I should say the Clinic. She says it's an awfully nice place, like a family hotel, except for a rather odd man who kept dropping on his knees and begging for sugar."

"How disconcerting," Eddie tittered.

Colin: "You must come to dinner, Elinor. We'll phone.

Now Eddie, no more chatter! To the Post Office. . . . We both need stamps. Thank you, Mr. Goggins, how kind of you." He spoke to the shopkeeper who was tottering behind him with a carton of provisions. "We'll charge that if you don't mind. Yes, we'll put it in the boot." The Boys drove a large station wagon which was parked outside the supermarket.

Miss Mairin O'Kelly was making out a postal order and that meant a long wait.

"Mr. Fox, Mr. Evans, good morning." She stared at them over her spectacles. "You heard Mrs. Musgrave was given up. She's in the Fungusport Hospital in Extensive Care."

"We did. Sad. I wonder if I might have two books of stamps, Miss O'Kelly?" Eddie put on an ingratiating smile; you had to woo that fierce woman.

"Just a moment." A yellow finger was wagged at him. The nail, he noticed, was long and curved, black-rimmed and could have come in as a handy weapon. "We go slow, Mr. Fox, we go slow." She turned from him haughtily. "Now Mr. Doogan?" Mr. Doogan who was trying to put through the postal order was taken by surprise. "Your name?"

"I don't rightly know," stammered Doogan. "Oh, begod, Doogan's the name!"

The business with poor Doogan, who was almost totally illiterate, took up so much time Colin wandered out into the street. The rain was clearing and patches of blue sky could be seen behind the clouds. Good Lord, could he believe his eyes, two sheep emerged from Monaghan's drapery shop and made their way dreamily down the street, oblivious of traffic. What on earth? Ah, a small boy came out of the shop with a stick and urged them towards the footpath. But what on earth were they doing in the draperies? It was always thus in Ireland, pondered Colin, orphaned livestock everywhere and nobody cares. He was interested to see Liz Atkins parking her car outside the supermarket and who was that slender, dark, handsome stranger beside her? Who could it be? Had someone supplanted the gorgeous hunk of middle-aged manhood, Tom Nolan? Not possible? He was, at that moment, joined by Eddie.

"That old bitch in the Post Office," fumed Eddie. "Practices torture. They could get her under some act or other. I believe her sexual appetite was roused by keeping me waiting."

Colin directed Eddie's attention to the supermarket. "See what I see. A toreador attending Liz."

"Wish I had my field glasses," sighed Eddie. "He looks like one of the Chilean refugees from Shannonside House. Surely Liz hasn't latched on to one of them." Suddenly there was a tremendous explosion; the whole village seemed to shake and quiver.

Colin gripped Eddie's arm. "Not another bomb?" he exclaimed. A young lad came towards them nonchalantly eating an ice-cream cone as if it were July.

"What was that?" Eddie asked him excitedly.

"Fallon's men is bringing down the Castle. Demolishment that's what it is." He grinned at them.

Though he was in his early teens, Colin noted that the lad had already lost most of his teeth and would shortly require dentures.

"Bringing down the Castle. So the engines of destruction have moved in," sighed Eddie with a mournful look; a cloud of dust was billowing over the rooftops.

"And they'll be cuttin' down Balooly Woods next, that's what me Daddy told me." The youth moved on, throwing the ice-cream stick and wrapper gaily on the footpath.

"I don't know which is worse in this country." Colin looked after him, "litter or dental problems."

"Tott is here with wife and child. I heard the gorgon in the Post Office telling a suppliant for stamps. Alicia says Tott and wife are starving. Come let us hasten home."

That night, Muriel Musgrave passed peacefully on to a higher life. From house to house the news flashed around the county, mainly with the assistance of Mrs. Walsh. By the time she arrived at the De Bracey bungalow her voice was almost gone. She was quite exhausted and had to be revived with strong tea. "Went off like that," she snapped her purple claw with a horrid gesture. "They was givin' her the bedpan when she gave a great gullup, turned blue from head to foot and when they looked at her next she was gone. It was the legs went to the heart, like."

"That's dreadful," sighed Lady de Bracey. "She was a nice little woman actually. Not a great help to the Archdeacon though. Sad. No children. Poor chap, he will be jolly lonely now in that enormous Rectory."

"He was cryin' his heart out, they tells me. If he weren't a Christian I'd be afraid for his life." (This was a great advance in Mrs. Walsh's thinking; she usually did not include Protestants in the Christian community.) "You know you'd be afraid of what they does in India, throws themselves into the oven when the wife dies, don't they? But sure, them's heathens. The funeral's of a Tuesday in the Cathedral. Bishops is comin' from all over. The Archdeacon's askin' a few friends back after the funeral, you'll be gettin' a ring. A sort of a Protestant wake, do you know? He's asked me in to help like, and Miss Atkins is lendin' Tom Nolan for the drinks." Mrs. Walsh lowered her voice and looked around as if enemies were lying in wait and Lady de Bracey nervously did the same. "There's queer doins' at the Old Mill." She paused, pursed up her lips and looked hard at her employer. Now Lady de Bracey knew that she should not encourage Mrs. Walsh's revelations, it was "simply not cricket," but somehow she couldn't resist. There was always a grain of truth in the fantasies.

"Well there's a foreign fella there that Miss Atkins met over at Shannonside and she has him at the Mill mornin', noon, and God forgive me, I was about to say night. Poor Tom Nolan's fit to be put away. Last night when I was helpin' up at the Mill she had them artists from London to dinner. Declare to God, before I was goin' I hid all the sharp knives, when I saw poor Tom's condemned face and the two glarin' eyes on him. 'I'm off to Australia to work for me brudder,' says he. 'A sure what would keep me now with the wife gone and no children.' I hope he goes before murder's done. Remember old Carmody fed his wife's fancy man to the pigs? Where's the young ones and the babby?"

"They're out shopping."

The telephone rang sharply at this point, bringing Mrs. Walsh's horrific flow of gossip to a halt. Lady de Bracey heaving a sigh of relief hastened to answer it. The phone was right beside her bed. This ensured some degree of privacy. She lifted the receiver. It was Eddie Fox who was in his own way just as informative as Mrs. Walsh when it came to gossip. "We want you for dinner tonight, Alicia. We both think you need cheering while you're within earshot of the bombardment. The Castle's coming down. Bulldozers, cement mixers, battering rams, you name it, have all moved in."

"Fallon's a damn rotter," exclaimed Lady de Bracey forcibly. She sat down on the bed. "Of course he does own the Castle; he bought it and that's what I'm living on," she added sighing.

"And, my dear, I want to warn you." Eddie lowered his voice. "He's after the Woods again. Isn't Mrs. W. there? It's your day, isn't it? Has she told you Muriel Musgrave passed away last night?"

"Very sad. What will poor George Musgrave do?"

"Nicely," Eddie sniggered. "Mark my words he will marry again." Again he lowered his voice. "Has she said anything about Liz and her new man?"

Lady de Bracey kicked the door shut. "Yes, she did as a matter of fact. She said Tom was desperately jealous. Isn't Liz dreadful?"

"Insatiable. Sad about Muriel, but what a relief. Those legs can't have been fun to live with. Tott and Fiona are with you, I hear."

"They're all three in the guest room. It's a shambles, and, oh Eddie you won't believe it, but there are enormous mushrooms in the built-in cupboard and another crack in the ceiling." Lady de Bracey's luxury bungalow, though hardly fifteen years old, was slowly disintegrating, a drifting wreck breaking up on the rocks. "Eddie, I'd love to come tonight."

"Bring the young folks. I've made a large lasagna."

"I'm afraid not, Eddie. No baby-sitter."

"Bring the baby too; we can always drug it."

"They're out shopping now but I'll ask them when they come back. Thanks awfully, Eddie. Ripping of you! I'll phone you."

Tott and Fiona were reputed to be paupers, nevertheless could be seen at the ballet, the opera and various other expensive social events. Tott earned a few guineas, as he put it, sitting in the Lords, and Fiona was learning to play the harp, with a view to a professional career, but then the baby came. They steadfastly accepted no money from her father. Shortly after her marriage Fiona was summoned back to Dublin. Her mother had died of an overdose — whiskey and drugs — and there were wild rumours flying around. Fiona and her elder brother refused to admit their father and stepmother into the church for the service, where ugly scenes took place in spite of the presence of a bishop and two important politicians. Everything was hushed up, which meant it was the talk of Dublin for at least six weeks. Auntie Alicia as we know adored Tott and now adored Fiona and was prepared to adore the baby. She was delighted when they announced the proposed visit at Easter. Things were rather cramped; there was only one guest room and the rising damp caused worry because of the baby, but on the whole it was very pleasant. Fiona immediately took over the cooking because Auntie Al was such a disaster in the kitchen, though she and Tott were still so happy nothing really mattered. In fact, their extraordinary connubial bliss caused a great deal of amusement amongst their sophisticated friends. The baby, who had been christened Beowulf, nobody quite knew why, was nicknamed Piddles, which was easier on the tongue and on the whole more suitable. As soon as they returned from shopping Auntie Al greeted them all smiles and gave them happy news of the invitation to the thatched mansion. They were delighted; Eddie's cooking was famous, as good as "Batty Betty's."

"We'll take Piddles with us," crooned Fiona. "I will have to feed him at nine anyway."

She had changed in appearance since her first momentous arrival in Ballyfungus. The light brown hair was cut very short; she was wearing blue jeans tucked into high boots and a very tight fitting blue sweater, which certainly reassured one as to her sex. Tott, on the other hand, wore his black hair long; he also were blue jeans and high boots but his check shirt was open at the neck, displaying a long gold chain and a locket which contained a miniature of Mr. Gladstone.

"Piddles is much too young to leave around don't you think, Mrs. Walsh?" Mrs. Walsh nodded approvingly and plugged in the Hoover and the young mother sat down, took off her sweater, and began feeding the baby from the breast. Mrs. Walsh looked at her in shocked surprise; she had to hang on to the Hoover to keep herself from fainting. Was she dreaming or was it real? She knew nothing of the light-hearted manner in which this natural function was carried out nowadays. Fiona had fed her child on buses, in tube stations, at art exhibitions and in the Tate Gallery without causing comment. Nobody could afford baby-sitters, let alone nannies.

Mrs. Walsh paid her usual visit to the Post Office that evening. "I tell you I couldn't believe me two eyes. Pulled the breast out into the open for all the world to see."

Miss O'Kelly tossed her head. "Ah sure, none of them Angular Irish would know decency if you showed it to them."

"And what's goin' on in the Old Mill I wouldn't tarnish me lips be repeating." Mrs. Walsh pursed up her mouth; the nose twitched violently; these were the well-known signals that something atrocious was coming. "She's got a new one."

"Who? Oh that brassy bitch Atkins. T'wouldn't surprise me."

"A Spanish fella; nice lookin' enough but talks foreign. He's a Chillun refugee. Young enough to be her grandson."

"Ah, that's where she'll meet her well-earned calvary. Tell me, how does Tom take it?" Miss O'Kelly leaned forward eagerly; the dentures had descended onto the lower lip; the Dracula stare was there.

Mrs. Walsh averted her gaze and stared at a picture of the Sacred Heart. "He says nothin' but he's looking plenty. Dr. Browne has him on pills." In the distance the angelus was tolling. Both ladies crossed themselves. It was in fact the TV in the next room heralding all the news from the Christian battlefields.

Miss O'Kelly snorted, "I don't rightly approve of Tom adulterating with her, but sure he's a decent Irishman, a good Catholic boy, until he took up with Atkins, but when she takes up with a dirty black foreigner and a Red into the bargain, somethin' should be done."

Mrs. Walsh hastily put on the cycling helmet, as usual she was beginning to repent her own loquacity. "God Bless . . ." She escaped into the street.

Eddie and Colin welcomed the family from the bungalow and didn't even wince when they saw the baby in the carry-cot. The infant was placed on the huge canopied bed in the guest room and then Eddie's well-known dry martinis were shaken up and administered. Later they adjourned to the dining room and enjoyed the deliciously cooked Italian dinner. Conversation was relaxed, and everyone talked at the same time. Tott gave forth a monologue on the London Intelligentsia; Eddie confessed at length that he had just bought a small Picasso drawing and hoped God and Colin would understand. Colin had laid in a quantity of French and German wines and discussed their merits at length with Tott. Fiona talked about the baby's high IQ and Auntie Al rambled on about quilting. All through this Eddie's Siamese cats stalked around the house, ferociously waiting, and the baby was hurriedly rescued from the guest room and later was given the breast, as they say, without any ceremony. The bachelors, though slightly amazed, didn't show it.

"Balooly Woods are under fire again." Eddie brought the dangerous subject up rather tentatively because of Fiona's relationship to Fallon.

"I knew he'd have revenge on Tott after the funeral," Fiona said. As if echoing her, the baby gave vent to an enormous belch.

"We'll fight it again!" exclaimed Tott. "I don't know how, but we'll fight it. Twenty-four Georgian villas are being built where the Castle stood. Land has been acquired near the restoration of the Abbey. The Canon says he'll lie down in front of the bulldozers and let them crush him before they lift a sod near the Abbey." Tott thumped the side of his chair. "Fiona, one thing puzzles me. Why hasn't your Daddy moved into Ferncourt? What did he buy it for?"

"And he bought the cook, Betty," Auntie Al broke in. "I don't mean he bought her, of course. She was the best cook in the county and he snatched her. She's in Dublin now with the Fallons, I hear."

Eddie rose and poured some brandy into the snifters. "Rooney the publican knows a great deal about this. I imagine he has a small share in the scheme. He tells me Ferncourt will have to come down because of its proximity to the Woods. They'll put a road through it. We'll have to move out if things get worse. I've heard of a villa near Verona suitable for two gentlemen."

"Oh, don't," cried Auntie Al, rising in her agitation and clanking her bracelets. "We musn't desert the sinking ship. We must fight on for Beowulf's sake if not for our own." She looked fondly down at the baby who was lying in Fiona's lap, stupefied with food. "Incidentally we'll all meet at Muriel's funeral. We've been asked to the Rectory afterwards. I presume you have too."

"Your presumption is correct," Colin nodded. "All Ballyfungus will be there. Nothing draws us together like a good funeral, provided you're not the corpse."

Colin was right. Mrs. Musgrave's funeral proved to be a splendid opportunity for the Ballyfungus Community to get together in a big way. Everyone had a hand in it. The Miss Croziers arranged the flowers, all white. They had worked all the previous evening in the Cathedral, assisted by Mrs. Walsh and some of her cohorts.

"Very tasty bokays and the wreaths is out of this world," remarked Mrs. W. eyeing the results critically.

"So's poor Mrs. Musgrave," was Tom's cynical retort. He had come over with an offering from the Old Mill. "And maybe she's better off."

"Don't be frettin', Tom. You're well out of it. The Mill I mean, not the world, of course," she tittered. She patted his shoulder. "I told the Archdeacon I'd take some of the wreaths over to the Old People's Home. They'll come in handy there. We can sneak them off the grave when they've all gone."

The beautiful little eighteenth-century Cathedral, just on the other side of the road from the Rectory, was packed with mourners. The service by special request was ecumenical, so one never knew what was coming next, but it provided interesting variety. Muriel's favourite hymns were sung or rather shouted by the congregation.

"When this passing world is done, / When has sunk yon glaring sun," and "Oh what joy and glory must be / Those endless sabbaths the blessed ones see."

The Bishop of Wexlow and Upper Mohare delivered a short but telling eulogy which centred round "our sister Muriel's legs, a burden bravely borne."

The Archdeacon's widowed sister, Violet Something, nobody caught the name, acted as hostess in the Rectory, where a repast of tea, coffee, sherry and sandwiches was served and enjoyed. A low murmur of gossip dominated the proceedings. As Mr. Green, father of six, the Rector of Ballyfungus,

Kinealy and at least two other parishes observed sorrowfully, "even in this hour of sorrow, tongues, alas, wagged."

The Archdeacon's sister was much older than he, and was severely handicapped by deafness and a total ignorance of Ballyfungus social life. Halfway through she was reduced to vague smiles, sign language, and wild guesses. The Archdeacon moved around, just his own big breezy self, in fact, a few meanies remarked, he'd never looked better. His main worry seemed to be the search for a housekeeper, someone who could cook for him. Muriel's legs had not prevented her preparing interesting meals. Then the Rectory was so big and all previous incumbents over the last hundred years had bred enormous families. He would be very lonely now; he did dread the coming years. Suddenly his attention was caught by a familiar face. It was Felicity MacCrea who was assisting Mrs. S., his widowed sister, in pouring tea. How she had changed. A ghost of her former self. She was still pretty though. The sad affair with the powerful stable lad, who now owned his own stud farm, had almost ruined her. Brute! The Archdeacon pushed his way through to her and took her hand. He felt an urge to help her in some way.

"I'm so sorry, Archdeacon," came very softly from Felicity. She looked up at him sadly, the blue eyes brimming with tears. "You will be so lonely."

"Alas, yes," sighed the Archdeacon. "I must look around for someone to housekeep for me."

"Housekeep!" exclaimed Felicity. "I'm out of a job. I can cook for you." She said long afterwards that Muriel must have prompted her from Heaven.

"You," exclaimed the Archdeacon. "You? Housekeep for me?"

"Why not?" said she calmly. "I can ride over on my bike every day, give you lunch and dinner, and ride back."

The Archdeacon gazed at her. Poor little thing. Life had not been kind to her. That wretched cad had hurt her deeply. He felt a sudden surge of hope. Might he not be the instrument, sent by a higher power, to help this sad little creature, fallen as it were, by the wayside. Who could cast aspersions if she came to cook for him? Not even Emerald Walsh — he hoped. "Let me think it over," he said and pressed her hand. "I will phone you. My sister returns to Tunbridge Wells tomorrow. Good Heavens!" the Archdeacon started. He couldn't believe his eyes. Felicity followed his gaze and found it hard to restrain her laughter. Fiona was seated in the bow window feeding the baby, both breasts fully exposed, and the two Catholic curates beside her quite unconcerned. Auntie Al had arrived with the baby after the service; it was felt it might be unwise to bring him into the church.

"They all do it nowadays," murmured Felicity. "Nobody can afford wet nurses or dry nannies." She moved over to the table to assist poor Mrs. Violet S., who was having trouble with the Bishop and the exact amount of sugar he needed in his tea.

"Tott's son will be a highborn anarchist," Colin remarked. He addressed the Archdeacon who was still in shock.

"Do you think so?"

"Undoubtedly. The brutal way he grabbed the breast is extremely characteristic of the genuine terrorist. Very different from his grandfather, Fallon, who would have made no noise at all and rapidly drained it dry. Incidentally, what is Fallon's background? I know he comes from these parts."

"I know very little really except what the old Bishop told me. His father was a small farmer who drank. John was the youngest of eleven children. The Christian Brothers spotted his ability very soon and hoped he would train for the priesthood. I'm told the old Bishop financed him through college but he decided to go into business, luckily for the priesthood," said the Archdeacon drily. "Yes Tott, you want me?" Tott had been hovering in the background.

"Just a few moments, if you don't mind."

The Archdeacon moved away with Tott, and Eddie was joined by Liz Atkins. She was trying to escape the Canon, who was on his favourite subject — the ruins — and on the subject the Canon was a walking sedative.

"The restoration is proceeding slowly but surely. The President is due next week to inspect progress. We have uncovered some interesting titbits about the rich and powerful provost, Alain." He droned on, his cavernous eyes staring into her face. "Not laudable, I fear. In fifteen forty-nine, a tragic year for the True Faith, he rejected the venerable title of Abbot, and the Chronicler tells us gave way to worldly lusts and begat children illicitly."

"How dreadful," murmured Liz and clutched at Eddie as if he were a life jacket. "Oh, Eddie do you want me? Excuse me, Canon, that was fascinating."

She moved away and the Canon undaunted slowly crossed the room to the tea table and addressed himself to the hostess. "It was not until the year sixteen forty-nine when Cromwell's troops arrived in County Wexlow . . ."

"Did you say two lumps, Father?" Mrs. Violet S. looked up at him smiling.

"Sixteen forty-nine," rejoined the Canon, placing his cup on the table.

"Three, four?" the hostess held up the sugar tongs and looked questioningly at him.

"No, Madam. Nine. Sixteen forty-nine," repeated the Canon.

Meanwhile Liz contrived to whisper in Eddie's ear, "I want to ask your advice. Will you be in this evening?"

"Certainly. You needn't tell me. It's about the new boy friend."

"How did you know?" asked Liz wonderingly.

"My dear, nothing in Ballyfungus goes unnoticed. We'll see you about nine."

Suddenly the Archdeacon clapped his hands. He had been deep in conversation with Tott. "Good people," he shouted, "may we have your attention." Everyone was startled into silence except for the deaf hostess who was still trying to get some sense out of the Canon.

"Nine lumps you say, Father?" She was hushed by those nearest.

"Tott, excuse me, Lord Tottenham wishes to make an announcement."

Tott, who was looking very respectable in the well-known business suit, climbed up on a dining room chair. "The Archdeacon, in spite of the sadness of the occasion, has kindly allowed me to say a few words. Balooly Woods are again in danger. We must unite to withstand this threat. I know that four of our bravest and best, though somewhat mistaken in their methods, I allude, of course, to the Ferncourt conspiracy, are not with us. Indeed they begged to be let out on parole or bail, I'm not sure which, to attend the funeral of their good friend, Mrs. Musgrave. Bail was not allowed." (There were cries of shame mingled with some hisses.) Tott continued, "But they urged us to keep the flag flying and we must go on. You will hear from me shortly. Thank you." Discreet muted clapping followed, after all it was a funeral, but most of the company gave the clenched fist and vowed to fight on.

In the kitchen, meanwhile, the recruited helpers were assembled. Mrs. Walsh, Tom Nolan, John Colley, the Rectory gardener and handyman; also Mrs. Walsh's husband Seamus, the bus driver; it was the latter's half day. The kitchen was large, looked out on a gloomy stable yard, and in spite of being April, was very cold. The helpers were all busy helping themselves to a prodigious amount of cakes and tea. Mrs. W. had also smuggled in a bottle of sherry.

"Did ye take them wreaths over to the Old People's Home like I told you?" Mrs. Walsh snapped at her husband. He winked at the others and grinned insolently at his wife.

"I did so," he said. "I gev them to Mother Agatha herself. Oh, they comes just at the right time ses she. One old one went off this mornin'. I'll pop it on her now, ses she, and another is due to go off tomorrow, so I'll lay it beside her on the bed — she's in a coma — and sprinkle a little holy water on it, to keep her, and it, fresh. Me wife," he looked round at the others and winked again, "me wife wants to get her old auntie into the Home, so she's suckin' up to the Reverend

Matron." There was a roar of laughter but Mrs. Walsh tossed her head frowning. She had hoped to preserve the image of simple goodness.

John Colley was padding around in a pair of fiery orange socks. He always took off the gum boots before entering the Rectory. Most of his fellow workers wished he would keep them on; the smell of unwashed and overworked feet was overpowering. "I do be dreadin' a new housekeeper," he groaned. "Poor Mrs. Musgrave, God rest her, let me do as I wished. I've a terrible fear some smart madam will come along and have everyone hoppin'. What do you think, Tom?"

Tom, who was gloomily getting through a raisin loaf and half a pound of butter, said dejectedly, "The whole world is changin' and goin' to rot. I can't do nothin' but eat, the Doctor says it's impulsive and nothing on God's Earth can stop it."

"They're all goin'," Mrs. Walsh jumped up. "Come along we'll be collectin' the things for washin' up."

She popped a few cakes and a loaf or two into the black bag, put it aside, and then rushed into the drawing room.

Punctually at nine Liz arrived, wearing what Eddie described as her thematic robes, grey cloak, black sombrero. The Boys were wearing Victorian smoking jackets, smoking cigars with a bottle of brandy and glasses on the small table beside them.

"How I adore this room, Boys." She clasped her hands and looked around, as if she hadn't seen it at least twice a week for the last seven years. "Eddie you clever thing! I smell hyacinths. Yes, you have pots and pots of them. No perfume like it." She removed the sombrero, threw off the cloak, and sank languidly into a chair. Eddie handed her a glass of brandy.

"What can we do for you?"

"It's like this, Boys. I'm leaving Ballyfungus, selling out."

"Good God!" Colin exclaimed, sitting up. "Why?"

"I've bought a house on the Isle of Man. The Mill will be up for auction next week."

"This is shocking. Why the Isle of Man? Not that you don't belong there," added Eddie drily.

"It's a tax haven. And I have a friend who's going there too."

"Who is this friend? Come to think of it we haven't seen much of you lately."

Eddie leaned forward and stared in her face. Liz winced slightly and looked away.

"My friend is a Chilean refugee. His family was wiped out when Allende was assassinated. He was living with a group of other refugees near Shannon but there didn't seem to be any job for them so they are going away. However, thank God, Fernando has got a job teaching Spanish at a college on the Isle of Man. Colin and Eddie, I want you to meet him." Liz blazed into life. "He's so cultivated so — how can I put it — so strong. We speak the same language."

Eddie snorted. "What did you use with Tom? Signs?"

"That's what I've come about. How can I get rid of Tom?" She held out her glass. "Give me some more brandy, for God's sake, I'm so nervous. Poor Tom, it's like getting rid of a sweet old dog. Eddie, would you break it to Tom?"

Colin burst into laughter and Eddie jumped and waved his arms. "I will not, you wretched woman. Listen stupid, Tom knows. Everyone knows. That's why he's eating himself to death, it's cheaper than drinking."

"He will send you back your presents soon and your letters all tied up with blue ribbon," suggested Colin maliciously. "One thing he won't give back are those excellent dentures you paid for."

Liz sighed. "There were no letters, Colin, he can barely sign his own name, poor thing. Boys, do you think I can take Fernando in soon? He's so lonely."

"You shock me, Liz."

Eddie sat down again and relighted his cigar which, in his excitement, he had allowed to go out.

"That would be a public humilation for Tom. All Bally-fungus would be laughing. Can't you hear Emerald Walsh?

Allow Tom his rights until you go, at least." He quoted, "Poor Tom's a cold."

"Eddie, I couldn't put my heart in it."

Colin, who had been silent, remarked, "Nobody asked about your heart, dear, because like most artists you haven't got one, apart from your work. The heart, all of it, goes into the work. Eddie knows that. Look what he takes from me."

"How horrible!" moaned Liz. She stood up and flung on the cape and the sombrero and stared morosely in the mirror. "And how true!"

"We're all horrible," Colin repeated and smiled complacently.

"Why pretend? Wait, I've had a letter from Doctor Josh. Would you like to hear it?"

Liz paused in the doorway and returned to her chair. "Yes, poor old darling. I miss him. Funny, you can say that about a murderer." She sat down and helped herself to another nip of brandy.

Eddie read slowly and with infinite relish: " 'Dear Boys, thank you for your good letter which we all four enjoyed. Too bad about Muriel but she was never much good to the Archdeacon. Let's hope he finds a more worthy bedmate, one who can open and close the legs. Your account of the funeral made us all homesick. My most enjoyable memories of Bally-fungus were the funerals; usually because the deceased was often a public nuisance and the world was much better off without him — or her. Incidentally, how's Mairin O'Kelly? Now *there's* a funeral I would have revelled in. I am persecuted here by one of the patients who's a religious maniac! He walks around all day singing hymns and chatting with the Deity about this and that. He begged me to come up to his room and take holy communion. Poor fellow, all he can procure for the ceremony is grape juice and Jacob's cream crackers. "Listen," I said to him, his name is Talbot, he's a brewer, "I consider religion of any kind to be the root of all evil. Take a look at the planet! Everywhere someone is fighting or killing in the name of religion. They invented God because they needed some father figure to heap all their guilt onto and then whine to for forgiveness. How often do you hear those sickly phrases: God willing, God save us, God help us, God be with you, or the parting shot over the shoulder God bless. . . ." He threw the grape juice at me. Hopeless. I very much fear the girls are failing; slowing up. Her psychiatrist told Albie to leave off the wigs. "You're hiding behind them," he said, "it's a form of infantilism." She's out in the open now, wigless, but still infantile. The biting and scratching and slapping over the bridge game is no better. Mabs has receded further and further back into her African past. Addressing the resident psychiatrist as "boy" doesn't help. Thanks for the books. *Some Victorian Poisoners* I enjoyed, but it made me sad. Poor old Toegreen. How we fumbled our job.' "

Eddie folded up the letter and put it away. "Fine old fellow. A totally independent spirit. You're off Liz?"

"Yes, I have so much business to do; it's frightening."

"And that's the end of her," said Eddie when the door closed upon Liz Atkins. "And that's the end of the Old Mill. Colin, do you think we can take it without her — and the Ferncourt foursome — who is there left?"

A week later all Ballyfungus was shocked by the news that the Old Mill was up for sale. There was no question of rumour, there it was, photograph and all, advertised in the Irish *Times* and also in the English papers. What was Liz doing? Who was this handsome Chilean and what would poor Tom do? They discussed the matter one evening after dinner at Racketstown House. They were all seated in the dim library drinking instant coffee — nobody could possibly afford the real thing; Goggins was charging £3.00 a pound. Alexis was present for one night only, tomorrow he was flying to the USA with loot for his gallery.

"I don't see how Liz affords this sort of thing. She's just paid an enormous sum for a mansion on the Isle of Man, Eddie tells me," sighed Mother MacCrea.

"She'll get fifty thousand for the Old Mill. And then she

sells well. She's rated as one of the top British painters. Liz has no problems except her nymphomania. Even though she's gone conceptual. Mother, do you have to keep all these boring dogs?" Alexis kicked a very old corgi away from him.

Mrs. MacCrea looked up startled, she was picking fleas off a basset hound. "Darling, they're so sweet. Such dear old friends!"

"I must say, Felicity, the cuisine has improved since you came home," remarked the brother patronizingly. "You learned something in the Silver Platter."

"I could make a casserole of cockroaches now and you wouldn't know," said Felicity proudly. "They often did in the Platter. Incidentally, Mummy, I'm going to be the Archdeacon's housekeeper. He phoned this afternoon and suggested we should try it out."

"What!" the whole family exclaimed, even Father MacCrea woke up into a semblance of life. "You don't mean live there?" squeaked Mrs. MacCrea.

"No," Felicity laughed. "He's much too proper. I will bike over in the mornings and bike back in the afternoons."

"I suppose it's all right," Mrs. MacCrea said slowly. She was thinking with some trepidation of Felicity's stable-girl job and the resulting scandal. But surely the Archdeacon was a man of honour.

Felicity jumped up and faced her family. What a shabby lot they were. She hated the crumbling old house which smelled of dry rot. That's what the MacCreas and many others like them were, dry rotten. She looked at her feckless father, who had let an inherited estate slip through his nicotine-stained fingers. Her silly mother, who was totally incapable, and her two spoiled snobbish brothers, who had never done an honest day's work in their lives. Anglo-Irish gentry who believed life owed them everything. At least her old lover Paddy worked and achieved success through his own efforts and the Archdeacon was a good man and greatly loved in the Diocese.

"I'm going to do it," Felicity stamped her foot and glared at her brother. "I will give him a good meal in the middle of the day, and leave a light supper for him in the fridge. If the weather's bad he will fetch me in the car."

"He's paying, I presume," asked Alexis. "The old bugger can afford it. He has substantial private means."

"Twenty pounds a week, what the Platter paid me for slave labour and he's not an old bugger." She looked scornfully at her effete brother who was languidly stretched out on the sofa.

"How do you know, dear?" Alexis smiled at her.

"I just know." She sat down breathing hard.

"Well, there's only one way to find out," Alexis laughed, and his laugh, as many people remarked, was worse than his bite.

Mrs. MacCrea looked at her son reproachfully. "How can you be so coarse, Lexy? The Archdeacon is old enough to be her father and he's a very good man. Keep still, Reggie. Do stop scratching. I'm only trying to help you dear." She was addressing the basset hound who was snarling in the most unpleasant manner.

"But Felicity is not a good girl." Alexis stood up and stretched, yawning prodigiously. "Never mind, Felly, I'm only joking. You could do worse than marry him. He's a big healthy old fella and he has money and there is some valuable silver there. I wonder has he thought of selling?"

"No, he hasn't, Lexy, and I'm not going to suggest it. No, I will have a nice job. I love cooking and he's so sweet to work for."

"Even if you don't marry the old chap he might leave you money, so stick around."

"You're disgusting, Lexy."

"My dear sister, I'm just practical. Somebody has to be around here."

The news of Liz Atkin's departure was received in the presbytery with infinite sadness. Father Kevin had come to depend on her for generous help and encouragement with

243

the Hodge Podge Players, and then think of all those wonderful parties in the Mill to which the young curates were always invited! Even the Canon lamented. In spite of her scandalous love-life he liked Liz and deeply appreciated her openhandedness where the restoration of the Abbey was involved. No, the general concensus was one of deep loss. Nobody could take her place and everyone wished the Chilean refugee had never been born. "It's down, down, down," groaned Father Kevin one morning in May. He was putting on his raincoat as he spoke for he had been summoned to a cottage in the mountains to administer the last rites to a dying man.

Father Dermot was setting out also. He had to visit the Old People's Home, where, if they weren't actually dead, they were certainly dying.

"Never has there been two years like the last two," said Father Kevin, and he tapped the barometer. "Down, down, down! Will you listen to this?" He held up his hand and ticked each horror off on his fingers. "Lady Vigors always good for a laugh, gone; the old Doctor the kindest of men, gone; the General a decent sort, gone; Mrs. Travers, her sister, all four locked up in Dublin. The Archdeacon widowed . . ."

"Muriel was no loss," commented Father Dermot. "He's looking great, breezed into the Boys Club last night, fit as a fiddle! Incidentally, Miss MacCrea is housekeeping for him," Father Dermot smiled, a rather naughty smile.

"Why not?" said Father Kevin shortly. "She's also stage manager for the Hodge Podge. She only works at the Rectory by day."

"Glad to hear it," replied the unquenchable Father Dermot. "I wouldn't want her to be there at night."

"Heavens man, he's old enough to be her father."

Father Dermot laughed. "My grandfather sired a son when he was over seventy, and wasn't Michael Collins' father in his late seventies when the great man was born. I tell you there's nothing can't be done if you have the will and," he added mischievously, "a young wife."

"It's disgusting," moaned Father Kevin, not to be comforted, "but then everything's disgusting. The old Castle a pile of stones; Ferncourt about to come down; Balooly Woods to be blasted. Tott is still fighting that. I'm lunching at the bungalow tomorrow to discuss another anti-Fallon Campaign."

Father Dermot slapped his gloomy colleague on the back. "Cheer up, man. Tott's always worth a bit of gas!" He opened the hall door and peered out. " 'Tis the merry month of May and the sky is black and the rain lashing. James' Street, it's the original flood." He pulled up the collar of his raincoat.

Father Kevin followed him. "Send out a dove Lord upon the waters," he shouted up at the sky.

Father Dermot put up the umbrella and stepped gingerly over a puddle; he looked back at his companion. "You're facing due North man. No dove will fly in from there."

The De Bracey bungalow was throbbing with life when Father Kevin arrived for lunch the next day after serving Mass. The table was laid in the small dining room. Fiona was moving around in the kitchen and Auntie Al was reading the Sunday paper. It was a sunny spring day, the hall door was open, and there was a branch of apple blossom in a vase on the mantlepiece. Tott, who had been, as usual, reading on the toilet seat in the bathroom, emerged to greet the curate. He was in blue jeans, a silver chain with a large silver cross around his neck."

"Well Tott, you're looking great. Marriage suits you." Father Kevin shook his hand warmly and saluted Fiona who was peeping around the kitchen door, smiling at him. She was wearing an enormous butcher's apron and a white kerchief concealed her hair.

"I'm feeling very well," said the Earl dolefully. "It's just that we don't have any money. When single I could rattle along on my income but two more mouths to feed and you're on the breadline."

"Oh Tott," cried Fiona reproachfully; she was in the room

now, staggering under the weight of a huge frying pan. "Our flat in London is charming. High ceilings, a bow window, and a stained glass window in the lavatory; you couldn't ask for more. And we do have enough to eat. People ask us out, though not so much since the baby," she sighed.

Tott kissed her. "Goodness, the weight of that pan. I'll carry it back for you."

"It's a relic of the Castle." Auntie Al looked up from her knitting. "Everything in the kitchen was over life-size including the cook Mrs. Flynn."

Tott returned from the kitchen with a bottle of sherry. "Sit down, Father Kev. Sherry? *Voila*. What's the news of late, apart from the Balooly horror."

"Ballyfungus is facing total disaster and spoliation, that's all I can report." The curate perched himself on the well-known piano stool. "The Fungusport fiasco was apparently only a prelude to worse." He sighed deeply.

"That was a shocker. I'd like to have met the crazy girl director, Lesley something. Auntie Al told me all about her."

Father Kev coloured. "She was not crazy," he said shortly. "She was a —" he paused, "a great director." He still could hardly bear to hear Lesley's name mentioned. Tott who was sensitive to other people's vibrations felt he should change the subject.

"Demonstrations don't get us anywhere; the last if you may remember was a total bust, though I must say it did delay things, but here we are up against it again. The awful thing is, Kev, that we're fighting unseen forces. Who are these men? How does one get to them? Is their buying power so vast, so worldwide that the little people are swallowed up? Those unfortunate people in Limerick were licked. They had to accept the asbestos factory. That town whatyoumaycallit in Connemara had to accept the Japanese factory which we are told if there's one leak the whole countryside will be poisoned for years. I know John Fallon is one of the power men but compared with the biggies he's a pygmy. Sometimes

I wonder if Fiona should," he sank his voice, "try to see her father and appeal to him on behalf of Balooly."

"I think she should, Tott. I really do. Has he seen the baby?"

Tott finished his sherry and poured another for himself and Father Kevin. "No, she won't go near him since her mother died."

Lady de Bracey flung down her knitting and rose from her chair. She was in a state of unusual agitation. "I won't have Fiona given the rotten job of asking her father for anything after what she's been through with him. Listen Tott, in my lifetime I've seen my whole world vanish. The Castle is gone, we have no money. The Fung once so clear and beautiful is hopelessly polluted. The poor women at Daisy Lodge tell me they're ruined. No one can fish in the Fung anymore so they have no guests. I don't say my world was a good one, in many ways it was a bad world, but when it went one did hope for something better and there is nothing better. It is worse. I feel as if Ireland is hopelessly corrupted by greed and marauding foreigners and as for beauty who cares. No, Fiona must not humiliate herself. Though I must say," here Auntie Al wiped the tears from her eyes, "I do believe John Fallon must have some good in him or he would not have a daughter like Fiona."

Fiona impulsively flung her arms around the old woman's neck and kissed her. "Thank you, Auntie Al. Oh I do so love you."

Father Kevin, a feeling man as we know, felt a lump rising in his throat. Why, he thought sadly, should a simple declaration of love bring forth tears? Maybe because there's so little of it. Then they all four started laughing and crying and Auntie Al said she was starving. Fiona recollected lunch and hurried back into the kitchen. In a few minutes an enormous Spanish omelet was placed on the table accompanied by potato chips and salad.

"I don't know what to say about anything anymore," exclaimed Father Kevin, "except of course my Faith." He added.

Tott was tossing the salad and Fiona was dishing out the omelet. Father Kevin's stomach was rattling with hunger. "I could eat a horse," he murmured pulling up to the table.

"Too expensive," said Tott severely. "We can't even afford carrion. I found myself looking hungrily at a tinker's pony the other day!"

The baby woke up in the other room and began crying. The fond mother hastened into the bedroom and returned carrying the heir to nothing slung across her shoulder. "Poor little man," she crooned, "his own grandfather is going to murder him with fumes from a poison factory. Tott, bring in the caramel custard darling while I feed Piddles."

"You're a great cook, Fiona," exclaimed Father Kevin patting his stomach. "That was a gorgeous meal."

Fiona nodded proudly. "I'm thinking of giving up the harp and going into cooking. Though Tott was writing lovely laments for me."

"Talking of laments," exclaimed Auntie Al, "I had a letter from poor Mabs Vigors. I must read it to you all; it's so interesting. Now where are my reading glasses. They're on Dr. Johnson, Tott. Thank you." She put on the glasses and read, occasionally looking up and uttering cries of distress or sympathy. She commanded a most attentive audience; it's not often you hear from a convicted murderess.

" 'Everything goes well here if being in a madhouse can be called well. The men Artie and Josh I fear are failing fast. Men do decay faster than women. Josh shouts terribly and I dare not describe his dental problems. His dentures are constantly turning up in saucers and ashtrays. Yesterday there had to be a prodigious search, the whole Clinic was alerted and a reward offered. They were found in the pocket of his dressing gown. As for Artie's swollen feet he cannot wear any form of footwear now. The Clinic found things for him like huge sponge bags which I believe are used on the feet of elephants in the circus. There are at least three poets here. Alcohol need I say. One of them Fergus Maloney has taken a fancy to me. He tells me all his problems and they *are* problems. "Why Fergus," I asked, "why have you tried to kill yourself?" "Don't you understand, Madame V.," that's his silly name for me, "don't you know that the only way for a poet to get published is to perish — preferably by his own hand. You are then discovered but dead of course. First you write intensely personal frank poems about your death wish and then comes wish fulfillment. I myself tried drowning four times; I've been dragged out of gas ovens barely breathing; cut down from hanging almost dead, and then dammit didn't I lie on the railway track on the right side while the express thundered past me on the left. Somehow or other I'll do it." He's given me a whole bundle of his gloomy poems to hold in case of a successful attempt. A retired witch — she's in for senility — has taught me how to make a wax figure, utter the right incantations and I stick a pin in it every evening. It's a wonderful likeness of John Fallon. Albie sends love.' "

Fiona screamed, "I don't like that. If she puts a curse on Daddy it might descend to Piddles. Do tell her not to do it, Auntie."

"I'll write this evening. Don't worry, dear."

"I must say I think Fergus Maloney is right. A lot of women poets have done it in the US with considerable success. Lately my poems have been rejected by everyone. Maybe I *should* kill myself." Tott threw himself into a chair, the picture of gloom.

There were of course cries of "don't be an idiot" from everyone and Auntie Al changed the subject by calling for coffee.

During the weeks that followed Felicity MacCrea found her new job extremely pleasant. The Archdeacon was so undemanding, and so impressed by her cooking, she could not help but feel consoled, more sure of herself than she had been for many a long day. One wet cold morning she arrived at the Rectory drenched (she had stopped off to shop on the way) and the Archdeacon ran into her, as she was putting her bicycle away in the potting shed. "My dear child," he exclaimed. "This is dreadful. This cannot be allowed. Why didn't you phone me? I would have gone for you."

Felicity removed the kerchief and shook out her yellow locks. Looking at her in dismay the Archdeacon's heart smote him. Was she overworked? Was he exploiting this frail creature? "It's all right, Mr. Musgrave, really. I don't mind the wet and you must be fed."

"My dear child, not at that price. I won't have it. You simply phone me when the weather is like this, and I will fetch you. Understand?" He took her by the shoulders and shook her gently. (Good Lord, how thin she is!) "Now Felicity, I must assert myself. This is not to happen again." He was holding her by the shoulders and gazing down into her upturned face when John Colley suddenly appeared at the door of the potting shed. He surveyed the scene, first with incredulity, and then with cynical amusement.

"Oh, Colley, is that you?" the Archdeacon backed away from his young housekeeper. "I'm looking for some strong string, or better still, some wire. A picture has come down in the library."

"More than the pictures comin' down," said Colley to himself. He was the father of fifteen children and a man of strong, primitive urges. According to Colley there was only one approach to women, instant coition. The Archdeacon, in spite of his clerical background, was normal, and simply acting like any man should with a young pretty girl. He mentioned the scene to his wife that evening.

"The ould cock's in heat and it won't be any time before she drags him to the altar."

"Well, don't be lettin' on about it John; not a word before that bitch outa' hell, Emerald Walsh. The Archdeacon's a decent enough man and he never got much canoodling from the wife. Sure they slept in separate beds as long as I was cleanin' for them." Mrs. Colley peered into a large pot which contained a monstrous stew.

"What's in that?" Colley peered into the pot and sniffed.

"Innerds," was the laconical reply.

Then came the afternoon when a gale blew in from the Atlantic during the afternoon, without any warning. Felicity, looking out of the kitchen window at the lashing rain was really afraid to ride home. What was she to do? There were several spare bedrooms in the Rectory and plenty of blankets and bed linen, but what would her mother say? Her reputation was so shaky since the affair with the stable lad, but surely nobody thought of that anymore. She dialled Racketstown and the tremulous voice of her mamma answered. "Mummy, I have to spend the night here; some trees have come down across the avenue."

"Oh, dear, but what does the Archdeacon say?"

"He says I'm not to go home under any circumstances and I'm to spend the night here." This was a lie; she had not yet consulted the Archdeacon.

"Well, I suppose you better stay. It is a dreadful storm. I'll see you sometime tomorrow. Take care."

Take care of what? One would think the poor harmless Archdeacon was a sex maniac. She opened the door of the library and peeped in. He was at his desk administering the affairs of the diocese with an open Agatha Christie thriller beside him. He looked up at her.

"Mr. Musgrave, I dare not ride back in this storm. If it's all right with you, I'll spend the night here. And I'll make you a lovely dinner. Truly."

"I was thinking the same thing, my dear." The Archdeacon rose and peered out of the window. "Indeed, yes. It's quite impossible. They've cancelled a vestry meeting in Fungusport. Did you phone your parents?"

"I did, and they thought it was a wonderful idea. Thank you." She paused at the door and turned to him smiling. "Isn't it fun?"

"Fun?" the Archdeacon looked at her surprised.

"Yes, think of it, we will be alone together."

She closed the door and vanished. Fun? Alone? The Archdeacon sent up a short prayer for guidance and slowly returned to his letter writing — and Agatha Christie. At seven o'clock she called him into the dining room. She had lighted four massive Victorian candlesticks and there was a delightful meal awaiting him. The table was so long (it seated twenty in the old days), Felicity sat beside him on his right. He appreciated it even more because he usually had his supper on a tray in the library. There was a chicken curry with rice, crispy string beans, perfectly cooked, followed by a raspberry mousse and cheese and crackers. Feeling slightly insane the Archdeacon opened a bottle of wine (he had an excellent cellar) and later, after she'd done the dishes, Felicity brought the coffee tray into the library. Though it was early June the Archdeacon lighted a fire because of the dampness and pulled the curtains across the bow window. It was then that Felicity broached a delicate subject.

"The Archdeacon of Ballyfungus, the venerable George Musgrave," she quoted at him smiling. "I can't think of you as venerable. It sounds like Father Christmas."

"It is rather oppressive," he agreed, lighting his pipe.

"You certainly don't look at all venerable. You look years younger than my father." She paused a moment and then knelt down beside the fire almost at the venerable feet. "May I call you something besides Archdeacon? It's so longwinded. I obviously can't call you Sir or Master. Could I just call you by your Christian name, George?"

The Archdeacon puffed on his pipe for a moment. "Well, I don't know . . ."

"What about Uncle George or Cousin George?"

"That would be a subterfuge. There is no relationship involved."

"What about Archie, short for Archdeacon?" she asked wide-eyed.

At that the Archdeacon burst into laughter. "I think George is best," he agreed but added in more cautious note. "But only while we're together. I think it would be wiser to be formal in public."

"Oh, thank you."

She sprang up and sat down on the sofa facing the fire-place. Here Muriel, he remembered, used to loll with her stubby legs up, snoozing, sometimes snoring. There was noth-ing wrong with Felicity's legs and she was obviously wide awake and pleased to be with him. Being human the Arch-deacon was flattered.

"George darling, have you any old photograph albums I could look at? I adore old albums."

The Archdeacon dazedly walked to a bookshelf and picked out some albums (must tell her not to say darling). It was very cozy, he couldn't help thinking, sitting there in the fire-light, the curtains shutting out the storm. She might be my daughter, he thought, well not exactly a daughter, more what the Victorians called a valued friend. There she sat huddled in a curious position on the sofa, her legs tucked under her, poring over family groups, snapshots of people long since dead, characters she had never known. She must be half my age thought the Archdeacon sadly. He had just struck fifty and she, he knew, was only twenty-five. There were a great many photos of the Archdeacon at school and college and lots of him when he played rugby football for Ireland. How did he come to marry that deadly little Muriel, Felicity was pon-dering, because the Archdeacon was very attractive then and not really so bad now. He had not put on weight, his hair was plentiful, a nice iron grey, and he was in very good condition. The Boys Club, which he administrated with Father Dermot, provided plenty of exercise. She sighed as she looked around the warm spacious room. The Rectory was very comfortable; it spoke loudly and clearly of money. Alexis was right; there's security behind the Rectory, and she hated Racketstown; she really did. Since she had taken the job with the Archdeacon her brothers had been so boringly, coarsely jocular. They would taunt her with, "Is there a wee one on the way yet?" or worse: "Has the Archdeacon laid rude hands on you yet?" Would she ever live down that wretched affair with Paddy?

The Archdeacon rose and threw another log on the fire.

"Do you have any night things?" he asked delicately. "I'm sure there are some of Muriel's things around still."

"No thanks, George, I never sleep in night things, in the summer, only in the winter."

"I see. Yes." He moved over to the window and peered out. "The Fung is in spate but the wind seems to be abating."

"Don't you think, George, it would be best if I slept here all the time?" Felicity assumed a business-like air. "It would be more professional."

The Archdeacon was genuinely puzzled. "Professional? I don't understand."

"I'd be a real housekeeper then. You see, George," she came closer and looked up at him, her pink mouth a little open. "You see, George, I'd be up in the morning to give you a real breakfast. You wouldn't have to creep around at dawn boiling dreary eggs. . . . See."

"But my dear . . ."

"Truly, it would be best. You don't know how I hate home. They couldn't afford to send me to college, so I have no profession, and I'm not clever. I'm only good at housework and cooking. And as for Dublin it was sheer hell in that basement. Please."

She moved towards the perplexed Archdeacon and put her arm through his and with the other hand patted his chest. "Please George!!"

"People might — well — say things. There would, I fear, be a great deal of gossip. Ballyfungus is a small place and my position . . ."

"But you're above suspicion."

Anybody looking in on the scene might have thought differently; to all intents and purposes the young housekeeper appeared to be in her employer's arms.

"No one is above suspicion," said the Archdeacon sadly.

"Oh, yes, yes," still clinging to him she looked at him pleadingly. "You see I've always looked up to you ever since I was a little girl. You were like a big teddy bear, the sort you sleep with, I have one still . . ."

The Archdeacon started. He removed himself from her innocent embrace and sat down at his desk. "I'll say good night, my dear. I must work on my sermon."

"You're not angry with me?" She crept over to his chair and stood behind him.

"No, no, of course not."

"I do love this house. It's been full of good people all its life. I don't mean saints or religious fanatics, I mean good people, who do their best, like you George."

Who could resist this? The Archdeacon was deeply moved. He reached up, felt for her small cold hand, and pressed it. "I'll talk to your mother tomorrow morning and see what she thinks."

"I don't care what she thinks. I'm grown up and can decide for myself. Don't treat me as a child. I've had a bitter experience and learned from it."

She snatched her hand away and moved towards the door. "You see I could make a little self-contained flat in what used to be the maid's room and I can lock the doors between."

"Between what?"

"Between us, so nobody can talk. That's the professional attitude." And she added. "I can often have people to stay."

"People to stay?" the Archdeacon raised his voice almost to a shout; he swiveled around in the chair and faced her. "What sex?"

"Girls, of course. Friends of mine from Dublin." She turned on the Archdeacon fiercely. "You don't think I'd have men in. . . . How cruel. I thought better of you, George, to throw the past at me!!!"

The Archdeacon rose from his chair and walked quickly towards her, he caught her before she could open the door. "My darl . . . my dear child, I didn't mean to. Of course not. God bless you." Gently, daringly he kissed her forehead. "This can be worked out."

Though the mice were positively rollicking behind the wainscoting, and the wind still moaned around the Rectory, Felicity slept soundly curled up in the foetal position with her arms round a late Victorian bolster. The Archdeacon, however, had a wretched night; for some reason when he did drop off to sleep he moved into nightmares of satanic revelry merging into what seemed to be a reenactment of the rape of the Sabine women, in which he was playing an active part. Not good.

The weeks rolled by, and a long hot summer, which gradually developed into a drought, settled down on Ballyfungus. Many letters were written to the papers from concerned citizens protesting against the proposed factory in Co. Wexlow. The Government spokesmen said it was perfectly safe and that extraordinary precautions would be taken to prevent accidents. They dwelt long and lovingly on the employment it would provide and the great boost it would give to Irish industry. As to where the profits would go a discreet silence was maintained and any explanations were so convoluted it was impossible for the ordinary man in the streets to understand them. Meanwhile the "Save Balooly Woods" Committee formed by the Earl was drifting away and sinking into the usual state of apathy and despair common to such well-meant but off-beat causes.

Sinister changes were taking place in Ballyfungus itself heralding worse to come. Goggins supermarket was enlarged and became the first Irish Supersonic Market because, as Goggins put it, of the boom, business was booming, which meant customers were being steadily and systematically robbed under rising inflation. It was not booming at Daisy Lodge. The lack of visitors to the guest house was put down to the pollution of the Fung, which precluded any fishing. No anglers came.

"We'll have to tighten our belts," said poor Maud ruefully. "No holiday for us this winter."

The Boys received letters from the Isle of Man describing Liz Atkins' sinful bliss and the beauty of the scenery, and she was painting six hours a day as if inspired. To the rage of The Boys the Old Mill had been purchased by two more tax evaders. An author who specialized in science fiction and his sixth wife who had been an Australian ballet dancer.

"Primus balletina," explained Mrs. Walsh who had already been hired to clean. "That's what she is. Stands on her tiptoes half the day. Has a neck like a giraffe. You could see her eatin' the tops off trees and wears them black skin-tight bathin' dresses. No class reely. No children. Can't have them. Too deesicated says she. He can only write when he's drunk. I never seen the like."

Lady de Bracey was worried, dreadfully worried. The Art Centre was almost bankrupt. Nobody could afford to buy any luxuries and she, if things went on like this, would not be able to pay her helpers. Tott, Fiona and Piddles were still in the bungalow. They had broken it to her in an absentminded manner that the flat in Clapham had been rented to an Arab, a minor member of the entourage of an oil sheikh. "Only for a few months. He's a junior oily Arabian. The rent we get from him will almost pay our debts. We'll be out by October, Auntie dear."

One beautiful golden evening they sat out on the little terrace, eating ice cream, and debated the future, which looked very bleak. "The rumble and thunder of those cement mixers and bulldozers is so wearing," lamented Lady de Bracey. She had aged in the last months. "They've surrounded dear Ferncourt with a ring of steel."

"I've lost hope, Auntie," Tott buried his face in his hands. "I can't get anyone to fight, and I don't know who to fight."

"I owe Goggins two hundred pounds," moaned Auntie Al. "And I simply can't pay him."

"I'm sorry, dear Auntie. I haven't a bean till next month when the Arab pays me. I'll hand it all over to you. Where the dickens does the money go? We don't smoke. An occasional glass of wine is all we allow ourselves. I might get a job on the Georgian building site. I've always craved to wear a hardhat."

"I won't let you, you might get killed," said Fiona. "Why don't I try for a job singing laments to my harp in the Grand

Hotel in Fungusport. I forgot, Daddy owns it. That wouldn't be good. What would you all like for supper? We'll eat it out here, it's so warm."

"Pheasant under glass, asparagus with hollandaise sauce," said Tott sadly. "That's what I'd like."

"What you'll get darling is cold ham and the spaghetti that was left-over from Monday night. Do you hear a motor bike?"

Tott rose, walked down to the gate and looked towards the village. "As I live and breathe the Emerald Bile is approaching. What does she want? It's nearly six o'clock."

Sure enough the great woman dismounted at their gate, parked her machine and approached them, obviously pregnant with bad news.

"Well, how's yous all? And how's the doatie babby?" She put on an air of great concern about the child though they well knew she couldn't be less interested. Animals and children were not Mrs. Walsh's speciality. News, and news alone was her contribution to society. "Well, hell's broke loose at last." She sat down in a deck chair, and removed the helmet. "The news that's goin' you wouldn't believe. Hold on to your hearing aids. Christmas is coming. Did you happen to hear the ambulance a couple of hours back?" Nobody it seemed had heard any strange noises. "That's odd now. Well I'll tell you. I was on my way back from Mr. Fox and Mr. Evans, it's their day, when there was a terrible commotion in the village. Traffic all tied up and Gardai everywhere. Wasn't a letter bomb received in the hotel addressed to the company offices what's taking down Balooly. It blew the fingers off of the sekaterry what opened it. She was took off to the orspital."

"How awful," exclaimed Lady de Bracey. She was echoed by Fiona and Tott, who were listening fascinated.

"And if that wasn't enough, didn't one of the fellas workin' on the development have cement poured on him and they can't even find the body!"

"I never heard such a thing," exclaimed Tott. "Are you sure it's true?"

"True as God. And they tells me the first tree to be

chopped down in Balooly is tomorrow or the day after. Ah, poor Tom Nolan always said there's a curse on anyone who touched the trees. Poor Tom, God rest his soul."

"Is he dead?" asked Tott in horror.

"Gone to Australia. Same thing. We'll never see him again."

"How did he get there?" asked Tott, who was beginning to feel as if he was living in a science fiction world.

"Wouldn't ye know." Mrs. W. pursed up her lips and twitched her nose. The only creature in the animal kingdom who could beat her at nose twitching was a domesticated rabbit. "Miss Atkins paid for his air ticket, single one-way, and he's gone to his brother. A place with an odd name. Bangbang. Poor Tom. Ah well, he's a fine figure of a man, he'll pick up something out there. There's nothing Tom can't put his hand to . . ."

"Well he certainly put it to Miss Atkins," commented Tott cynically.

This witticism was received with a hoot of laughter from Mrs. Walsh and shocked murmur from Auntie Al. Mrs. Walsh rose regretfully and moved towards the door.

"Ta now. I'll be seeing you next Saturday. Oh and Mrs. Tott dear, there's an awful lot of mumps around. An emperdermic. Keep the babby home. But if he does get it don't worry your head. Me ould Granny said, and there was nothin' she didn't know about sickness, she said wrap the child in a blanket, take it to the pigsty, rub the child's head to the back of a pig, and the mumps will leave it and pass from the child to the animal. Cheerybye!" Mission accomplished she was off, speeding homewards.

Fiona rose from her chair, where she had been sitting transfixed by Mrs. Walsh's reminiscences. "It makes me sick to think of a pig with mumps. I must beat up some sort of supper. Salad with hard-boiled eggs. I'm so frightened, do you think Piddles could get the mumps?"

"No, but I could," said Tott, "and at my age group it hits a vital spot."

259

Fiona paused at the kitchen door. "Your heart?"

"No, me balls," said Tott, jumping up. "Excuse me, Auntie Al, I didn't mean to be so coarse, it's Mrs. W., she does things to me. I'm going to take a walk before supper. I might walk as far as Ferncourt and see what's going on."

It was Saturday evening so the road between Ballyfungus and Balooly was deserted. Blackberries were ripening in the hedges. We can always live on berries, reflected Tott ruefully and they say nettles make a tasty soup. For half a mile across the fields yellowed by the drought, he saw the distant outline of the Woods. Tott jumped across the road-side ditch and stood for a while leaning his arms on the loose stone wall, gazing out upon the landscape. In spite of the calm loveliness of the summer evening he felt as if he were shrouded in unhappiness. What was it? Intimations of mortality? Suddenly Tott smiled. Two herons were standing by a small pond in the lower field silently contemplating the water. Suddenly one of them uttered a wild cry, flapped his widespread wings, rose in the air, and flew towards the Wood. There used to be a heronry near here, Tott remembered. Could be one still. But you're doomed old heron, you're doomed. He reflected then, as he leaned on the wall, of all the wild creatures which were vanishing from the world. Golden eagles, the swift hares, secretive otters in the river banks and all the creatures of the seven seas, whales, baby seals, the intelligent innocent dolphins, the wild seabirds drowned in oil, dying on the beaches. And what of the pink and silver salmon leaping the weirs, ah yes, what of them? Thousands had already died in the Fung, poisoned by the effluent from some wretched factory. But how can I fight it, he thought despairingly. This infernal factory may poison all of us. I am an unarmed soldier fighting a faceless enemy. My enemy, thought Tott turning away, has bought the world and I have no weapons with which to fight him. He trudged along the road, his shoulders hunched, his hands sunk in his pockets, and within a short time the gates of Ferncourt were in sight. A few yards further was the entrance to the main trail through Balooly. Already the enemy was massing his weapons; bulldozers, haulage trucks, electric saws were there waiting. Slowly Tott walked up the melancholy avenue. The lawns so trimly tended in the old days were now unkept meadows. He peered in the downstairs windows. The rooms were bare, stripped of trappings. Carpets, pictures, silver, china had all gone under the hammer. Children and grand-children could not afford to live in the house and they certainly couldn't afford the taxes so it had fallen into John Fallon's rapacious hands. Or worse to the property developers. Squatters might come! Squatters! Why hadn't he thought of it before? He, and Fiona and the baby would move into Ferncourt, squat there, and the house could not be torn down over their heads. It would hold up the destruction of the house and possibly the Woods. And the piquant fact that Fiona was Fallon's daughter would make very unpleasant publicity for the Combine. Tott's mind was made up. He charged down the avenue and sprinted all the way back to the bungalow, arriving breathless. He was surprised to see Mrs. Walsh's motor scooter was parked outside. What was she up to? What meant this second coming? She greeted him at the door.

"Left me specs behind. I forgot to tell yous all John Colley says that the Archdeacon is going to marry Miss MacCrea this autumn, and his wife not seven months gone. They say them that marry in autumn die in the spring."

"Men have married their cooks before this, but not for love. For food," said Tott. Exhaustedly he sank into a chair. He inadvertently sat on the harp which emitted an unearthly twang.

"There you are," cried Mrs. Walsh alight with triumph. "That's a soul passing."

"Mrs. Walsh," Tott jumped up and grabbed her by the arm. "Mrs. Walsh, I want you to spread the news. Fiona, and I, and the baby, and possibly, Auntie Al will move into Ferncourt tomorrow morning, early before the men arrive and we will squat there, and we won't move, even if they pull the place down over our heads and kill us."

Fiona shrieked and hugged the baby to her breast and Auntie Al exclaimed, "Tott, you're mad."

"Mr. Tott you're right," said Mrs. Walsh. "You was right last year and you're right this year. They've destroyed all Ballyfungus, so they have. I'm off and I'll get the town on your side, so I will. God bless." She was off like a flash and riding hell for leather, a winged messenger of the gods.

"I can trust her to do a job. She'll have the whole county alerted."

"Oh, Tott, is it all right for the baby? Even though it's early September it will be cold there, and no furniture."

"We'll bring mattresses along and there are plenty of fireplaces. We can buy turf and bring loads of candles." He was already in their bedroom packing a suitcase.

"What will we buy it with?" asked poor Fiona looking dolefully down at the sleeping Beowulf. "We've no money."

"People will give us some. You will see. I'm going to make a few phone calls now. Is the phone working, Auntie Al?"

"Miraculously yes, up to a few minutes ago."

"I'll phone Eddie Fox first and then the Canon, and oh dear I wish Liz was here. You will see Ballyfungus will rally behind me."

True to her mission Mrs. Walsh was already at the Post Office. She had to ring the upstairs bell because, being Saturday, the office itself was closed. Her excitement was so intense she could hardly get the words out.

"Lovely news!" she panted. "Mr. Tott and his wife and Auntie is movin' into Ferncourt tomorrow mornin' and they're goin' to stay there, squattin' they calls it, until Balooly is preserved. I'm goin' to clean there tomorrow after I finished Racketstown. The floors must be rotten and the kitchen a dirt heap. I'm not takin' a penny because it's for the Cause." If cross-examined Mrs. Walsh could not for the life of her have explained the aims and objectives of the

Cause but that it meant trouble, disruption and excitement, and above all news was enough for her.

Miss O'Kelly also showed interest. "Well I wouldn't have thought that Tottenham would have shown so much spunk. There was a letter bomb this morning they say." The upper dentures had descended and the Dracula look had taken over.

Mrs. Walsh glimpsing it murmured a short prayer to herself. "There'll be another, or worse, mark my words, and that may help matters. Nothin' like a bomb for gettin' things done. I'll send my newphew Ignatius over to lend a hand at Ferncourt." Emerging into the street Mrs. Walsh was lucky enough to meet John Colley on his bicycle. "John Colley is it yourself?"

"I hope so, I was till this minute missis!"

In a few breathless sentences, she was now hiccuping, Mrs. Walsh gave him the news. "And mind, you be sure and tell the Archdeacon himself. How's things there John?"

"Nicely ma'am. They was walkin' round the garden holdin' hands this afternoon." Colley broke into crude laughter, mounted his bike, and rode towards the Rectory.

The Archdeacon and his seductive housekeeper were seated on the terrace which looked out on the River Fung, enjoying a glass of sherry before dinner, when John Colley delivered the news with many respectful nods, winks, and asides. As soon as he'd taken his departure Felicity jumped up. "Oh, George darling, I must go over and help them tomorrow. I could cook for them in the evenings. You wouldn't mind?"

"Yes I would," replied the Archdeacon.

"George! I'll leave the dinner cooked and ready you'd only have to heat it."

The Archdeacon said firmly. "It's not the food, it's you."

"George, what do you mean?" She knew well what he meant, but now that she saw it actually coming, she was frightened.

"Come into the house," said the Archdeacon commandingly. "I can't tell you out here in full view of those people in the canoe." He walked into the library, through the french window, pulled Felicity towards him and kissed her. The kiss was not avuncular neither was it paternalistic, it was just plain passion as of man to woman. "We must get married, this can't go on. You do love me?"

"I do George. Really."

He kissed her again, then he sat down on the sofa, and pulled her onto his knees. "You better go home tonight. I'll drive you back. You can't stay here under these circumstances. Tell your parents, but we must keep it a secret. We can be married quietly in Dublin in October. I couldn't have the ceremony here. It's only six months since Muriel's death." He tried to assume an expression of deep sorrow, but failed dismally.

"I'm so glad you're not bald." Felicity stroked his hair. This evoked such a violent response that she cried out for mercy and said he was choking her. "Tell you what, George." She struggled out of his embrace. "I could cook the dinner over at Ferncourt for you and the Tottenhams."

"I couldn't go against the law, darling, in my position. I will see you at Racketstown every day. But I will send them a cheque to buy food."

He was kissed again and his ears nibbled. "Then I may cook for them? It's a splendid cause. You know you approve of it. I can't bear to think that I won't be here for so long. October? I hate Racketstown. Oh God, the meat will be overdone."

She jumped up and ran for the kitchen leaving the Archdeacon staring bemusedly into space. What a wife she will be, he thought. I'm greatly blessed.

By Sunday evening the squatters had moved in (Tott broke a window, flouting the law) and opened up the house. Quite a crowd of well wishers arrived to cheer them on. Mrs. Walsh had circulated through the congregation coming out of twelve o'clock Mass, spreading the news and causing considerable excitement.

Monday midday, Colin and Eddie arrived with enough

tinned food to last a month. There was no gas or electricity laid on but Father Kevin said that was no problem at all. By Tuesday he got the old kitchen range going with a load of coal which had been bought with the Archdeacon's generous cheque. Felicity and Fiona organized the kitchen with stuff brought over from the bungalow. Workers had appeared to begin blasting Balooly and adding to the mystery a Gardai Squad Car drove in on Thursday afternoon. Tott watching from the window fully expected to be arrested, but nothing happened, they simply drove away again.

Felicity arrived every evening to help cook dinner, because volunteers, and there were never less than six, had to be fed also. On the Saturday she announced the Conglomerate personnel had moved out of the hotel and were now in Dublin, she also shocked Fiona with a more personal announcement. "I thought I ought to tell you I'm going to marry George."

"George who?" asked Fiona innocently.

"The Archdeacon, of course."

Fiona looked at her amazed and said without thinking. "But he's so old."

Felicity tossed her head. "I can tell you he's not old when it comes to lovemaking. Of course it's a secret. Please don't tell anyone."

News of the engagement had already leaked out. John Colley had reported it as definite to Mrs. Walsh.

"Men is all dirty," commented the virginal postmistress when Mrs. Walsh told her. "Do you remember Father Kevin was struck on that disgusting jade who came down to help with the filthy play. A collar doesn't restrain them, not anymore."

The two Catholic curates were over at Ferncourt every day; the Canon had allowed them to go as observers. He, of course, had to stay away because the operation was illegal, but he was supporting the Cause in spirit. It was well he did not see Father Kevin stoking the stove or hoovering the rooms; or Father Dermot cutting the grass and weeding the flower beds. Mrs. Walsh came twice a week to polish non-existent brasses and retail Ballyfungus gossip.

Still no work had begun on the Woods and Father Kevin said, "If you ask me the Conglomerate itself is up a tree. You notice they've made no statement to the press."

The squatters had already been dealt with by the media. Journalists had been sent down to see for themselves and TV crews from RTE had appeared and added to the public interest. The fact that Lady Tottenham was the daughter of John Fallon, the notorious industrialist, was played up to the hilt. All this caused a rather wearing lack of privacy. Ferncourt was in a constant state of interesting commotion resembling an airport in a fog. Far-out Socialist students from all the universities had arrived to squat with the Ballyfungus rebels and on Saturdays and Sundays carloads of sightseers arrived and strolled around as if it were a public park. Auntie Al had brought her quilters over to work in the mornings and the Hodge Podge Players were rehearsing *You Never Can Tell* in the evenings. The excuse being that Felicity was stage managing. Felicity was never happier. All this business took her away from dreary Racketstown but the Archdeacon was getting restive. Hurried caresses at lunchtime didn't satisfy him at all, though he was allowed some amorous evening dalliance in the Woods on their way back to Racketstown.

One morning, three weeks after the squatting began, Tott looked out of their bedroom window and remarked, "There are two more tents on the lawn and you can't move in the stables. The dust in the kitchen is shocking. I'm bound to say, darling, I'll be glad to see Clapham again."

"I will too," Fiona agreed, "or at least be in a place of our own. Why haven't we heard from Daddy?"

"None of us can understand."

In order to continue writing his poetry Tott had to lock himself into what had once been the linen room. That afternoon he was irritated almost into using strong language when there came a loud bang on the door and the voice of a resident Socialist called Tony shouted, "Your wife is in the drawing room with Fallon."

"Gracious!" The Earl threw aside his manuscript and rushed downstairs and entered the living room wearing, he hoped, an intimidating stare. John Fallon was there, calmly inspecting the baby. Fiona also showed no sign of fear or embarrassment. Outside the window Tott could see a menacing crowd of fellow squatters carrying banners with insulting slogans.

"Lock the door and pull over the shutters," commanded Fallon. "I don't want those fucking asses to interrupt our talk." Dazedly Tott obeyed him. There was a roar from the mob outside when the shutters were bolted.

"I hope you have some protection," Tott addressed his father-in-law.

"I have plenty of security. Sit down, Tottenham. I want to talk business with you."

"Daddy has come up with an idea." Fiona kissed the top of the baby's head. It might have been Tott's overheated imagination but he fancied the child fixed a rather suspicious stare on his grandfather.

"I'm sure Mr. Fallon has an idea, a profitable one, no doubt." The Earl sat down.

"It's this. If you move into Ferncourt I will make a gift of it to Fiona and I will call off work on the Woods."

"What?" Tott stared at him blankly.

"I want you to live here. I had thought of the Castle but then you put on that silly protest two years ago and I dropped it."

"What about your German partner's sad end in the well? I thought that was why you dropped it."

"It may sound strange but family feeling is involved. I don't want my daughter living like a tinker. You move in here, I'll have the place done over and I will give you both an adequate allowance."

"No." The Earl sprang up. "By God, no!"

Fiona looked at him in astonishment. Tott never spoke like that before in her hearing.

Fallon rose and reached for his hat. "Then the Woods go and I'm afraid the police will evict you all and Ferncourt will come down. Work will commence next week."

"Wait. Give me time to think. One thing. Do you give me your word of honour as a — " Tott hesitated. Fallon looked at him sardonically, "as a gentleman that you will leave Balooly intact, that is if I consent to your terms."

"Even though I'm not a gentleman I will sign a written agreement if you consent to these terms."

"I must consult my fellow squatters. I'll call a meeting for this evening and let you know our decision at once. Are you at the Grand?"

"Yes. The sooner the better. I must let my partners know too. I better go before I'm lynched. The baby looks healthy." He paused hat in hand and looked down at the child who looked back at him with a fearful scowl.

"He looks like you, Daddy," Fiona murmured. "Smile Piddles, smile at Gramps." She looked up at her father and two pairs of brown eyes confronted each other. (She is very like him, thought Tott sadly.) "How are the boys?" asked Fiona.

"All right. I wish you'd see them oftener. The little fellow could do with some mothering."

"And my poor mother isn't there!" Fiona suddenly broke into tears.

For a fleeting moment the hard set mask of greed and power cracked on Fallon's face and a spasm of something like pain was visible. "That's why I want you here." he said. Then he walked to the door, opened it, and moved contemptuously through the crowd of youthful Socialists that was milling around in the hall. The Rolls was waiting for him below the steps with two security men, one being the driver. Hisses and groans disturbed him not; as usual he remained passive, unmoved and sure. As the car moved down the avenue he was shaken with silent laughter. He was thinking with cynical amusement how easily he had foxed them all and how true it was that anyone and everything could now be bought. The fact was the factory would go up within the year; it simply meant a problem of rerouting the road. The Woods therefore could remain intact, though a couple of unpleasant experts had warned that the fumes might endanger the surrounding vegetation. Meanwhile, Fallon smiled again, he had bought Fiona back and he would have the gratification of a son-in-law who had background and snob value. The strange fact was that self-made millionaires like Fallon craved the mystique of social uplift. Even though the Irish Republic did not, like the UK, hand out titles to their money moguls, there were other ways of attaining social distinction, such as the acquiring of rundown castles and aristocratic sons-in-law. Permission to build the factory had already been given. Politicians, County Council, health authorities had all been paid off. Fallon was due in Tokyo for an important meeting next week. He had no doubt in his mind what the result of the emergency meeting would be.

The emergency meeting was held in the Ferncourt dining room and overflowed into the well-known conservatory now buzzing with bloated bluebottle flies and little else. The sickly vine had passed on; the geraniums had withered away. It was the last time this particular group of concerned citizens would come together before their little world irrevocably changed. Father Kevin and Father Dermot sat on either side of the Canon with Father Hannigan looming in the background. The Archdeacon sat beside his beloved who was flashing a large diamond ring. She was the target of many rude stares and coarse comments. Mairin O'Kelly had brought her knitting and was ensconced between her nephew Iggy and Mrs. Emerald Walsh; the latter was dangerously alert and of course in her mind preparing news bulletins. Auntie Al shared an old sofa with Attracta Mulcahy and behind them were the two Miss Croziers full of apprehension as to their very chancy future. Tott, of course, was in the chair.

269

Grouped around were the Socialist splinter groups, who could not agree on any issue but were full of ebullience leading nowhere.

The Archdeacon opened the proceedings, first of all giving them a rundown on Fallon's offer and the resulting complications. "Personally Tott, I think you should accept it." The truth was the Archdeacon found it hard to keep his mind on anything except his approaching marriage. The Canon, who hoped for money from Fallon towards the restoration fund, echoed him as did Father Hannigan, who also had monetary plans. Sadly enough practically everyone at the meeting had their own personal motivation.

"What about the factory?" asked Eddie. "Did he assure you that plans for the poison outfit had been abandoned?"

"Well I took it for granted. No road, no factory." Tott was feeling more and more depressed. Fiona who was seated modestly in the background, watching her husband, thought with a mixture of pity and love how innocent poor Tott was; anyone could fool him and he was certainly no match for her father, that master of corruption, John Fallon. So she remained silent — all she craved for herself and Tott now was a home and some security and for that she was willing to sell out her youthful ideals and also Tott's. She'd had enough of squatting and she feared a future with a non-earner. The Archdeacon continued regardless of some hostile booing from the younger squatters. "I honestly think Fallon means it. After all Tott, you are married to his daughter. All he asks is that you live here and keep up Ferncourt. It's his house of course but forget that . . ."

"That's just what I can't forget," snapped Tott angrily. He was cheered by the mob.

Father Kevin rose now and addressed his friend. "But Tott, we will have Balooly. We're sure of that. Think again. It's for the common good."

"Work for the common good usually foretells an assassination or a civil war," murmured Colin cynically. "You may be sure Cromwell, Hitler and the Grand Inquisitors felt they were working for the common good." Now a spirited onslaught was launched upon Tott urging acceptance of Fallon's terms.

"Tott, you belong here," begged Father Kevin; he had in mind interesting outdoor performances of Shakespeare's comedies in the Ferncourt gardens.

"Tott darling, we need you," cried Auntie Al who was prejudiced.

"We can't let Ferncourt go," cried Miss Clara Crozier and she was echoed by her sister.

Even Eddie piped up, "It's quite a pleasant life here, Tott, and with that money you can make Ferncourt a show place."

"There's nothing to stop you writing your poetry," said Father Hannigan whose motivation as we know was not pure.

Just then a scuffling could be heard near the dining room door and Old Jamesy appeared pushing his way through the mob; he was brandishing a green envelope. "Mr. Tott sir, Mr. Tott," he bawled, "a tellygram for you, a tellygram. 'Tis a death rattle the young lad said what brung it." A low murmur went through the room. What in heavens name could this be?

Tott read the telegram through once and then read it aloud. "Fear personal sacrifice required stop Keep Balooly at all costs stop We paid the price stop It was worth it stop We would all four do it again stop All's well that ends well stop Mabs Josh Artie and Albie."

This poignant communication as might be expected evoked cheers. Even Mrs. O'Kelly dropped her knitting and clapped long and vigorously; she whispered to Mrs. Walsh, "I always says physical extermination goes a long way."

Mrs. Walsh said, "Aye, into the next world."

"The taking of human life cannot be applauded," boomed the Archdeacon, "but in the case of our absent friends the motives were laudable. Now Tott, the main objective has been to save the Woods and we seem to have achieved that objective."

"Yes, at Tott's expense," shouted an honest Socialist in the back of the room.

At that moment another Socialist who had been sitting near Fiona stepped forward and pushed a piece of paper in front of the harried Earl. He read it without looking up. "I'm pregnant. The Doctor told me this afternoon. I love you. Fiona."

The Earl looked up, he was very pale. "This is a private matter," he said and thrust the message into his pocket. A silence fell upon the gathering during which one could hear the horrible buzzing of bluebottles eating up the smaller flies Tott looked hurriedly around for Fiona but she had disappeared. He opened his mouth to speak, but no words came.

"Who was the Greek king who was torn apart by the Bacchae?" whispered Eddie to his friend.

Pentheus King of Thebes, why?"

"We're looking at his modern counterpart now. Poor Tott! Poor fellow!"

The Earl lifted his head and faced the crowd. An expression of the most dismal acquiesance was written on his face. He stood there the picture of defeat. "Friends, perhaps I should say comrades, but it's all the same, it has never changed in two thousand years. 'Who groans beneath the Punic curse and strangles in the strings of purse before she mends must sicken worse.' " He paused and looked around. ("Who said that?" Eddie pinched Colin. "I think *I, Claudius*, Robert Graves.") The Earl continued, "Fiona and I will stay here, confined during my father-in-law's pleasure is the right way to put it. Yes, you may have the woods and I trust you will be saved from the poison factory."

There were cries from the more committed Socialists, "It's a bloody shame," "Don't give up comrade," "We're with you."

Tott lifted his hand for silence. "I had other plans but that's all over. In a sense we've won a victory but in another sense we've been bought. But the fight against the despoilers of this planet earth must continue. Bribery and corruption

272

are the enemies and I've been bribed. Yes that's the truth. I want to thank everyone who helped us in the fight to save Balooly, especially the students. It's up to you boys to carry on the fight. I put my faith in you."

He sat down and shamelessly wiped his eyes. Everyone else was doing the same and the cheers even drowned out the thunder of the rain which was pouring down on the conservatory roof.

Coffee was then served; harps and guitars were brought forth and the revels lasted until dawn. The Archdeacon however thankfully removed Felicity and deposited her in Racketstown with her watchful parents.

"Only two weeks more and then we are together," murmured the venerable man as he kissed her lingeringly. "I'm aching for it," he added with truth. There were times however after dalliance in the Woods when he saw himself with horrid clarity as a middle-aged satyr pursuing a rather naughty little nymph, and he didn't care for that at all.

The next morning the squatters all streeled away, leaving a hideous mess behind them and the Tottenhams returned to Clapham until Ferncourt could be made fit for human habitation, courtesy of John Fallon, who spared no expense.

In the five years since the memorable Poetry Festival Ballyfungus has changed and not for the better. Once a charming rural village it has mushroomed practically overnight into an ugly country town. The advertised Georgian village with Georgian village green is a monstrous settlement of small redbrick houses all exactly the same, the Green is a Georgian carpark. There is nowhere for the children to play, so they assuage their boredom by throwing litter around, smashing public phone booths, and breaking other people's windows. Twenty-five stately homes have appeared in the fields round Racketstown House which has been pulled down. The MacCreas sold out and settled in Dublin. Even more menacing to behold are four blocks of five-story slummy flats looming up behind the main street. The Old Mill has become a pottery factory run by a Japanese company which succeeded in dealing the final death blow to Lady de Bracey's crafts in the Town Hall. Even Goggins supermarket has been swallowed up by a large shopping centre on the outskirts of Ballyfungus owned by a Canadian company. All the cozy friendliness of the Friday morning shopping in Goggins has gone forever. Also the road between Ballyfungus and Fungusport has become a dual carriageway, the scene of many fatal accidents. The saddest of these perhaps was the death of Bejasus that "poor innocent cratur," who was knocked down and killed by a drunk hit-and-run driver. He was found lying in the ditch into which he had crawled clinging to his cross. "Blessed are the meek," not anymore: the march of progress has seen to that. His funeral expenses were subscribed for by a little group of persons mostly underprivileged who were only a little better off than the victim but they happened to be practising Christians and wished him well. The worst loss was suffered when the two lively young curates were transferred to other parishes and two dull holy plodders took their place. Father Dermot was deputed to a red-brick rash outside Cork and Father Kevin to a similar fungus operation north of Dublin. The Hodge Podge Players and the footballers (the Archdeacon was unable to go it alone), having no incentive to do otherwise, drink the hours away in Rooneys. On the other hand Father Hannigan is now leading a successful boycott of the family planning clinic in Fungusport. He also collected half a million pounds to build a new church near the shrine where Our Lady appeared to the two teenage girls (one of them was a Goggins), some thirty years ago. This infuriated the Canon. He had to wring every penny out of the authorities for the restoration of the Cistercian Abbey, and even then it was not enough. "But then," he added bitterly, "I don't use intimidation." Auntie Al, courtesy of John Fallon, has moved into a cozy little flat in the stables where she conducts a teeny-tiny weaving industry assisted by Attracta whose three little lads are thriving wonderfully.

Soon after the Tottenhams moved into Ferncourt the factory was built just the other side of Balooly, two miles outside Kinealy. Permission was obtained after interviews with the necessary authorities; great emphasis was placed on employment and the extraordinary efficiency of the Far East. Experts who were called in assured the residents that everything was perfectly safe. The most far-reaching precautions had been taken, even human error was ruled out. A highly paid Divine Providence it seemed would take care of everything and what providence neglected to do John Fallon would overcome. Tott knew then he had been fooled, they had all been fooled and he has given up the fight. He once burst out to Auntie Al when they were alone, "I paid for the Woods, you know. I was the burnt sacrifice offered up to the gods."

Auntie Al began to cry and told him he mustn't talk like that. "You have your poetry darling."

"I haven't, not anymore."

Fallon talks a great deal about his son-in-law the Earl and his daughter the Countess and his unruly sons spend much of their time in Ferncourt; the whole outfit is owned by Fallon and the inmates are his creatures.

"Welcome to the court of King Midas," was Tott's bitter greeting to Father Kevin, who had come to visit them. "Step right in; you're walking on gold."

Tott is not the only casualty. The old men who used to sit gossiping on the bridge over the river no longer do so; the traffic is too noisy, too frightening. Rooney's pubs have become so grand, the humbler folk are afraid to enter them. Both of them boast discotheques which over the weekend render life almost impossible for the residents what with the drunken rows, stabbings, and rapes. The Boys have long since fled to a Caribbean island where the weather and the taxes are kinder; their thatched mansion has been taken over by the Japanese potters and is used as a storehouse for markdowns. Liz is still on the Isle of Man with her Chilean, who, we are told, is showing signs of wear and tear. Nine months after their wedding Archdeacon and Mrs. Musgrave's child was born: a girl christened Euphrosnye. The MacCreas assured everyone the child was premature, but John Colley in jocular mood told Mrs. Walsh it could spell its own name when it was born, which was more than anyone else could!

Balooly Woods are still intact. It is now a national park and bird sanctuary, a gift to the nation from John Fallon. Some ingenious tax arrangement facilitated this generous offering. Balooly still remains a haven for innocent people who value Nature above quick profits; who love the majestic trees, who gaze delightedly upon primroses and daffodils in the spring; of children who love to scrunch the fallen beech nuts under foot, collect bagfuls of useless chestnuts and chase each other down the green glades. It is a haven for lovers who lie together in the bracken, while millions of leaves from the ash trees drift softly sighing down on them and a magic world for those who can with quickened imagination still hear the antic rout of Comus and his crew, while high in the branches above, the birds trill songs of thankfulness and praise. Ah heaven! but Mrs. Emerald Walsh like Cassandra knew better. "The smoke belchin' up out of that high chimney from the factory in Kinealy looks like it's stokin' the fires of hell." And a premature autumn descended this year on Balooly; the leaves on many of the trees displayed an unpleasant sickly fungus. . . .